HER
DEADLY
GAME

Center Point
Large Print

Also by Robert Dugoni and available from
Center Point Large Print:

Close to Home
A Steep Price
The Eighth Sister
A Cold Trail
The Last Agent
In Her Tracks
The Extraordinary Life of Sam Hell

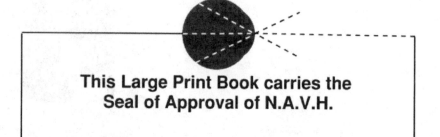

**This Large Print Book carries the
Seal of Approval of N.A.V.H.**

HER DEADLY GAME

ROBERT DUGONI

CENTER POINT LARGE PRINT
THORNDIKE, MAINE

To Jim Fick. Strong mind. Strong will. Strong body. Looking forward to watching you climb mountains at ninety. And to Doug Harvey, mentor and friend. Gone too young.

The truth is rarely pure and never simple.

—Oscar Wilde,
The Importance of Being Earnest

PART I

PROLOGUE

April 1, 2022
Seattle, Washington

Seattle Violent Crimes Detective Frank Rossi drove over the street curb onto the Pioneer Square plaza pavers, the black Chevy's headlights reflecting the heavy rain, its windshield wipers slapping left and right in a futile effort to clear the glass. Ambulance lights pulsed red and white on the Pioneer Building's first-floor gray sandstone, and the fifty-foot, red cedar Tlingit totem pole overlooking the square. The eyes of a raven, the lowest carving, stared at Rossi, as if to question his early-morning presence.

"Right there with you," Rossi said, turning off the engine.

Being the on-call detective team was like being an on-call doctor. Rossi and his partner, Billy Ford, could be summoned at all hours of the day and night, though unlike a doctor, they never had the chance to save a life.

Rossi's day began when the victims' days ended.

The wind gusted, causing water from the sodden leaves of a maple tree to fall like hail on the car's roof and hood. Rossi noted two additional pool cars in the plaza. That would be his sergeant, Chuck Pan, and Ford. No matter how quickly Rossi responded to a homicide scene, he had never beaten Ford in the two years they had been a Violent Crimes team.

Rossi draped his Gore-Tex jacket over his head, pushed from the car, and hurried up the marbled steps where a uniformed officer stood seeking refuge beneath the arched building entry. Rossi flashed his credentials and stepped inside the foyer. He shook the rain from his jacket while considering the directory of commercial tenants in the glass case mounted on the wall. He found Cliff Larson Accounting on the fourth floor. The name pinged his memory, though at four in the morning, his addled brain couldn't place why.

He looked up at the peaked glass roof. Vines stretched over each landing, a curtain of green hanging in an atrium. The tenant offices were situated on the periphery of the landings, which were accessed by a staircase or a tiny cage elevator—a death trap, in Rossi's opinion. He climbed the ornate, marbled staircase with the decorative, wrought-iron handrail, passing framed photographs on the wood-paneled walls that documented the building's 130-year history at First and Yesler. The interior's musty odor reminded him of the smell inside his grandfather's closet.

On the fourth floor, Rossi followed the sound of

hushed voices to the building's northeast corner. Two paramedics stood alongside a uniformed officer—presumably the first to respond—and Billy Ford. Red crime scene tape had been strung across the office entrance. Cross it and you were obligated to file a report documenting your purpose at the scene, what you encountered, and with whom you spoke. Most officers avoided it like the plague.

Ford glanced at his wristwatch as Rossi neared. "Beat you by six minutes. You're getting slower," he said, his baritone voice as soothing as a deep saxophone.

"I'm beginning to think those rumors about you sleeping at Police Headquarters are true," Rossi said. "Either that or you're a superhero."

Rossi scribbled his name on the log held by the uniformed officer, noting Chuck Pan's and Ford's names beneath the signatures of the two first responders. Pan used his middle name, and with good reason. His parents, first-generation Vietnamese immigrants, gave their son an American name, hoping he'd better fit in at school. Not aficionados of children's literature, they had named him Peter. Everybody at SPD called him "Pan."

Rossi could empathize. His Italian parents had named him Francesco. He'd endured bullying until he shortened his name. "You been in?" Rossi asked Ford.

11

"Waiting for you," Ford said.

"You confirmed the victim is dead?" Rossi asked the paramedics. They looked remarkably young, and shaken, as did the officer holding the clipboard. At thirty-eight, Rossi had reached the pinnacle of investigations, with nowhere left to ascend, unless he had an interest in a desk job. He didn't. He became a cop to avoid a desk. Homicides were now his job.

"Vic is in the office in back," the young officer said. "It's gruesome."

They almost always are, Rossi thought but did not verbalize. "Did you or your partner touch anything?"

"No," the officer said.

"Step in or on anything?"

"Nothing."

"Who found the body?"

"Building superintendent. The victim's wife called in just after two, said she couldn't reach her husband."

"Why'd she wait so long to call?"

"Husband said he'd be working late. She said he'd worked late all month."

Tax season, Rossi thought.

"The super is in the office down the hall." The officer pointed over Rossi's shoulder with his pen. "My partner is taking his statement. You'll find some vomit in the reception near the desk. That's the super's."

"The super let you in?"

"Door was open. He was waiting out here. Pretty shaken up too."

The super had likely touched the doorknob. They'd get elimination prints. "You do anything else?" Rossi asked.

The officer shook his head and gave a slight shrug. "Nothing else to do."

"Pan called CSI and the ME," Ford said.

"Let us know when they arrive," Rossi said to the officer.

Ford opened their go bag. Made of black nylon, the bag had multiple exterior pockets, like a tool bag. Inside were notebooks and pens, a small tape recorder and batteries, disposable gloves and booties, a flashlight, a folded pocketknife, a small medical kit, zip ties, duct tape, business cards, a laminated card with a suspect's Miranda rights, a magnifying glass, and extra ammo for their Glock handguns.

Rossi and Ford slipped the gloves and booties on. Before stepping inside the office, Rossi read the stenciled lettering on the fogged-glass door pane:

CLIFF LARSON, ACCOUNTING

The name still nagged at him. Still didn't have time to consider why.

The office walls were red brick. Framed photographs hung by picture wire from the wooden molding high up on the wall. Rossi noted a reception desk piled with manila folders and documents, tax forms. *There but for the grace of God,* he thought. His mother was a CPA, as were both his sisters and his older brother. Family business. Rossi had taken all the classes at the UW and passed the CPA exam's five sections in just two tries. But he got cold feet. Couldn't picture himself sitting at a desk surrounded by numbers.

You'll never be out of work, his mother had told her children. *Two things are certain in this life. Death and taxes.*

Three certainties, actually. His mother had left out crime. Sadly, every day, someone, somewhere committed a crime. Law enforcement called to Rossi. A passion, he supposed, though his mother didn't like his choice. "I'll go to bed worrying about you every night."

She called frequently.

Rossi noted the puddle of yellow vomit on the beige rug. Blinds covered the windows of the two offices behind the reception desk. Pan stepped from the office on the left. Their sergeant was built like the brick walls—square and sturdy. Rossi couldn't help but think Pan's build was related to his given name. Kids could be cruel, until they feared for their safety.

Pan, almost never at a loss for words, grimaced. "This one is brutal," he said softly.

"Gunshot?" Rossi asked.

Pan nodded to the office. "Tell me what you think, but from a distance. You'll want to put on a Tyvek suit." Which meant there was a lot of blood and likely bodily fluids.

With growing trepidation, Rossi stepped to the office door. He noticed blood spatter on an exterior window, which was partially open, and the manila files atop the desk. A rainbow-shaped swath of spatter cut across a framed print by Ansel Adams—a lone tree crystallized in winter snow, the beautiful image a stark contrast to the violence Rossi took in. The room held the metallic tinge of iron.

Pant legs protruded from behind a desk. Khakis. Rossi took one careful step to his left. The person, presumably Cliff Larson, lay facedown. His green leather chair had been upturned, and blood, a burgundy red, pooled on the plastic mat beneath his misshapen head. Rossi initially thought gunshot wound, but a longer look revealed that wasn't the case. He stepped back out into reception, where Pan and Ford waited.

"Someone beat him to death," Rossi said.

"Thinking the same thing," Pan said.

"Not sure with what, but to inflict that much damage . . ."

Rossi didn't finish his sentence. He didn't need to. Pan and Ford knew what Rossi had been about to say. The killer had struck Larson repeatedly,

15

hitting him long after Larson's skull had caved in and death had been certain. An act of rage. Rossi now knew why those assembled outside the office could barely talk.

This was a nightmare, one that would linger in their memories every time they closed their eyes to sleep.

Rossi would share their nightmare.

CHAPTER 1

June 2, 2023
Seattle, Washington

Keera Duggan peered across the King County courtroom to the swinging wooden door and willed her father to walk in. Leaving him to lunch alone had been a mistake.

The bailiff entered from a door behind the elevated bench and commanded the courtroom to rise as Superior Court Judge Ima Patel retook her seat behind her desk, instructed the three people in the gallery to sit, and invited Officer Greg Walsh to retake the witness stand. Walsh pushed through the railing gate and made his way past the jurors. He looked official in his navy-blue uniform and utility belt. His SPD badge glistened. Walsh wore the belt at the request of the young prosecutor standing at the adjacent table. Keera used to give officers the same advice, despite the efforts of many judges to prohibit weapons in their courtrooms.

Patel turned her attention to Keera. "Counsel," she said. "Will Mr. Duggan be joining us this afternoon?"

Patrick Duggan had sparred with King County prosecutors for four decades, including Ima Patel before she ascended to the bench. "Sparred" was a polite term. Patsy had routinely knocked out prosecutors, earning his nickname, the Irish Brawler, a moniker he wore as a badge of honor. The prosecuting attorney's office felt differently. Patsy had not been opposed to hitting below the belt, throwing elbows in the clenches, and rabbit-punching out of the break. He defended his clients the way he'd won a Golden Gloves boxing tournament as a young man—any way he could. But alcohol abuse had softened Patsy's punches and slowed his reflexes, if not yet his razor-sharp mind, and prosecutors and jurists on the King County bench knew well his binge drinking. When she'd been a prosecutor, Keera had heard colleagues in the office say, "If you want a chance to beat the Brawler, save your best witnesses for the afternoons, and hope Patsy Duggan goes on a bender."

Clancy Doyle, apparently now Keera's client, looked at the empty chair at counsel table with genuine concern. With good reason. Keera sat second chair at this DUI trial only at the insistence of her eldest sister, Ella, now the managing partner of Patrick Duggan & Associates. Babysitting duty. Ella had suspected Patsy to be on the brink of a binge. Damned if she hadn't been right.

Keera knew almost nothing about the details of Doyle's case.

"Counsel?" Patel asked, sounding impatient.

Keera rose and tugged at the lapels of her black suit. "Mr. Duggan has been detained," she said, as if her father had a dental appointment that had run long. "I'll conduct the cross-examination of Officer Walsh."

Patel's lips nearly inched into a grin. Keera clearly wasn't fooling at least one person in the courtroom. "Proceed," Patel said.

Officer Walsh looked tightly wound as Keera approached. He expected a confrontation. The prosecuting attorney, also young, inched to the edge of her chair, prepared to stand and defend Walsh with objections and interruptions intended to throw Keera off her game.

They wouldn't.

Keera approached the podium without notes. She smiled. "Good afternoon, Officer Walsh. How was your lunch?"

Walsh hesitated. "Too short." His response garnered a few smiles from the jurors.

"You're tired, I assume, from working the Third Watch last night—the graveyard shift." Keera knew this because of Walsh's age—twenty-three. He was years from pulling more reasonable watches. She also knew no officer got used to working the graveyard. Officers had told her their bodies adapted, but their internal clocks longed for normalcy.

"I'm eager to get home and sleep." Walsh

glanced at the jury. His boyish good looks and aw-shucks smile played well.

"I'll bet it can be difficult to concentrate when your internal clock is thrown off."

"You get used to it," Walsh said, cautious, as the young prosecutor had certainly prepped him to be. Keera empathized with her. She was about to lose this case, and her supervising attorney would not be happy.

"You still have your officer's report?"

"I do." Walsh held up the multipage document.

"You testified on direct examination that your report was complete, accurate, and honest."

"Truthful," Walsh said.

Keera had deliberately misquoted Walsh. "Complete, accurate, and *truthful*," she repeated, for the jury's benefit. Each question was strategic. Keera thought several questions ahead, choosing the next one depending on Walsh's answer. Walsh had found Doyle asleep behind the wheel of his car on a county road. Doyle had blown a .08 on the Breathalyzer and been charged with drunk driving, his second offense in two years. He faced a $5,000 fine and thirty to 364 days in jail. Patsy had the Breathalyzer test thrown out since Doyle hadn't been operating the vehicle at the time Walsh confronted him, but the PA chose to move forward with evidence Doyle also failed the field-sobriety test.

"Let's get to it, then," Keera said. "At the

academy and at roll call before each watch, you are taught that officer safety is priority number one; aren't you?"

Walsh looked surprised by the question. "Yes."

"And in keeping with rule number one being *your* safety, you are taught how to interact with people in all kinds of situations, including a possible DUI stop; correct?"

"That's correct."

"Remind me. Your police training at the academy is about seven hundred hours; isn't it?"

"Seven hundred and twenty." He smiled.

"Of those seven hundred *and* twenty hours, how many hours are devoted to pulling someone over for a possible DUI?" Keera knew the answer from a class she took while at the PA's office, but the answer was better coming from Walsh.

"I don't know," Walsh said.

Keera gently pounced. "The class didn't make much of an impression, then," she said.

Walsh stumbled to correct his mistake. "It did. I just don't remember how many hours it was."

"The DUI class I took at the police academy was two hours. Does that sound about right?"

"I'll take your word for it," he agreed, his smile becoming tentative.

"At the academy you're also taught that approaching a vehicle can be dangerous; correct?"

"It can be, yes."

"Even more dangerous when you come upon

a car at night, on a county road, in pitch-black darkness; correct?"

"I have a lamp I shine through the back windshield," Walsh said.

"You're alert, then, maybe even nervous?"

"I'm not nervous. You get used to it," he said. He thought he had figured out Keera's next move.

"Really? With all the negative publicity police officers have recently received, you're not nervous when you approach a car parked along the side of the road, alone, late at night?"

"There are always some nerves, but you deal with them." Walsh glanced at the prosecutor, who gave him a subtle nod of approval.

"Okay. You're also taught the person inside the car might be nervous, correct?"

"Correct."

"A specific protocol exists on how to proceed with a night stop; doesn't it? You call in the stop and provide your location to police headquarters."

"Dispatch. Right."

"You don't jump out of your car with your gun drawn, do you?"

Walsh chuckled. "No. I check the license plate to determine if the driver has any warrants."

"Did Clancy Doyle have any warrants?"

"No."

"Then you jump out?"

"No. You position your vehicle at an angle in

22

case the patrol car were to be rear-ended, it would not strike the parked car. Then you light up the person or persons inside the vehicle to determine if they're trying to hide or grab anything. Any suspicious activity."

"You didn't observe Mr. Doyle doing anything suspicious, did you?"

Another pause. "No."

"And when you approached Mr. Doyle's driver's window and questioned him, he didn't argue with you, did he?"

"I don't think he did."

"If he had argued with you, you would have written it in your complete, accurate, and truthful report, wouldn't you?"

"He didn't argue with me," Walsh said.

"He was cordial. Polite. Reasonable."

"I guess so." Walsh shrugged this off as inconsequential.

"You asked him to exit his vehicle, and he did that with no problem, correct?"

"I don't recall any problem."

"You didn't note any problems in your complete, accurate, and truthful report, did you?"

"No."

Keera picked up Officer Walsh's report. "On direct examination you said the first thing you did after ordering Mr. Doyle from his car was put a pen in front of his eyes and ask him to visually track it. Did I read that correctly?"

"You did. And he didn't." Another smile for the jurors.

"You didn't consider the fact that Mr. Doyle had bright lights shining in his eyes on a pitch-black road just seconds before you administered that test, though, did you?"

"Well . . ."

"It's not in your complete, accurate, and truthful report."

"Okay."

"Let's talk about what else is not in your report . . . and feel free to refer to it. I don't want to mislead you." She noticed several jurors suppressing grins. "Mr. Doyle did not have red, bloodshot eyes."

"No."

"He did not have glassy eyes."

"No."

"His skin was not flushed."

"I couldn't really see."

"It's not in your report."

"It's not."

"He did not slur his speech."

"No."

"He did not stumble, fall over, or lose balance when he exited his car."

"No."

"He didn't throw up or look sick."

"No."

"You testified that you considered 'each

piece of evidence' to conclude my client was drunk. I assume you considered this evidence that indicated Mr. Doyle was not drunk; didn't you?"

"When I gave him the field sobriety test, he did not step straight."

"You're saying Mr. Doyle, who admitted to being nervous, and after you had shone a bright light in his eyes, didn't step perfectly straight while trying to follow your instructions that he walk heel to toe, with his hands at his side, along an imaginary straight line, on an uneven dirt-and-gravel shoulder?"

Officer Walsh sighed. "He stumbled."

"But he did follow your instructions correctly, and he did count nine steps, turn, and count exactly nine steps back; didn't he?" Keera demonstrated the walk.

"He followed the instructions I gave him, but he wove."

"You considered his accurately following your instructions as evidence he was not drunk; didn't you?"

"I considered the things he did wrong."

Keera frowned, as if sorry for what she was about to do. "Then you *didn't* consider each piece of evidence, as your report states. You *didn't* consider all the evidence that indicated Mr. Doyle was not drunk; did you?"

"I considered everything, but I was *focused*

on the things he did wrong," Walsh said again, becoming recalcitrant.

Another mistake. "Then leaving out all the evidence you observed indicating Mr. Doyle was not intoxicated was inadvertent and not a deliberate attempt to mislead this court and its jurors?"

"Objection," the prosecutor said, standing. "Argumentative."

Patel sighed. "Overruled."

"I'll withdraw the question," Keera said. She didn't need the answer. "You also wrote in your report the car smelled of alcohol?"

"That's correct," Walsh said.

"You didn't write Mr. Doyle smelled like alcohol."

"What? I—"

"Was the car drunk?"

"Objection, Your Honor."

"What's the objection, Counselor?" Patel asked.

"Sarcasm?"

"Overruled."

"He was the only one in the car," Walsh said, his tone combative.

"You were taught at the academy, during that two-hour class on DUIs, that alcohol has no smell, weren't you?"

"I don't follow."

"You were taught alcohol has no smell." It was technically true. If the officer smelled an odor on the driver's breath, it was the flavoring added to the beverage.

"I know what beer smells like, and he smelled . . . hoppy . . . Like hops."

"Did the car smell like peanuts?"

Walsh paused. "I don't recall."

"My client had a bag of peanuts in the car, didn't he? It's in your report."

"He did."

"So you smelled peanuts, or maybe hops, but not alcohol, because you were taught at the academy that alcohol has no smell."

The prosecuting attorney stood. "Objection, Your Honor. The witness said the defendant smelled like beer."

"I don't believe he did, Your Honor. Officer Walsh said the witness smelled 'hoppy.' "

"Overruled," Patel said.

Keera made a face like Officer Walsh's answers pained her, but she'd have pity and not embarrass him further. She turned to Judge Patel. The jurist no longer looked as though she was holding back a smile.

Though several jurors did.

CHAPTER 2

The prosecuting attorney gave her closing argument, and Keera followed with a short summation. Judge Patel moved to adjourn for the day, but the jurors expressed a desire to deliberate, so they wouldn't have to return in the morning. Patel, knowing what was to come, capitulated. The jury came back with a not-guilty verdict in less than half an hour.

As Keera packed her laptop, Clancy Doyle profusely thanked her. "I'm going to recommend you to all my friends," he said. "You're even better than your father."

"Please don't," Keera said.

Doyle looked confused. "I didn't mean—"

"You dodged a bullet, Mr. Doyle. The officer and the prosecutor were young and inexperienced. They made a lot of mistakes. You may not be so lucky next time. Beyond that, you could hit another car, or someone walking along the road, and you won't be looking at a DUI. You'll be looking at vehicular homicide and spending the rest of your years behind bars. Do you really want to do that to your wife and children? Your grandchildren? I noticed neither Dolores nor your children were in court today." She let the unspoken inference remain that way.

Doyle looked like he'd been slapped. "I'm going to give up the drinking this time, Keera. I swear it."

Her father had made similar promises so many times it no longer even angered her. It was just sad. Empty promises only made afternoons like this more painful. "Do me a favor. Don't lie to yourself. You're not going to give up drinking."

"I . . ."

"The next time you drink, do it at home. Or hand the bartender your car keys at the start of the evening and tell him to call you a cab. Put the Uber and Lyft apps on your phone. The cost of a ride will be a small fraction of what you paid my father. And it may save a life. Possibly yours." She slid her briefcase strap onto her shoulder and stepped past him, carrying her father's box of binders and documents. "Say hello to Dolores for me."

Keera put her back to the tall doors and pushed out into the marbled hall. When she turned, Miller Ambrose, her former boss and lover, pushed away from the wall he'd been leaning against. He tried to make his presence look like a coincidence, but he was a second too late initiating his first step. He'd been waiting for her. Keera ignored him and walked to the bank of elevators.

"You beating up on the rookies now?" Ambrose said.

"What are you doing here, Miller?"

"Get over yourself. I have a trial down the hall."

She adjusted the box on her knee to press the elevator button. "Muni court? Is that where the most dangerous offender cases are now being tried?"

Ambrose was a senior attorney in the Most Dangerous Offender Project, or MDOP. In Seattle, a senior prosecutor was sent to the most serious crime scenes to help detectives with evidence issues and provide advice on subpoenas and other legal technicalities. The intent was to eliminate mistakes a good defense attorney could exploit.

"Where are you headed? Maybe we could have a drink, for old times' sake."

"That would certainly be like old times," she said.

An elevator pinged. The doors slid apart. Keera allowed those people inside to exit.

"Is this your career now? DUI cases? Beating up rookie prosecutors and police officers?"

She stepped inside. "Just happened to be walking by, huh?"

"I expected so much more from you."

Keera spoke as the elevator doors closed. "Really? I always expected so much less from you."

She sighed and leaned against the back wall.

Keera and Ambrose had quietly dated for eight months. Keera had been initially attracted to Ambrose's legal mind and unwavering self-confidence. At times, he controlled the courtroom more like a judge than an advocate. And Ambrose knew his way around a woman's body as well as he knew his way around the courtroom, but his self-confidence was narcissism, and too many of their nights had been fueled by alcohol and primal urges—red flags Keera eventually noted. A nightly cocktail before dinner. A good bottle of wine. A port before bed. Keera had no interest in becoming her mother, a drunk's caretaker. She told Ambrose her concerns. He told her he could stop drinking. But he didn't. Then came the familiar excuses. He drank to be social, to keep her company, to take the edge off a difficult day. The apologies followed. She'd heard those too.

When she tried to discreetly end their relationship, he became verbally abusive and confrontational. She gave him every opportunity to stop harassing her. When he showed up outside her home, she had the locks changed. When he waited after work to talk to her, she changed parking structures. When he persisted, she threatened to get a restraining order and make his actions public. In this era of the Me Too movement, it would have ended his career. Many said Ambrose would be the next King County prosecuting attorney. Maybe mayor. He backed off, but her caseload changed to prosecuting misdemeanors. Keera had no future in the PA's office. She languished another month, then tucked her tail between her legs and asked her father for a job. Patrick Duggan & Associates had been a place she had sworn she would never work.

She stepped off the elevator and walked outside. A stiff, warm breeze blew east up James Street from Elliott Bay. The weather had been unseasonably hot for Seattle; meteorologists predicted several more days of temperatures exceeding one hundred degrees. More days in one week than Seattle had recorded in the last one hundred years combined.

By the time she reached Occidental Square, she dripped sweat beneath her suit jacket and was ready to dump her father's box of binders into a garbage bin. The heat had sent most sane people indoors in search of air-conditioning, the light-blue tables and chairs beneath the trees in the square vacant.

Keera approached the Paddy Wagon, an Irish pub on the first floor of the building her father obtained from a client who couldn't pay his legal bill some thirty years ago. Having a pub just three floors beneath her alcoholic father was like having a candy store in the same building as a diabetic. Liam called out to her from the pub's patio, as he usually did.

"Hey, Keera. Stop by for something to eat," Liam said, his Irish accent lyrical.

She smiled and lifted the box. It seemed to gain weight with each step. "I'm working."

"All work and no play make for a boring Keera. You have to eat."

"I'm in trial." She smiled but hoped her definitive declination would discourage Liam. His persistence was both flattering and annoying.

Keera rested the box on a knee, punched in her secure access code, and stepped inside the lobby to the caged elevator. She dropped the box, shut the gate, and made the sign of the cross before she pushed the third-floor button. No way she was lugging that box up three flights of stairs, no matter how finicky the elevator car could be.

Part of her hoped the cage got stuck.

The conversation she was about to have would not be good.

Keera stepped from the elevator into the lobby of Patrick Duggan & Associates. Her father, she knew, had envisioned the firm to someday be Patrick Duggan & Sons, but her two older brothers, Shawn and Michael, had chosen only one of their father's passions—drinking, though Michael had been sober for fifteen years.

The family legal mantle had fallen to Ella, child number three, and it had been a heavy load. Ella was part lawyer, part caretaker, a task she shared with daughter number two, Margaret. Keera had been unexpected, born ten years after Maggie. With an infant at home, their mother could no longer function as Patsy's caretaker. Ella and Maggie filled that role. Ella had never married. A relentless worker, she professed to have no time for boyfriends. Keera had thought Ella gay, but she now believed the fallout from their father's drinking had soured her on men, the institution of marriage, and raising a family. She had trysts to satisfy her biological needs, but never anything more.

As Keera approached the lobby, Maggie hurried to the reception desk. She looked harried and upset, never a good combination. Maggie lifted the telephone receiver. "Duggan & Associates. Please hold." She glared at Keera. "Why the hell did you let him go to lunch alone?"

"You're blaming me?"

"You were supposed to keep an eye on him."

"No. I was supposed to sit second chair at a DUI trial. Patsy said he had a meeting and wanted me to take Clancy Doyle to lunch."

"And you still don't know what that means?"

"We were in trial, Maggie." Keera tried to maintain her composure. "I told Ella—"

"Since when did that stop him? When did anything ever stop him? You should not have left him alone."

"I should not have sat second chair. We enabled him. Ella enabled him. I told her—"

"Take that up with your managing partner. Thanks to you two, I'm late for a date. It's a miracle I even have a relationship, dealing with this family crap all the time."

Keera bit her tongue. Maggie went through boyfriends the way some women went through shoes. She wore them out. "Where is he now?"

"Patsy? At home. Yours truly had to hunt for him at his usual watering holes and drive him there, drunk as a skunk. Brought back some fond memories."

The job of bringing Patsy home had often fallen to Maggie. At eighteen, Ella had left for college at Notre Dame, their father's alma mater. In the Duggan house, attending Notre Dame was as expected as attending Sunday Mass. Keera followed Ella twelve years later. Margaret, who suffered from anxiety and bouts of depression, had not been a good student. Notre Dame was out of the question. She went to community college, obtained an AA degree and ultimately her paralegal certificate. She blamed just about everything on the way she'd been raised.

"Thanks for getting him," Keera said.

"Save it," Maggie said.

"I'm just trying—" Keera started.

"I don't need to be patronized."

"I wasn't patronizing you," Keera said, but there was no reasoning with Maggie when she got like this.

Ella hurried down the hall. "Hey. Hey!" she said. "It may be after hours, but this is still a law firm. Conduct yourselves accordingly."

"The queen bee comes out of her hive," Maggie said.

"Can it, Maggie," Ella said. "This hasn't been an easy day for any of us." Maggie gave Ella a look like she had to be kidding, but Ella got the final word. "Go home. It's after five."

Maggie reached under the desk for her purse and her jacket. She skewered Keera with a searing look on her way to the elevators. Ella said, "You should know better than to engage her when she's in one of her moods."

"*I* should know better?"

"Maggie feels put-upon by the entire world, Keera. Finding scapegoats for every perceived wrong is her survival mechanism. Always has been." She nodded for Keera to follow her down the hall to her corner office. Patsy's adjacent office was dark.

Ella sat behind her desk. Their offices weren't the behemoths of wasted space lawyers in modern offices favored; the building had been built during a different era. Ella had made her office homey with Tiffany lamps, potted plants, colorful paintings, and trinkets from her travels abroad. Keera disregarded the two chairs across from the desk and moved to the brown leather sofa against three western-facing arched windows. With the removal of the earthquake-damaged Alaskan Way Viaduct, Ella now had a view of Elliott Bay, Bainbridge Island, and the distant, snowcapped Olympic Mountains, though there wasn't much snow, given the persistent warm weather.

"Thank God I insisted we put in air-conditioning when we did. A hundred and six degrees in Seattle? This place would have felt like the inside of a brick oven," Ella said. She sighed. "So, what happened?"

"We won." Keera slumped onto the sofa. "I crossed the officer. The jury deliberated less than a half hour."

"I know that already."

"What? How?"

"Clancy Doyle called to complain about you."

"He did what?" Keera sat up. Her voice rose. "That ungrateful son of a bitch."

"He said you insulted him, told him he drank too much and next time he'd kill someone and go to prison."

"If he took the truth as an insult, too damn bad."

"How did you intend it?"

"Constructive criticism."

"Clancy's seventy-two. Same age as Patsy. Have any of our interventions worked with Patsy?" She put up a hand before Keera could answer. "Your job is to defend them, not to chastise them."

Keera bit her tongue. "My job was to sit second chair and keep an eye on Patsy, which you asked me to do. My job wasn't to bail Clancy Doyle out of a conviction."

"Well, you failed the first job but succeeded at the second. You're even."

"Failed the first job?"

"You were supposed to make sure Patsy didn't go on a bender."

"He said—"

"I know what he said. You don't think I've heard all his excuses and justifications before? Next time you tie yourself to his leg."

"There won't be a next time," Keera said. "We enabled him by having me there. We've always enabled him."

"We?" Ella arched her eyebrows.

Keera just wanted to get home, take off her suit, and sit beside a fan. "Are we done?"

Ella leaned back. Her leather chair creaked. "Is that what you think we've done all these years? He's a drunk, Keera. He's been a drunk since he was seventeen. His alcoholism is an illness. It isn't going to change."

"Not now."

"We adapt and try to limit the damage. It isn't perfect, but it's the best we can do."

"Okay," Keera said, not wanting a lecture.

"He can't do what he once could," Ella said.

"Meaning what?"

Ella sighed, then looked at the clock on the wall. "It's late. Go home. Nice job today."

Keera started for the office door, wondering what Ella had been about to tell her.

"Keera?"

She turned back.

"Dinner at Mom and Dad's this Sunday."

She groaned. "This Sunday?"

"First Sunday of the month. You'll be there?"

Ella phrased it as a question, but it sounded like an order. "Aye, aye, Captain." Keera issued a faux salute before departing.

CHAPTER 3

June 4, 2023
Denny-Blaine Neighborhood, Seattle

Frank Rossi noted the camera mounted atop the garage roof's peak, centered over a basketball hoop positioned between two garage doors. He stepped from his car and looked back up the sloped driveway to the street. He'd driven past a patrol car, an unmarked car from the motor pool, an ambulance, and neighbors lining the sidewalk. The CSI Unit's gray van and the medical examiner's blue van, as well as additional motor pool cars driven by the standby detective team, and possibly police brass, would soon join them.

Along with reporters and news vans.

God almighty.

The circus was coming to the upscale Denny-Blaine neighborhood. Rossi might as well find a top hat and red tuxedo jacket. As lead detective, he would be directing this show like Hugh Jackman as P. T. Barnum in *The Greatest Showman*. No way he'd convince Ford to take the lead on this one, not unless it turned out to be a grounder—straightforward and easily resolved. Rossi's gut, for no particular reason, told him that would not be the case.

Speaking of Ford, where was his maddeningly punctual partner?

The lone motor pool car Rossi had passed undoubtedly belonged to Chuck Pan.

Rossi noticed a uniformed officer moving the sawhorse barricade blocking the driveway entrance just before a black motor pool car descended. Ford parked beside Rossi's 1969 Pontiac GTO, custom painted British racing green. Yeah, Rossi had exceeded a few speed limits getting here, but sometimes you had to let the horses run when trying to beat a superhero.

Ford unfolded from his car like the beanstalk grown from Jack's magic beans. He just kept rising, all six foot eight inches of him. At five foot ten, Rossi looked up to him. Literally.

Ford nodded to Rossi's car. "You just had to finally beat me; didn't you? Couldn't stop to get a pool car?"

"I was out to dinner in Madison Park," Rossi said. "I didn't want to drive downtown to get a car and drive back out here. Figured it will be a late enough night as it is."

"Bullshit. You wanted to beat me."

Rossi couldn't conceal his smile. He did. And he had. He liked to win. Finally.

"Damn, it's hot," Ford said. "I moved to Seattle to get away from this kind of heat." Ford had grown up in Texas.

"Supposed to remain hot for another week."

Rossi fanned his shirt. "Read that the smog and particulates from the fires in California and Eastern Washington are creating a pressure system."

"All I know is it's hot." Ford sighed. He paused and looked about the yard. "Thought we'd make it through the week unscathed." Just a few more hours and Rossi and Ford would have been off the clock. The apparent homicide would have belonged to the next-up detective team. Ford pointed to the peaked roof. "Smile."

"Saw that. Hope it works."

In Rossi's experience, many homes had security cameras, but they didn't always function. Most were set up with good intentions but served mainly as deterrents.

"Who's standby?" Ford asked. The standby detectives would assist at the crime scene and canvass the neighboring houses to determine if anyone saw or heard anything.

"Heard it was the Italian Stallions," Rossi said, using one of Vic Fazzio and Del Castigliano's nicknames. "You want the lead on this one?"

"Fat chance. This bad boy is all yours, partner. Luck of the draw, my friend."

"Rock, paper, scissors?"

"Bet against myself? I don't think so."

"Double or nothing."

"Nothing."

Rossi glanced at the basketball hoop. "Game of

one-on-one? Backboard looks freshly painted."

"Hell, the basketball hoop at my house looks unused, and it isn't fresh paint. My kids take after me. Couldn't hit the broad side of a barn if I was sitting on it." More than once people had assumed that because Ford was Black and tall, he had played basketball, but Ford might just be the most unathletic person Rossi had ever met. Ford's talent was music. The man played piano, guitar, bass, saxophone, and trumpet, and he could play any song by ear. "I don't think so."

"Had to at least try."

Ford bent and retrieved their go bag from the back seat of his car, then they walked toward two regal stone lions adorning each side of three stairs descending through an eight-foot laurel hedge. A ramp had been built over one side of the staircase, which led to a stone walk. Two more lions guarded the front door beneath a portico. The house, which Rossi would describe in his report as English Tudor, had pitched, gabled roofs with slate tiles. Timber beams protruded from yellow stucco, and the windows were narrow leaded glass.

"What do you estimate, five to seven million dollars?" Rossi asked Ford.

"Maybe in a normal real estate market," Ford said. "My guess, seven to ten million."

"Getting so that a hardworking public servant can't afford to own a home where he works,"

Rossi said. Neither Rossi nor Ford lived in Seattle.

They went through the usual ritual with the uniformed police officer standing outside the front door and holding the sign-in log. Rossi noted the names of two paramedics who stood off to the side, Pan, and the two first responders. He signed in and handed the clipboard to Ford. "No brass."

"Not yet." Ford scribbled his name and his badge number and returned the board. "Murder in this neighborhood bound to make the news, and that's like catnip to the brass."

To discourage the attraction, Rossi would have the redline strung across the entire property.

"Where's your partner?" Rossi asked the uniformed officer.

"In the living room with your sergeant, talking to the husband."

"The husband is talking?" Ford asked.

"Appears to be," the officer said. "He was waiting for us on the driveway."

"How'd you get in?"

"Front door was open. Husband led us. It's not pretty."

"You confirmed the victim is dead?" Rossi asked the paramedics.

They each shook their head. The officer at the door said, "There was no need."

Rossi knew what that meant. He'd had his fill of gruesome with the Cliff Larson case a year ago. Every time he worked that case, and reached another dead end, it reminded him of the beating death's brutality. Two dozen blows according to the ME. They'd had a few suspects—disgruntled former clients—but each with an alibi Rossi and Ford had been unable to crack. About the only thing Rossi had solved was why the name Cliff Larson sounded familiar. Clifton Larson Allen, or CLA, was one of the largest CPA firms in the country—a far cry from Cliff Larson's small accounting office in Pioneer Square.

Before stepping across the threshold, Rossi observed a keypad on the door and made a mental note to find out who had the entry code. Neither the door nor the casing looked damaged. No forced entry.

Inside, the house décor was understated and the furniture sparse. The floors were hardwood and marble. No carpeting. Windows provided a view east across Lake Washington's gray-blue water to the homes in Medina, Clyde Hill, and other cities too expensive for Rossi to even dream about.

Definitely $7 million to $10 million.

In a room adjacent to the sitting room, Pan and a uniformed officer spoke to a man who looked to be early to midforties, with a youthful face, and brown hair graying at his temples. He wore the remnants of a black tuxedo, his jacket and tie removed, shirt collar open, several buttons undone.

Rossi considered the built-in shelves on the southern walls. The books, sculptures, and framed photographs looked undisturbed, as did the furniture and the magazines neatly arranged on the coffee table. No evidence of a struggle in this room.

Rossi nodded to Pan, and their sergeant directed them back to the foyer. "One victim, a woman," Pan said, lowering his voice. "Shot once in the back of the head."

"Where?"

"The kitchen." Pan gestured across a dining room to a swinging door with more red tape strung across it.

"I take it we don't need SWAT to go through the house," Rossi said.

"The two uniforms went through it when they arrived. It's clear."

"And the guy in the tux is who?"

"Victim's husband, Vincent LaRussa. Claims he got home from some gala at the Four Seasons and found his wife dead."

"Should be easy enough to confirm—the gala part at least," Rossi said. "I'll get a search warrant and include his cell phone." Cell phones provided geolocation records revealing where the phone, and presumably the owner, had been. Detectives used them to help build a timeline and possibly catch a suspect in a lie. "Noticed a camera over the garage."

"Security system," Pan said. "I've asked for the footage. Should confirm the time he got home."

"Just visual or audio as well?" Rossi asked. If the victim had been shot, and the video included sound, it might have picked up the gunshot, documenting the specific time of death.

"Didn't get that far," Pan said. "Ask him. Patrol set the perimeter atop the sloped driveway, but I'm having them move it down the block, given the likely media draw."

"Let's expand the red tape also," Rossi said.

"Already ahead of you. Be sure you conduct yourselves accordingly." Pan made eye contact with each of them. "I don't want to see any smiling faces in tomorrow's newspaper or on the six o'clock news."

"Why is it so hot in here?" Ford said. "Thought we might catch a break and get to work in air-conditioning."

"Husband doesn't know. Said the house has air-conditioning but someone turned the thermostat switch off."

"If there was ever a day to use it," Ford said.

Pan checked his watch, then took out his cell phone. "I'll call and get an ETA on CSI and the ME."

As Pan left, Rossi and Ford approached the officer and the husband, introducing them-selves. LaRussa looked spent, eyes bloodshot. He did not offer his hand in greeting. Perhaps a lingering habit from the Covid pandemic. Perhaps something else. Rossi's gaze roamed to LaRussa's white shirt, looking for blood spatter. He did not see any.

"You're homicide detectives?" LaRussa asked.

"Violent Crimes," Rossi said, "but yes, homicide. Our condolences. I have to ask you some questions during this difficult time, Mr. LaRussa. Are you up to answering them?"

LaRussa nodded.

"Can you tell us what happened when you got home?" Rossi asked.

LaRussa inhaled a breath and said, "I don't know what happened. I was at a charitable event downtown, and when I came home . . ." LaRussa's words caught in his throat. Rossi looked for tears. Didn't see any. "I came home and found Anne. Someone shot her."

"Anne is your wife?"

"Yes."

"Where was she shot?"

"I . . . I don't . . . the back of the head?"

"Where in the *house* was she shot?"

"I'm sorry. The kitchen."

The uniformed officer pointed with the pen in his hand. "Through the swinging door off the formal dining room."

"Do you have any children, Mr. LaRussa?" In Rossi's peripheral vision he saw Ford scan the framed photographs on the shelves.

"No."

"Anyone else live in the house besides you and your wife?"

"No."

"Any regular visitors—relatives, house cleaner, pool guy?"

"No relatives, well, Anne's family but . . . The house cleaner comes on Thursdays. We don't have a pool."

"A gardener?" Considering the manicured yard, Rossi figured the gardener to be a given.

"He comes once every two weeks."

"Did he come this week?"

"I'm not sure."

"I'll need his and the housekeeper's names."

"I can get them to you."

"Can you think of any reason why someone would shoot your wife?"

He shook his head. "Anne was a gentle soul."

"Is there anything missing? Does it look like any of the rooms were tossed?"

"Tossed?"

"A robbery," Ford offered. "Drawers opened, books pulled from shelves, a wall safe cracked."

"I haven't really looked," LaRussa said. "I just called 911, and the person told me to step outside and wait for the officers to arrive."

Rossi would check the camera footage to see if that statement was true and verify the amount of time LaRussa had spent in the house before coming back outside. "How did you come into the house when you got home?"

"The front door."

"Was it opened?"

"No. I used the code."

"Was it locked?"

"I don't . . . I assume so. It locks automatically when the door shuts."

"Does it register each time the door is opened?"

"I don't understand."

"Is there a computer chip that records the date and time when the door is opened and closed?"

"I don't think so. I don't know."

Rossi made a note to find out for certain. "I noticed a security camera over the garage. Are there other cameras?"

"A second camera covers the backyard." The house had homes on each side, but Rossi knew from experience that neighbors didn't take well to having security cameras pointed at their homes.

"Do they pick up sound as well as video?"

"No," LaRussa said.

Del and Faz would check if the neighbors heard a shot or had security cameras and, if so, whether those cameras recorded sound.

"How long does the video remain on the system?"

"I don't know."

"Where are the feeds stored? On the cloud?"

"The cloud and a DVR box in the mudroom off the kitchen."

"You said you were at a charitable function?" Rossi asked.

"I sit on the board of Seattle Children's Hospital. The hospital held its annual fundraising dinner tonight. The first we've had since the pandemic."

"Where was that?"

"The Four Seasons Hotel downtown."

"And your wife didn't go with you?" Rossi asked.

"My wife doesn't go to those events, no," LaRussa said.

That struck Rossi as odd. "People will verify your presence at the event?"

"I was a speaker," LaRussa said. "I can provide names."

"How long were you there?"

"I went from my office downtown. I arrived around six thirty, during the silent auction."

"And what time did you come home?"

"Sometime after nine o'clock. Nine fifteen."

Again, they'd check the geo records on LaRussa's cell phone and the security tape to confirm where he had been and when. The ME would provide them with a window of time the victim had died. "What time did the event end?"

"I don't know. They have a live auction after dinner and a band. Dancing."

"Your wife doesn't like to dance?" Rossi asked to push LaRussa a bit and see what kind of reaction he got.

LaRussa gave him a look, though Rossi couldn't quite discern its meaning. "No," he said. "My wife doesn't dance."

"Okay, Mr. LaRussa, I'm going to ask you to go through the house with the officer and determine if any windows or doors were broken or pried open, or if you notice anything missing," Rossi said, wanting to keep LaRussa around, but not in their way, in case they had questions. "Don't touch anything. Just do a visual observation. If you notice anything out of the ordinary, tell the officer. Does the officer have permission to go through your house with you and take photographs?"

"Yes, of course."

Rossi would contact the on-call homicide prosecutor and put together a broad search warrant for the home and the yard, in the event LaRussa suddenly became uncooperative. The prosecutor would transmit the warrant to the on-call judge and get email confirmation approving the warrant or approving it with limitations.

"Have you washed your hands since you've been home?" Rossi asked LaRussa.

"Washed my hands?"

"A Crime Scene Investigation team is on their way. They're going to swab your hands for gunshot residue." This was a ruse Violent Crimes detectives used to gauge how the suspect reacted. Detectives had stopped doing GSR swabs because the test was not reliable, but suspects didn't know this.

LaRussa's eyes narrowed. "Do you think I shot my wife?"

The husband was always the first suspect.

"It's a way to eliminate you as a suspect," Rossi said. "We'll need to also take your fingerprints, get a shoe impression, and get a DNA swab for the same reason. Do we have your permission?"

"I guess so. Anything to determine who did this."

Rossi and Ford handed him business cards, then LaRussa and the officer stepped past them. Ford said, "Mr. LaRussa?" LaRussa turned. "I understand the home has air-conditioning."

LaRussa nodded. "It kicks on and off automatically when the rooms reach a certain temperature."

"So the air-conditioning should be on, I assume, given how hot it is?" Ford asked.

"It should be. Someone turned it off. I noticed when I got home."

"You're sure someone shut it off? It's not broken or, maybe . . . I don't know, the electrical grid went down from people plugging in too many fans?"

"I don't know," LaRussa said. "I thought maybe

Anne turned it off. She got cold sometimes, but . . . I really don't know."

"Did you try to turn it back on?" Ford said.

"No."

"Can we? To see if it works."

LaRussa walked down the front hall to a wall thermostat. Rossi took several pictures to record the temperature in the house, then said, "Give it a try."

LaRussa punched the keypad. After a few seconds, Rossi heard air flowing from a nearby vent. "Sounds like it's on," LaRussa said.

"Odd," Ford said after LaRussa and the officer left. "Why would someone turn off the air-conditioning on the hottest day of the year?"

"I don't know," Rossi said. "You catch the look he gave me when I asked him if his wife danced?"

"You know I can't catch. But yeah, I saw the look. I don't think he appreciated the question."

"I don't either."

Ford pulled out the Tyvek shoe coverings and blue nitrile gloves from their go bag and they each slipped them on. "I have a feeling this is going to give me more nightmares," Rossi said.

"You and me both," Ford said.

They walked through the formal dining room. Large abstract paintings hung on the walls.

"Whoa." Ford stopped to admire a bronze sculpture on the sideboard—a cowboy on a horse descending a steep incline, a pack mule following.

"No pun intended, right?" Rossi said.

"That's a Remington."

"The rifle?"

"The sculpture."

"Is it expensive?" Rossi asked, though he assumed that much from Ford's reaction.

"If it's an original stamped Remington it is. I just read about some selling for more than ten million."

"For that kind of money, I'd prefer a 1967 Chevy Corvette Sting Ray—convertible."

"Art is lost on you," Ford said.

"Beauty is in the eye of the beholder, my friend, and I like to drive my beauty."

Rossi pushed open the swinging door and stepped carefully on the black-and-white checked tile. A center island the size of an aircraft carrier, with a sink and four barstools, dominated the space. Behind the island was a stainless-steel range top, two stacked ovens, a refrigerator, a microwave, and cabinets to store enough food to feed the crew of that aircraft carrier.

He stopped when he could see over the center island. Anne LaRussa sat with her head and upper body slumped to the left. She faced away from the counter, as if she had been looking out the sliding glass door leading onto a deck with an expansive view. A picturesque setting but for the blood matted to the back of her head and sprayed on the counter.

Rossi stepped around the counter. Anne LaRussa sat in a wheelchair. The reason for the ramp down the steps outside the front door was now apparent.

My wife doesn't dance.

"Shit," Rossi said.

"Partner, when you step in the shit, you do so up to your ankles," Ford said.

CHAPTER 4

June 4, 2023
Seattle, Washington

Keera left her house for Sunday dinner before she lost track of time and missed the monthly event. Tempting, but Ella and Maggie would skewer her, and her mother would inflict Irish guilt—similar to Catholic guilt, which her mother was equally adept at inflicting, and just as insidious.

She picked up a blueberry cheesecake from the bakery in Madison Park and minutes later pulled to the curb at the base of her parents' sloped driveway—in case she needed to make a quick getaway. She didn't want any late-arriving lunatics blocking her in, though a quick car inventory indicated she was the last lunatic to arrive at the asylum.

A counselor once labeled her family "enmeshed" and not in a flattering way. Despite their seeming animosity, they lived near one another, worked together, and remained intimately involved in each other's personal lives, far too intimate for Keera's tastes. She'd never mentioned Miller Ambrose to any of them, or why she left the PA's office.

Keera had temporarily escaped the inquests while attending both college and law school at Notre Dame. She believed she'd maintained her independence by declining to work at the family law firm, then had to slink back to the sticky web when her ill-conceived relationship with Ambrose fell apart. She also lived in a house owned by one of Patsy's clients and endured these monthly inquisitions that would have broken even the most resolute Salem witch.

Why?

Because avoiding them would be worse. Her mother had decreed the first-Sunday-of-the-month dinners sacrosanct. Nothing short of a medical emergency, a vacation to a foreign country, or death excused your presence. And, although the attendees were crazy, they were family. She loved her siblings, though she didn't always like them. She was as different from them as water from oil. They didn't mix well.

Keera reached into the glove box and squirted two peppermint bursts of breath freshener into her mouth, then exhaled into cupped hands. She didn't smell her late-afternoon glass of Scotch to help her get through this evening. She pushed from the car onto the tree-lined street and navigated the pavers between the expansive lawn and manicured flower beds. The temperature still hovered in the midnineties.

She climbed the front steps to the wraparound

porch, took a deep breath, opened the door, and waded into shark-infested waters.

Inside was chaos. She dodged Lucas, her brother Michael's son from his second marriage, then Nicholas and Sophia, Shawn's son and daughter from *his* second marriage. Shawn apparently had custody this weekend.

"Hi, Auntie Keera," Lucas said as he sped past the staircase banister.

"Hi, Auntie Keera," Nicholas and Sophia mimicked.

Keera lifted the cheesecake out of harm's way.

"Michael and Isabella, Shawn, come feed your kids," Keera's mother yelled as she came down the hall from the kitchen. "Keera. When did you arrive?" She made a point of looking at her wrist, which didn't bear a watch, then the grandfather clock in the hall. "You're late."

"Ella told me seven o'clock."

"Liar," Ella called out as she came down the hall. "Don't throw me under your bus's wheels." She turned and spoke to their mother, Bernadette. "I have to make a phone call."

"Don't be long. We're ready to eat."

Her mother leaned in to allow Keera to kiss her cheek. She took the cheesecake from Keera's hands. "Is it homemade?"

"By someone," Keera said.

"I'll see if I have some fruit to spruce it up.

Help your sister set the table. She's in a mood again. She broke up with that boyfriend."

"The painter who was going to be the next Pablo Picasso?"

"No, the mechanic with the bad teeth."

"What happened to Pablo?"

"I don't know. I can't keep up."

"Keep up with who?" Maggie stood in the threshold holding forks and knives as if she might throw them.

"These kids," Bernadette said. Keera had once wondered how her mother made up excuses so quickly.

A lot of practice.

"Nice of you to show up when all the work is done," Maggie said.

"Ella told me we were eating at seven," Keera said.

"Eating at seven. Do you think the food gets cooked and the table set by magic?"

"Enough," their mother said. "No fighting at Sunday-night dinners."

"Since when?" Maggie said.

"Since I said so. Finish the table. The roast is done."

Keera followed Bernadette into the kitchen, which always held the aroma of warm food and spices. Her mother's cooking, these Sundays, was what held the family together.

Bernadette set the cheesecake on the tile

counter. She handed Keera a decorative plate, then rummaged in the refrigerator, producing blueberries and strawberries. "Put these around the edges," she said, stepping to the oven. "I heard what happened in court Friday with Clancy Doyle."

"That was a lot of fun," Keera said.

"He's having a tough time, honey."

"Clancy?"

"Your father."

"When hasn't he had a tough time?" Keera said.

"This is different," her mother said, always making excuses for their father.

"Different how?"

"Because he's starting to slip." Her words had a bite that caused Keera to stop decorating. Her mother looked sad, though Keera saw no tears. The Irish didn't cry. They were stoic.

Keera had thought Patsy had been off his game the morning of the Doyle trial. He'd missed a few objections Keera would have raised, and his cross-examination of witnesses had lacked a punch.

"Law is all he's ever known," her mother said. "I accepted him having this mistress because he loved it so much. Now, he doesn't think he's the lawyer he once was. He's lost confidence and he's feeling useless. That's a horrible feeling for someone getting old, Keera."

"Is he sick?"

"He's been sick his entire life." Bernadette audibly exhaled. "He's old, Keera. The alcohol has aged him. He sees the end. Just have some empathy. That's all I'm asking."

Keera wondered how the law firm would survive if Patsy could no longer try cases. His reputation was the firm's lifeblood. Keera had already noticed fewer big felony trials and more petty crime cases since she'd arrived.

"I know he feels bad about what happened. Go say hello to him," her mother said, taking the blueberries. "I'll finish in here. Go on. He's in the back, watching the Mariners game with your brothers and Isabella. I'm sure he could use a distraction from those three."

"You know she doesn't know a baseball from her ass," Maggie said, entering the conversation. "She just pretends to be interested to get out of doing any work."

"Better that way. She couldn't fold a napkin with instructions." Bernadette smiled. "Go say hello to your father. He misses you."

Keera dodged her niece and nephews and made her way to the den. Her father sat in his leather recliner, a Rainier beer resting on the arm. Shawn sat on one side of the red leather sofa, looking miserable and staring at his cell phone. Two open Coors Light beer cans rested on the end table. He'd brought his own beer. Not a good sign.

Michael and his second wife, Isabella, sat on the other end. Isabella stared at her freshly painted nails. Michael stared at the television with a ghostly gaze. They'd met in rehab.

"This is a lively group," Keera said. "Did somebody die?"

"The Mariners," Michael said. "They're about to lose five to one."

Her father smiled. "Hey, kiddo," he said.

She bent and kissed his forehead. "Hi, Daddy."

He lowered his voice. "Thanks for covering for me Friday. I heard you were magnificent."

"Not from Clancy Doyle's perspective, apparently," Keera said.

"I made sure Clancy got some religion," her father said. "He won't be a problem."

"Clancy Doyle? What's that jackass done now?" Shawn asked, looking up from his phone.

"Leave it alone, Shawn," Patsy said.

"Mom wants you to serve your kids," Keera said to her brothers.

Shawn stood. "Might as well. This one is over. Someone dig the grave and bury this team." Michael and Isabella followed him from the room.

Patsy smiled. "It was nice working a case with you," he said.

"Would have been better to have finished together," Keera said.

Her father sighed, and Keera got the impression

he wanted to say something more but refrained. "Maybe you could spend the night. We could play chess by the fireplace. Like old times."

"It's ninety degrees out, Dad."

"So, we won't light a fire."

"We'll see," she said, because it was easier than saying no.

They stepped into the dining room. Her mother served French bread, and the beef with mashed potatoes and baby carrots. Ella had made the salad, which included cucumbers, watermelon, and feta cheese.

"Do we have any ranch dressing?" Shawn asked.

"I put dressing on the salad," Ella said.

"I can't taste anything. Can you taste anything?" Shawn asked Maggie, who sat beside him.

"It's a summer salad," Ella said. "It's supposed to be light."

"I can't taste any dressing." Isabella poked at the leaves with a fork.

"Keera, get your brother some ranch dressing," Bernadette said.

"No," Ella said. "He can eat the salad as it is, or he can not have any."

"What do you care how I eat it?" Shawn shot back.

"It's an insult to the chef who prepared it."

"I don't see a chef, and I don't see how putting

dressing on a salad is an insult," Shawn said.

"Ella, let it go," their mother said. "Shawn, if you want ranch dressing get it yourself."

Shawn pushed back his chair and put his napkin on the table.

Ella dropped her fork in her plate. "Really?" She yelled over her shoulder. "Hey, Shawn, grab the ketchup while you're up. I want to put some on my beef."

"Don't you dare," Bernadette said.

Patsy tapped the side of his glass with his knife. "I have an announcement to make. Actually, Ella and I have an announcement." The cutlery silenced. "Ella and I have agreed to make Keera a partner of Patrick Duggan & Associates."

"Non-equity partner," Ella quickly added.

"Are you shitting me?" Maggie picked up her full wineglass and drained it.

"Language, Margaret," Bernadette said.

"She's been here barely a year. What about my raise and promotion?" Maggie said.

"To what? Queen of the receptionists?" Shawn laughed.

"Pretty funny coming from someone who drank his way to the warehouse and takes orders from a twenty-year-old."

"He's the boss's son . . . Oh, wait a minute. You're the boss's daughter; aren't you?" Shawn said, needling.

"Hey!" Patrick Duggan rapped his knuckles on

the table. "This is Keera's moment. Not either of yours. So shut your traps." He raised his glass of wine to Keera.

She felt nauseated.

"When has it ever been my moment?" Maggie mumbled. She turned to Keera, raised her empty glass, and gave her a painful, faux smile.

Keera felt the sticky Duggan web entombing her.

"Speech. Speech," Shawn said.

"Yes, share a few precious words, golden child," Maggie said.

A cell phone rang in the kitchen. Keera didn't recognize the ringtone, but she was grateful for the interruption, nonetheless.

Ella pushed back her chair. "That would be my phone."

"Saved by the bell," Shawn laughed.

"I thought cell phones were outlawed at the table during family dinners," Lucas said, coming in from the kitchen. "Dad, can I have my cell phone? Auntie Ella has hers."

"That's because the rules don't apply equally," Maggie said. "You'll learn soon enough."

CHAPTER 5

The circus had arrived.

Rossi and Billy Ford worked with the CSI sergeant, directing the videographer and CSI detectives marking potential evidence with placards. Darkness had fallen, but not the temperature, which remained stubbornly in the upper eighties. Thank God they got the air-conditioning working.

Two CSI detectives used total station surveying equipment to create the crime scene diagram to scale. The detectives in the kitchen wore booties, N-Dex gloves, and Tyvek suits. Personnel from the medical examiner's office waited to take photographs of the body and record its temperature to get an estimate on the time of death. Latent fingerprint and DNA experts also awaited Rossi's instructions, and the next-up detectives, Vic Fazzio and Del Castigliano, canvassed the neighborhood. Rossi had called in to the prosecutor and secured a search warrant signed by a King County judge.

Rossi stepped back and took a moment, as he did at each murder scene, to remember that the victim had once been a living, breathing human being. He didn't need that reminder in this instance. Something about Anne LaRussa's circumstance, being confined to a wheelchair, made him even more empathetic. It seemed more horrific to kill someone already so defenseless.

"How you holding up, partner?" Ford asked.

"Something about her being in a wheelchair . . . You feel it?"

"I feel it. Shot her in the back of the head. Coward."

"You think it was the husband?"

"Isn't it always? No forced entry."

Rossi stared at the crime scene, trying to figure out what had happened, trying to put himself in the killer's shoes and walk through what he or she had done. When he and Ford had stepped farther into the kitchen, Rossi had noticed a gun on the floor beside the wheelchair, along with shattered glass and what appeared to be water. What didn't make sense was the water on the kitchen counter behind LaRussa, which dripped over the edge and puddled on the floor. They'd also found a bullet cartridge about ten feet to the right of the gun. The bullet's exit wound had removed a large portion of the right side of Anne LaRussa's face, and CSI had dug out a bullet from a hole in the wainscoting beside the sliding glass door on the opposite side of the room. On the counter behind Anne LaRussa burned a small aromatic candle in a glass jar. The room smelled of vanilla.

"It's like that riddle we used to try to solve as kids," Ford said.

Rossi shrugged and shook his head.

"You know. The riddle in which Mary is found dead beside a table and an open window. There's glass on the floor and a puddle of water. The autopsy determines Mary died of shock and loss of oxygen. What happened?"

Ross gave the riddle a moment of thought, only because he knew Ford expected him to. "I don't know."

"Mary was a goldfish. The glass was her bowl. Strong wind blew it off the table. Sometimes the riddle involves a cat, but I always thought that made it too easy to solve."

"How does the candle fit?"

"No idea. That's part of our riddle."

"You think she could have done this?" Rossi asked, doubt creeping into his question. He'd initially thought suicide, but the location of the wound at the back of the head seemed to make that unlikely.

Ford shook his head. "Would depend on the extent of her disability. Look at her hands." Anne LaRussa's fingers looked like Rossi's grandmother's, twisted with rheumatoid arthritis. In the end they had resembled claws more than hands.

Rossi considered a laminated placard he kept in his go bag, a checklist to ensure everything that needed to be done was being done and done properly. "You remind CSI to go over the bathrooms?" Rossi asked.

"Toilet's clear, but I asked CSI to fingerprint the doorknobs anyway and the toilet handle, as well as the refrigerator door handle in the kitchen."

Murderers, like the Golden State Killer in California, had been known to open the fridge to eat, or to use the bathroom before departing a victim's house, leaving fingerprints and sometimes DNA. Checking the bathrooms and appliances had become standard protocol.

"What's your theory?" Rossi asked.

Ford sighed. "She's sitting, facing the view, drinking a glass of water. Killer walks in, comes up behind her . . ." Ford made a pistol with his index finger and thumb. "Shoots her in the head, tosses the gun."

"Could she hold a glass of water?"

"Don't know," Ford said.

"And the water on the counter?"

"Working on that as well."

"No forced entry at the front door," Rossi said.

"She let them in, or they let themselves in," Ford said. "Or the husband. He did call it in, so . . ."

"Why leave the gun?"

"What else are you going to do with it?" Ford said. "How often do we get a conviction because the killer kept the gun, or was a dumbass and stashed it in a place where we could find it?"

Rossi looked to the gun on the floor. A 9-millimeter semiautomatic. They had photographed it in place and from half a dozen different angles before examining it. They did not find a serial number on either side of the slide along the barrel, or any indication a serial number had been removed. "Ghost gun?" Rossi asked.

"Bet on it." Ghost guns were the bane of police officers, made from a kit that could be purchased online or at gun shows without the buyer providing identification and without a background check. They also did not have a traceable serial number. In 2019, Washington State had passed a law banning plastic weapons made using a 3D printer, but the legislature did not go so far as to ban ghost guns.

"Premeditated then?" Rossi said.

"Seems likely." Ford looked at the gun. "Feels like it's baiting us, doesn't it, just lying there?"

The videographer approached. "We're good," she said.

"I'll let the CSI sergeant know they can get to work—tell them to be careful about the water and the pieces of broken glass," Ford said. He bent and touched the water with his gloved finger, then smelled the tip. He shrugged. "Smells like water."

As Ford headed outside, Rossi walked into the sitting room. Vince LaRussa and the first officer on scene had returned from their inspection of the house. "Anything?" Rossi asked.

The officer shook his head. "Mr. LaRussa did not notice anything out of the ordinary."

Rossi would bring in Kaylee Wright, a tracker, to look for signs of an intruder outside the house. "Is that correct, Mr. LaRussa?" Rossi asked.

LaRussa looked up as if uncertain of the question. "What's that?"

"You didn't notice anything out of the ordinary? No broken windows, locks undone, doors or windows jimmied open."

"No," he said, seemingly deep in thought. "Nothing like that."

"Do you or your wife own a handgun?" He thought maybe for self-defense but, again, those hands.

LaRussa shook his head. "My wife really didn't have the ability to fire a handgun," he said. "She had nerve damage in her hands and her feet."

"I wanted to apologize for my comment earlier about your wife not liking to dance."

LaRussa shook his head and waved off the apology.

"Could she hold a glass of water?" Rossi asked.

"Yes," LaRussa said.

"A gun?"

"Hold? Yes. Pull the trigger . . . I don't know. I don't think so, but . . ."

"Can I ask how she became wheelchair bound?" Rossi thought perhaps she had advanced cerebral palsy.

"A horse-riding accident a few years go. My

wife showed horses—jumpers and hunters. Do you know horses?"

"Nothing beyond the merry-go-round," Rossi said.

LaRussa didn't smile. "Anne almost made the Olympic team twice. During a competition, the horse spooked and threw her. Anne injured her spinal column. We thought she was fully paralyzed, but with intense therapy and massage she recovered limited movement in her lower extremities, arms, and hands."

"When did this occur?"

"August 15, 2018. It changed both our lives, forever."

"I'm sorry."

LaRussa scoffed. "It seems inconsequential now."

"Was your wife expecting any visitors this evening?"

"She didn't mention she was expecting anyone."

"She was home alone then, to your knowledge?"

"It's the reason I wanted to come home after giving my speech. I don't like leaving Anne home alone. After the accident I worked more out of a home office, and I cut back on many after-hours obligations to be here with her." LaRussa let out a breath. "I've done very well. I didn't need to keep the same pace."

"What is it you do, Mr. LaRussa?"

"Wealth management. I oversee investment funds and decide which securities they should hold and in what quantities."

"Mutual funds, exchange-traded funds, money market, hedge funds?" Rossi asked.

LaRussa didn't immediately answer. Then he said, "You invest?"

"I have an accounting background. I do my own investing."

"Open-ended investment funds," LaRussa said. "Real estate—flipped homes, retirement homes, and commercial properties, mortgage-backed securities, and seller-financed real estate contracts, or private mortgages. I don't have to be in the office to do much of what I do. It allowed me to stay home more with Anne."

"Was your wife involved in the business?"

"No. Anne was busy with her horses and the shows. It kept her occupied, and she loved it."

"And the name of your business?"

"LWM. LaRussa Wealth Management."

"And after the accident? What did your wife do?"

"The accident was . . . like a car crash. That's the best way I can put it. One moment I'm kissing my wife goodbye, and the next I'm outside a hospital room and the doctors are telling me Anne may never move her extremities again."

"It must have been difficult for you both," Rossi probed. LaRussa was doing a good job painting a picture as the doting, caring husband, but maybe he'd grown tired of caring and wanted to use some of his money to travel to exotic places, eat at fine restaurants, and do so with a fully functioning companion. "How was your wife's mental health after the accident?"

"Spotty."

"Can you explain?"

"I don't know. Initially, Anne couldn't imagine living the rest of her life disabled. But as her rehabilitation progressed and she recovered some use of her arms, hands, and legs, she became hopeful."

"She could walk then?"

"No. She was determined though. I think she fully believed she would one day step out of that chair and get back up on her horses."

"And when that didn't happen?"

"Reality can be harsh. Anne's progress plateaued. The doctors told her further progress would be limited."

"How did she react?"

"Not well."

"Meaning?"

"Bouts of depression. Panic attacks. Anxiety."

"Suicidal thoughts?" Rossi asked. LaRussa paused and broke eye contact. "Mr. LaRussa?"

"It's possible. My wife was in constant physical

pain. I hired a therapist to come to the house four mornings a week to massage and stretch Anne's limbs, but that only did so much."

"When was the last time that therapist came to the house?"

"It's been weeks. Anne didn't want to do it anymore."

"I'll need his name."

"Her name. I can get it to you."

"Was your wife seeking treatment for her mental health?"

He shook his head. "She was, but she also recently stopped going to her doctor."

"How long ago was that?"

"Maybe a month. Six weeks."

"Was she medicated?"

LaRussa nodded slowly. "Her medicine cabinet resembles a pharmacy."

"Could I see that medicine cabinet?"

"Sure," LaRussa said.

"Before we do, there was a candle burning on the kitchen counter."

"Anne has them all over the house. I believe it's called 'aromatherapy.' The smells were supposed to calm Anne when she became anxious."

Rossi clicked his pen. "You mentioned showing me your wife's medicine cabinet?"

"It's this way."

Rossi turned to Ford, but his partner already had his telephone out to call and get the search warrant modified to specifically include anything in Anne LaRussa's medicine cabinet.

LaRussa led Rossi down a marble hallway and through a master bedroom seemingly as big as Rossi's home. From the bedroom they stepped into a bathroom, white marble on white marble, that had been remodeled for a person bound to a wheelchair. Two sinks, one lower than the other, with a medicine cabinet.

Rossi pulled it open using his nitrile gloves. The sheer number of prescription bottles caught the detective by surprise, despite LaRussa's statement that it resembled a pharmacy.

Rossi looked to LaRussa. "I'm going to have a forensic pharmacist document what's here."

"They can take it," LaRussa said. "I have no need for it."

"I'll need to have you sign a statement to that effect."

A knock on the bedroom door drew their attention. Ford. "MDOP just arrived. Wants to speak to you outside."

"I'll be right there." Rossi picked up on the subtle tone in Ford's voice and his expression. They hadn't pulled their top choice of MDOP attorneys. "Mr. LaRussa, there are going to be a lot of people here. Do you have someplace where you can spend tonight?"

"I have a condominium downtown. I haven't had much use of it lately. I could stay there."

"Okay. Let me meet with the attorney. I'll let you know when we can release you."

"Am I a suspect?"

"Not at this time."

"But I could be in the future?"

"At present our job is to gather evidence that will lead to a determination of what happened to your wife," Rossi said, hoping the statement didn't sound rote, though it was a standard line.

LaRussa looked him in the eye. More than a look. He engaged Rossi, so much so that Rossi felt a chill along his spine. "I didn't kill my wife, Detective."

"I didn't say you did, Mr. LaRussa."

"You didn't say I didn't either."

CHAPTER 6

Keera parked in her driveway adjacent to the elevated front walk leading to the nine-hundred-square-foot brick rambler she rented in the North Beacon Hill neighborhood once called Boeing Hill, because the homes were built in the 1950s and '60s for people going to work for the aerospace company.

"Welcome to my brick oven," she said.

Most Seattle homes did not have air-conditioning. Seattle was synonymous with rain. Not heat. Keera would have to fire up fans and try not to melt.

Inside, she dropped her keys in the glass bowl on the entry table. In the dining room she removed the bottle of Dalmore Port Wood Reserve Scotch from the sideboard cabinet and fished a glass from a kitchen cabinet, pouring two fingers. She added an ice cube and a splash of water and heard one of her father's mantras. *Just a splash. Don't baptize it.*

It had been another mentally exhausting family meal. In between the family griping over salad dressing, she'd almost forgotten that Patsy and Ella had made her a non-equity partner.

Why?

She'd been at the firm less than a year, and she

certainly wasn't bringing in much business. She thought of what had happened in court—Patsy not showing up in the afternoon, Ella looking like she had something to say, the conversation in the kitchen this evening with her mother.

He's old, Keera. The alcohol has aged him. He sees the end. Just have some empathy. That's all I'm asking.

Keera couldn't help but feel as though she'd been brought on board a sinking ship and handed a bucket.

Needing to relax, she walked back to the dining room table, where she kept a glass chessboard beside her laptop computer. She played online against anonymous opponents but used the chessboard to better evaluate the moves. She opened the chess app and entered her password, along with her chess name, Seattle Pawnslayer. A tournament director had bestowed the name on her when Keera had competed in tournaments in her teens. She had achieved the title of expert from the United States Chess Federation with a rating of 2192, just eight points below master. But titles had never been her goal. She started playing chess to spend time with her father. Her brothers and sisters had moved out, and her mother volunteered long hours at the local church. Patsy agreed to teach her, but only if she committed. He told Keera chess was more than a game. Chess could be a way to live her life.

They had played at night, after dinner and homework. Before a crackling fire, Patsy taught Keera to evaluate before reacting to an opponent's moves. He taught her to strategize, to consider not just her next move, but her opponent's options and how she would counter each. He told her the best trial lawyers were strong chess players.

When she regularly beat Patsy, he entered her in tournaments. She did not just do well. She won. Until Patsy showed up at one of her tournaments drunk and embarrassed her. She gave up the game and her last real connection with her father.

On her computer, she pulled up her game in progress against the Dark Knight. The names could be a bit melodramatic, but this player was better than competent, though he'd yet to beat Keera.

From: Darkknight
To: SeattlePawnslayer

A most ambitious move, Slayer.
I respectfully resign.
If you are so willing, a rematch?
I believe I have the first move . . .
Pawn d2 to d3.

Keera sipped her Scotch and reset her chessboard. She moved the Dark Knight's light-colored pawn from d2 to d3 and considered his move. Conservative, which was rare for someone playing the light-colored pieces. A strong player making the first move usually sought to control the center of the board. In their three prior games, the Dark Knight had come out aggressive, bold, even careless. Perhaps he had decided to take a defensive tactic.

Keera typed.

From: SeattlePawnslayer
To: Darkknight

I accept your resignation and your rematch.
Pawn to e5.

She took control of the center of the board.

The Dark Knight responded pawn to c3, continuing his conservative play. Keera responded pawn to d5, to gain more space in the board's center. The Dark Knight played pawn to g3, pushing to the right side of the board. Curious to see where this was going, she advanced her knight to c6. The Dark Knight responded bishop to g2, putting some pressure on the center and making Keera wonder if, perhaps, the Dark Knight had some other intent. Attacking with his bishop allowed his queen to slide out and pressure the center.

This could be a trap.

She decided to be conservative. Knight from g8 to e7.

Her cell phone rang.

She checked caller ID and groaned. The law firm call service. She was the attorney on call for the week. If anyone phoned after hours seeking a criminal defense attorney, or advice, Keera handled the matter. She hoped it was something simple. Something that could be put off until tomorrow.

Keera instructed the operator to put the call through. A click indicated the call had switched over, but the caller did not speak. "Hello?" Keera said.

"I'm calling for Patsy Duggan."

"Let's start with your name and why you think you need a criminal defense attorney."

"My name is Vince LaRussa. I'm at the Seattle police station downtown. Someone murdered my wife."

Keera recognized the name, though she couldn't recall why or from where. She asked LaRussa if he had been read his Miranda rights. He had not. The police said he wasn't a suspect. He was. She advised LaRussa to tell the detectives that, upon the advice of legal counsel, he declined to answer any further questions. Then to shut up.

She disconnected and jumped in her car without

calling Patsy or Ella, which only would have sent Ella into managing-partner mode, trying to control everything, and likely relegating Keera to some minor role. Not if Keera could help it.

She was qualified to defend persons accused of murder—though she'd never done so. She had sat second chair to Miller Ambrose on multiple aggravated-homicide prosecutions, including death penalty cases, and she had been the lead attorney on a dozen serious felony cases. She had also completed defense penalty seminars while at the PA's office.

If, in fact, Vince LaRussa faced such a charge.

The husband was always the prime suspect.

A senior prosecutor had kept a sign in his desk drawer—he'd been told not to hang it on his wall.

RULE NUMBER 1:
IT'S THE HUSBAND OR THE BOYFRIEND
RULE NUMBER 2:
SEE RULE NUMBER 1

More than 60 percent of violent crimes against women were inflicted by the husband or a live-in boyfriend. Another 20 to 25 percent were by men the women knew—a relative or family friend. If the police had taken LaRussa to Police Headquarters, they suspected him. The police never questioned you with the intent to eliminate you as a suspect, no matter what they told you. Nothing a suspect could say would improve his defense. Each time he opened his mouth, it was a mistake.

As she drove, Keera punched in "Vincent LaRussa" on a search engine on her phone and considered dozens of hits, including the one hit that jarred her memory.

Seattle Magazine.

LaRussa had been profiled on the magazine cover for his wealth-management and investment firm LWM, and for his philanthropy. Keera read as she drove, a no-no for certain, but on a Sunday night, traffic was light. The article said LaRussa had the Midas touch, consistently earning his investors healthy returns—he'd raised more than half a billion dollars in his investment fund. He sat on the boards of half a dozen companies and charitable organizations, including Seattle Children's Hospital, to which LaRussa and his wife, Anne, had donated generously.

All of which meant a potentially high-profile case, and a potentially high-profile client able to afford the very best representation, if in fact he needed it. That representation was Patsy Duggan. At least it had once been.

Because he's starting to slip. He's lost confidence and he's feeling useless.

Keera parked on Fifth Avenue, where spaces were plentiful. The glass doors to the main lobby of Police Headquarters were locked. No one sat at the desk. Keera called up to the Violent Crimes section and spoke to the on-call detective. She did not recognize the name but told him her business. He said someone would be down to let her in.

As she waited, Keera went through the sixteen Violent Crimes detectives in her head. She had a strong rapport with most, but a few would not be her first choice. When she heard the door rattle, she looked through the glass at Detective Frank Rossi. Her stomach dropped.

Rossi opened the door. "Keera." He sounded surprised.

"What the hell, Frank?" She stepped inside. "You know better than to question someone without an attorney present."

"He isn't under arrest."

They moved toward the bank of elevators. "Is he under suspicion?" Rossi didn't answer. "I take it you haven't read him his Miranda rights."

"As I said, he isn't under arrest."

They stepped onto the elevator and the door closed. "Then what is he doing down here at Police Headquarters?"

"His wife has been murdered. His house is currently a crime scene."

Something about Rossi's tone didn't sit right with her. She knew Rossi to be a straight shooter, even with public defenders. On the witness stand he didn't fudge the truth. He wasn't about to burn his integrity. "And you decided to provide him a quiet place for the evening?"

"Just listen for a moment, okay? You and I have worked a lot of cases together."

They had. Tough cases resulting in good sentences. They'd had a good rapport, a professional respect. Rossi worked hard, laughed easily, and didn't pull punches. He also listened. But Rossi had mistaken a professional relationship for something more. After a particularly hard-fought conviction and drinks to celebrate, Rossi told Keera he had feelings for her. At the time, Keera had not yet ended her clandestine relationship with Miller Ambrose, and she wasn't looking to start another, especially not with someone with whom she worked. Frank Rossi wasn't the wrong type. He was the wrong profession at the wrong time.

Rossi called her the next morning and apologized, said it had been the alcohol talking and hoped it didn't impact their professional relationship. An invisible wall now separated them and, though unseen, neither would cross it.

"LaRussa claims he came home from a charitable event and found his wife shot in the back of the head. He has a home security system so it's all easily verifiable. He consented to a DNA swab, and we took elimination fingerprints. I explained each to him fully, and in each instance, he said he wanted to cooperate. He signed consent forms."

"Then why did he call and ask for Patsy?"

"Look, Keera, it wasn't my decision to bring him down here for further questioning. The MDOP made that decision."

"You're not holding him, then?"

Rossi shook his head. "We're not."

"Where is he?"

"He's in the conference room down the hall."

"The soft interrogation room?" Keera knew the lingo in the police department. The soft interrogation room resembled a small conference room with a round table and chairs. The hard interrogation rooms resembled cramped jail cells and were designed to intimidate. Regardless, the goal was the same, to keep the suspect talking and catch him in an inconsistency or a lie.

The elevator stopped and the doors opened. They stepped off. "Get him, please. We're leaving."

"Something else," Rossi said, but he never got to finish his sentence.

Miller Ambrose stepped into the hall and smiled at her. "Keera Duggan."

She hadn't seen him in person in months. Now she'd seen him twice in three days.

"Miller's the MDOP attorney handling this matter," Rossi said.

CHAPTER 7

A part of Keera believed Ambrose had orchestrated this encounter, but that was just her anger. Ambrose being the MDOP on call had simply been the luck of the draw. Bad luck. Regardless, Keera knew Ambrose well enough to know from his shit-eating grin that he was enjoying the irony—and her uncomfortableness.

"We're not done questioning Mr. LaRussa," Ambrose said.

"Question him all you like, but he's done answering," she said.

"We can hold him for up to seventy-two hours," Ambrose said.

"Only if he's suspected of a crime." She turned to Rossi. "Is he suspected of a crime, Detective Rossi?"

"Not at this time," Rossi said.

"Then we're leaving. Unless you wish to discuss something else, Counselor?" Ambrose didn't.

"I'll get him." Rossi left Keera and Ambrose alone in the lobby.

"You know the statistics," Ambrose said. "It's always the husband."

"Not always. Sometimes it's the boyfriend who's abusive; isn't it?" she said.

Her comment seemed to rock Ambrose on his

heels, but only for a moment. "You just can't get over me, can you?" he said.

Keera smiled. "I think you got that wrong, Miller."

"You think I can't get over you?" He gave a sarcastic scoff.

"No, I think you can't get over yourself."

Rossi appeared in the hallway with a good-looking man wearing the remains of a tuxedo. They both looked from Keera to Ambrose, whose face had flushed red, and his jaw had set as if his molars had locked.

"Mr. LaRussa? Keera Duggan. Duggan & Associates." She extended a hand. "We're leaving."

In the elevator, Keera told LaRussa it was important they speak while the night's events remained fresh in his mind and suggested the conference room at Patrick Duggan & Associates. LaRussa said he had only briefly spoken to his wife's family and friends and needed to let them know what was happening. He suggested a downtown Seattle condominium he kept for when he worked late, which would allow him to make calls, since the police had taken his cell phone.

"They had a search warrant," LaRussa said.

The prosecutor ingrained in Keera couldn't ignore the possibility that LaRussa had killed his wife, though she also knew the large percentage of murderers didn't kill again. She agreed but told LaRussa she needed to let her office know what had transpired and her location. She didn't actually call Patsy or Ella. She phoned the call service, identified herself, and provided the location of LaRussa's condominium.

When Keera and LaRussa stepped out the glass doors of Police Headquarters, Greg Bartholomew, the *Seattle Times* courthouse reporter, snapped their picture with his cell phone, then proceeded to ask questions. Lawyers learned to walk away from Bartholomew. Keera offered "No comment" to each of his questions, ushered LaRussa into the passenger seat of her car, and hurried around the back to the driver's seat. She pulled from the curb, leaving Bartholomew on the sidewalk.

Minutes later she parked at the Residences at Rainier Square at Fourth Avenue and Union Street. The building looked like a long waterslide, the kind kids plunged down holding a rubber mat. Bathed in purple light, it rose high above the adjacent buildings.

LaRussa instructed Keera to give her keys to the valet, then led her inside the building lobby to an elevator bank. He used a card key to call an elevator, and they ascended to the fifty-eighth floor. Keera followed LaRussa inside an immaculate apartment with an open floor plan. She considered the space while he left the room to make his phone calls. A large living area flowed into a dining room adjacent to a pristine kitchen with appliances that looked unused. Floor-to-ceiling glass offered a view of the darkened waters of Elliott Bay—the surface mirroring the lights of the downtown office buildings, anchored cargo ships, and a crossing ferry. Red lights atop towers on Bainbridge Island flashed a warning to passing planes.

LaRussa returned just minutes later. "That was rough," he said with a long sigh. "Anne's father is going to call Anne's extended family and friends. I told them I'd provide more information as I obtained it. I offered to come over tomorrow morning, but they suggested I wait until everyone had more information."

Keera thought the family's reaction odd. "What's your relationship like with Anne's family?"

LaRussa shook his head. "We're cordial but we've never been close."

"Why is that?"

"I don't really know. Initially I think it was because they had money. Anne had a trust. I don't come from much. I think they were just trying to protect their daughter."

"And they never warmed to you . . . even after your success?"

"Some," LaRussa said. "I've made them a lot of money over the years, but it's more of a professional than a personal relationship."

He pulled two glasses from a cabinet. "Drink?" He sounded exhausted.

Keera gave the bottle of Scotch on the counter a long look, too long, before declining.

"Do you mind?" he asked. "I'm not sure how I'll sleep."

"No."

LaRussa poured himself a Scotch and added a single ice cube. He carried it back into the living area, slumping onto a white leather couch, and balanced his drink on his lap. Keera took a seat across a layered coffee table of white, beige, and gray blocks.

"I just can't believe it," he said quietly.

"Mr. LaRussa, before we get started—"

"Vince," he said. "I'm assuming from the last name that Patrick Duggan is your father?"

"He is."

"Is he going to meet us here?"

"I can call him if you'd like, but I don't think we need to do that tonight." Not after the number of glasses of wine her father had consumed at dinner. He was likely passed out asleep. "I do, however, need to confirm that it's your intention to retain the law firm, though you haven't been arrested."

"Yes, of course."

"I'll have an agreement drafted tomorrow and sent over for your signature, but the relationship starts now. What we talk about is covered by the attorney-client privilege. Anything you tell me I'm obligated to hold in strict confidence. I want you to understand that you can be truthful. I cannot disclose what is said, not to the police, the newspapers, not to anyone."

"I didn't kill my wife," he said.

Keera paused. Then she said, "I don't care."

LaRussa gave her an inquisitive look.

"The prosecutor cares. My job as your attorney is to represent you to the best of my ability, regardless of your guilt or innocence. My job is to ensure that, should the prosecutor file charges, your constitutional rights are protected, and that the prosecutor follows all state and local rules. You are innocent of all crimes until proven guilty after a fair trial, were it to come to that."

"I understand. But I think it's important for you to understand that you are not representing a man who killed his wife."

"Okay." She removed a pad of legal paper and a pen from her briefcase. "I'd like you to take a step back and tell me exactly what you remember. Where you were tonight, during what period of time; when you came home; what you did, what you saw. Everything and anything."

For the next half hour, LaRussa reconstructed his evening, starting with his appearing at the Children's Hospital fundraiser. "I was the first speaker after the silent auction closed. I think that was at around eight o'clock. I requested to talk first so I didn't leave Anne home alone all night."

"Were you concerned about her for some reason?"

"No more than normal." He sipped his whisky.

Keera's lips moistened. She cleared her throat. "What do you mean by that?"

"Anne had emotional mood swings. Some days were worse than others. We'd recently received a diagnosis that Anne's progress in her rehab had likely reached its limits. Any further improvement would be incremental."

"What type of rehab was your wife undergoing?"

LaRussa closed his eyes. "I'm sorry. I've answered the question so many times tonight I forgot you weren't there. You don't know."

"That's all right."

LaRussa explained his wife's paralysis following a horse-jumping accident, and that she was confined to a wheelchair. "When her progress plateaued, her mood plummeted, especially these last few weeks."

"In what way?"

"She was in a dark place, irritable, short-tempered, frustrated, depressed." He rose from his seat and crossed back to the bar.

"Were you worried your wife could take her own life?"

He poured another finger of whisky, then walked back to his seat. "She'd never expressed anything like that to me, and frankly I don't know how she could have."

"What do you mean?"

"Anne's paralysis included both hands. It wasn't total . . . Have you seen the hands of someone with severe arthritis?"

"I have."

"I don't know how Anne could have even held the gun. She could barely hold a glass. And then to squeeze the trigger . . . I don't think her fingers had the strength."

None of which helped LaRussa's cause, though Keera didn't say that.

LaRussa sipped his drink and set it on the table between them. The ice rattled. "I arrived home at around nine fifteen. The security cameras will confirm the exact time."

Keera's interest picked up considerably when she heard "security cameras." She spent the next twenty minutes asking what the cameras covered, where the video was stored, whether they recorded audio as well as video, and made a note to view the tape, though Rossi likely had the copy from the house, and LaRussa's laptop had also been taken. Keera made a note to view the tape ASAP.

LaRussa told Keera the police asked him about the entry pad at the front door and had him and an officer search the house for any evidence of a forced entry.

"Was there?" she asked.

"No."

"What did you do when you arrived home?"

"I called out to let Anne know I was home. I went into the family room because the television was on, but Anne wasn't there. I shut the television and the lights off, then looked down the hall to the master bedroom. The door was ajar. I could see a faint light. I figured Anne had gone to bed early. I went into the kitchen to get a glass of water, a nightly routine. Anne sat across from the kitchen counter in her wheelchair. She had her back to me. She was slumped to the right. I thought she was asleep; she'd fall asleep in her chair frequently. I said something. I don't recall what exactly." He paused and looked to be fighting tears. "Anne didn't answer." He exhaled audibly. "Just need a minute."

"Take your time."

"I said, 'Anne? Anne?' She didn't answer. I flipped the light switch for the four pendant lights over the counter. That's when I saw . . ." LaRussa shut his eyes and lowered his head. He sipped his drink. After a moment, he opened his eyes and looked up at the ceiling. His voice broke. After another moment, he said, "It looked like she'd been shot in the back of the head, but . . ."

Which would also dictate against a suicide and potentially be evidence that Anne knew the person and had not been concerned turning her back to the person. LaRussa?

Keera gave LaRussa a moment. Then she asked, "What did you do next?"

"I don't recall. At some point I looked down and saw a gun on the floor."

"Did you touch it?"

He shook his head. "I don't believe so."

"This is important, Vince."

"I didn't. I didn't touch it."

"Did you recognize the gun?"

"I don't own a gun. Neither did Anne. So, no. I didn't recognize it."

Keera searched her databank of tried cases. She could think of just two instances in which the defendant had left the gun behind. In one, a murder in the woods, the killer had panicked and dropped the gun, then couldn't find it in the dark. In the other, Keera's private investigator believed the killer had worn gloves when loading the magazine and when he fired the weapon. The gun had no connection to him. He didn't own it and he hadn't purchased it. Leaving it behind meant it couldn't be found in a place to which he had some connection. Slick.

So had Anne LaRussa's killer been careless or slick?

"Then what?" Keera asked.

"I reached for my cell phone, but I had put it on the counter when I came in the door, along with my car keys. My routine. I backtracked from the kitchen, called 911. The person told me to go outside and wait for the police. She stayed on the line with me."

"How long before the police arrived after you called 911?"

"I don't know. Minutes that felt like hours. The rest is a blur. They asked me questions, and I answered them until the attorney showed up, and they brought me to the station downtown. When they took my phone and computer, the fog I'd been in lifted, and I realized I needed a lawyer."

"The husband is always a suspect," Keera said.

"I loved my wife."

"It doesn't change the probabilities, I'm afraid."

LaRussa made a face. He looked beat. Spent. He had a right.

Keera checked her watch. It was after midnight. "Do you have a computer here?"

"No. I usually just bring my laptop."

"I'll let you get some rest."

He gave the wisp of a smile as if to say, *Yeah, like that is going to happen.*

She stood. LaRussa followed her to the door. "Did you or your wife have any enemies? Anyone who would want to harm you?"

"I make people money, Keera. Most people are happy about that."

"I'll get into the office tomorrow and begin to

put together a plan of action. I'd like to hire a private investigator to work for us."

"Can we get the police detectives' investigation? Aren't we entitled to it?"

"Not if you haven't been charged with a crime."

"They kept asking for my permission," LaRussa said. "I just thought they would provide me with the results of what they were doing."

"I've asked the detectives to notify me when you can get back into your house. If they call you, do not talk with them, and don't go into your house without me. I want things to be undisturbed as much as possible. The press will be hunting you, as you've already experienced. A shooting in your neighborhood is rare. The killing of a prominent businessman's wife is going to garner a lot of interest and speculation. I'd suggest not watching the news or reading the newspapers. Say nothing to anyone—not to family, employees, or friends. Reporters might camp out at your home and outside your office building. You might want to hire private security. I can help set that up." She reached into her purse and pulled out a business card, leaving it on the marble countertop near the door. "Tomorrow, call the receptionist at your office. Tell her if anyone calls for you or wants to know your whereabouts, she is to give them my name and my telephone number. Do you have any questions for me?"

"Probably, but right now my brain is fried."

"You have my number." Keera opened the door.

She stepped into the hall. "I'm very sorry about your wife, Vince." She hoped it sounded sincere, but the prosecutor in her couldn't get past rule number one.

Keera returned home at just before one in the morning, her adrenaline still pumping and too amped to sleep. She needed a drink. She picked up her drink from earlier in the evening, refreshed it, and took a sip. The subtle nectarine-and-raisin taste rolled over her tongue and warmed her throat and stomach.

She hit the space bar of her keyboard, bringing the computer to life, hoping the Dark Knight had at least made his next move.

From: Darkknight
To: SeattlePawnslayer

Knight to f3.

Keera moved the piece on her chessboard and studied it. The Dark Knight had finally put pressure on the center squares.

"Okay," she said. "Maybe there's a method to your madness."

She moved her pawn to g6.

To her surprise, she got a response. She wasn't the only one not sleeping.

His sixth move, the Dark Knight castled his king—his rook and king switching places on the board, the only move in chess that allowed a player to move two pieces at the same time. A strategic move strong players used in almost every game.

Keera moved her bishop to g7—what was referred to in the chess world as a "fianchetto bishop." The Dark Knight moved his knight from b1 to d2.

Keera responded pawn to h6.

The Dark Knight was either studying his board or had the good sense to go to bed. Keera sipped her Scotch and waited. She thought about Vince LaRussa. He seemed sincere. He seemed to be telling the truth. So did many of the men she'd prosecuted who had been found guilty.

She'd find out soon enough.

CHAPTER 8

June 5, 2023

Keera awoke early, despite not getting to sleep until after two. She wanted to beat Ella into the office and speak to Patsy, who usually arrived before seven, even after nights drinking. His daughters called his ability to quickly recover "the Irish curse"—no hangover, and thus no pain to dissuade him from overindulging again. That, and a good wife who always made sure Patsy ate, kept him functioning.

Before departing her house, Keera brought her computer to life. The Dark Knight had made his eighth move late the previous night.

> From: Darkknight
> To: SeattlePawnslayer
>
> Pawn to c4

She smiled. "What do we have here?"

This signaled a major strategy shift. The Dark Knight had gone on the offensive, unlocking his knight and his queen to attack. Keera had a visceral reaction, as she had at her championship matches, but she remembered Patsy's tutelage.

Evaluate. Consider. Then move. She did so and moved her bishop to e6. It appeared to be another defensive move, but again, Keera had a different intent—preparing to attack the fortress the Dark Knight had built around his king.

Keera had no sooner stepped off the elevator than Patsy came down the hall, the *Seattle Times* newspaper in hand. At that same moment, Ella, uncharacteristically early, hurried into the office from the elevator, her hair still wet. She wore jeans, a T-shirt, sneakers, and otherwise looked disheveled. A suit and blouse on hangers hung over her shoulder.

"Holy shit, did you see the inside page of the metro section?" Ella said.

Keera didn't receive a hard copy of the newspaper. Hers was a generation that obtained news from their computers and cell phones. Patsy held up the metro section. Beneath a headline was the picture of Keera and Vincent LaRussa leaving Police Headquarters.

Seattle Wealth Manager Questioned in Wife's Death

"Why do you think I'm in early?" Keera said innocently. "The call came in over the answering service late last night."

"And you didn't call us?" Ella asked.

"I didn't see the need to call last night and wake everyone."

"You didn't see the need?" Ella shot Patsy a look, then said to Keera, "Do you know who Vincent LaRussa is?"

"I'm aware, yes, and I have it under control."

"He's estimated to be worth a hundred million dollars and runs the biggest investment fund in the state."

"I know," Keera reiterated. Ella had no doubt looked up LaRussa on the internet.

"And you didn't see the need to call me or Patsy?"

"Let's take this in the conference room," Patsy said.

"I have work I need to get done, calls to make," Keera said.

"Conference room. Now," Patsy said. Discussion over. He turned and headed into the glass-enclosed room.

Windows provided a western view of Elliott Bay, glass calm from the persistent heat wave. A stain of rust-colored haze lingered on the distant horizon, a rarity for Seattle. Ella draped her business clothes over the back of a leather chair.

"Sit," Patsy said.

Keera and Ella dutifully sat. Patsy stood at the head of the table. "Now tell us what happened," he said to Keera.

Keera had decided on the drive into the office

to keep her explanation simple. She told them about the call to the switchboard and said she had handled the situation. "Did you tell him you have never defended a client accused of murder?" Ella asked.

"You're jumping the gun here, Ella. He hasn't been accused of murder."

"Not yet," Ella said. She shifted her attention back to her father. "I made a call this morning to a contact. I'm told the MDOP on the file is Miller Ambrose."

"I'm aware," Keera said, not wanting to be ignored. "Ambrose was at Police Headquarters last night. And maybe you're unaware, but I was qualified at the PA's office to try murder cases."

Patsy and Ella exchanged another glance. Patsy spoke in a patronizing tone. "But you've never defended one, and a case this high profile isn't one to cut your teeth on."

Keera didn't appreciate being treated as his little girl. "I'm not cutting my teeth on anything. I told LaRussa over the phone to not say anything to anyone except that he wanted a lawyer. Then I pulled him from questioning at SPD and spoke with him for nearly two hours."

"And?" Ella asked.

"And I'd like to get to my office to start checking out his alibi and working on his defense. I'll dictate my notes of the conversation and have my assistant provide you each with a copy."

Patsy spoke again in his concerned-father tone. "Keera, these cases can take on a life of their own. There is a lot of ground to cover."

"*If* he is accused, there will be more than enough for all of us to do. Maggie included."

"Maybe more than we can handle," Patsy said, looking uncomfortable.

"More than . . . Look, I think we should at least meet with LaRussa," Ella said to Patsy, as if Keera wasn't in the room.

"I told you, I met with LaRussa," Keera shot back. "At the moment, he's speaking to family and friends, and he's got a funeral to plan."

"What's he telling them?"

"Only the facts as he knows them. I'm going to set up a meeting with JP and get back into the house to conduct our own investigation," she said, referring to JP Harrison, their private investigator. She looked at her watch. "Frank Rossi told me they will release the site later this afternoon. In the interim, I have calls to make to confirm that Vince LaRussa spoke last night at a Seattle Children's Hospital fundraiser at the Four Seasons, as well as the time he left that event and says he drove straight home. His home has security cameras, and Rossi and Ford are already ahead of me."

Keera and Ella looked to Patsy. Though Ella was ostensibly the managing partner and handled the day-to-day firm management, Patsy's opinion still carried more weight. "All right. Keera, you'll run with this, for now. But with the understanding that if you get in over your head, you will ask for help." He put up a hand to keep her from responding. "Clients don't need heroes. They need competent, well-reasoned representation. Remember. Evaluate and consider before you make a move. Don't rush. And don't let your desire to win influence the moves you make."

"I won't," Keera said.

"*If LaRussa is charged* . . . we'll have to make a decision then on what to do," Patsy said. He let out a breath, then he stood from the table and walked out the door.

After he had departed, Ella shut the door. "I'm still the managing partner of this firm. You will keep me updated on what is going on."

"I just said I would."

"Did you and LaRussa discuss a billable rate?"

"No."

"Good. It's six hundred dollars an hour."

"Six hundred dollars an hour? I've never billed out at that high a rate."

"You've never had a client worth a hundred million dollars. If he bitches, tell him prisoners make twelve to forty cents per hour. Look, Keera, we need this case. The firm needs this case."

"What's going on, Ella? You started to say something yesterday but stopped. Then Mom told me last night that Dad's slipping. That he hasn't been himself. He hasn't had a big case since I arrived."

"He's turned down several significant cases," Ella said.

"What? Why?"

"Because he doesn't think he can handle them. He had a couple of panic attacks in court, and he's gun shy. I'm sure that's why he didn't show up to cross the officer in Clancy Doyle's case."

"That was a routine DUI. He's crossed police officers hundreds of times."

Ella shrugged. "I'm just telling you what's going on."

"Where does that leave us?" Keera asked. "If Patsy's reputation is the firm and he's turning down cases, then what's left?"

"I'm not sure. The firm has always been Patsy's. Putting 'and Associates' after his name hasn't changed that. Clients still want the Irish Brawler. I'm just not sure he exists any longer, and without him . . ." She paused. "Look, we own the building, but we'll be doing DUIs, low-level possession charges, and petty thefts."

"So we need this case, then," Keera said.

"We need to win it," Ella said.

No pressure, Keera thought.

She went to her office and got to work. She reached LaRussa at his condominium and went over the terms of their agreement. He agreed to the hourly rate without question. Keera had a secretary draw it up, then messenger the agreement to LaRussa for a signature. He asked about Patsy. Keera told him she had brought Patsy up to speed on all the details that morning, and they had discussed a road map going forward.

Next, she got in touch with JP Harrison, whom she woke, and it didn't sound like the bachelor was alone. Harrison told Keera he'd be at her office within the hour. She then called Seattle Children's Hospital and reached the fundraising event chairman, who confirmed LaRussa spoke at the event, but couldn't recall specifically when LaRussa arrived or left. She did state LaRussa had asked to speak first, after the silent auction and dinner.

Next, Keera called the Four Seasons, asked for the security desk, and, after starts and stops, spoke to its head of security, Amar Dalal. Dalal said the luxury hotel had security cameras, including a camera that monitored the front entrance portico where attendees dropped off and picked up their cars. Keera asked that Dalal take possession of the tape for Sunday evening to prevent it from being erased or filmed over.

"One step ahead of you," he said. "I got a call from a detective, just before you called, asking that I secure the tape. I have done so."

Rossi. Keera was on the right path but a step behind. She swore under her breath at Ella for delaying her. She advised Dalal she would send him a subpoena requesting the film, to satisfy hotel management protocols, then provided her email information. She hung up, called her assistant, and told him to prepare and send the subpoena.

Next, she called and asked the Washington State Department of Transportation about traffic cameras between the Four Seasons and LaRussa's home. A manager directed Keera online to street cameras and advised her on how to get specific camera footage for the particular day and time. She again instructed her assistant to get the footage. LaRussa drove a 2022 silver Porsche 911. It would not be difficult to spot the $120,000 automobile. Once she had the footage, she would have Harrison drive and time the route LaRussa said he took from the Four Seasons to his home. The home security camera would document LaRussa's arrival, and she should have her timeline. She'd also confirm this through the geo records on LaRussa's cell phone, when LaRussa got his phone back.

Which was an excuse to call Detective Frank Rossi.

"Wow. Seven minutes after nine. What took you so long?" Rossi said.

She pictured Rossi checking his wristwatch. "When can we get back into Vince LaRussa's house?"

"We should be out this afternoon."

"And when can Vince LaRussa get back his cell phone and laptop?"

"When TESU is finished," he said. Keera had worked with Andrei Vilkotski, head of the Technical and Electronic Support Unit. Vilkotski would create a forensic image of Vince and Anne LaRussa's laptop computers' and cell phones' hard drives and memories, capturing their emails, internet searches, photographs, text messages, browsing history, and documents, including deleted files.

"Vince LaRussa wants to call his wife's friends and doesn't have their numbers," she said, making it up.

"Again, not my call entirely, but hopefully TESU will be finished soon."

"Are you going to provide copies of the CSI reports?" She knew Rossi's answer but figured it couldn't hurt to ask.

"I told you last night, your client hasn't been charged with a crime."

"You asked LaRussa for his permission to be fingerprinted and to provide DNA."

"And he gave it."

"He believed he'd get copies of the reports."

"Not my call, Keera."

Ambrose. "Those are SPD reports," she said.

"Everything has to be run through the PA."

"Why is he keeping such a tight lid if LaRussa isn't being charged?"

"You know why, Keera." She did. The husband was always the primary suspect. Ambrose would not give the defense squat, and definitely not until and unless LaRussa was charged and arraigned. He'd make it difficult for her even if that occurred. He'd withhold evidence Keera did not specifically request, and he'd do everything he could to mentally wear her down. Keera didn't like starting on the defensive, but she had no choice. At present Ambrose controlled the center squares. So be it. She'd look for her moments to attack.

"Sorry, Keera. Wish there was something I could do," Rossi said.

She almost said, *Grow a pair, Frank.* But she knew that wouldn't help her situation.

CHAPTER 9

Forty minutes later, Keera looked up at the sound of three sharp raps on her office door. JP Harrison knocked as if he was trying to take the door off its hinges—an old habit from when he served search warrants as an SPD detective. He entered looking stylish, as always, in slim black pants rolled at the ankles, white tennis shoes with no socks, and an untucked light-blue dress shirt, sleeves rolled to his elbows.

"Hey," she said, not completely suppressing a smile. "Hope I didn't interrupt anything this morning."

Harrison returned the grin, though his was more subtle. A good-looking, fifty-year-old Black man whom Maggie called tall, dark, and hand-some, Harrison had a smile and personality that could charm the queen of England out of her knickers. Born in Liverpool to parents who had been Beatles fans and shared the same last name as the guitarist, George Harrison, he had been named John Paul after John Lennon and Paul McCartney. After enduring beatings from schoolmates, Harrison went by the moniker JP—and learned how to fight. In the United States, he was picked on for his flamboyant fashion and his accent. He graduated high school, studied criminal justice in college, and served twenty-five years at SPD, making Violent Crimes detective. He retired to do private consulting. Patrick Duggan & Associates was one of his regular clients.

"There will be other mornings." He slid into a chair across Keera's desk and looked about. "Don't think I've ever been in your office. Understated furnishings. Not nearly as lived in as Ella's office. Or Patsy's."

"Ella and Patsy live here. I'm trying not to."

He pointed to the ego wall behind her that included framed diplomas from college and law school and her legal certification to practice in Washington State. "I'd ask if they misspelled your name, but since it's uniform on every document, I'm guessing they didn't."

Her parents named her Ciara Katherine Duggan, but since no one outside her family could spell or say the Gaelic version of her name correctly, she used the phonetic spelling: Keera. In Gaelic her name meant "dark," which fit her coal-black hair, though not her crystal-blue eyes. "Black Irish," her mother had said.

"Made a few calls," Harrison said. "Rossi and Ford are the investigating detectives—"

She grabbed her briefcase and jacket. "Three steps ahead of you. Just talked to Rossi. They're turning over the house. You have all your equipment?"

"In the car."

"I'll fill you in on the drive." She took out her cell phone and called Vince LaRussa's condominium, telling him to meet them outside his house.

The television news vans remained, now parked farther down the street from LaRussa's driveway. The reporters peered at Keera and Harrison as they drove past. Two men wearing suits and sunglasses greeted them atop the driveway. Private security. LaRussa had taken her advice.

LaRussa waited outside his front door, as Keera had instructed. Keera made the introductions. Harrison offered his condolences. LaRussa reiterated he'd spoken with Anne's father and the family was justifiably upset and wanted answers. LaRussa had told them he would keep them abreast of the situation.

Keera quickly told LaRussa about calls she had made to the Seattle Children's Hospital and to the Four Seasons, as well as to Frank Rossi, hoping her diligence would impress him. "We won't get any of their expert reports, not unless they decide to charge you. I asked, but they are not yet under any obligation to turn over those reports. Hopefully, it will never be an issue."

"What about my computer and cell phone?"

"Their electronic support unit is downloading

the information from both. I've asked them to expedite their return."

They walked down the steps to the front door.

"Is this how you entered the house last night when you arrived home?" Harrison asked. He carried a dark-brown leather backpack with the gear he anticipated needing.

LaRussa said it was, entered the code, and pushed open the door. Harrison asked him who else knew the code, whether his wife was expecting any visitors that evening, and many of the same questions Keera had asked the prior evening. LaRussa patiently answered each question and told Harrison of his discussions with the detectives—before his instincts caused him to stop talking and call a lawyer.

Inside the house, LaRussa pointed to the kitchen beyond a swinging door in the dining room. "If you don't mind, I'd prefer to wait out here. Once was enough."

"Certainly," Harrison said. "Let me ask, when you arrived home, did you notice anything out of the ordinary?"

LaRussa told them the air-conditioning had been turned off, and at Harrison's request showed them the keypad in the hall.

"I felt the change in temperature as soon as I got inside."

He said Rossi and Ford had wondered if the system could have shut down during a power outage, and he told them the lights and the tele-vision were on when he arrived home.

Keera made a note to call Puget Sound Energy and determine if there had been any electrical outages during the heat wave. "Had your wife ever turned off the thermostat before?"

"Not that I recall."

Keera and Harrison shared a look. It could be nothing. It could be something.

"I have another job for you," Keera said to LaRussa as Harrison got his equipment together. She opened her laptop and entered her pass code. "Since the police have your and your wife's com-puters, I need you to access your account on the cloud and obtain the security camera footage for Sunday evening from whatever time you left the house until you returned."

LaRussa took the laptop into his study.

Harrison and Keera slipped on disposable gloves and booties before they entered the kitchen. The wheelchair remained, though Keera assumed it had been moved when the ME took control of Anne LaRussa's body. The black-and-white checked tile was smeared with blood near the chair. Harrison shook his head. "Like a herd of elephants," he said.

"Vince said he found his wife sitting in her chair facing the view."

He pointed. "And the broken glass and water on the floor?"

"I'll ask," Keera said and explained what LaRussa told her the prior night.

"Ask him about the candle and the towel on the counter also," Harrison said, nodding to the counter.

The walls, appliances, and countertops were covered with black fingerprint dust.

Harrison took another step into the room. "Where exactly was the gun?"

"The floor on that side of the counter, according to Vince."

The gun's location would be documented in photographs in the police report. She told Harrison that LaRussa said his wife was not capable of holding a gun and pulling the trigger because of her disability, and that she was shot in the back of the head. "Both of which would seem to rule out suicide."

"Not his or his wife's gun? So, the killer left it?" Harrison asked.

"Seems that way."

"Hmm."

"What?"

"Just something to consider." Harrison squatted to examine blood spatter on the back side of the kitchen island and floor, though the blood on the floor looked to have been diluted by water. "Much of the water probably evaporated if the thermostat was off, given how hot it was Sunday. Do we know the caliber of the bullet?"

"Not yet."

He removed a small plastic ruler from his go bag and measured the diameter of a few spatter drops. The diameter was a means to determine the distance between the victim and the weapon, as well as the caliber of bullet. "Less than a millimeter," Harrison said. "It wasn't a peashooter. Nine millimeters or more. Shot at close range."

"How close?"

"Don't hold me to it, but five to seven feet, give or take."

Which again ruled out suicide, though Keera didn't say that out loud, not wanting to influence Harrison's investigation. As part of his SPD experience, Harrison had, like all detectives, worked as a CSI detective for two years. He knew their routines, making it difficult for a prosecutor to attack his techniques, methods, or practices without attacking his own CSI detectives and their conclusions. CSI's mantra was to assume nothing and gather all available evidence.

Harrison removed a camera, notebook, and tape measure. He snapped photographs and took measurements. He then opened a black case containing a digital room scanner he'd use to measure the entire room from different points and obtain a 3D model.

"I'll leave you to it," Keera said. She exited the kitchen to find out how Vince LaRussa was doing.

Harrison, already knee-deep in his work, grunted a reply.

In the study, LaRussa worked at an ornate desk. He looked up as Keera entered. "I accessed the home security system. The front door was opened and closed six times between 6:00 and 9:34 Sunday night. I've written down the exact times." He handed her a piece of paper. "I have no idea why the door was opened and closed the first four times, or if anyone entered."

"Was the code entered?"

"I don't know. That isn't recorded. No other door or window on the security system was opened during that time."

"What about the security cameras?"

"That's the problem. I can't access the video."

"What do you mean you can't access it?"

"I mean the cloud indicates the video was removed," LaRussa said, visibly frustrated.

Ambrose. Bastard.

"Call the security company. Tell them who you are . . . You must have an account with a user-name and password."

"I do."

"Tell them the video you want and ask them if it is still somehow available, if you can somehow still access it from the cloud."

"Okay."

She asked LaRussa questions that Harrison had asked her.

"I assume Anne dropped the glass when shot," LaRussa said, confirming his wife could hold a glass. He explained to Keera that the detectives had asked him about the candle, and he had told them it was part of Anne's aromatherapy. Keera also asked him about the distance of the gun from the wheelchair, and about the towel on the kitchen counter. LaRussa clarified where the gun was on the floor but had no explanation why the towel was on the counter or why it was wet. "Maybe Anne spilled something, maybe the water in her glass. Simple tasks were not simple for Anne."

Keera returned to the kitchen uttering profanities.

"What's wrong?" Harrison asked, shooting measurements.

Keera told him what LaRussa had determined about the security system and the video.

"It's not a police-generated report. The owner clearly has a right to access it."

"Ambrose is going to make everything a dogfight. It's what he does." She took a breath. "How are you doing?"

"You said the wife was shot in the back of the head?"

"That's what LaRussa said. I haven't verified it."

"The blood spatter certainly does. The spatter on the countertop is considerable, while the spatter on the wall beneath it is not as much, indicating the victim was close to the counter when shot, which means the shooter had to be on the other side of the counter. If I'm accurate, then the question becomes: Why was the gun found on the floor near the wheelchair? If the shooter intended to leave it, a natural sequence would be to fire the weapon, drop the gun, and leave. There would be no reason to toss a loaded gun over the counter."

"Except to make the shooting look like a suicide," Keera said.

"Perhaps, but if that was the intent, why shoot the victim in the back of the head?"

"Good point." She thought again about where the gun had been found. "He might have come around the counter to ensure she was dead, then dropped the gun."

"Maybe, but someone being that careful, it doesn't seem likely they'd risk leaving shoe prints. Something else I noticed." Harrison walked behind the counter to the upper oven. "Look here."

Keera looked from the other side and noticed a black mark. "Looks like a wear mark," she said.

"It looks like a burn mark to me. I've taken a scraping to analyze. Also, the oven was locked shut. We need to determine why."

"How did you find that?"

"When I was a detective we made it a habit

123

to check the refrigerator door handle and the bathrooms. Killers would often open the fridge and use the toilet. I got in the habit of checking the other appliances as well."

"Vince said they have a housekeeper. I'll find out if she locked the oven to clean it. What are you thinking?"

"At this point, nothing concrete," Harrison said. "But this seems to be anything but a grounder, Keera."

CHAPTER 10

Frank Rossi cued his desktop computer and pulled up the LaRussas' home security video for Sunday. Miller Ambrose had told Rossi and Ford to make reviewing the video a priority. The two detectives didn't appreciate Ambrose telling them how to do their job, or what to prioritize. It made Rossi want to do the hundred other things on his plate first, but he had to forget about Ambrose and think of Anne LaRussa, the victim of a brutal crime.

Ambrose's abrasive and demanding demeanor was one reason he was not well liked by most Violent Crimes detectives. Female detectives in particular considered him arrogant and condescending. Ambrose too often discounted the detectives' opinions on how best to investigate their cases.

Rossi had other reasons for disliking Ambrose. For one, he did not appreciate the way Ambrose had treated Keera Duggan at Police Headquarters, which seemed to confirm the unstated reason why Duggan, once a rising star in the PA's office, had abruptly left. Rossi initially thought it had been his ill-timed confession of feelings beyond their professional relationship. Keera's demeanor, which had been outgoing and extroverted, changed about that time. But Rossi had then started hearing the rumors that Keera and Ambrose had been an item, that Keera ended the relationship, and Ambrose, not happy about it, made her life difficult. Rossi surmised that Ambrose's current orders that Rossi keep his investigation close to the vest were more about payback than good police work, and the motivation didn't sit well with him.

Rossi fast-forwarded the tape, watching with one eye while considering emails, text messages, and telephone calls that TESU had captured from Anne and Vince LaRussa's computers and cell phones. Movement on the videotape caught his attention, and he stopped the tape and rewound, then hit play. A maroon Model X Tesla drove down the LaRussa driveway and parked. He jotted down the time, 6:07 p.m., as well as the license plate number. A man got out of the car wearing a button-down shirt, slacks, and brown dress shoes. Rossi's pulse quickened. The man looked to be of average height, with thinning silver hair. He leaned into his car interior and retrieved a lawyer's-style briefcase, then headed to the front door.

"Interesting."

Roughly twenty-five minutes later, at 6:31 p.m., the man emerged from behind the laurel hedge with a cell phone pressed to his ear. He paused in the driveway, looking about for several seconds, before he lowered the phone and returned to his car. He sped backward up the driveway.

Rossi hit fast-forward and expected to next see Vince LaRussa's silver Porsche. Instead, a blue BMW drove down the driveway and parked. Again, Rossi noted the time, 7:03 p.m., and the license plate. Again, his curiosity was piqued.

The driver was a tall, blonde woman also dressed in business attire—navy-blue slacks and a cream-colored blouse. She opened the back door and slid the strap of a large handbag, bigger than a purse, more the size of a beach bag, over her shoulder. The woman stepped between the two lions and disappeared behind the laurel hedge.

Twenty-six minutes later, at 7:29 p.m., the woman hurried up the steps and tossed her bag in the back seat. She got into her car and nearly backed into the curving, rock retaining wall. She jerked to a stop, corrected, and sped up the driveway to the street. Something had clearly unnerved her, but there had been no 911 call from a woman reporting a dead body, which meant Anne LaRussa had been alive when the first visitor had left the home.

LaRussa drove his Porsche down the driveway at 9:17 p.m. and parked in one of the two garage bays. He emerged in his tuxedo but with his back to the camera. He walked down the stairs in no apparent hurry with his jacket draped over his shoulder and disappeared behind the laurel hedge. At 9:34 p.m. LaRussa came back up the stairs to the driveway, his cell phone pressed to his ear. He'd reached 911 at 9:24, the call recorded. He paced the asphalt and kneaded his brow until a patrol car arrived. LaRussa quickly led the two responding police officers to the front door.

Billy Ford came into the C Team's four-desk cubicle area and leaned against Rossi's desk. "Just spoke to Del and Faz. LaRussa's neighbors did not hear a gunshot, and none had security cameras with audio. Those neighbors living closest to the house were either on boats on Lake Washington or in air-conditioned restaurants. One owner was home but in the back of the house with fans going while he watched the Mariners game on the television."

"I just watched the videotape from the camera over the garage," Rossi said.

"Anything of interest? LaRussa's timeline check out?"

"His timeline checks out, but the wife had two visitors before LaRussa arrived home."

"No shit?" Ford said, suddenly interested.

"A man, then a woman. The woman left looking upset."

"No call to 911 by a woman," Ford said.

"I know," Rossi said. "Both the man and the woman looked affluent, at least based on the cars driven and their dress. The man carried a briefcase." Ford bent down to view Rossi's computer screen as he rewound and fast-forwarded the tape. "I got clear captures of each license plate. I'm about to have them run."

"You watch the rest of the tape. I'll run the plates," Ford said. "Then we'll take a drive and talk to them both."

Rossi handed Ford his page of notes. "See if the ME has an estimated time of death yet?"

"Roger that. Damn . . ."

"What?"

"I thought we were going to have a legitimate mystery. Starting to feel like it will be a routine grounder to short, doesn't it?"

"Maybe. Sometimes those routine grounders can hit a rock, skip, and hit you in the eye."

"Anyone ever tell you you're a ray of sunshine?"

"Every day."

"Liar."

CHAPTER 11

After speaking to the LaRussas' neighbors, Keera returned to the house with no new information except that Violent Crimes detectives Del Castigliano and Vic Fazzio had visited their homes late Sunday night, leaving business cards, which meant they were the next-up detective team.

Harrison was finishing up his work in the kitchen. "Anything?" he asked when Keera entered.

She shook her head and told him what she had learned. "No security cameras with audio." Then she asked, "What do we know?"

"Not likely a suicide, though one never knows for certain until one analyzes all the evidence. I have the scraping from the oven door handle and a sample of what was left of the water on the floor."

"Why the sample?"

"Because it was there."

"Very scientific. How much more do you have to do?"

"Just about done."

"I'm going to go find LaRussa; has he come into the kitchen at all?"

Harrison shook his head. "Can't say I blame

him either. I don't think I'd ever come back to this house if it had been my wife."

Keera found LaRussa in his den. He sat back from the computer when she entered. "The PI is almost done," she said. "Any luck with the cloud service?"

LaRussa looked troubled.

"I don't know what to think. This is all very strange. Take a look." LaRussa got up from his leather chair so Keera could sit. He hit play on the security tape from the front of the house and narrated for her and JP, who had just arrived in the room. "That's Syd Evans," he said as a maroon Tesla drove down the driveway, and a silver-haired man parked and got out.

"Who is Syd Evans?"

"Anne's parents' personal attorney."

Keera looked up at him. "And you were not expecting him at the house?"

"No," LaRussa said. "I don't believe he's ever come to the house."

"How long have you known him?"

"Since before Anne and I married. He prepared a prenuptial agreement."

"Was that Anne's doing?"

"Her parents."

On the video, Syd Evans came out the front door of the house in just under twenty-five minutes with a phone to his ear. "And you haven't heard from him?"

"Nothing," LaRussa said. "He didn't call me. There's more." LaRussa reached across her and hit fast-forward, stopping the tape when a blue BMW drove down the driveway, seemingly in a hurry. "That's Lisa Bennet. Dr. Lisa Bennet. Anne's best friend."

Keera checked the doctor's time of arrival. "And you had no idea Anne was meeting her either?"

LaRussa again shook his head. "No."

"What kind of doctor is she?"

"She's an oncologist, but she's been involved with Anne's medical care since the accident. She's treated Anne for her depression and anxiety, as well as for her chronic pain."

"And you haven't heard from this doctor? She hasn't tried to call you?"

"No," LaRussa said.

"Have you tried to call her?"

"No. I assume Anne's parents contacted her and let her know what happened."

Controlling the narrative perhaps, Keera thought. "Have you spoken to your wife's parents since last night?"

"No."

Keera thought it odd that Anne LaRussa's closest friend would not reach out to Anne's husband. She couldn't very well claim she didn't know what had happened, given that the death had been covered in both the newspapers and on television. "How close were she and Anne?"

"They've known each other since college. They were sorority sisters at the U Dub."

"And the two of you? Did you get along?"

"Seemed to. Lisa lost her husband to cancer, so doing things as a couple was awkward. Anne usually spent time with her one-on-one."

Keera sped up the tape. Lisa Bennet left the house, sunglasses again in place, blocking much of her face. She tossed a bag in the back seat and hurried off, nearly backing into a rock wall.

"Send me a copy of the tape," she said, handing him a business card with her email address. "I take it you have an address for Dr. Bennet."

"I do. And if you're planning to talk to her or Syd Evans, I want to be present."

"Not a good idea, Vince. I don't want a prosecutor intimating that you somehow influenced what either had to say."

"Influenced? She was my wife's best friend. I want to do something other than just sit here," LaRussa said. "Anne was my wife. I want to find the person responsible. At least let me introduce you. If at any point you want me to leave the room, I'll do so."

"All right," Keera said. "But no matter what she says, I don't want you to confront her. You have to anticipate that anything you say will get back to the police. Do you understand?"

"Absolutely. Should I call and let her know we're coming?"

"No," Keera said, wanting to gauge Bennet's behavior in person. Something had clearly upset her at the LaRussa home, but if she had found her best friend dead, she wouldn't have stayed in the house twenty-five minutes, and she would have called the police.

A second option was that Bennet had killed Anne LaRussa.

LaRussa provided Keera and JP with directions to Lisa Bennet's home on Capitol Hill. She parked in the street in front of a cutout in the sidewalk and they accessed concrete steps along the side of the garage leading up a slope to a front porch. Potted annuals wilted in the excessive heat.

Keera knocked, heard footsteps inside the home, then silence. After a beat, the door pulled open. The blonde woman who had exited the BMW on the video looked at Keera with red, tired eyes and slumped shoulders, obviously physically exhausted. Then she looked past Keera to Vince LaRussa and JP and sighed. "Vince," she said, softly, closing her eyes as if she'd been caught.

"Can we have a minute, Lisa?" LaRussa asked.

Another pause. Then she nodded and pulled open the door.

They entered a well-kept Craftsman home with intricate hardwood floors, crown molding, and small but quaint rooms. Bennet directed them to the living room. LaRussa and JP Harrison sat side by side on a plush, burgundy sofa, partitioned windows behind them. Keera took a seat in one of two white upholstered chairs across a coffee table. Bennet grabbed tissues from a box and sat in the second chair.

"I was going to call," Bennet said. "I'm so sorry, Vince. I'm so sorry," she said, wiping tears.

"Why didn't you call?" LaRussa asked.

"The police told me not to."

"The police have been here?" Keera asked, though Bennet would have been the first witness on Keera's list, followed by Syd Evans.

"They left a short while ago," Bennet said.

"Did they leave business cards?" Keera asked.

Bennet retrieved cards from the mantel above the fireplace, which was lined with framed photographs of Bennet and a man with three girls of various ages. She handed the cards to Keera. Frank Rossi and Billy Ford.

"Dr. Bennet, I'm—" Keera started.

"I know who you are. I saw your picture in the paper this morning with Vince." She looked to LaRussa. "I spoke to Anne's family. Her father called. The police haven't arrested you?"

"Why would you think they had arrested Mr. LaRussa?" Keera asked.

"I guess . . . the picture was at the police station; wasn't it?"

Keera said, "Mr. LaRussa has not been arrested.

135

He was brought to Police Headquarters for questioning."

"You don't know, then?" Bennet said to LaRussa.

"Know what?" LaRussa asked.

Bennet sighed. "This is ridiculous." She stood from her chair and walked into the dining room, retrieving a manila envelope from the table. Returning, she handed it to Keera. "Anne called me yesterday evening. She was upset, but she wouldn't say what about over the phone. She asked me to come to the house. I was worried about her. She didn't sound well."

"You were her doctor?" Keera asked, looking up as she opened the envelope.

"Foremost I was her friend."

Keera pulled out eight-by-ten photographs from the envelope. She'd seen photos like these before. Photos taken by someone close enough to get details but far enough so as not to be seen. A private investigator. Butterflies fluttered in her stomach.

"The detectives wanted to take them, but I told them I would make copies. I had a hunch you would be here, and I felt you had a right to see them. The detective took pictures with his phone."

The persons of interest in the photos were clear. The first showed Vince LaRussa getting out of his Porsche in a suit, open-collared shirt. He wore sunglasses. Another showed him near a restaurant with sidewalk seating. The third showed Lisa Bennet seated at an outdoor patio table beneath a white awning. A wineglass on the table. She, too, wore sunglasses. In the fourth, LaRussa looked to be greeting Bennet, reaching out and leaning in to kiss her cheek. In the final photograph, LaRussa had his elbows on the table, holding Bennet's hands. Keera handed each picture to JP Harrison, who used his camera to photograph them before he handed them to LaRussa.

"What am I to make of these?" Keera asked.

"The paranoia of a once strong mind," Bennet said. She directed her gaze to LaRussa. "Anne thought you and I were having an affair. She accused me last night at your home."

CHAPTER 12

LaRussa looked up from the photographs. "What?"

"Anne was convinced you and I were having an affair," Bennet said again.

"Were you?" Keera looked between Bennet and LaRussa. "If you were, Vince, I need to know."

"No," they both said.

"How do you explain these?" Keera asked, taking back the photographs and holding them up.

"Anne clearly hired someone to follow me," LaRussa said.

Keera looked to Bennet. "Why didn't you call Vince and let him know what Anne had accused you of?" Keera asked.

Bennet spoke to LaRussa. "Anne told me you were at a charitable function Sunday night. I was going to call you this morning, and then I saw the news . . . I thought you'd been arrested. I didn't know what was going on. Then Larry called me."

"Who's Larry?" Keera asked.

"Anne's father," LaRussa said.

"He told me Anne was dead and said Anne called their attorney, Syd Evans, Sunday night. That she was upset and asked Evans about the prenuptial agreement. How it could be activated."

"Oh shit," LaRussa said quietly.

"What?" Keera said.

"Syd Evans," LaRussa said. He looked to Bennet. "He's the reason why Anne's parents were so reserved Sunday night when I spoke to them, why they didn't want to see me."

"What is the reason?" Keera said.

"If Anne thought I was having an affair, then she called Syd Evans to get his opinion on how much evidence she needed to trigger the forfeiture clause in the prenuptial agreement. If the photographs were enough."

"Enough for what? What does the clause state?" Keera asked.

"It states that if either party is found to have cheated during the marriage, the cheating party forfeits all of the marital assets."

"Do the marital assets include the assets of LWM?" Keera asked.

"Everything," LaRussa said.

JP gave Keera a knowing look she read instantly because she'd had the same thought. Ambrose now had a hundred million reasons why Vince LaRussa would have killed his wife.

Keera did not want Vince LaRussa to discuss the matter of Syd Evans any further in front of Lisa Bennet. She changed subjects quickly.

"You're an oncologist?" she asked. "Why were you treating Anne?"

"Because I have experience treating people in pain. I was primarily trying to help Anne mentally come to terms with her condition. When she learned that her physical therapy would not help her to progress further, she stopped all treatment and went into a dark depression. She became paranoid."

"What do you mean by paranoid?"

"She imagined people were out to get her, conspiring against her."

Keera held up the photographs. "Cheating on her."

"Apparently," Bennet said. "Vince and I met that afternoon because Anne had stopped her therapy and had increased the amount of opioids she was taking for her pain."

Keera looked to LaRussa, who acknowledged what Bennet said was true. A thought came to her. "Did you prescribe the opioids?"

"I did, and I wanted to move Anne back into physical therapy and counseling and use muscle relaxants to relieve her spasms instead of the opioids. I didn't want to have this discussion in front of Anne, who was already becoming combative."

"I suggested we meet for lunch in Madison Park. Someplace close," LaRussa said.

"How many times did you meet?" Keera asked, skeptical that a PI would catch them the one time they met.

"Twice," Bennet said, looking to LaRussa for confirmation.

"We discussed how best to reduce the amount of opioids Anne was taking," Vince said. "I suggested we not tell Anne; she had so many drugs in her medicine cabinet I don't think she knew what she was taking."

Bennet said, "I told Vince we had to wean Anne off the opioids, for her sake, before it got any worse. My suggestion was to gradually reduce the milligrams she was taking."

Keera looked to JP, who she knew wanted to ask more questions to gather as much evidence about the crime scene as possible. "When you arrived at the LaRussa house, did you notice anything out of the ordinary?" JP asked.

"Like what?"

"The temperature inside the house."

"It was hot," Bennet said.

"Did you ask Mrs. LaRussa about it?"

"I don't recall getting the chance. When I stepped in the door I tried to hug Anne but she pulled back. I knew something was wrong."

"Anything else you found odd?"

Bennet slowly shook her head. "Not that I can think of."

"Where did you talk to Mrs. LaRussa?"

"In the entry when she let me in. Then in the kitchen."

"What else did Anne say to you Sunday night

other than accusing you of having an affair with Vince?"

Bennet shook her head. Tears rolled down her face. "Nothing. She just kept asking me how I could betray her. Nothing I said could convince her otherwise. I finally left. I thought I'd call Vince and the two of us would talk to her when she had calmed down."

Back inside her car, Keera felt gut punched. JP was also uncharacteristically quiet. She tried to absorb what she'd been told. LaRussa sat in the passenger seat looking numb. "I didn't kill Anne."

"It doesn't matter. The prosecutor now has opportunity and motive," Keera said. "A significant motive. He will look at this case in terms of what he can prove. He will put on Syd Evans to say Anne wanted advice on divorcing you and invoking the forfeiture clause in your agreement because you were having an affair with Lisa Bennet."

"But Lisa will testify there was no affair."

"What matters is what Anne *believed*. The prosecutor will argue she confronted you, threatened to take the marital assets, and you killed her." Keera needed to slow her thoughts. She needed to consider and evaluate before acting. "Did you seek to have the prenuptial agreement altered after you became successful?"

"How was I supposed to do that?" LaRussa

shook his head. "I'm not being flippant, but how do I go to Anne and say, *Remember the agreement that punishes me if I cheat? I'd like to alter it.* What would she have thought? Then she had the accident and . . ." He broke off, let out a held breath. "I couldn't very well bring it up to her after her accident. But honestly? I never intended to cheat on Anne; the agreement wasn't an issue when I signed it, and it wasn't something I thought much about."

Maybe not, but it was an issue now.

Keera called Syd Evans on her cell phone. To her surprise, he answered. She was not surprised when he declined to meet with her or to answer any of her questions. His refusal to talk to her was potential grounds to get a court order under Criminal Rule 4.6 and seek to take his deposition, but she'd cross that bridge at a later date. Besides, she had a strong understanding of what Evans would say, given what Anne's father had told Bennet.

When they arrived back at LaRussa's home, LaRussa said, "If you don't mind, I don't feel like talking anymore."

Keera did not push the matter. She assumed LaRussa, an intelligent man, understood the ramifications of what they had learned—and the likely consequences. Then he confirmed it.

"I'll let you know when I hear from the police

". . . when they come. Do you think they'll let me at least plan Anne's funeral?"

Ambrose would, but out of sympathy for Anne's family, not for LaRussa. Ambrose would imply that LaRussa's attendance, his playing the grieving husband to a woman he had murdered, was further evidence of his callousness and his deception. She didn't want to tell LaRussa that, however. Instead, she said, "Ambrose will wait until they have the medical examiner's report and toxicology screening. That takes time, though he will no doubt expedite it." Most prosecutors were usually cautious about getting their ducks in a row before acting. But Ambrose had an ax to grind, and he was arrogant, having never lost a murder case.

"I didn't kill my wife," LaRussa said for at least the third time.

Keera also didn't tell him that, at present, the evidence indicated he had, and that was all that mattered.

She drove JP Harrison back to his car in the parking lot behind the office building in Occidental Square.

"If Washington still had the death penalty, he'd get it for certain, killing a wheelchair-bound wife . . . after cheating on her," JP said.

"Do you think LaRussa and Bennet were having an affair?"

144

Harrison tilted his head. "He'd been through a lot. It was not just his wife that went through the trauma and all the pain and the rehabilitation. He was likely right there beside her through it all. Who else was present, maybe offering her support?"

"Her best friend, Lisa Bennet."

"And Bennet was also in pain," Harrison said. "You saw the pictures on the shelves in her living room. Losing a husband had to be devastating for a young woman and her daughters."

"Ambrose isn't going to allow LaRussa to turn himself in. He wants the spectacle. This kind of case is perfect for a guy seeking a future political office." *Not to mention a guy seeking retribution,* Keera also thought but did not say.

She drove home rather than return to the office, which would have started the royal inquisition, and that could last hours. She needed time to think and evaluate what she had learned and decide what she could do. In chess terms, Ambrose had a strong grip on the center of the board. She had to find a way to move him off those squares and, if she couldn't, then a way to bait him into moving. She thought of the Dark Knight and wondered if, after losing three successive matches, he was taking a different tack, relinquishing the center squares and giving Keera a false sense of security.

At home, she changed and went for a five-mile run, which always helped to relax her and to clear her head. She returned home an hour later dripping sweat. She'd brought a water bottle with her but should have brought two, given the persistent heat. She tapped the space bar on her keyboard and pulled up the chess match. Then she filled a glass with ice water from the fridge and returned to her dining room table.

From: Darkknight
To: SeattlePawnslayer

Queen to a4

The Dark Knight had moved his most powerful piece, signifying his intent to come for her. She couldn't help but think that Miller Ambrose was about to do the same thing.

She castled her king and put him in a safer place, while activating her rook to protect him until she could determine what the Dark Knight was up to. She'd have to think of a similar strategy for defending Vince LaRussa.

The Dark Knight swiftly moved his pawn to d5 and took the first piece off the board.

Keera had multiple options, but she chose to move her bishop to put tension on the board's right side while preparing to break down the fortress the Dark Knight had built around his king.

Bishop takes pawn at d5.

Were LaRussa and Bennet having an affair and presenting a unified front, like the Dark Knight's bishop and the queen? If they were, Anne LaRussa had outplayed them by calling Syd Evans and asking about how to initiate the forfeiture clause and take all the assets. It had been a deadly game she had played, and she'd paid the ultimate price.

Keera's computer pinged. She was surprised the Dark Knight would respond so quickly. But the ping had been her server at Patrick Duggan & Associates. She'd received an email from a name she didn't recognize. Reading, she felt her pulse quicken.

CHAPTER 13

At the conference room table in the prosecuting attorney's offices, Rossi and Ford filled in Miller Ambrose on their interviews of Lisa Bennet and Syd Evans, as well as their interviews of Anne LaRussa's mother and father, and other evidence they had gathered, like the ghost gun. Needless to say, the interviews had been enlightening.

Ambrose sat, reading glasses perched on the tip of his nose, scribbling notes. Rossi could tell he was tempering his emotions. "What's the ME's estimated time of death?" Ambrose flipped pages. "Arthur Litchfield." He looked up at the two detectives. "He's new; isn't he?"

"Been with the ME's office about a month," Ford said. "Came from Tacoma." Litchfield was one of nearly a dozen on the King County staff with the official title of medicolegal death investigators, a mouthful the department simplified to forensic medical examiners or just MEs.

"What's his estimated time of death?"

"Somewhere between six and nine thirty that night."

"What time did the husband arrive home?"

"Nine seventeen."

"And when did he make the 911 call?"

"Nine twenty-four. He claims he did not find

his wife's body right away. Said he went into the family room because the lights and television were on and then his bedroom before he went to the kitchen to get a glass of water."

"Why can't the ME be more specific as to the time of death?" Ambrose asked.

"According to Litchfield, the loss of body core temperature was likely impacted by the temperature inside the house, which was more than one hundred degrees, making the ETD less certain. The wife was also thin, which Litchfield said can impact heat loss," Rossi said.

"What about lividity and rigor mortis?" Ambrose asked.

"Consistent with the ETD," Rossi said.

"Any further explanation why the air-conditioning was off?" Ambrose asked.

"Husband said somebody had to have shut it off," Ford said.

Ambrose rocked back in his chair. "And no electrical surges or power outages?"

"I checked with PSE," Ford said. "They had no power outages in that area that evening. Someone had to have manually shut the system off."

"The husband? Perhaps trying to confuse the time of death," Ambrose said.

"Not unless he shut it off before he left the house earlier that day," Rossi said. "The house would not have heated quickly enough to make a notable difference in the brief time he was home. And one has to presume if he shut it off before he left that morning, the wife would have checked it. It was like a sauna in there."

"What about turning it off remotely?"

"Not set up."

"Let's check both phones to be certain." Ambrose shifted gears. "Bennet testified Anne LaRussa was alive when she left the house?"

"That's what she said," Rossi said, not convinced.

"Weren't she and the victim friends?" Ambrose asked.

"Anne believed the doctor was screwing her husband," Rossi said with a shrug. "I don't think we should rule her out just yet."

Ambrose held up copies of the photographs Rossi had taken with his phone of the photos of the meeting between Dr. Bennet and LaRussa. "How did the doctor explain these?"

Rossi filled in Ambrose about what Bennet had told them.

"Okay, so she'll testify that she wasn't having an affair?" Ambrose said. "That doesn't really matter; does it?"

"Nope," Ford said.

"What matters is that Anne LaRussa believed Bennet was having an affair with her husband," Ambrose said. He flipped through his notes on a yellow legal pad. "And hiring a private investigator is hard evidence she believed the two were having an affair. So is calling the attorney . . . What was his name?"

"Syd Evans," Ford said.

"So is calling him to the house yesterday to discuss the terms of the prenuptial agreement if one spouse cheated," Ambrose said.

"We don't know yet that the wife hired a private investigator," Rossi said, feeling like a man trying to stop a boulder rolling down a hill and picking up speed. "That's what the doctor *said* Anne LaRussa told her."

"Who else would it be?" Ford asked.

"Let's be certain, then," Ambrose said. "Check the wife's credit card charges, checks, Venmo account, phone numbers. She certainly didn't take these photographs herself."

"No, she didn't," Ford said.

"The photographs aren't exactly intimate either," Rossi said. "Two friends can certainly kiss on the cheek and hold hands during a difficult conversation."

"The point is," Ambrose said, "the photographs and the discussion with the attorney substantiate what Anne LaRussa believed. And that gives her husband a hundred million reasons to kill her," he said, referencing the LaRussas' estimated net worth.

"Why shoot her?" Rossi asked.

"What?" Ambrose and Ford both said.

"Why be so obvious? Why not just overdose

her on pain pills and make it look like an accident or a suicide?" He looked to Ford. "You saw the medicine cabinet."

"Looked like the back room of a pharmacy," Ford agreed.

"What specifically did they find?" Ambrose asked.

"Muscle relaxants, pain medication—opioids. We have a forensic pharmacist cataloging the contents now," Rossi said. "Safe to say there was more than enough to kill her."

"Let's stick to what we know and can prove," Ambrose said. "Anne LaRussa wasn't overdosed. She was shot."

"We don't have toxicology back yet," Rossi said.

Ambrose continued as if he didn't hear him, reading from his notes. "The lawyer confirmed Anne LaRussa texted him asking for an urgent meeting. When he arrived, she asked about a poison pill in the prenuptial agreement, which would have given her control of the marital assets. That same evening, she confronts Lisa Bennet with the photographs, and we can presume at some point on Sunday . . . maybe earlier, she confronted her husband, can't we?"

"Seems a logical next step," Ford said.

"As for why Vince LaRussa didn't choose some other methodology to kill her . . . He was at a charitable function where dozens of people saw him and thought that was a sufficient alibi. So he decides to say he found her shot when he got home. The gun is untraceable so he sets it on the kitchen floor. He didn't know the doctor and the lawyer had shown up at the house to ruin his alibi," Ambrose said. "He thinks he got away with it, but the wife beat him at his own game."

Except the wife was dead, Rossi thought. "How do you explain the gun? A ghost gun would indicate premeditation, not a spur-of-the-moment killing," Rossi said.

"Maybe he bought the gun for some other reason and had it on hand," Ambrose said with a shrug.

"And no blood spatter anywhere on his clothing?" Rossi said. "No fingerprints or his DNA on the gun. A guy that smart . . . wouldn't he also check the security cameras? Not having anybody show up is worse than having two people show up; isn't it?"

"He could have wiped the gun clean. He could have put on gloves. This is all happening fast. It was twenty minutes, wasn't it?"

"Seventeen," Ford said. "He stepped back outside at 9:34 p.m."

"So he arrives home at 9:17 p.m. and calls 911 at 9:24. He's moving quickly. He isn't thinking about the security system cameras," Ambrose said.

"And his clothes?"

"He gets home, shoots her. Sees the blood on his clothes and changes them either before or after he calls 911. That maybe explains why he didn't step outside until when?"

"Nine thirty-four," Rossi said.

"How many tuxedos does he own?" Ambrose asked. "Guy that rich could have half a dozen tux shirts and pants."

"Shit." Ford looked to Rossi. Neither had considered that possibility, and neither had checked the closet.

"I don't know," Rossi said, not convinced.

"Let's not complicate this," Ambrose said. "We have motive, and we have opportunity. We have two witnesses who saw Anne LaRussa immediately before Vince LaRussa got home who will each testify Anne LaRussa was alive when they left the house. The security cameras don't reveal anyone else coming to the home. I've obtained convictions with a lot less. You spoke to the parents?"

"Father confirmed Syd Evans called him from the house and said Anne asked him about the prenuptial agreement," Rossi said.

"So we have independent verification. What did the family have to say about Vince LaRussa?"

"Father never liked him, but he tolerated him for his daughter's sake," Ford said. "Said he didn't trust him when he first started coming around. Thought he could be a gold digger. It was

154

one of the reasons for the prenuptial agreement. Also, he said that after her accident Anne became more reclusive. Vince started to work from home and seemed to always be present when they went to visit their daughter to find out how she was doing. Father said he got the sense something was wrong, but never got the opportunity to find out what it was, if anything. Neither did Anne's friends, at least according to the father. He gave us names. I got ahold of two. They said they hadn't seen Anne in several weeks. Father wasn't surprised when the attorney called and told him about the meeting with Anne."

"Not exactly the happy couple Vince LaRussa painted then," Ambrose said.

"We have too many variables we can't account for," Rossi said, again trying to slow the rolling boulder. "A good defense attorney will use them like darts to poke holes in our theory."

"A *good* defense attorney," Ambrose said.

"What's that mean?" Rossi asked.

"Keera Duggan has never defended a murderer. She's never prosecuted a murderer."

"Patsy Duggan—" Rossi started.

"Is an old drunk. Heard he's trying drunk-driving cases now and didn't make it through his last trial. We're going forward." Ambrose stood from the table. "I'll prepare the charging document, but we'll wait to arrest Vince LaRussa until after his wife's funeral. Let him play the grieving husband. The jurors will hate him even more. In the interim, eliminate the variables."

Ambrose was making this case personal. He was rushing the prosecution because he wanted to stick it to Keera Duggan in court. He likely also wanted the publicity such a trial could bring for his future political aspirations. Rossi wanted to tell Ambrose to grow up. He wanted to tell him that he was moving this case too quickly. But Ambrose wasn't listening, and Rossi wasn't interested in talking to himself. The PA had near unlimited power to make the most consequential decisions in a criminal case, including whether to charge LaRussa.

His call, Rossi thought.

Maybe his mistake.

Rossi had sat through trials with Keera Duggan. She was a chip off her father's block, a brawler.

And definitely not someone to underestimate.

CHAPTER 14

Keera answered her front door after the no-doubt-about-it knock. JP Harrison stepped inside.

"Thanks for coming," Keera said.

"No problem."

Though almost nine o'clock at night, it remained dusk and the temperature warm. Oscillating fans moved the heavy air and offered some relief. Harrison wore loose-fitting pants and a white linen shirt. With his long legs and arms, the clothes looked good on him. At just five foot six, Keera feared she'd look like a round Oompa-Loompa from Willy Wonka's chocolate factory. She stepped to her laptop on the table and hit the keyboard.

"Nice place." Harrison clearly wasn't referring to Keera's spartan furnishings. He saw the potential in the crown ceiling molding, the elaborate window trim, and the inlaid hardwood floors. "You play chess?" He nodded to the board and glass pieces on the table.

Keera looked over her shoulder. "Just for fun," she said.

"We should play sometime. I was pretty good when I was young."

Keera smiled. "Yeah. Me too." She pulled up her emails on her computer. "Take a look at this."

157

She stepped back, giving Harrison room to read her computer screen.

From: Worthing, Jack
Sent: June 5, 2023
To: Keera Duggan
Subject: The Game of Your Life

I understand you're a chess player. You're in the game of your life, so play like your life depends on it . . . because it very well might. Don't speak to anyone about this email until you understand. Trust no one but yourself. Everything will soon become clear.

Harrison studied the email for a moment, then said, "Who is Jack Worthing?"

"No idea," she said.

"Did you try to respond?" Harrison asked.

"It came back undeliverable."

Harrison tried and received the same response. "Couldn't have been sent by mistake," he said.

"Not given the chess reference. Few people know I played competitive chess—they'd have to dig for that information. It's out there, but not easy to find."

"What do you mean it's out there? On the internet?"

She leaned back against the edge of her kitchen

table and told Harrison about playing chess in her youth. "I gained some notoriety. I was considered somewhat of a prodigy."

"I'm glad you told me before I embarrassed myself. You still play?"

She shook her head. "Not competitively."

"What's this game then?" Harrison asked, giving a nod to the chessboard.

"I play online under a chess name a tournament director gave me. Seattle Pawnslayer."

"Very chic."

"My father thought it sounded intimidating."

"Could this email be related to this current game?" He motioned to the board.

"I thought of that but . . . I've played the Dark Knight several times before this game."

"The Dark Knight?" Harrison smiled. "This keeps getting better."

"Players use all kinds of monikers. My point is, there were never any emails during those prior games. I think this email is talking about the Vince LaRussa case. The timing is just too big of a coincidence to ignore. Whoever sent it knows I'm representing him."

"That could only be a handful of people though. I mean—"

"No," she said, shaking her head. "I thought of that too. The picture in the newspaper was a clear signal I would be representing LaRussa, or could be."

"It could be anyone, then," Harrison said. "Though I'd start with people who knew your chess affinity."

Keera pushed away from the table. "Can we find out who Jack Worthing is from the IP address?"

Harrison frowned and rubbed the stubble on his chin. "You could ask law enforcement to track it down, but if this person is being this careful, I'd suspect he or she got an address from a VPN company so the email can't be traced. And most VPN companies won't respond to a subpoena."

"And I don't have a strong reason to involve law enforcement. It isn't like this is a threat of any kind."

"Says here it could be the game of your life."

"Not enough," she said. She knew because she had made an anonymous phone call to the police when Ambrose's stalking was at its worst, and she didn't get far seeking help.

"What are you going to do?" Harrison asked.

"Nothing at the moment, but if the person provides more information, as the email implies, I don't have the luxury of ignoring it," she said. "Right now Ambrose controls the center of the board."

"Center of the board?"

"Chess terminology. It means he has the stronger position."

"You want me to try to find this Jack Worthing?"

"Poke around, but don't waste time. I don't want this to become a distraction or a wild-goose chase. I'd rather you concentrate on finding the PI who took the photographs of Lisa Bennet and Vince LaRussa, and on the crime scene evidence. We're going to need to move quickly. Ambrose isn't going to wait to charge LaRussa. When he does, I'm going to call his bluff and convince LaRussa not to waive time." Meaning she was going to press the matter forward by having LaRussa not waive his right to a speedy trial.

"Could be risky."

"Could be," she said.

"Maybe you don't push too hard, take the additional time."

"It's been one of my father's trial tactics when he believes the prosecution is moving too quickly and doesn't have all the evidence. It puts tremendous strain on the prosecutor."

"And the defense," Harrison said.

"My father always bet on himself," she said. "The sooner he had the prosecution's evidence, the sooner he could poke holes in it. Ambrose will think he's in the driver's seat because of what Bennet and Evans had to say, and he thinks of me as naïve and inexperienced. I'm hoping to use that against him."

"I can see that underestimating you would be a

mistake. You're as competitive as your old man. I guess we really do have a game, don't we?"

Keera looked at the email. *The game of your life.*

Whatever that meant.

PART II

CHAPTER 15

June 12, 2023

Monday morning, Keera studied the chessboard as she sipped a cup of chamomile tea and tried to calm her nerves. Chess had always forced her to concentrate, despite outside distractions, and she needed to focus this morning.

"Train your mind," her father had taught. "Have a singular purpose, a strategy, then execute your game plan. If you can focus in the difficult times, you will become a champion."

As Keera had predicted, Miller Ambrose filed a charging document and had Vince LaRussa arrested after his wife's funeral late Friday afternoon, ensuring LaRussa would spend at least the weekend in jail, and that his arrest would be covered in the *Seattle Times'* increased weekend circulation. To ensure media attention, upon LaRussa's arrest, the King County prosecuting attorney and Chief of Police Marcella Weber held a televised press conference to announce the charges, and that Senior Prosecuting Attorney Miller Ambrose, who stood alongside Frank Rossi and Billy Ford, would try LaRussa on a charge of first-degree murder.

Keera filed a notice of appearance for Patrick

Duggan & Associates. Court Operations called her cell phone to advise that LaRussa's arraignment would be held by Judge Laurence Valle, but moved from the traditional arraignment courtroom on the twelfth floor to room 854E, one of the larger courtrooms at the King County Courthouse. A room next door would provide closed-circuit television coverage for any overflow.

Keera had appeared before Valle multiple times, mostly as a prosecuting attorney but once as a defense attorney. She found Valle to be fair in his rulings and had come to admire the judge. Unfortunately, because Judge Valle would preside at the arraignment, he would not be the trial judge. The trial judge would be assigned after the arraignment.

Keera was surprised to learn when she turned on her computer that the Dark Knight had made a move at 5:15 a.m. Rook to b1. She responded pawn to a5. The Dark Knight countered knight to e4, occupying an important center square and freeing his bishop to join the attack. To temper his attack, Keera responded boldly, knight to d4, threatening the Dark Knight's pawn, his knight, and his king while also preventing his queen from swinging to the opposite side of the board to help with the defense. The Dark Knight, perhaps sensing something he had not considered, moved his knight to take Keera's knight at d4. Keera's pawn took his knight. The Dark Knight moved his pawn to a3. Keera responded king to h7, as if she feared his attack. She didn't. She had her own plan. The Dark Knight just did not know it.

From experience, Keera knew Ambrose would also go on the offensive at the arraignment and play to the big media presence. He would attempt to scare and intimidate. Like the Dark Knight, he would fail. Keera had her own plan to be bold.

Before leaving the house, Keera checked her appearance in the full-length mirror. She, Patsy, and Ella had met over the weekend with a jury consultant the law firm regularly used in big trials. The consultant advised that much had already been written about Vince LaRussa's personal wealth, and any attempt to paint him as a pauper by dressing down would be perceived as disingenuous. She wore her best Hugo Boss black skirt and jacket, a beige chiffon blouse, black pumps, little makeup, and gold stud earrings. The consultant also said Ambrose was planting seeds in the media, insinuating to the potential jury pool that LaRussa was a coward—a rich and powerful man who had shot his disabled wife in the back of the head as she sat in her wheelchair. Unless Keera came up with a better story, how she dressed would matter little to the outcome.

The consultant could have solved their bigger issue—who would try the case? He cautioned that, given the gender and the frailty of the victim, the defense needed to avoid a male-dominated counsel table and present a softer appearance. He said that Keera, a young female, would play better to the jury. The logical choice to sit second chair in that scenario was Ella, but Ella was not a great trial attorney. She was steady, deliberate, and reliable, qualities that also made her predictable. In chess, this was the easiest opponent to defeat. Ella didn't have Patsy's instincts, or his ability to think on his feet, anticipate arguments, and get ahead of the prosecution's moves. Patsy also wasn't afraid to take calculated chances—at least in the past. That was no longer a guarantee. Keera knew firsthand that Patsy could go off the rails at any moment. As Keera's mother had said, his mind and his instincts were not what they had once been.

This left Keera with several problems: how to tactfully pass over Ella, how to let Patsy know she needed him sober and how to make that happen, and, most importantly, how to convince Vince LaRussa that she was the right choice to lead his defense. Patsy solved her first problem by telling Ella the firm needed her to run the office and manage their other cases. Ella didn't put up much of a fight, an indication, perhaps, she knew her limitations.

As for LaRussa, Keera and Patsy met with him in an attorney-client consultation room at the King County jail and explained the jury consultant's opinion and reasoning. LaRussa listened attentively but said he would wait until after the arraignment to make a decision.

Which meant Keera needed to convince LaRussa at the arraignment that she was up to the fight. The jury consultant suggested she imply to the media, without overdoing it, that LaRussa had already suffered the horrific loss of his wife, and now he suffered the further indignity of being the prosecutor's scapegoat in a rush to judgment. She might not change Ambrose's narrative completely, but she might, at least, temper it.

As if that was not enough pressure, Ella again told Keera how much the firm needed this case, and how important the media coverage was to the firm's future, if they were ever going to be more than Patsy Duggan's associates.

"Knock, knock."

Keera looked up from her desk. Patsy entered her office in his finest navy-blue suit. He'd had his hair cut over the weekend and looked like the Patsy of old, the Irish Brawler.

"You ready to go, kiddo?" he asked.

She looked at the clock on the wall, not realizing how much time had passed since she had come into the office. "Just going over the recent cases on bail," she said.

"Judge Valle won't grant it."

Patsy was right—Judge Valle would be hard-pressed to grant bail to a man with millions of dollars and access to a private jet. Valle, while fair, was an elected official, and he wouldn't take a chance a man charged with murder might escape prosecution because of one of his rulings.

"I know," she said. "But I want to lay a foundation to maybe convince the trial judge."

"About that." Patsy grimaced. "My contacts are indicating the trial will be assigned to Judge Hung."

"Damn," Keera said. "Maximum Maxine would not have been my first choice."

"Or mine," Patsy said.

"But I'm sure Ambrose is thrilled."

Maxine Hung had obtained more death penalties than any other King County prosecutor before she rose to the bench. The judicial robe had not tempered her. She was a prosecutor's judge. Since the Washington Supreme Court abolished the death penalty, Judge Hung had repeatedly delivered maximum sentences to those convicted in her courtroom.

"But if she *is* our judge, know that she does not tolerate nonsense or incompetence in her courtroom from either side," Patsy said. "And she'll hold you, as a woman, to a higher standard."

"You still have your spies, then," Keera said.

"A few," Patsy said.

"Let's go find out how good they are." Keera stuffed her materials into her briefcase.

"Hey, kiddo," Patsy said, his tone changing.

Keera sensed what was to come. Another apology, or another assurance.

"Don't worry about me, okay?" he said. "You just do your job. I'm going to be here for you."

Keera wanted to believe him, but she also knew her father, and his string of broken promises, too well. In his day, Patsy had been fearless and unpredictable. Now, she feared he was just unpredictable.

"Don't make promises you can't keep, Patsy," she said. "And do not embarrass me. I'll win this case with or without you. But that's not up to me. That's up to you."

When Keera and Patsy turned the corner onto Third Avenue, news vans, more than half a dozen, greeted them. Reporters angled for live shots with the King County Courthouse as a backdrop, and a long line of people seeking to watch the trial had formed on the sidewalk outside the entrance.

"Come on, kiddo," Patsy said. "If you stand in that line, you won't make next Monday's arraignments."

Keera followed Patsy up the block and across the street to the county administrative building on Fourth Avenue. Once through a metal detector, Patsy led Keera down a stark white tunnel to the courthouse. Keera knew of the tunnel, but she hadn't thought of it, nor had she ever used it. The prosecuting attorney's offices were inside the King County Courthouse.

When they stepped off the elevator onto the eighth floor, voices filled the hallway, and the volume increased as she and Patsy approached the crowd waiting on the white marbled floor outside the courtroom door. Reporters wasted no time.

"How will your client plead?"

"Mr. LaRussa is eager to get these proceedings underway to prove his innocence," Keera said. "This is a travesty. The man lost his wife to a violent crime and is now suffering the indignity of being the prosecuting attorney's scapegoat in a rush to judgment."

"Can you comment on the evidence against your client?"

"The prosecutor has presented no evidence," she said, following the script Patsy had helped to write. "All I have are the unsupported statements in the charging document. We'll request that the prosecution provide us with evidence. Until I evaluate that evidence, I can't comment."

Keera and Patsy ducked inside the outer wooden door manned by a marshal with the King County Court Protection Unit. A second marshal waited at the interior door with a raised hand, then lowered it with an acknowledgment to Patsy.

Inside, spectators filled the gallery pews and stood in the back. Members of Anne LaRussa's family sat in the first pew on the courtroom's far side—her mother and father, with her two siblings and their spouses. Anne LaRussa's father glared at Keera as she entered. This was the difficult part of being a defense attorney. Everyone professed to a belief in an accused's right to counsel, but the attorney became synonymous with the accused, and sometimes even more reviled.

Miller Ambrose was not yet present. He liked to make a late entrance. Patsy had told Keera being late was a mistake. He said prizefighters also liked to make their opponents wait, an intimidation tactic, until Muhammad Ali got to the ring early and worked the crowd into a frenzy in his favor. Patsy told Keera to use the time to get comfortable, to greet the court reporter and the bailiff, and to let the spectators and the media see her unconcerned demeanor, a reflection of her innocent client.

Keera followed that script now, forcing herself to look relaxed and at ease while approaching the well beneath the elevated judicial bench. She had a casual conversation with the clerk, then Judge Valle's bailiff, an elegant-looking Indian woman she'd met once before.

Shortly after she'd returned to counsel table and took her seat, the courtroom door swung open. Miller Ambrose entered dressed in a light-gray checked suit. April Richie, who had arrived at the prosecutor's office about the same time Keera departed, followed him. Young and attractive, Richie had become Ambrose's newest protégé.

Ambrose set his briefcase on the prosecutor's table and greeted the judge's bailiff and court reporter as if he owned the room and had invited them as his guests. Keera had seen it before. He was good. He was very good.

Moments later, three correctional officers escorted Vince LaRussa into the courtroom. He held his head high and kept a neutral expression, as Keera had counseled. The room fell silent, the spectators evaluating the wealth advisor's every move. LaRussa was handcuffed at the waist with a belly chain. He wore red prison scrubs, white socks, and slippers. After an officer removed the handcuffs, LaRussa sat between Keera and Patsy. As the jury consultant had instructed, Keera put a hand on LaRussa's shoulder and leaned close for those in the gallery to see that this was not a man that a woman needed to fear. She asked in a low whisper how he was holding up.

LaRussa nodded. "I'm okay."

Valle's bailiff had left the courtroom when LaRussa arrived. She reentered, followed by the judge, who was short, balding, and wore wire-rimmed glasses.

"All rise," the bailiff said.

Valle wasted no time getting down to business. "Be seated. Good morning, Counsel. Ladies and gentlemen. I want to remind you all that although we are in the ceremonial courtroom, this is a judicial proceeding and I expect decorum. Mr. Ambrose, let's get started."

Ambrose stepped around counsel table with his reading glasses perched on the end of his nose. "Number twenty-seven on the arraignment calendar, Judge. State of Washington versus Vincent Ernest LaRussa—"

Keera also stepped from behind the table, not about to cede the center of the courtroom to her opponent. "Good afternoon, Your Honor, Keera Duggan and Patrick Duggan of Patrick Duggan & Associates appearing on behalf of the accused, Vincent LaRussa. A notice of appearance has previously been filed, Your Honor."

"The clerk will enter the notice of appearance of Ms. Duggan and Mr. Duggan of Patrick Duggan & Associates," Valle instructed. "Let the record reflect that Patrick Duggan is present in the courtroom this morning. Good morning, Mr. Duggan," Valle said.

Patsy slid back his chair and stood as if to greet the king of England. "Good morning, Your Honor."

Ambrose took another step forward, remaining on script. "Defendant is present in custody—"

Arraignments were often cattle calls with the prosecutor running the roundup, and the defense attorney ignored, but Patsy had instructed Keera not to let Ambrose treat her like some vestigial organ. She, too, stepped forward. "Your Honor, the defense acknowledges receiving the charging document, agrees to accept service, and waives a formal reading of the charges. The defendant, Vincent LaRussa, is a United States citizen. He enters a plea of not guilty."

It felt, for a moment, as if Keera had sucked the oxygen from the courtroom, which had been her intent. Patsy instructed her to enter the plea quickly to prevent Ambrose from reading the charges in open court to the media.

After a moment's hesitation, the members of the gallery exhaled and stirred.

"A plea of not guilty will be entered," Valle said.

Keera said, "Your Honor, the defense wishes to discuss the issue of bail."

Ambrose took another step forward, now directly beneath Judge Valle. He placed his file on the railing near the court clerk, a subtle hint this was his courtroom. "The State objects to bail. This is a first-degree murder case. The murder was premeditated, calculated, and cowardly."

Keera advanced, standing elbow to elbow beside Ambrose. "Your Honor, the prosecutor has misspoken. There is no *case* yet. We are here for a murder *charge,* and that is all it is, a charge. Mr. LaRussa has not been convicted of any crime, let alone the charge of murder. He is innocent until

proven guilty, and that presumption of innocence applies here, at his arraignment. As for the
prosecutor's inappropriate personal opinion, the
defense requests his comment be stricken from
the record and that the court admonish him to
keep those opinions to himself."

"The reference to the defendant is stricken. Mr.
Ambrose, please refrain from offering personal
opinions."

"My apologies, Your Honor."

It was a minor victory, but a victory nonetheless. "Now, as to the matter at hand," Keera said.
"The prosecutor is well aware that every person
in the state of Washington is entitled to bail. The
only relevant issues are Mr. LaRussa's ties to the
community, and whether he is a flight risk or a
threat to the community in which he has lived for
twenty years."

A smirk crept across Ambrose's lips, as if he
found Keera's argument painfully juvenile—and
misleading. "The murder of which the defendant
is accused was premeditated," Ambrose said.
He'd once told Keera to never use a pronoun
like "it" for a specific crime, particularly murder.
"The victim was shot in the back of the head with
a handgun found at the crime scene. A ghost gun,
Your Honor."

That piece of evidence, an untraceable gun,
had been advanced for the media's benefit, and it
caught Keera by surprise, but she willed herself

not to react. Ghost guns had become every police officer's and prosecutor's nightmare. More important to the issue of bail, a ghost gun could indicate premeditation.

Evaluate. Consider. Then respond.

Ambrose pushed forward another square. "Witnesses will testify the victim was alive shortly before the defendant arrived home and provide motivation for the murder of his wife. As for the two issues raised by defense counsel, the defendant has substantial financial resources and access to a private jet capable of flying him to countries that do not recognize US extradition treaties. Beyond that, he is now widowed, has no children, and has no family living in the area."

Ambrose had purposefully stated the alleged evidence Keera had sought to avoid having read out loud. He had advanced, but he'd left an opening. Keera made a move to fill that opening.

"Your Honor, with all due respect, the prosecutor is incorrect on a number of counts. While the nature of the weapon may be of interest, no evidence will be presented that it was owned or fired by Mr. LaRussa, which I assume the prosecutor would have improperly told the court and the gallery, given his liberal recitation of other unproven allegations. Premeditation? By someone, perhaps, but not by Mr. LaRussa." Just as it appeared Valle was about to cut her off, Keera moved on. "Now, as for the *pertinent* issues regarding bail, it's specious for the State to argue that Mr. LaRussa has no ties to the community. Mr. LaRussa sits on the boards of, and contributes millions of dollars to, charitable organizations, hospitals, and other civic causes. He is the managing partner of LaRussa Wealth Management, with an office in Pioneer Square, and he remains committed to his company employees as well as his clients even during this difficult time. Moreover, he has no prior criminal record that would make him a risk to the community. He should not be penalized simply because he is successful. He will surrender his passport. He will wear an ankle monitor and agree to be confined to home. He is eager to appear in court and defend against this charge so that the person who killed his wife can be pursued and apprehended. The court must honor his presumption of innocence."

If Valle was disturbed by the attorneys' bickering over LaRussa's guilt or innocence, he did not display it. He raised a hand and cut off further argument from Ambrose. "I am going to deny the defense's request for bail at this time. If the defense wishes to raise the matter before the trial judge at a later hearing, I'm sure the trial judge will entertain it." In other words, Valle shrewdly kicked the can down the road. "I find that because of his substantial resources and access to private airplanes, and his lack of any immediate family, the defendant is a potential flight risk. Moreover, this is a serious charge, and it would be a disservice to the people of King County to not treat it as such."

Keera understood Valle's decision and had even predicted his ruling when she and Patsy spoke to LaRussa, but she still didn't like losing the first fight to Ambrose.

"Anything else from the State?" Valle asked.

"No, Your Honor." Ambrose turned from the bench.

Keera, however, was not finished. Patsy had advised Keera that the presiding judge, responsible for assigning judicial caseloads, had recently mandated a fast-track system to expedite legal matters and reduce the backlog of those persons held in custody.

"Your Honor, Mr. LaRussa requests the court immediately set a case-scheduling conference to be held within the next seventy-two hours."

Ambrose wheeled. "Your Honor," he started, then perhaps perceiving the game of chicken, said, "the State has no objection."

Valle, however, leaned forward. "Are you saying the defendant does not waive his right to a speedy trial, Ms. Duggan?"

"He does not. He wishes to move this matter forward expeditiously to clear his name."

"Very well." Valle set the case-scheduling conference for Thursday, June fifteenth. "Any other matters?"

Keera drew the court's attention to her motion to discover the evidence within the police file. She could surmise some of it, but she did not want to be surmising or assuming at trial. In keeping with Patsy's tutelage, she needed to know the evidence better than anyone, and sooner rather than later.

"Any opposition, Counsel?" Valle asked Ambrose.

"None, Your Honor," Ambrose said, pleasant. "The prosecution is pleased to share the evidence with defense counsel . . . when it is ready."

"Then we're dismissed." Valle rapped his gavel.

As they turned from the bench, Ambrose uttered under his breath, but loud enough for Keera to hear, "I'm not sure, however, the defense will be pleased to receive it."

CHAPTER 16

Ambrose's cryptic comment and his quick departure from the courtroom confirmed Keera's justification for filing a pleading requesting the evidence as quickly as possible. She didn't trust Ambrose as far as she could throw him, and she wondered what else, besides the ghost gun, she'd have to deal with.

She didn't rule out that she'd need to seek a court order to compel the evidence's production. She hoped she did. The Sixth Amendment granted a defendant the right to view evidence gathered against him, and Keera doubted Judge Maxine Hung would respond favorably to Ambrose wasting her time by forcing Keera to bring a motion.

After the hearing, Keera advised LaRussa she would move to seek bail when the trial judge was assigned. "I'll also get the police reports and the evidence as soon as I can and keep you fully advised."

LaRussa thanked her.

She put her hand on his shoulder and leaned close. "Do you know anything about the gun?"

"No," he said.

She patted his shoulder before the marshals reapplied the bellyband and handcuffs and escorted him from the courtroom. Keera noticed JP Harrison standing at the back of the courtroom. He nodded—an indication he wanted to talk.

"You go ahead," Patsy said, also noticing Harrison. "I'll handle the press."

"Patsy—" Keera started.

"I've done this a few times," Patsy said. "Tell them everything without telling them a thing." He smiled. "Go."

Keera met Harrison, and they moved to a vacant corner at the back of the courtroom. "A ghost gun," Harrison said. "That complicates things."

"You're a master of understatement," she said.

"Good to be a master of something."

"Going to need you to go through their financial records again and rule out any third-party purchases or purchases made at gun shows or from online dealers."

"Made a note to do so. A lack of evidence won't exonerate him though. That is the purpose of a ghost gun—no record of a purchase or sale."

True, but Keera could also argue the State lacked evidence Vince LaRussa had purchased the weapon.

"Have something for you," Harrison said. "Let's go someplace where there aren't so many ears. I take it you walked?"

"It's the only exercise I've been getting."

"Good. I'll drive."

Keera approached her father and they stepped aside. "JP has something for me. I need you to look into getting the evidence. You'll be all right getting back to the office?"

Patsy smiled. "I think I can make it."

On their walk to his car, Harrison told Keera he'd found the PI who took the pictures of Vince LaRussa and Lisa Bennet.

"How'd you manage that?"

"As I said, people talk, especially when the case is this public. It's good for business."

"Have you spoken to this PI to confirm?"

"And possibly spook her? No. I assumed you would want to be present."

"Her?"

"Her."

Like Patsy, Keera preferred interviews in person, so she could evaluate the witness's physical demeanor while answering questions. She pulled open the passenger door of Harrison's 1972 BMW his father had originally bought for $12,000. Harrison had recently been offered more than $100,000. Keera called the car color red, but Harrison told her the color was Verona. Looked red to her.

As they drove, Keera said, "You reviewed the videos I sent you from the Four Seasons and traffic cameras?"

"And made the drive last night at eight forty-five," Harrison said, confirming he'd viewed the camera footage, and had retraced LaRussa's exact drive home at the time he left the Four Seasons on a Sunday evening. "LaRussa arrived at and left the hotel at the times he said and drove straight home. No detours."

Keera had a thought. "Do me a favor. Confirm that LaRussa didn't have a package delivered to the hotel. That he didn't have a room there."

"The ghost gun?"

"Just making sure. That gun had to come from somewhere. I want to eliminate any argument he had it delivered to the hotel."

"Will do," he said, dictating a note into his phone.

"Who's lying, JP? Somebody's lying."

"Don't know," he said. "But Vince LaRussa is the only one so far with a reason to lie."

"That we know of," Keera corrected. "Bennet could be lying about leaving Anne LaRussa alive that night."

Harrison looked over at her. "The SODDI defense?" he said with skepticism. SODDI stood for Some Other Dude Did It. Often a defense of last resort.

Keera shrugged. "Need to create reasonable doubt. We argue Anne threatened to expose Bennet for overprescribing opioids."

"And Bennet just happened to be carrying a gun in that bag of hers?"

"Right now we don't know where the gun

came from. So it remains possible. Maybe Anne previously threatened Bennet. Maybe Bennet shot her after weeks of accusations and threats Bennet isn't telling us about."

It wasn't a strong argument, Keera knew, but at the moment it was all she had come up with. "I'll talk to Vince and get a list of his and Anne's friends. Let's find out if any of them is aware of animosity or friction. Maybe Anne told someone besides Bennet that she suspected Vince was having an affair."

"You indicated Anne had become a recluse . . . at least according to the father."

"And Vince," Keera said. "But Ambrose will certainly do the same."

"He's got opportunity and motive right now," Harrison said.

"Ambrose will dot all his i's and cross his t's," she said. "He won't leave anything to chance."

The private investigator's office was on the first floor of a brick apartment complex in Madison Valley, not far from the LaRussas' home. The area had been refurbished over the prior decade with apartments, duplexes, commercial space, and a supermarket. Harrison drove by the space to confirm the office was open before he pulled into a parking garage beneath the building.

"You called to make sure the PI is here?" Keera asked.

"Michelle Batista," Harrison said.

"You know her?"

"No," Harrison said. "And not much about her on the internet or her website. Never heard of her while I was in law enforcement either."

Private investigators, more knowledgeable than most about how easily criminals could gather personal information, guarded their privacy. Most had law enforcement experience or a legal background, since much of their bread-and-butter involved serving legal papers and performing background checks. Harrison claimed he did not own a computer, except for his smart phone, and he refused to do bank transactions unless physically inside a bank. He did not advertise on the internet, had no social media presence, and he would not purchase anything online unless certain he could return it and get a refund. To Keera's knowledge, he utilized three different PO boxes in three different neighborhoods.

"How do you know she took the photographs if you haven't spoken to her?" Keera asked.

Harrison gave Keera his million-dollar smile. "Like I said, this case is free publicity. That's the best kind." Harrison left several spaces between his BMW and the nearest parked car to prevent door dings.

They rode the elevator to a lobby. Glass doors with stenciled gold letters identified the offices of SRI, LLC. Whatever that meant.

Inside, they approached a Black woman seated behind a beige faux-wood counter in a generic-looking office.

"Can I help you?" the young woman asked Harrison, doing her best to hide a smile.

"I believe you can," Harrison said, his accent more pronounced. "Would like a moment of Michelle Batista's time."

The woman stumbled to get out her next question. "Do you have an appointment?"

"We don't, but I'm sure she'll want to see us."

"Can I tell her your names?"

"Tell her Vincent LaRussa wishes to speak to her."

"Are you Vincent?" the receptionist asked.

"I'm a lot of things." Harrison and Keera stepped back from the desk as the young woman picked up the phone.

"Including old enough to be her father," Keera said under her breath.

"You want to speak to someone, you first have to get past the gatekeeper," he whispered.

The young woman hung up and gave them a sheepish smile. "Ms. Batista is busy," she said.

Keera smiled at Harrison. "Score one for the gatekeeper." She redirected her attention to the receptionist. "Please tell Ms. Batista that counsel for Vincent LaRussa is in her lobby, and I would appreciate five minutes of her time, otherwise

I'll subpoena her computer and phone records, as well as her appearance for a deposition. All of which will take her away from money-generating files."

The woman looked stunned.

Keera nodded to the telephone. "She'll want you to make that call."

The receptionist picked up the phone and repeated what Keera had said, listened for a moment, then hung up. "Ms. Batista will see you now," she said.

Keera turned to Harrison. "Sometimes you have to threaten the gatekeeper to get them to open the gates."

Inside an office as spartan as the reception area, Michelle Batista stood behind a desk. A fake but real-looking fern took up one corner near a window. Batista's desk and the shelving behind her contained no family photographs. Nothing personal.

Keera introduced herself and JP Harrison.

"I saw your picture in the paper and on the news this afternoon," Batista said. "Figured it was only a matter of time before you came around." She looked to Harrison. "How did you find me?"

"People talk," Harrison said.

"Especially in this business." Batista gestured to two chairs, and they all sat.

"What does SRI stand for?" Keera asked.

"Seattle Research Institute," Batista said.

"Do you have a background in law enforcement?"

"Hardly. I have a master's degree in library science from the University of Washington."

"How does a librarian end up doing PI work?"

"My last years as a librarian I spent most of my time at the downtown library policing the homeless and mentally ill. Don't get me wrong. Many came to the library seeking help getting jobs and getting back on their feet. They weren't the problems I had to deal with. The problems were those who came to use the computers to watch porn, play with themselves, and defecate all over the bathrooms. When I stepped in, they threatened me. When I complained to my boss, he told me to deal with it. When I called the police, they told me they wouldn't touch the situation, not with the current city council espousing a mantra that anyone who confronts the homeless is an insensitive fascist." She shrugged. "I got tired of that fight. Tired of seeing a therapist. I decided to get out when my pension fully vested. But I like to work. I like to research. I'm kind of a nerd that way."

"You took the photographs of Vince LaRussa with Lisa Bennet?"

"I contracted with someone to physically take the photographs, but . . . yeah. That was my contract."

"It's not exactly research," Keera said.

"No, but I've learned that catching cheating spouses is a lot more lucrative than finding out the history of Charlemagne for someone writing a novel set in the Middle Ages. And I have a mortgage to pay."

"How much were you paid?"

"That I won't reveal. No sense telling my competitors my price structure, and I can't see the relevance to your criminal case."

"And if we said we won't tell anyone?" Harrison said, smiling.

"Like you said, people talk."

Keera said, "You met Anne LaRussa?"

"No."

"Spoke to her on the phone?"

"No."

"Emails?"

Batista shook her head.

"Then how did you get the job?"

"I got an email asking if I could follow a spouse and determine if he was cheating on his wife. I said I could for a price, and I received a second email with the spouse's name."

"How'd you get paid?" Harrison asked.

"PayPal," Batista said. "If you're looking to identify the person, forget it. They used a VPN to hide their IP address."

"You still have the emails sent?"

"Electronic copies stored on the computer and printed. As I said, when I saw the news, I knew the police and the attorneys would eventually come knocking. I don't want to get involved, but I guess I'm beyond that. Makes research into Charlemagne look a lot more enticing."

"Have the police been here yet?"

"You're the first."

"Can I see the emails?"

Batista opened up a manila file on her desk and handed two pages to Keera. The email was from Jack Worthing, and the name hit Keera like a dart. She turned to Harrison, who had also taken notice. The email said basically what Batista had told them.

"I take it from your reaction that you might know a Jack Worthing?" Batista said, looking between Keera and Harrison.

"I don't," Keera said. "Did you ever meet him?"

She shook her head. "Personally, I don't think he exists. I think the name is made up. That's why I asked."

"You tried to find him?"

"I did when the news of the murder broke."

"What did you find?"

"He had a short but notorious life in 1895 at the St. James's Theatre in London."

"I don't understand," Keera said.

"That's because you're not a research nerd." Batista pulled out a manila file from beneath another on her desk. "Jack Worthing is the protagonist in the play *The Importance of Being Earnest* by Oscar Wilde. It opened to great aplomb. Then the marquess of Queensberry learned Wilde was gay and his partner the marquess's son. He tanked the play and Wilde's career. So, unless the person sending those emails actually shares the same name, which is possible, my guess is he's fictitious. Someone using an alias. I bought a copy and read the play. It's a commentary on the institution of marriage, its perception, which might be relevant to your case. I don't know. As for the plot, Jack Worthing creates a fictitious brother, Ernest, to do all the hedonistic things Jack wouldn't do. The title is intended to be ironic."

"You have a copy of the play?" Keera asked.

Batista pulled a small, thin booklet from the manila file, handing it to Keera.

"Can I borrow this?"

"You can keep it. I have no further use for it. Just wanted to satisfy my curiosity."

Keera thanked her. She thought of Jack Worthing's email to her, the detail about her having once played chess.

"Did Jack Worthing ask you to research me?"

"No. Why?"

"He sent me an email also."

"I don't know anything about that," Batista said. "Though it certainly adds another wrinkle; doesn't it?"

More than a few, Keera thought. "Can I make a copy of the email?"

"Ordinarily I wouldn't turn over a copy of a client's file without a court order, but since my client is likely fictitious, I believe that abrogates any concerns I have to protect his privacy." She handed Keera the file. "Seems we're both involved in some sort of game."

CHAPTER 17

Keera needed a quiet place to go through Michelle Batista's Jack Worthing file, what little there was, read the play, and think through what it all could mean. On the drive back to her office to retrieve her car, Harrison said what Keera had been thinking. "It has to be the wife, doesn't it?"

"Can't be. That message I received from Jack Worthing was sent after Anne LaRussa died."

"You can set up the email to be delivered at a future date and time."

"But Anne LaRussa would have had no idea I would be representing Vince LaRussa. Not even an educated guess."

"So it's an intermediary, then; someone Anne LaRussa hired?"

"Why would Anne LaRussa go to such an extent to keep secret that she hired a private investigator?" Keera asked. "She called out Lisa Bennet and Vince."

"Maybe she feared her husband learning she was checking up on him."

"Maybe, but that choice of name, this play." She held up *The Importance of Being Earnest*. "She either knew the play, or she chose it and the character after she did some research. Maybe she wanted it known that their marriage was not as it appeared, that there was something sinister beneath the façade."

"Okay. Let's assume that premise. Then why send an email to Vince LaRussa's defense counsel indicating more information is to come? If she had information on something sinister in their marriage, why not send that email to the prosecution?" Harrison asked.

Keera gave it some thought, then recognized it to be a waste of time and energy that she didn't have to spare. "We're speculating about speculation here," she said, recalling another of Patsy's mantras. *Control what you can control. Deal with what is in front of you.*

"What can we control? Let's find out Anne LaRussa's major in college. Maybe she had theater experience," Keera said, making a note to ask Vince.

When she arrived at home, Keera picked up her mail, slipped through the mail slot in the door, from the floor. She set it on the dining room table and hit the space bar on her keyboard and checked the game in progress. The Dark Knight had retreated his queen to c2, perhaps now realizing a straightforward attack would put his queen in peril. Keera moved her pawn to b6. His sixteenth move, the Dark Knight slid his bishop to f4. Keera moved her rook to a7, continuing her defensive façade, but opening a diagonal path she was certain the Dark Knight had not anticipated.

The Dark Knight moved his rook from f1 to c1, doubling down on the queen's side of the board. His two rooks, now side by side, appeared to be a powerful battery with his queen and his bishop, but he had sacrificed one of the three defenders protecting his king, weakening his defense.

Keera responded pawn to c5, another seemingly innocuous move, but it released her rook to slide over for the future attack.

She shut down the game and methodically went through her current case files to clear her deck if Vince LaRussa agreed to have Keera defend him. She did what she could to clean up her files and made a comprehensive list of her cases, upcoming court appearances, deadlines, and other tasks that needed attention. She forwarded a copy of the document to Ella and to her assistant, and told both she'd be in early, after she spoke to Vince LaRussa at the jail. She then methodically checked emails that came in while she had been out of the office. Near the middle of her newest emails she noted a name, opened the email, and read.

Jack Worthing had made the first move.

CHAPTER 18

June 13, 2023

The following morning, Tuesday, Keera met with Patsy and JP Harrison in Patsy's office, which was cluttered with knickknacks, most provided by grateful clients. The clutter included paintings and framed photographs of Seattle icons, a wooden Indian, a crossbow and arrows, an antique rifle, and a framed four-leaf clover.

"What did you learn?" Keera asked. She had forwarded Jack Worthing's most recent email to Harrison. Worthing had advised Keera, cryptically, to talk with someone named Mary C. Bell in Beaverton, Oregon.

"All I can tell you is Mary C. Bell is a retired elementary school teacher with a recent Facebook presence started not long after the death of her husband," Harrison said. He looked like a Los Angeles celebrity in white linen pants rolled at the ankles, no socks, and brown leather loafers. The sleeves of his light-blue shirt gripped his biceps. Ray-Ban sunglasses hung from a pocket. "They apparently took motor-home trips before he passed. Now she reads cozy mysteries, likes to quilt and garden, and watches her two grand-children."

"You spoke to her?"

"Yesterday afternoon," Harrison said. "She was Vince LaRussa's grammar school teacher."

"Grammar school?" Keera said.

"That's what she said. She also said I was the second person to call and ask her about Vince."

That was of significant interest to Keera. "Let me guess the first. Jack Worthing?"

"Bingo. Said Worthing called about six months ago. Asked her all kinds of things—what kind of kid Vince was, whether he ever got in any trouble. His family. She also said that she couldn't be sure, but she thought maybe the person was disguising his voice."

"You can do that?" Patsy said.

"There are all kinds of devices on the internet," Harrison said. "But since she had never spoken to Jack Worthing before, she couldn't be sure. Said the person also asked about others who might have known Vince growing up."

That was a potential problem, if Jack Worthing was also speaking to Ambrose. "Could she provide other names?"

"One. Eric Fields. Also still lives in Beaverton. He owns a garage specializing in antique cars. That alone is worth the drive."

Keera had debated whether to pursue Worthing's email at all. A trial attorney's job was prioritizing the myriad of things needed to prepare a case for trial by minimizing wasted

199

time and maximizing effort. Keera didn't want to send Harrison on a wild-goose chase, but she also didn't want to leave a stone unturned and later have Ambrose throw that stone and shatter her case.

"What do you think?" she asked Patsy.

"I'd at least dip my toe into the Jack Worthing water, if for no other reason than to possibly learn his identity. I'll go with JP and gauge Mary Bell's and Eric Field's reactions to questions and determine if Ambrose has spoken to them, and what type of witnesses they might be, should we or Ambrose call them as witnesses at trial. We can head out as soon as traffic clears."

The drive south to Beaverton, Oregon, a city twenty minutes outside Portland, was about three hours.

"What did you learn about Jack Worthing?" Harrison asked Keera.

Keera had spent the better part of an hour and a half the prior evening reading and analyzing the play *The Importance of Being Earnest*. "Batista got it right. The play is a debate about marriage."

"I don't like it already," Harrison said.

"No, you wouldn't, but it is interesting."

"The play or the institution?" Harrison said.

"The subject matter. In some respects, this case is about marriage, isn't it? On the surface, at least, the LaRussas appeared to have a strong marriage . . . Vince the doting husband, concerned about his disabled wife."

"You don't think he was?" Patsy said.

"I'm worried about the father saying Anne had become a recluse, that maybe it was indicative of a problem in their marriage."

"Could have been due to her injuries, the realization she wasn't going to get better," Patsy said.

"Or the controlling nature of her husband who perhaps knew she was on to something," Harrison said. "Disabled women have a forty percent greater chance of experiencing domestic violence than able-bodied women. Her becoming a recluse could be a red flag."

"And we can be sure that is the picture Miller Ambrose will paint for the jury," Patsy said. "And that he'll be looking for witnesses to confirm it. He wants to tell a story of a husband who *appeared* to dote on his disabled wife but was actually cheating on her with her best friend. I think it's worth the drive, if for no other reason than to be sure these people can't come back to bite us in the ass."

"Is that what Jack Worthing did in the play— killed his wife?" Harrison asked.

"No. Nothing like that. A man discovered Jack Worthing as an infant in the cloakroom of a London railway station, brought him home, and raised him to be a seemingly respectable young man and a pillar of the community."

"But that was just a façade?" Harrison asked.

"Worthing led a double life, pretending to be someone he was not."

"Ah. The plot thickens. Who does he pretend to be?" Harrison said.

"His irresponsible younger brother, Ernest, whom Jack is always bailing out of trouble," Patsy said.

Both Keera and Harrison stared at him.

"What? I have an artistic side," Patsy said. "Your mother and I had season tickets to the Seattle Rep for years. That was one of the plays we saw."

"You could have saved me the trouble of reading the play," Keera said.

"That's all I remember," Patsy said.

"So who, then, is Ernest?" Harrison said.

"Ernest is the name Jack goes by when he escapes his responsibilities and goes into London to indulge in the behavior he pretends to disapprove of," Keera said.

"Ah," Harrison said. "Sort of like *The Fabulous Mr. Ripley*. Tom Hanks pretends to be some rich guy, but things go sideways, and he ends up killing the rich guy in a rowboat."

"The movie was *The Talented Mr. Ripley*. And it was Matt Damon, not Tom Hanks, but other than getting the name of the movie and the actor wrong, I agree," Keera said. "The two stories are similar."

"A man pretending to be someone he is not. Vince LaRussa?" Harrison said. "I take it this Jack Worthing is eventually exposed?"

"He is," Patsy said. "At least, that's what I remember."

"Maybe that's a harbinger of things to come in our case," Harrison said.

"A line in the play jumped out at me," Keera said. She opened the book to where she had dog-eared the page. " 'The truth is rarely pure and never simple.' "

"Seems that quote would apply equally to the playwright, Oscar Wilde, wouldn't it?" Harrison said. "A gay man pretending to be something he is not. The question is, what is the truth in the LaRussa case?" He shook his head. "Well, I can honestly say I have never had a case that referenced literature."

"Nor have I," Patsy said. "Changing subjects, I spoke to Rossi. He said we'd get the police files tomorrow, though toxicology has not yet come back." Toxicology reports on victims could often take weeks.

"And speaking of reports," Harrison interjected. "I got the report back from the lab on the sample of water we collected from Anne LaRussa's kitchen floor."

"Let me guess, it's water," Keera said.

"Well, it's sort of like your Jack Worthing; it appears to be water, but it's more interesting."

"What's the interesting part?" Keera asked.

"The lab detected potassium nitrate."

"Which is . . . ?"

"An oxidizer, according to my research. I looked it up. It accelerates burning when a fire is lit."

Interesting indeed, Keera thought. "Where is potassium nitrate found?"

"I had to look it up. It's found in deposits crystallizing in cave walls from bat guano."

"Bat guano?" Keera said.

"Bat guano. It's one of several nitrogen-containing compounds collectively referred to as saltpeter," Harrison continued.

"I meant where would someone find it here, in this country?" Keera asked.

"Fertilizers, stump remover, rocket propellants, fireworks. It's a basic component of gunpowder. I also looked it up," Harrison responded.

"So then it could have come from the gun on the floor," Keera said.

"Maybe. Except that doesn't explain the burn mark on the oven door handle, which also tested positive for potassium nitrate," Harrison said. "And the water on the floor also had microscopic cotton fibers in addition to the potassium nitrate."

"Could the cotton fibers have come from Anne LaRussa's clothing?" Keera asked.

"I'm not sure how," Harrison said. "She wasn't shot through her clothing."

"Could someone have fired the gun and touched the oven handle for some reason, transferring the potassium nitrate to the handle?" Patsy said.

"Could have, but that wouldn't explain the burn mark," Harrison said. "And my high school chemistry instructor, Mr. Cobalt—"

"Seriously? You had a chemistry teacher named Cobalt?" Keera said.

"As God is my witness," Harrison said. "Mr. Cobalt said, 'A theory isn't a theory if it doesn't explain every variable.' "

"You have a theory?" Keera asked.

"Hell no. Not yet, anyway. But I am working on it."

After Patsy and Harrison left for Beaverton, Keera made the walk up the hill to the King County jail, filled out forms, presented proper identification, and placed her belongings in a locker. Inside the jail, the aroma of soiled clothes dominated, along with the noise—inmates shouting and the rhythmic sound of someone dribbling a basketball. A corrections officer led Keera down a narrow hall, used a key to unlock a heavy metal door, and ushered her inside a windowless room with battleship-gray walls, a table two feet square bolted to the floor, and two chairs.

"Keep the door open," the officer said.

A few minutes after her arrival, a different

corrections officer escorted LaRussa into the room in his red prison scrubs, white socks, and slippers. He was belly chained at the waist.

"Can the handcuffs be removed?" Keera asked.

"Nope," the officer said. "I'll be outside the door if you need anything."

After the officer departed, Keera asked LaRussa how he was doing.

LaRussa shrugged. "Sometimes I'm okay. Sometimes I feel like I'm living in a nightmare that I can't wake from."

"I'm sorry about bail," she said.

"You told me it would be a long shot, given the charge."

"I'll raise the issue again with the trial judge."

"Do we have a judge?"

"I'm told it will be Maxine Hung. I'm going to be honest with you. She wouldn't have been my first choice. She's a former prosecutor who earned the nickname 'Maximum Maxine' when she tried murder cases. That moniker has followed her to the bench."

"So bail isn't likely," LaRussa said with a waning smile.

"She's tough but she's fair," Keera said, repeating what Patsy had told her.

"But she won't grant bail."

"In a first-degree murder trial, given your considerable wealth and resources, it's unlikely."

"So where do we go from here?"

"The case-scheduling hearing is Thursday. I'm told we'll get some of the prosecution's evidence this afternoon, and I'll evaluate it. I also have JP Harrison putting together the evidence he independently obtained when we went to your home, to determine if anything doesn't match up. We're hoping to come up with evidence to support our own theory of what happened."

"Such as?"

Keera shook her head. "I'm not going to lie, Vince. We just don't know yet. Harrison did obtain the Seattle street-camera footage, and the video footage from the Four Seasons for that Sunday night, and he's driven the route confirming your timing getting home. And we found the private investigator hired to take the pictures of you and Lisa."

"What did he have to say?" LaRussa said, clearly interested.

"She. The PI is a she. I'll get to what she had to say in a minute. Have you given any more thought to the jury consultant's advice about my defending you?"

LaRussa sat back. "It makes sense, and I was impressed by you in court. I've never seen your father in action, but from what I've heard, you're cut from the same cloth."

"I won't let you down, Vince. I can't promise you anything except that I'll give you my very best and fight every step of the way."

LaRussa smiled, but again it faded. "I can't ask for anything more than that; can I? Okay. Let's move forward."

Keera felt relief, and she knew Ella would also. She couldn't predict Patsy's reaction, but given what Ella and their mother had said about his recent court appearances, she suspected he, too, would be relieved.

Keera filled in LaRussa on what Michelle Batista had told them. Then she said, "The email wasn't sent by Anne."

"Who sent it?"

"Someone named Jack Worthing." Keera had been trained from her youth to evaluate her chess opponents' body language—how they sat, their facial expressions, whether they had any tells like licking their lips when nervous, a tug on an ear when bluffing, a false smile. She studied LaRussa.

His brow furrowed and his eyes narrowed. "Who?"

"You've never heard that name?"

"No. Who is Jack Worthing?"

"We believe it's an alias. One hypothesis was that it was a way for your wife to keep her identity secret."

"She made it up?"

"Not exactly." Keera told LaRussa about the play *The Importance of Being Earnest* and its main character. "What was Anne's major in college?"

"She was a literature major."

"Do you know what era of study?"

"No."

"So she could have read and studied the play in college."

"I suppose," he said.

Keera nodded. Something about LaRussa's physicality struck her as less than genuine, though she didn't know why. "There's something else," she said. "I also received an email at work from a Jack Worthing."

"How can that be? Anne's dead."

"We're trying to figure that out," she said. "He directed me to speak to someone in Beaverton, Oregon."

"I grew up there," LaRussa said. "Who's the person?"

"A grammar school teacher named Mary Bell."

"Mary Bell? What the hell could she have to do with any of this?"

"You know her?"

"She was my fifth- or sixth-grade teacher," LaRussa said, clearly perplexed.

"I sent JP Harrison and Patsy to talk with her and someone named Eric Fields."

"I knew Eric in grammar school and high school."

Keera told LaRussa that Worthing had asked Bell about others who might have known him. "It could be nothing, but I didn't want to ignore it and find out at trial that the prosecution spoke to them for some reason. You have no idea why someone would want me to talk to Bell?"

"None," LaRussa said. "If Anne used the name Jack Worthing to hire the investigator, who's using that name now?"

"Good question," Keera said. "We don't know."

CHAPTER 19

Frank Rossi paced the glistening linoleum floor in the King County medical examiner's waiting room. The offices were located in a fourteen-story, tinted-glass and natural-light building of the Harborview Medical Center at Ninth and Jefferson Street. Rossi had driven to the office upon email receipt of Arthur Litchfield's autopsy report on Anne LaRussa. He could have walked the four blocks up the hill and got outside and enjoyed some exercise, which was rare during a full-blown investigation heading to trial.

But not this morning.

Not after he'd read Litchfield's report.

This morning he was more interested in answers, and he wanted them quickly. He'd tried calling Litchfield but got his voice mail. That was not unusual. The ME's office was usually under siege. Returning phone calls and responding to emails was often put off to the end of the day—not that Rossi would have put anything in writing. Emails were paper trails, and Rossi knew not to leave one, or a phone message for that matter.

Rossi had not expected to find anything of particular interest in Litchfield's report, given Anne LaRussa's obvious cause of death—gunshot wound to the back of the head. He expected the report to confirm the caliber of bullet, checking one more thing off his list of things to do. Upon receipt of Litchfield's report, Rossi had put his feet up on the corner of his desk and skimmed the sections noting rigor mortis and lividity, the body's rectal temperature, and Litchfield's conclusion that Anne LaRussa had died between six o'clock and nine thirty at night. Rossi knew Ambrose wanted something more specific, but he wasn't going to get it. He'd have to deal with it at trial, get Litchfield to discuss how the room temperature impacted how quickly a victim lost body temperature, make him look smart before the jury.

Rossi confirmed Litchfield had complied with law enforcement requirements in the processing room, noted the appearance of Anne LaRussa's clothing, jewelry worn, and any markings on her body, including surgical scars to her cervical spine, her throat—a tracheotomy—and her right arm, incurred at the time of her horseback-riding accident. He found no puncture wounds indicating any injections. No tattoos. He noted no scratches or bruising of her skin, no missing fingernails, no skin under her nails to indicate a struggle or a fight. In other words, no evidence of domestic violence, which would seem to rule out that Anne became a recluse because Vince had abused her. Litchfield had also performed X-rays and a CT scan.

Rossi skimmed the case summary until he arrived at the cause of death. Litchfield described the damage the bullet caused upon entering the skull and the more considerable damage caused upon its exit above the right eye socket. He concluded from the wound location, the bullet trajectory—depicted with a dotted line—and from the lack of GSR on the victim's scalp that she had been shot at a distance of between three to five feet.

He ruled her death a homicide.

That was all well and good . . .

The door to the processing room swung open. Litchfield stepped out, pulling the light-blue surgery cap from his bald head, then removing his gown, throwing both in a laundry bin. The two men had never met. Rossi introduced himself and said, "Need a moment of your time to discuss the Anne LaRussa autopsy."

Litchfield scratched the back of his neck, looking chagrined. He adjusted round glasses and, with a nod, turned and led Rossi down the hall to an office that looked unused. No photographs or paintings hung on the walls or adorned the desk or the shelving, which did, however, contain thick medical textbooks on anatomy, biology, chemistry, and other subjects. No plants or knickknacks decorated the room or revealed anything personal about the man. Litchfield either hadn't yet had time to decorate, or he didn't see the point. Stuart Funk, the King County chief medical examiner, kept an office just as spartan. Rossi wondered if that was because nothing could beautify their job, or maybe it was because their office was not within these four vacant walls, but within the cold and sterile processing room where they hunched over stainless-steel tables with drains and traps, removing and weighing organs.

Rossi held up Litchfield's multipage report before Litchfield's ass had hit the seat of his ergonomic chair. "Anne LaRussa had stage-four pancreatic cancer?"

"That's what Anne LaRussa's remains *told me*," Litchfield said with little emotion.

"Explain it to me," Rossi said.

Litchfield exhaled a long sigh, as if perturbed by the interruption, and again rubbed the back of his neck. "I found multiple tumors that I believe metastasized from her pancreas to her lymph nodes, to her other organs including her lungs, and her bones."

"Any indication she had received treatment?"

"None that I could determine."

"Could she have not known?"

"Possible, but given the progression noted, the fact that it had invaded her bones, I would be surprised. She would have been in significant pain, which is likely the reason the toxicology report indicated the presence of opioid analgesics."

Rossi thought of Anne LaRussa's stocked medicine cabinet and wondered if she had mistaken the pain associated with her cancer for the pain from her continuing disability injuries. "How long did she have to live?"

"Not really my bullfight," Litchfield said.

"Wave a red cape at the bull and give me an educated guess, Doc," Rossi said, not liking the attitude.

"Educated guess, I'd say not long."

"And the translation of the medical term 'not long' is what? A month, six months?" Rossi asked.

Litchfield looked to be doing math in his head. "An educated guess would be a month, perhaps six weeks, assuming no treatment. If treated, maybe three months. She would have gone very quickly, regardless."

"She was dying. Treatment or not. She was dying."

"Yes."

The information rattled in Rossi's brain. He thought of Lisa Bennet, an oncologist and Anne LaRussa's friend—at least she had been a friend at one time. Had she known?

He knew one thing for certain. Keera Duggan would pounce upon the information. She'd argue that Anne LaRussa, knowing she was dying, took her own life. She'd have an uphill battle, given Anne LaRussa's physical impairment. It made the argument seemingly far-fetched, but Rossi had witnessed jurors respond to all kinds of crazy arguments.

"My suggestion," Litchfield said, "would be to subpoena her medical records. Find out who, if anyone, diagnosed her cancer and what steps were taken, if any. She had a world-class facility at Seattle Cancer Care. Perhaps she sought treatment there?"

"But treatment would not have made any difference?"

"In my opinion, the chances of her surviving were minimal; no more than three to five percent. Could treatment have prolonged her life? Again, perhaps. But we're talking weeks. Not months. And she would have suffered."

"Either way, Anne LaRussa was going to die," Rossi said, trying to get his head around this unexpected turn of events.

"Either way," Litchfield said.

An hour later, Rossi hung up his desk phone and swiveled his chair to face Billy Ford, who had his back to him, seated at his desk in their bull pen. The television mounted overhead spewed some late-afternoon news, and Rossi could hear a smattering of telephone conversations, punctuated by bursts of profanity.

"Hey," he said, gaining Ford's attention. "Ambrose wants to talk."

"You tell him about the ME's report?"

"I told him. He said he was out and would come here."

Ford made a face like he didn't believe it. Ambrose never made it easy on the detectives he worked with. "What was his response to the news?"

"Just asked if we'd sent over the police file to defense counsel."

"Did we?"

Rossi shook his head. "I was about to until I read the ME's report. Decided not to send anything before Ambrose took a look," he said. The file also did not yet contain the final toxicology or DNA reports. "Had to come as a surprise to Ambrose. Sure as shit came as a surprise to me."

"But Litchfield concluded homicide," Ford said.

"Ambrose isn't likely worried about what the ME concluded. He's worried about how Keera Duggan might use this information in her arguments to the jury. At least he should be."

"Meaning what?" Ford asked.

"Why would Anne LaRussa's husband kill her if she was already dying?"

Ford looked to be contemplating the question.

"I'm no doctor—" Rossi said.

"—Far from it."

"But I've had a friend and an uncle die from pancreatic cancer. It's one of the worst forms, almost always a death sentence. Remember Patrick Swayze?"

"The actor. Did the Chippendales skit with Chris Farley on *Saturday Night Live*."

"I think he died from pancreatic cancer, but don't quote me on it."

"Like the *Hollywood Reporter* is gonna call you?"

"Litchfield said Anne LaRussa had weeks to live. How long does a divorce take?"

"You don't think Anne LaRussa would have had enough time to divorce her husband and trigger the clause in the prenuptial agreement."

"And if she didn't have sufficient time, there goes Ambrose's argument that LaRussa was motivated to kill his wife. At a minimum, it gives Keera Duggan a plausible argument the jurors can understand."

"Maybe Vince LaRussa didn't know about the cancer either."

"And maybe cows can fly," Rossi said.

"She could have kept the diagnosis from him," Ford said.

Rossi didn't buy it. "Why?"

"To set him up . . ." Ford stopped himself, perhaps realizing that the more layers he added the weaker the argument became.

"Like I said. Keera Duggan will argue Vince LaRussa had no reason to kill his wife if she was already dying. Simple. Straightforward. Easy for jurors to follow and understand," Rossi said.

"Which are the best arguments," Ford agreed.

"Common sense," Rossi said.

"But there's still the problem of Anne LaRussa's physical disabilities," Ford said. "How could she have physically shot herself? Let alone shot herself in the back of the head?"

"Duggan doesn't have to prove Anne LaRussa did it. She doesn't have to prove anything. She just has to deflect Ambrose's evidence that Vince LaRussa was motivated to kill his wife and get one juror to find reasonable doubt."

Rossi's desk phone rang, an interior line. Ambrose had arrived.

"Speak of the devil," Ford said.

"Meet me in the soft interrogation room," Rossi said. "I'll go get the Prince of Darkness."

Rossi walked from his desk to the elevator bank. He wasn't smiling because he hoped Vince LaRussa got off—if he was indeed guilty, and it certainly seemed that way. He was smiling because he knew how competitive Keera Duggan was, especially in trial. Give her an inch and she'd take a mile. And Arthur Litchfield had given her much more than an inch. Litchfield had given her something she could use to explain why technicians did not find blood spatter on Vince LaRussa's clothes or his hands; why his fingerprints and his DNA were not found on the weapon; why his finances did not indicate the purchase of a handgun. She could argue that LaRussa had no motivation to kill his wife, even if Anne LaRussa confronted him with the affair. Anne LaRussa would be dead in a matter of weeks, maybe a month. Litchfield had perhaps given Keera Duggan a defense attorney's best friend.

Reasonable doubt.

CHAPTER 20

June 14, 2023

Late the following afternoon, after taking a long deposition in another of her cases, Keera made her way to the conference room where JP Harrison was unpacking food from a brown bag. Harrison, too, had been working another case, and Patsy had been in court most of the day. They had not discussed Harrison and Patsy's trip to Beaverton, Oregon, in any detail. Harrison handed Keera a Greek salad and put a second salad on the table in front of him. He pulled out a Styrofoam box for Patsy, who entered carrying soft drinks and bottles of water.

After getting settled, Patsy said, "Bell isn't as old as her hobbies would otherwise indicate."

"Old is relative." Harrison stabbed at his salad. "She's sixty-two. Does look younger though. Judging from the multiple pairs of sneakers outside her front door, she's a runner. She'd read the story of Vince LaRussa's arrest in the newspaper and saw it on the news. Said she didn't believe it. Said Vince was a sweet boy and whip smart. Beguiling. A leader."

Patsy put down his gyro sandwich and washed down the bite he'd taken with a sip of Coke.

"Teachers are like women who have babies. After the students leave their classroom, even those students who were shits didn't seem that bad, and they're prepared to do it all over again in the fall. I asked her if she could recall anything not so wonderful." Patsy took another bite.

"Could she?" Keera asked.

Harrison answered, giving Patsy time to chew. "She said Vince wanted to put on a class play."

"What play?" Keera asked, though she knew *The Importance of Being Earnest* would have been far too ambitious for grammar school students.

"Great minds," Harrison said. "I thought the same thing, but couldn't see grammar school kids doing a play about marriage."

"She didn't recall the name," Patsy said. "A Christmas play of some sort. She couldn't provide all the details but said it was about an English family moving into a run-down cottage in the English countryside occupied by a family of ghosts. She remembered the play had two sets—a dark cottage covered in tarps, and the same cottage illuminated with candlelight and a warm fire in the hearth."

"One dark and one light," Harrison said, continuing to eat his salad. "Sort of like Jack Worthing and his brother, Ernest. Two sides of the same coin. Or am I reading too much into this?"

"What else did she say?" Keera asked.

"Some of the students accused Vince of keeping money they apparently raised doing car washes and bake sales for play supplies."

"And?" Keera asked.

"And that was the end of it," Patsy said. He picked up his gyro and took another bite.

"So a wild-goose chase?" Keera said.

"Not exactly," Harrison said. "We also ran down Eric Fields, the owner of the mechanic shop specializing in classic cars."

"JP was in hog heaven," Patsy said. "Fields apparently went to elementary, middle school, and high school with Vince LaRussa."

"Did he also speak to Jack Worthing?"

Patsy nodded. "About six months ago. Same as Mary Bell."

"Were Fields and Vince close?"

"Fields didn't say, but I didn't get the sense they were. He said they had different interests. I think he was being diplomatic," Patsy said. "His interest was cars. Said Vince's interest was making money. He said Vince always made money."

"Anything specific?"

Patsy nodded and flipped a page in a legal pad, reading for a moment. "He said Vince sold strawberries for his grandfather. He'd sell them for a couple of bucks more per basket than he was told to sell them and pocket the difference. Fields said Vince used to make up stories to get people to buy the strawberries from him—he needed the money so his mom could buy groceries, or to pay the rent. Said Vince was a 'gifted liar.' " Patsy put the final two words in air quotes.

"That doesn't exactly help us," Keera said.

"If Vince had any baskets left over at the end of the day, he'd lower the price so his grandfather would be proud he sold them all."

"Again, I don't see that as anything admissible. Did Fields have anything negative to say?"

"Other than that Vince LaRussa was a 'gifted liar'?" Harrison said.

Patsy ran a finger down his page of notes. "He said Vince was a good athlete, got good grades, class president. Editor of the paper. Had the girls after him. But that never seemed to be enough for Vince. He said Vince was always lured by the prospect of making money, that Vince told him he wanted to be a millionaire before he turned thirty."

"So he was ambitious," Keera said.

"Maybe a little too ambitious," Patsy said. "Fields recalled a high school incident also. Said a teacher asked Vince to tutor a student in math. Bingo. Vince gets the idea to start a tutoring business and hires the smartest kids in the school to be tutors."

"Let me guess. There was a money issue," Keera said.

Patsy nodded. "At the end of the year Vince stiffed some of the tutors, said some of the parents hadn't paid him, so he couldn't pay them. Fields said one tutor didn't take Vince at his word and checked around. Turns out the parents did pay."

"Vince kept the money," Keera said.

"Appears that was the case," Patsy said.

"You talk with anyone else?"

Patsy shook his head. "Fields said Vince didn't have a lot of friends and speculated that was why Vince had never gone to any of the class reunions, even though he's done so well. He said hard feelings tend to linger."

"Especially when the guy goes on to become a multimillionaire," Harrison said. "Like rubbing salt in the wound."

"Had either Bell or Fields spoken with anyone at the PA's office?" Keera asked.

"No," Patsy said. "And I don't think what they had to say is germane to a murder charge. We're talking about things from decades ago."

Keera agreed. They finished eating and continued talking and strategizing. As they cleaned up, Patsy said, "Have we received the police file yet?"

Keera checked her watch. "Should be here by now. My intent was to take it home where I can shut off the phone and better prepare for tomorrow's hearing."

"I'm happy to go over a copy," Patsy said. "Sometimes two pairs of eyes are better than one."

"I'll have a copy made for you," Keera said. "I'd like you to work with the jury consultant, focus on the types of jurors we're looking for and what questions we may want to ask to determine prejudices and weed out those most likely to convict, without it looking that way."

Patsy smiled and Keera knew she was not telling him anything he didn't already know. "Judge Hung keeps a tight leash on voir dire," he said, meaning the jury selection process. "She isn't going to let either side stray far from the straight line or even ask questions. She likes to have juries picked quickly and therefore asks most of the questions herself. I'll make some calls and determine other attorneys' experiences before her."

"We can also expect a slew of motions from Ambrose," Keera said. "He'll contest everything, try to make our lives miserable, distract us."

"Put Ella on motion duty," Patsy said. "That's where she thrives."

Ella was fast, efficient, and lethal when bringing or opposing motions, and judges appreciated brevity. They wouldn't thank you for it, but there'd be hell to pay if you wasted their time.

"What about the LaRussas' marital relationship?" Patsy asked.

"I'll get names from Vince," Keera said. "I also called Anne LaRussa's parents. They won't talk to me."

"Not surprising," Patsy said.

"And I tried Syd Evans again. He turned me down again. I told him we would get a subpoena. He told me to 'be my guest.'"

"I doubt there's much more to get than what we already know," Patsy said. "But I'll depose him to be sure."

Keera took a deep breath. "Anything else?"

Harrison and Patsy looked to one another, then shook their heads. Harrison left the conference room first.

"Hang on a minute," Patsy said to Keera. "I just wanted to make sure you're doing okay."

"I'm fine. Why do you ask?"

He gave her a painful smile. Keera knew why. Because Patsy was, first and foremost, her father, and she was his daughter. Because he longed for those better days they'd once shared. But the past was the past. No sense longing for something that no longer existed.

"Just making sure," he said, obviously not allowing himself to say what had really been on his mind.

Keera took the remainder of her Greek salad home to her dining room table. She glanced at the cabinet, felt the liquor's pull. It surprised and scared her. She hurried into the kitchen to grab a Diet Dr Pepper from the refrigerator and returned. She sipped her soft drink and hit the space bar on her laptop. Over the prior days, the Dark Knight had responded to Keera's attack head-on. His eighteenth move, pawn to h4, was even a bit cocky. He was either taking risks or hoping Keera would become distracted by the battle on the right side of the board. Underestimating her was his first big mistake. She unleashed what she had kept hidden. She moved her pawn to f5, signaling she had never been on the defensive. The gloves were off. The real battle was now on, and there would be no turning back for either side.

The mental break and the rest of her salad rejuvenated her. She shut down the computer and pulled out the police file, at least what currently existed. The final toxicology report would take time. She read the initial police report detailing Vince LaRussa's 911 call, the responding officers first to arrive, what they saw and heard, including what Vince LaRussa had told them. She noted slight differences from what LaRussa had told her, but nothing that couldn't be explained as a husband in a state of shock. She flipped to the report prepared by Rossi as the lead detective. Again, nothing alarmed her, though certain things made her job more difficult. LaRussa had readily told Rossi and Ford about the security cameras. She'd argue if he had been concerned about what they might reveal, he would not have been so forthcoming.

Rossi had sent LaRussa and the responding officer to check the other rooms in the house for signs of an intruder, but Keera knew that had been a ruse to keep LaRussa busy but not in Rossi's way. The lack of any signs of an intrusion refuted a defense argument that an intruder had broken into the home and shot Anne LaRussa. Rossi also had Kaylee Wright, a tracker, canvass the house exterior. She did not find footprints in the ground or in the grass to indicate a person lying in wait.

Keera would have preferred LaRussa had not consented to being fingerprinted or to providing a DNA sample, but technicians did not find his fingerprints or his DNA on the recovered gun. Again, she would argue his willingness indicated he was unconcerned. Ambrose would say LaRussa had wiped the gun clean, maybe even changed clothes, all of which supported a finding of premeditation, an intent to get away with the crime. Keera would talk to Harrison about potentially re-creating and timing whether LaRussa could have shot and killed his wife and done all of those other things between the time that he returned home and the time he walked back outside to await the responding officers' arrival.

Keera noted the Latent Fingerprint Unit had

affirmatively identified Syd Evans's and Lisa Bennet's fingerprints on the kitchen counter. Rossi and Ford had taken elimination prints from both, no doubt telling them they needed their fingerprints to eliminate them as the shooter. Keera lowered her plastic fork and sat forward when she read the next sentence. Bennet's fingerprints had also been found on the refrigerator door handle and on the handle of the upper oven.

She wrote a reminder on her legal pad to find out if Harrison had noticed this, and to ask Bennet about why she had opened the refrigerator, and whether she had also opened the oven, or at least touched the handle. It was one more variable for Harrison to consider in whatever theory he developed.

Keera flipped a tab and read the neighbors' statements collected by Vic Fazzio and Del Castigliano confirming they had not heard a shot, nor did they possess a video with audio recording the gunshot.

She skimmed the report from the Technical and Electronic Support Unit, as well as the LaRussas' financial records. She'd previously been through them, and again, nothing had alarmed her. No purchase at a gun shop or from an online gun dealer. No registration to a gun show.

She skipped the charging document and newspaper clippings, then flipped the tab to the CSI reports. She inserted a provided USB stick into a port on her laptop, and for the next half hour reviewed photographs, a crime scene video, and a 3D computer simulation. She'd have Harrison look more closely at the material, but from what she could tell, CSI had not noted the burn mark Harrison found on the oven door handle. They had tested the water on the floor, noted the presence of potassium nitrate, and attributed it to the discharged weapon and bullet casing.

The next report, from the Washington State Patrol Crime Lab's firearms section, confirmed the weapon recovered was a 9-millimeter handgun, recently fired, and that the bullet dislodged from the wainscoting had striations that matched the inside of the gun barrel. Barry Dillard, head of the firearms section, offered no opinions in his report, but Keera had put him on the stand in several cases and knew Dillard, if asked, would testify that a single bullet indicated the shooter had likely not been motivated by rage, vengeance, or anger. In such cases, victims were usually shot multiple times. This was not necessarily a good thing. Ambrose would argue it supported his argument that Vince LaRussa had planned the murder and not acted impulsively.

Dillard had interpreted work performed by Arthur Litchfield, a pathologist with the King County medical examiner's office, and concluded from the bullet hole, the lack of powder grains, burn marks, or mercury or lead on Anne

LaRussa's scalp, as well as from the lack of human tissue—otherwise known as blowback—in or on the gun barrel, that the gun barrel had been three to five feet away from the back of Anne LaRussa's skull. Keera looked for the tab to the ME's report. She wanted to see if the ME had provided an estimated time of death. If the ME estimated the time of death to be an hour or less before LaRussa called 911, sometime after eight fifteen, the SODDI defense would be on life support.

Her cell phone rang. "No report from the ME," Patsy said.

"Huh?" She flipped the tab but did not find a report.

"Dillard's report and conclusion that LaRussa was shot from at least three to five feet was based on the ME's findings. So where is the report?" Patsy said.

"They withheld it?"

"Seems that way," Patsy said. "Can't see why. Dillard's report seems to confirm this wasn't a suicide, but we already knew that. I'm wondering if the report says something about the time of death they're trying to reconcile."

"Thinking the same thing. Or maybe it contradicts something in the toxicology report, though I can't imagine what. Or it could just be Ambrose being an asshole, making our life difficult."

Patsy's chair squeaked. "I'll get Ella started

on a motion to compel to be heard tomorrow morning at the case-scheduling conference. This could be a blessing. Judge Hung won't appreciate it if Ambrose is playing games, maybe get him off on the wrong foot with her."

"I'm going to make a call and see if I can get to the bottom of this," Keera said.

"It's nine o'clock at night."

Keera looked up at the clock on the wall, unaware so much time had passed. "Tell Ella I'll be up working late, and in the office early tomorrow morning to go over the motion." Keera disconnected and debated what she was about to do, but she wanted to be able to include a declaration with any motion that she had tried to resolve the dispute before seeking a judicial ruling. Judges expected lawyers to work out their disagreements. She swore and punched in the cell phone number.

"Keera Duggan," Ambrose said. She heard ice cubes clink in a glass. "What a pleasant surprise."

"This is a professional call."

"To my cell phone?"

She ignored him. "I'm looking at the police file, Miller. I don't see the ME's autopsy report."

"He isn't finished with it," Miller said.

Liar. But Keera wasn't going to tell him she knew that. She'd also save that for a declaration in support of a motion to compel production, and

233

she'd seek sanctions. "So you haven't seen it either?" she asked.

"What in particular are you interested in?" he asked, too smart to answer her question.

"I'm interested in a copy of the ME's report. You've read it?"

"Let me check with the detectives and find out if it has come in or not and why they didn't include it."

He'd blame Rossi if he had to. "You haven't seen it?"

"I'll call you back . . . during work hours. I'm enjoying my evening." Again, the glass clinked. "You, on the other hand, are working awfully late. Perhaps you'd like to rethink your decision not to waive LaRussa's right to a speedy trial?"

"Don't make me bring an unnecessary motion, Miller."

"Good night, Keera. Sleep tight." He disconnected the call.

"Shit," she said. She stood and retrieved the bottle of Dalmore, pouring herself a finger, neat. She took a long sip and felt the burn down the back of her throat, which, after a moment, eased her adrenaline rush. She walked back to the table, picked up her cell phone, and made another call, this one to Frank Rossi's personal number.

"Keera?" Rossi said.

"I received the police file today," she said. "But not all of it."

"We're waiting on the toxicology report," he said.

"Anything else?"

"Not that I can think of."

"Where's the ME's report?"

Rossi paused. "You didn't get the ME's report?"

"You included it?"

Again, Rossi didn't immediately answer. "Let me check when I get in tomorrow."

"Ambrose said any mistake would be yours. So did you include it? Frank?"

"I'll check when I get in," he said again, and disconnected.

CHAPTER 21

June 15, 2023

Keera awoke early Thursday morning despite being up late talking on the phone with Ella and working to put together a motion to compel the ME's report. Ella had also filed a motion that Judge Hung reconsider the issue of bail, though that did not seem likely.

Keera showered, dressed, downed a cup of coffee, and ate granola and yogurt while thinking of the arguments she'd raise, each argument Ambrose might make in response, and how she would counter. Keera knew lawyers in private practice who billed their clients for the time they showered and commuted to work. Most people didn't understand that some days, the good lawyers spent every waking moment thinking about their cases. It explained why so many lawyers were divorced or had addiction issues. The law, she had been told, more than once, was a jealous mistress.

She picked out an outfit based on Patsy's admonition that Judge Hung expected lawyers to be professional and to show respect for the legal process. The judge believed lawyers had earned their bad reputation and would not change that public perception without also earning it.

Keera moved to her front door, catching the chessboard in her peripheral vision. The previous night, the Dark Knight had made another aggressive move, knight to d6. Keera had countered with an even more aggressive move. *Never back down from your opponent,* Patsy had instructed. Her bishop took the Dark Knight's bishop at g2, eliminating the last defender protecting his king.

She sensed his vulnerability and wondered if he did also.

When she stepped from the elevator, the office lobby lights, triggered by motion, had already been activated, meaning she wasn't the first to arrive. Maggie never got in early unless promised overtime pay. Ella could have beaten Keera into the office, but as Keera walked the hall, she noticed Ella's corner office remained dark. That left Patsy.

During a rare moment of honesty when speaking about their father, Ella had once said that, as a young girl tasked with retrieving a drunk Patsy from his office, the approach to his office door caused the greatest anxiety. She described it as approaching a bear's den. "You didn't know if the bear would be hibernating, or awake and angry."

No wonder Ella had sought counseling. "I wasn't going to cart around that luggage for the rest of my life," Ella had once told Keera. "I couldn't. It would have crushed me, the way it's crushed Maggie."

Keera stopped just outside her father's office. He sat behind his desk, his forehead resting in the cathedral he'd made with his hands. Steam wafted from a hot cup of coffee on his blotter, and Keera could smell the bitterness of the beans. She knocked gently three times to draw his attention. His eyes were clear and his cheeks ruddy. "Hey, kiddo. You're in early," he said. His voice was strong. He did not sound tired or hoarse. He'd had a good night's sleep. He had not been drinking.

"Thinking about the hearing." She settled into a chair across his desk. "Is that the motion?"

Patsy nodded. "Just doing a final read. I have a messenger set up to file it the minute the clerk's office opens, and to hand deliver a copy to Judge Hung."

"What do you think?" she asked.

"Strong on the facts, light on the law."

"Knowing Ambrose, I wouldn't be surprised if he presented the ME's report in Hung's chambers. He knows he kept us up late, and he knows Judge Hung won't issue sanctions so long as he delivers the report."

"So he's just screwing with us."

"It's what he does best." She paused to change subjects. "Got a question for you. JP said something the other day. Suggested maybe I pull back, not push so hard to get a trial date. Maybe we need more time to figure out the evidence. Was wondering if you had any advice?"

Patsy leaned back. "Where do you think Ambrose is at?"

"Last night Ambrose made the same sugges-tion, so I'm betting he's in the same place we are. Trying to figure out the evidence."

"His case is circumstantial," Patsy said, "though he's certainly got more evidence to argue that Vince killed Anne. Is it enough to get a conviction? I don't know."

"But at present, he's definitely controlling the center of the board."

Patsy smiled at the chess reference.

"His best witnesses will be Syd Evans and Lisa Bennet," Keera said. "They'll each say Anne LaRussa was alive when they left the house. Right now, I'd be trying a reasonable doubt case." Meaning she'd be attacking the prosecu-tion's witnesses and evidence hoping to plant a seed of doubt in at least one juror's mind. "I'd rather try my own theory, but . . . I'm waiting on the toxicology report. If it comes back showing Anne LaRussa had opioids in her system—I have circumstantial evidence to argue Bennet had a reason to kill Anne."

"Tell me the argument," Patsy said.

"Bennet was having an affair with Vince. So in

addition to threatening Vince with the forfeiture clause, Anne threatened to go after Bennet's medical license for overprescribing narcotics."

"That's a lot to lose for a single mother of three," Patsy agreed.

"But is it enough to convince a jury that Bennet was capable of shooting her friend?"

"It's a brutal act," Patsy said. "And, sadly, jurors are more likely to accept the spouse as the killer than her best friend, not to mention accept the loss of a hundred million dollars as opposed to a medical license. Have you found any witnesses who will testify that their marriage had problems?"

"No. But those we've spoken with confirm what the father said, that they hadn't seen much of Anne following her accident, less so the past six months," Keera said. "I'm worried Ambrose will argue Vince intended his wife's isolation. And Vince remains adamant there was no affair, as does Bennet, though Bennet will testify Anne *believed* there was an affair."

"What's your working argument?" Patsy said.

"Bennet's a survivor. She lost her husband early in life and has struggled to raise and educate her daughters on her own. She wasn't going to let anyone prevent her from doing that by ruining her career."

"It's thin," Patsy said, though Keera knew that already.

"What would you do?" Keera asked.

Patsy smiled. "I think you know what I'd do."

"The best defense is always a good offense. You'd attack."

"Sometimes you have to push forward with your strongest pieces and not fear the consequences. I wouldn't waive time either. I'd keep Ambrose's feet to the fire, play a little chicken, see who clucks first. A lot can happen between now and the trial date, and a lot more can happen during the trial. Our job, if our client refuses to plea, is to work with what we have and push it as far as we can. Good things tend to happen to people who are optimistic. Even the defeats don't feel so bad. Not that I'm saying you're going to lose."

Keera feigned being indignant. "I should hope not."

"I learned a long time ago not to bet against you, kiddo."

Keera stood. "Thanks, Dad."

Patsy smiled. "Thanks for asking for my opinion. Have you thought more about me coming to the hearing with you?"

She nodded. "I think it would look like overkill and, given your reputation, like you're holding my hand. Both the judge and the client need to believe I am capable of trying this case."

"We're well past that, Keera. I'm proud of the attorney you've become, but I'm prouder of the person you've become."

"I'll let you know how it goes."

"And I'll keep working like the wizard behind the curtain." He checked his watch. "At the moment, this wizard needs to get this motion finalized and filed."

Keera worked at her desk until roughly 8:30 a.m., then made her way up the hill to the King County Courthouse. She rode the elevator to the ninth floor, the highest floor in the courthouse with courtrooms. Patsy said the joke was no one ascended higher than Judge Hung. Keera pushed open the wooden door to courtroom W-941 and stepped inside. She had yet to appear before Judge Hung, but the courtrooms were mostly generic— modest in size and well worn, the gallery pews nicked and chipped, the dark linoleum floor bare in spots. On the wall to the right of the judge's elevated desk hung an oversized calendar. A woman, presumably Judge Hung's clerk, scurried about in the well beneath the desk.

When Keera set her briefcase on the defense table the woman took notice. "Are you Ms. Duggan?"

"I am."

"Judge Hung is holding the case-scheduling hearing in her chambers. Mr. Ambrose just arrived. I'll escort you back."

Keera thought it improper for a judge to invite back an attorney without opposing counsel present, even if only for a moment, but she wasn't about to open with that admonition. She followed the woman down a narrow hall to the judge's chambers. Ambrose sat in one of two leather chairs on a red Persian throw rug across the desk from Judge Hung. Behind him, windows faced downtown Seattle, patches of the blue waters of Elliott Bay visible between the buildings.

"Ms. Duggan." Judge Hung stood and extended a hand.

Hung, sixty-two, had no gray in her dark hair that curled at her shoulders. Soft facial features and few wrinkles made her look younger than her years. She was slight of build and wore a white, collared shirt, and no makeup or jewelry but for a silver wristwatch.

"You and Mr. Ambrose know one another, I presume?" she said in a voice an octave deeper than Keera had expected.

"We do," Keera said, finding her way to the chair beside Ambrose.

"Keera and I once worked cases together." Ambrose reached out his hand. Keera reluctantly shook it. Ambrose smiled. His grip was stronger than necessary and punctuated with a squeeze. Keera's skin crawled.

"Will Mr. Duggan be joining us?" Judge Hung asked.

"Not today," Keera said, sitting.

"His name is atop the pleading I have before me," Hung said, indicating the motion Ella had prepared and filed. "Will he be trying this case?"

"He's the firm's founding member," Keera said, though she was certain Judge Hung was well aware of this fact. "I will try this case."

"But Mr. Duggan will sit second chair?"

"That's correct." Keera sensed Judge Hung had concerns about her qualifications to defend a first-degree murder charge. Keera refused to give in to the temptation to further explain her qualifications, and a brief, uncomfortable silence hung between them.

"Let's get started, then," Judge Hung said, breaking that silence. She looked to the court stenographer, seated to the judge's right with the steno machine, which would capture everything said. After calling the hearing to order, and both sides stating their appearances, Judge Hung said, "I'm going to put over the defense's motion to compel until the end of the hearing and get some preliminary matters out of the way. Has there been any discussion regarding a plea?"

"There has not," Ambrose said.

"No, Your Honor," Keera said.

"There will be none?" Hung asked.

"We would accept a guilty plea, if defendant is so inclined," Ambrose said.

"Defendant is not so inclined," Keera said. "We will accept a dismissal of all charges."

"And your client is not waiving his right to a

speedy trial?" Judge Hung asked in a tone that sounded disapproving.

"He is not, Your Honor. The defendant is prepared to move forward to clear his name."

Hung made a soft noise that sounded like "Hmm." She looked down at pages on her desk, seeming to study them. After a moment she raised her gaze to Keera. "This is a murder-one charge. Your client understands he's looking at life behind bars without parole."

"If convicted," Keera said.

"And did you tell him the prosecution has not yet completed pretrial discovery and it's unlikely you'll get everything prior to the trial date if he does not waive time?"

That did not bode well for Keera's motion to compel. "I'm sorry, Your Honor? Why is that?" She regretted asking for an explanation the moment the question left her mouth.

Judge Hung wasted no time making Keera feel naïve and inexperienced. "Murder trials are fluid, Ms. Duggan. Witnesses and evidence often can't be located until the day the witness testifies. Witnesses get sick or have conflicts and must be taken out of order. If your client refuses to waive his right to a speedy trial, I want to be sure he understands that I won't look favorably on any requests for additional time during trial."

Keera thought of her father's counsel earlier that morning. "I'm optimistic the State won't unnecessarily waste court time with gamesman-ship requiring the defense to file motions to compel, Your Honor. We ask only that the State timely disclose witnesses, their expected testi-mony, and the evidence they intend to rely upon, so the defense can properly prepare, as required by Washington State law."

Ambrose, his legs crossed, formed a steeple with his hands just below his chin and said, "Your Honor, we certainly aren't hiding any information from defense counsel, as insinuated. We provided the lead detective's investigative file immediately following the defendant's arraignment, though we were under no such obligation to provide it so quickly. The current defense motion is a little bit of a damned-if-you-do motion . . . if you will. No good deed goes unpunished."

"I guess we'll go ahead and talk about Ms. Duggan's motion since you've both brought it up," Judge Hung said. "Ms. Duggan?"

"The investigative file produced omitted the medical examiner's autopsy report and the victim's toxicology labs, though several experts indicated the conclusions in their reports were premised upon the medical examiner's findings—like the ballistics expert's opinion. Those experts clearly had the report, which begs the question why it was not produced."

"Your Honor," Ambrose said. "I spoke with the detectives about this and understand that the medical examiner had not yet finalized his report but had provided several experts with his initial findings so as to, again, expedite getting this information to defense counsel. As for toxicology, counsel should know such a report can take several weeks to complete."

"Your Honor, the State's ballistics expert—" Keera began.

Judge Hung raised a hand. "I read your briefing, Ms. Duggan, and counsel for the State is correct, the investigative file was provided early. As I previously stated, all expert reports and pleadings identifying witnesses and what they're expected to testify about are to be provided and updated as we near trial. I think you jumped the gun here with your motion."

Keera bit her tongue.

Ambrose uncrossed his legs. "Your Honor, the prosecution does not want to unnecessarily take up the court's time. I have the medical examiner's report as well as the toxicology labs, which I received yesterday afternoon." He reached into his briefcase at the side of his chair and, as Keera had predicted, handed multipage documents to Judge Hung, making Keera look petty and himself magnanimous. Ambrose could have told Keera he had the reports and would produce them at the hearing when they spoke last night. He'd forced Keera to prepare an unnecessary motion and now sought to make her look unreasonable.

Keera knew arguing would do no good. Judges were often put in the role of a parent stuck between two fighting children. They weren't interested in who did what to whom; they just wanted the matter resolved so they didn't have to hear the fighting.

"So that's all resolved now, Ms. Duggan?" Judge Hung said.

"That appears to be the case," she said, "though I haven't yet read the reports."

"Good. Now, given that there will be no plea agreement and the defendant is not waiving his right to a speedy trial, I'm going to set an omnibus hearing and a trial date. I have a busy calendar but recently had an upcoming trial resolve when the defendant pled out."

"The State has no objection, Your Honor."

Judge Hung looked to Keera. "I assume the defense also has no objection?" she said.

"It does not, Your Honor."

Judge Hung reviewed her court calendar. "I was to have a trial starting at the end of next month. That's July thirty-first. Any objection to that date?"

The question was rhetorical.

"None, Your Honor," Ambrose said.

Keera pulled up her calendar on her phone, which was synced with her office computer. She quickly checked the date. Her father had a trial starting earlier that week. "Patrick Duggan has a trial that week in Judge McCormick's courtroom, Your Honor."

"A lot can happen between now and then, such as plea bargains," Judge Hung said with clear intent. "I'm sure Judge McCormick can move the trial date to accommodate us if necessary. Now, I expect, based on the defendant's arraignment, that a considerable number of media will be present. I have let court operations know I have no intention of abandoning my courtroom for the ceremonial courtroom. This is a trial, not a circus, and I will not have it become one. Both of you will be playing to me and to the jury. If I believe either counsel is playing to the gallery, I will put an end to it swiftly. Is that understood?"

Again, the question was rhetorical. Judge Hung did not wait for a response.

"Anything further?" Hung asked.

"No, Your Honor." Ambrose rose. "Thank you for your time this morning."

"The defense wishes to discuss the issue of bail, Your Honor. I filed a motion."

Ambrose stopped. He gave Keera a bemused smile before retaking his seat. He put out his hands. "Judge Valle denied bail, Your Honor, finding that because of the accused's substantial resources, access to airplanes, and lack of family living in Puget Sound, he is a potential flight risk. I don't believe any of those factors have changed since his incarceration."

"Have any of those factors changed, Ms. Duggan?" Judge Hung asked.

"Your Honor, the defense will need unfettered access to the defendant to prepare its case for trial."

"Have you had difficulties meeting with your client in the King County jail?"

"Not per se, Your Honor, but gaining access is time consuming, and the lack of privacy and limited facilities in which to work make pretrial preparation more than an inconvenience. The defendant could be monitored just as effectively with an ankle bracelet and home confinement."

Judge Hung cleared her throat. "My job, Counselor, is to ensure your client receives a fair trial, not to provide him conveniences. I am also obligated to protect the citizens of King County. Countless defendants and their counsel have managed to prepare for trial while the defendant remained in jail. You and your client will also. Your request that Judge Valle's ruling be reconsidered is denied. Anything further?"

"No," Keera said. She'd lost the first two battles.

"Good. Then let's discuss how I handle voir dire, as well as expected courtroom decorum."

Twenty minutes later, without Keera or Ambrose adding much to the lecture or asking questions, Judge Hung concluded. As Patsy said, Judge Hung would ask the jurors questions. If either side wished to put forward questions, they were to go through her.

As they moved to the office door, Judge Hung said, "Ms. Duggan?"

Keera turned.

"I expect to see your father in court the next time we meet. I don't want any post-trial motions concerning ineffectiveness of counsel." She put up a hand. "That is not intended to impugn your abilities, but, in my experience, convicted defendants will take advantage of any opportunity to appeal the jury's findings, including attacking their own counsel as inexperienced."

Keera nearly bit a hole through the inside of her lip. "As well as attacking the jurist who presided over the case as prejudiced, Your Honor. Also not intended to impugn."

As she walked from the courthouse, Keera chastised herself for what she'd said. She should have simply walked from the judge's chambers and proved her wrong at trial, but her competitive streak had kicked in, and now she'd said something she regretted, implying that the judge was prejudiced.

As she neared Occidental Square her thoughts turned to the ME's report. She didn't for a moment believe Ambrose's statement that Arthur Litchfield had provided other experts with *preliminary* findings. The pathologists in the ME's office didn't have the time to write up preliminary findings and wouldn't do so. A preliminary report, possibly different from a final report, could be used by the defense to suggest the PA had a hand in the conclusions in the final report. Beyond that, there was Frank Rossi's pause when Keera asked him about the ME's report, indicating he had provided it to Ambrose.

That left one inescapable conclusion.

Ambrose was hiding something.

She'd have to wait before she could dive in and find out what that might be. As soon as Keera stepped from the elevator car into the office lobby, Maggie looked up, as if waiting for her arrival. "Ella and Patsy want to talk to you in the conference room. I'll let them know you're here."

In the conference room, Keera downplayed much of what had transpired in Judge Hung's chambers. She didn't want to alarm Patsy, and she certainly didn't want to kick-start Ella's paranoia.

"She set the case for trial," Keera said. "July thirty-first. She's going to push us." She told Patsy of the conflict on his trial calendar.

"That's a drug-dealing charge. My guy will plea. If he doesn't, I'll get Judge McCormick to move the trial. It won't be a problem."

"She's pretty adamant about you being present in court with me. She said she didn't want any post-trial motions premised upon ineffectiveness of counsel."

"She said that?" Ella asked. "Out loud?"

Patsy sighed.

"What?" Ella said.

Keera suspected from the anguished look on Patsy's face that she knew what he was about to say.

"Judge Hung has a long memory, and is ultra-competitive, as are all good trial lawyers. She doesn't appreciate that I won each trial we had against one another, or the means I might have used to do it."

Meaning Patsy the Brawler had pushed the envelope, gotten away with it, and left some lingering resentment.

"Can we challenge her?" Ella asked. Counsel could ask a judge to recuse herself for prejudice.

"I have no proof beyond my intuition," Patsy said. "And she'd deny it. All we'd accomplish is to piss her off."

As Keera feared she had done with her comment. "And make it look like I can't fight my own battles," she added.

"Maybe. But maybe it would send a message we expect her to be fair or we'll be filing appeals during and after the trial," Ella said.

"She's a good judge," Patsy said. "Tough but fair, which could be a good thing if Ambrose is going to play games like he played this morning."

"Certainly didn't hurt him this morning," Keera said. Patsy continued to look anguished. "Something else?" she asked.

"I also suspect what happened at Clancy Doyle's trial the other day has made its way around the courthouse," Patsy said.

"What does that have to do with Judge Hung?"

"Many of those judges, including Judge Hung, were prosecutors I sparred with and beat. More than a few would not be disappointed to see me fall flat on my face," Patsy said, his voice soft.

Keera didn't think Judge Hung would be so petty, but she also recalled the look of hardly suppressed glee on Judge Ima Patel's face when Patsy failed to return to the courtroom to finish Clancy Doyle's trial. Patsy was likely correct. But Keera wasn't going to baby him the way her mother and sisters had babied her father's alcoholism, sweeping it under the carpet until they'd created a mound as large as an elephant. Patsy had made his own bed, and she had no intention of being the one to lie in it. "Maybe we should think about Ella sitting second chair. Take you out of the equation."

"You want to replace me?" Patsy looked devastated.

"What I want is irrelevant. Vince LaRussa deserves a fair trial. If your presence in Judge Hung's courtroom is going to jeopardize that, we have to consider other possibilities."

"I don't plan on embarrassing you," Patsy said.

Keera didn't respond. She didn't have to. Patsy knew both she and Ella had heard too many of his empty promises.

Ella looked between the two of them. "Keera isn't worried about you embarrassing her," she said.

"Don't talk for me," Keera said.

"I'm not talking for you. I'm the managing partner—"

"You are talking for me. You always have. You and Maggie."

"We only wanted to protect—"

"I'm a grown woman, and I'm a damn good attorney. And I will decide what is in the best interests of my client."

For a moment no one spoke.

Keera broke the silence. "Once the jury is picked, it will be next to impossible to bring some-one else in. I don't want to be Marcia Clark when Bill Hodgman had to leave the O. J. Simpson trial. If you are going to sit second chair, I need to know you're going to be there to the end."

"I'll be there," Patsy said.

"That's not good enough. I want your word that you won't drink, not a drop, until this trial is over. Not beer. Not wine. Not hard alcohol."

"Keera, you can't—" Ella started.

"Yes, she can," Patsy said. "It's a fair request." He looked at Keera. "You have my word."

"Good," Keera said. "Then you'll just have to disappoint Judge Hung again."

Both Patsy and Ella gave her confused looks.

"And not fall on your face. I want the Irish Brawler in that courtroom beside me, because we can damn well bet that Ambrose is going to come out of his corner swinging."

After she left the meeting, Keera stopped at her assistant's desk to have Litchfield's autopsy report and the toxicology report duplicated and working copies delivered to Patsy and Ella. Then she sat down at her desk and called Harrison to tell him about the trial date.

"You're shitting me?" Somehow the English accent made the expression sound less crude.

"Ambrose suggested I rethink my position not to waive LaRussa's right to a speedy trial, which could indicate he's not prepared, and we need to continue to push forward. I need you to come up with a theory to make Mr. Cobalt proud, or at least create reasonable doubt. And we don't have a lot of time to do it."

"I'm working on it," he said. "Any further emails from Jack Worthing?"

"Not yet, but you'll be the first to know."

Keera hung up the phone as her assistant entered her office and handed her working copies of the two reports. She'd read enough autopsy reports to know what to look for. Litchfield's report referenced the blood spatter, ballistics, wound location, and Anne LaRussa's lack of dexterity in her hands and fingers. He concluded her death to have been a homicide.

Keera felt a huge letdown. Given the gymnastics she'd gone through to get the report, and her personal knowledge of Ambrose and his trial tactics, she had been sure he had done something nefarious, but Litchfield's report contained no information to indicate that had been the case. She set the report aside and read the toxicology report from the King County head of forensic toxicology. She skimmed the testing methods and the patient data and more critically read the detailed lab results. The toxicology screening revealed high levels of opioids, including oxycodone, also known as Oxycontin, and hydrocodone, also known as Vicodin. That certainly helped her argument that Bennet had a motive to kill Anne LaRussa, but she remained a long way from reasonable doubt.

Still, as Patsy said, something was better than nothing.

It just didn't feel that way in this instance.

About to shut down her computer, Keera thought of something else. She pulled up the videotape from the security system at the LaRussas' home and fast-forwarded the tape until Lisa Bennet's car came down the driveway. She studied Bennet as she got out of the car, then opened the back door for her handbag. The muscles in her arm flexed when she lifted the bag from the back seat and slipped the strap over her shoulder. Keera hit fast-forward again and stopped the tape when Bennet came out the front door, again studying Bennet's arm holding the bag as she opened the driver's door and tossed the handbag onto the back seat. Keera rewound the tape and reviewed it several more times.

The bag seemed to be significantly lighter when Bennet left the house.

Keera made a mental note to ask Bennet about it.

CHAPTER 22

Late in the afternoon, Keera drove to the Seattle Cancer Care building on Aloha Street near Lake Union. She'd called Lisa Bennet's office and asked for a moment of her time. She didn't want to talk to Bennet over the phone, not for this conversation. She wanted to gauge Bennet's reaction, if any, when pushed.

She found street parking and walked up the hill to the brick-and-glass building that housed the cancer center that had saved so many lives. Inside, she rode the elevator to the fifth floor and approached the receptionist. A phone call later, he said, "Dr. Bennet will be right out."

Bennet came out of an interior door wearing a white doctor's smock over navy-blue slacks, and flats, her hair pulled back in a bun. "Ms. Duggan," she said, inviting Keera back.

Bennet led Keera down a hallway, past medical personnel at workstations. Bennet's office was small, with built-in shelving, a curved desk, and a computer screen that partially blocked a spectacular northwest view of Lake Union. Keera noted framed family photographs similar to those that had been on the mantel of Bennet's home.

Bennet moved behind her desk but remained standing. "Has something come up?"

"I have a few more questions about the night you went to see Anne LaRussa."

"I thought we covered that already."

"I know you're busy and I'll be respectful of your time." Keera pushed ahead. "You carried a large handbag into the house. It looked heavy. What was in it?"

Bennet broke eye contact and looked to the side. Stalling. Reengaging, she said, "I don't know. A lot of stuff I probably don't need. I try to consolidate. My purse, water bottle. Sometimes I bring home patient files."

"You didn't bring anything to Anne?"

"Like what?"

"Anything."

"No," Bennet said, again breaking eye contact. A lie. Why? Keera wasn't going to get an honest answer and decided to let it go for now.

"Anne let you in the front door?"

"That's right."

"And did you go into the kitchen immediately to talk?"

"I believe we spoke in the entry for a moment."

"You didn't linger in any of the other rooms?"

"Not that I recall, no."

Keera studied the two answers. *I believe . . .* and *Not that I recall.* Far more stilted and cautious than the first time she spoke to the doctor. The phrasing was how lawyers instructed witnesses to respond to questions. The lack of certainty allowed the witness wiggle room to later amend her answer, if necessary. Then again, Keera could have been reading too much into the responses. If Bennet had met with a lawyer, the first words out of any good attorney's mouth would have been: *Don't talk to anyone without me present.*

"Anne was upset?" Keera asked.

"Very."

"Were you able to calm her?"

"Some. I reminded her that we'd been friends a long time, that I wouldn't do something like that to her. That I wouldn't hurt her."

"Did she believe you?"

"Honestly? I don't think she did. Anne had become paranoid and upset. She wasn't thinking clearly."

"Was she drinking?"

"She had a glass of water. At least I think it was water. Is that what you meant?"

"She had that glass with her in the kitchen when you arrived?"

"I believe so."

"You didn't get her a glass of water from the fridge?"

Another look to the side. After a beat, Bennet said, "Now that you ask, I may have. I think I did get her a glass of water. Why are you asking me?"

"Just trying to reconcile a few things. One glass

was found. I'm trying to establish it was Anne's glass, as well as the contents."

"It was Anne's. I didn't get a glass of water myself. I wasn't there long."

"Twenty-six minutes."

"It didn't feel that long."

"You didn't open and close any cabinets, the stove, anything else?"

Bennet's facial expression changed, as if she was starting to understand or at least become suspicious of the purpose for Keera's questions. Keera had seen that look when she caught a witness not telling the truth. They looked at you as if a veil had fallen in front of their face. Bennet was no doubt weighing the consequences of what she was about to say. "I don't recall doing so, but I could have. I don't really remember."

More wiggle room.

Bennet had touched the refrigerator door handle and the oven handle, and she did recall doing so. She just didn't want to admit to it. Why not? Whatever Bennet's reasons, Keera wasn't going to get them now, not without some leverage. Bennet was guarded. "Was there a candle in the kitchen?"

"Yes. One of Anne's aroma candles."

"Was it lit?"

"I believe so."

"You didn't light it?"

"Why would I light it?"

"How did the conversation end?"

"Like I said. I assured Anne she was mistaken, that my meeting with Vince was innocent . . . that I was concerned she was taking too many opioids, that she was becoming addicted. I told her that if she needed help with pain management, I could find someone to help her."

"About the pain medications that you pre-scribed and ordered refills for. So you knew how much Anne was taking, right?"

"What exactly are you implying?"

"I'm not implying anything. It's just the toxi-cology labs are unequivocal," she said to let Bennet know she had independent evidence. "Anne had high levels of opioids in her system."

"As I said, I was concerned Anne was becoming addicted."

"Yes. I'm sure you were. You looked upset on the security video when you left the house that Sunday night."

Bennet's temper flared. "Of course I was upset. My best friend had just accused me of having an affair with her husband."

A good answer. A plausible answer. Reasonable emotion. But Keera didn't believe it either. Not fully.

Half an hour later, Keera entered the attorney-client room at the King County jail after going through the usual machinations. LaRussa entered as before and sat in a plastic chair across from her. "Did you speak to Mary Bell?"

Keera told him what Bell had said. "No one from the prosecution team has contacted her, and I'm not sure why anything she said would be relevant. We also spoke to Eric Fields."

"What did he have to say?"

"Nothing that alarms me." She told LaRussa the gist of the conversation. "I am concerned that Jack Worthing, whoever he is, also spoke to him."

"In person?"

"No, by phone. Bell said she suspected the person was disguising their voice, but didn't have any real basis that was the case. Again, nothing either person had to say alarms me, but I am concerned about who Jack Worthing is and his purpose."

"Has he emailed again?"

"No."

"Maybe he won't," LaRussa said.

"Time will tell. We also received the police report," Keera said. "The medical examiner concluded homicide and determined your wife was shot from a distance of three to five feet."

"We knew that; didn't we?" he said.

"Something else of interest. The Latent Fingerprint Unit found Lisa Bennet's fingerprints on the kitchen counter, the refrigerator door handle, and the handle of the top oven."

"Maybe she opened them. Why is that of interest?"

"She couldn't definitively recall opening the refrigerator to get Anne a glass of water, then said she did recall it. There'd be no reason for her to open the oven, or to lock it. I think she's hiding something. I'm a good judge of people's tells, their body movements. She kept breaking eye contact and pausing before she answered. I'm wondering if her fingerprint near the burn mark our investigator found on the oven door handle has some significance. If she locked the oven."

"Why would she open the oven, or lock it?"

"I don't know yet. Another thing. She arrived at the house carrying a large handbag that looked heavy. The muscles of her arm strained when she lifted it onto her shoulder. I'm wondering if she brought something with her."

"What did she say?"

"She became reticent and said she carries a lot of unnecessary stuff in that bag. Plausible, except when she left the bag appeared noticeably lighter," Keera said. "She came out of the house and threw the bag in the back seat."

"You think she brought something to the house? The gun?"

"She could have brought the gun, but that wouldn't be what made the bag heavy. If I'm right. Can you think of anything?"

LaRussa shook his head. "No."

Keera changed gears. "We also got back the toxicology lab work. Anne had high levels of Oxycontin and Vicodin in her system."

"Again, we suspected that was the case."

"We did, but what I don't understand is, if Dr. Bennet was concerned Anne was becoming addicted, why didn't she change the prescription? Fewer pills or a lesser dose? The prescription bottles and medical records don't indicate she did either, which makes her argument of concern less believable. What if Anne threatened to report Bennet to the medical board, putting her license in jeopardy?"

"It would certainly be a motive," LaRussa said, sounding upbeat. "But it's still a big leap to get a jury to believe she killed Anne; isn't it?"

"Maybe not," Keera said. "Bennet had lost a husband. She was her daughters' sole provider. She'd fight fiercely to protect them."

"I like it. It makes sense," LaRussa said.

"And she and Anne spoke frequently. I'm working on an argument that Anne made the threat earlier, which would have been motivation for Bennet to buy the gun. Did either Anne or Bennet mention the threat or anything like that to you?"

"No," he said.

"We don't have to prove the argument. We just have to raise it as a possibility, give the jurors something else to consider."

LaRussa let out a breath. "It doesn't sound like much."

It didn't, Keera knew. "Changing gears again. Our investigator had the water on the floor tested, and the lab detected potassium nitrate. It's an oxidizer. It accelerates burning when a fire is lit."

"Where did it come from?"

"Not sure, but potassium nitrate can be found in home products like fertilizers and tree stump removers, as well as fireworks. It's also a major constituent of gunpowder."

"So it could have leaked from the gun on the floor?"

"That was my initial thought, but Harrison said the lab also found potassium nitrate in shavings he took from the burn mark on the oven door handle, and microscopic cotton fibers in the water."

"Which came from where?"

"Again, we don't know yet, but we're working on it. Also, you heard Ambrose describe the gun as a ghost gun. Ghost guns can be bought over the internet or at a gun show and are assembled at home. They don't have serial numbers, and dealers don't require ID."

"How does that help us? Won't the prosecutor just argue it shows premeditation?"

"He will," Keera said. "But he can't tie the gun to you, which, again, gives us room to argue that Bennet purchased the gun and brought it that night. I know it doesn't sound like much, but all these unanswered questions together can help with reasonable doubt. I don't want to rely on that if we can help it. We're working on our own theory about what happened. I'd like to go back through your house and the garden. See if anything else turns up now that we have some additional information to work with."

"Anne liked to garden before her accident. She had a small greenhouse and a vegetable garden out back. There's a shed there. You might find fertilizer in the shed, though I don't know how it would explain the presence of potassium nitrate in the kitchen."

"I just want to be sure we haven't missed anything. What did Anne like to do after her accident?"

"She cooked," LaRussa said. "She was a good cook. And she read a lot. She couldn't hold the book in her hand, but she could swipe the page of a Kindle."

"Okay. I'll let you know if we find anything more. Last thing. Judge Hung set a trial date for July thirty-first. The only other issue is whether we need more time."

"Do we?"

"Patsy and I talked this through. More time also gives the prosecution more time to solidify their evidence. I'd like to keep pushing things until, or if, it becomes disadvantageous to do so."

"Then let's do that."

Keera stood to leave, then remembered something else and said, "We're going to need names of people who knew you and Anne, who could testify as to the type of relationship you had."

"Character witnesses?"

"We need to be sure the PA doesn't surprise us at trial with a witness who testifies that you and Anne fought."

"Can he do that?"

"Theoretically they have to disclose their witnesses at the omnibus hearing, but prosecutors have a number of different arguments to get around that."

"All couples fight," LaRussa said. "We had our disagreements, especially as Anne became more depressed and paranoid."

"Can you think of anyone who could testify positively or negatively about your relationship?"

"I didn't air our dirty laundry with others. I've never felt it appropriate. But her family was never one of my supporters. If they think I killed her . . ."

"Anyone besides Anne's family?"

"Anne became more and more of a recluse, especially the last two months. She didn't want to go out, and she didn't want to have friends over. The one person I would have suspected she spoke with was Lisa, but given what has transpired, it doesn't sound like that would be helpful."

That's what Keera had been afraid of.

CHAPTER 23

Late that evening, Keera arrived home and pulled a pitcher of lemon iced tea from the fridge, pouring a tall glass. The warm weather left her parched. She pulled out mini carrots, salami, crackers, and a brick of cheddar cheese. After trimming off mold, she set the cheese on a cutting board and returned to her computer. Her eyes drifted to the sideboard, but she resisted the temptation.

Wanting a break for a few minutes, she pulled up the chess game as she chewed on a carrot. The Dark Knight continued his aggressive tactics. His twentieth move was knight to b5. A mistake. He just didn't know it yet. She moved her bishop to a8, as if in retreat, but she was baiting the Dark Knight to use his knight to take her rook at a7. He did. Keera had sacrificed her rook for the greater good of her game. His knight was now stuck and of no import. She moved her queen to d7 and hit send.

She cut off a strip of cheese and laid it on a cracker along with a slice of salami. Her computer pinged, an incoming email to her work account. This time she wasn't surprised; she remained intrigued.

Jack Worthing.

"Well, well, well," Keera said. "What do you have for me now?"

Early Friday morning, Keera met Harrison outside the LaRussa home. After Keera and Harrison went over the property, Harrison would pick up Patsy and the two would fly east to Pullman, Washington. Jack Worthing had given Keera another name: Spencer Tickman. Harrison had performed some research. Tickman was a Farmers Insurance agent who had attended Washington State University and evidently never left the area, opening an insurance office on Main Street.

Upon her arrival at the LaRussa house, Keera again noted the security camera over the roof ridge. LaRussa told her during one of their discussions that he'd had the cameras installed after his wife's injury. He said he worried about her when he wasn't home to care for her. He wanted to install a gate atop the driveway, but said Anne had nixed the idea, telling Vince she already felt like a prisoner in her home. Keera hadn't given the statement much thought at the time, figuring it had to do with Anne being in a wheelchair. JP had also said that disabled women were more susceptible to spousal abuse, which made the cameras and the suggestion of installing a gate atop the driveway more ominous. What purpose would a gate serve?

Harrison stepped from his BMW in gold slacks that stopped above his bare ankles, leather loafers, and a loose-fitting white shirt with the word "Cuba" over an antique red car on the breast pocket.

Keera punched in the code on the front-door pad, and she and Harrison entered the house. Everything was as they had left it. She looked around the sitting room, living room, and dining room before she went into the kitchen. It struck her that the home had no plants or flowers.

"Nothing living," she said.

"Pardon?" Harrison said.

"The entire house. No plants or flowers. It's sterile and cold. I didn't notice that the last time we were here."

The paintings were cubist abstracts; the kitchen glass, marble, and stainless steel. No wonder Anne had felt like a prisoner. The rooms were sterile, like the attorney-client rooms at the King County jail.

Anne LaRussa's wheelchair remained, still facing the view—a world perhaps she had no longer felt a part of. Keera set her briefcase on the marble countertop, which still showed fingerprint dust. She opened her laptop and inserted the USB stick, studying the crime scene photographs before Anne's body had been removed.

"Any inspiring thoughts?" Harrison asked.

Something had struck Keera as odd and as

another potential problem. "If you were mad at someone, arguing with them, would you turn your back on them?" She looked up at Harrison.

He said, "I wouldn't, no."

"Lisa Bennet said Anne was upset and she was unable to calm her before she left."

"And you're wondering why Anne LaRussa would have turned her back on Bennet, giving Bennet the opportunity to shoot her?"

"Something to think about," Keera said.

Harrison thought for a moment, then said, "So maybe she had the gun when she came, left the room to get it, then came back in?"

"That's one theory, but it doesn't solve the motivation problem if Anne hadn't confronted Bennet about the affair until that night. And that's an argument that won't escape Ambrose. He'll drive a huge truck through it at closing, say we're grasping at things that don't make sense just to confuse the jury. It's a problem."

"The theory doesn't explain all the variables," Harrison said. "So then we're looking for evidence to help formulate a theory. What if we can't find it?"

Keera thought of her chess game with the Dark Knight. "We let the prosecution advance and make it look like we're on the defensive."

"We are on the defensive."

"But things can change with a single move."

"Move?"

"Piece of evidence," she said.

"I like the strategy in a vacuum, but it's a risk."

"I'm remaining optimistic," she said. "Besides, what choice do we have?"

Harrison looked to the oven. "I spoke with the house cleaner. Had to remember my Spanish. Her English isn't great."

"What did she have to say?"

"She and another woman cleaned the LaRussa home every other Wednesday. She said they focused on the master bedroom, bathrooms, living area, and kitchen. The spare bedrooms aren't used. She said she doesn't clean the oven. It cleans automatically, but she wipes it down before she locks the door latch and sets the knob to clean."

"The knob wasn't set to clean."

"No, it wasn't," Harrison said.

"Did she have any explanation why then the door was locked?"

"None. She said when she set the oven to clean, she always reminded Mrs. LaRussa. She didn't recall whether she'd set the oven on her last visit, but she started to get confused when I said the oven was locked. She said maybe she did clean it."

"So, she doesn't know for sure?"

"She doesn't. But if she did, she said maybe Anne LaRussa had not gotten around to unlocking the door."

"But moved the knob? That doesn't seem likely."

"It also doesn't explain the burn mark."

"I've been through the photographs. CSI didn't photograph it."

"Noticed that also."

They spent a few more minutes in the kitchen. "Let's go out back to the garden shed. Maybe we'll find fertilizer or something else that contains potassium nitrate," Keera said.

"I'd prefer to find gunpowder, whatever the hell that might mean. If Anne LaRussa liked to garden *before* her accident, doesn't that raise the same problem as Bennet having the gun before the confrontation . . ."

"Why would she have used fertilizer after the accident?" Keera said, noting where Harrison was headed and getting her first epiphany—why the lack of any living plants inside the home struck her. "No live plants," she said.

"What?"

"Anne would have had no use for fertilizer inside without any living plants."

"Good point. So why then would the lab find potassium nitrate in the water?"

"Let's go see what we find anyway, cross our t's and dot our i's before you and Patsy head to the airport."

The backyard lawn sloped down to a well-maintained and defined flower garden and a raised, rectangular dirt bed probably for a dormant vegetable garden. Beside the bed stood the eight-foot-wide yellow shed with white trim and barn doors. They put on blue nitrile gloves. Keera undid the clasp and opened the door. Inside, she flipped a switch, illuminating an overhead bulb. Gardening tools hung on pronged hooks or had been stored in white five-gallon buckets. Paint cans and bins with paintbrushes and rollers sat on shelves. Neatly organized steel shelves, seven feet tall, held gardening materials.

"You take one side. I'll take the other," Keera said.

She walked down her side, pulling products from the shelves and reading the ingredients for weed and bug killers, as well as for lawn fertilizer, but the ingredients didn't include potassium nitrate. Harrison walked down the other side doing the same thing.

Near the end of the rack, Harrison said, "Keera, take a look at this."

Keera walked around to where Harrison stood. He pointed to a black sixteen-ounce bottle on the top shelf. "Stump remover."

"I didn't see any stumps outside, did you?"

"No, I did not."

"Document where we found it before you bring it down," she said.

Harrison removed his telephone and took photographs of the bottle on the shelf. After doing so, he reached and lowered the bottle, turning it over to read the ingredients.

"One hundred percent potassium nitrate," he said to Keera.

Keera felt her pulse quicken. "Let's get the bottle checked for fingerprints. Seems like too big a coincidence to ignore; don't you think?"

"Seems that way. And what would Mr. Cobalt say?"

"He'd say we still don't have a theory," Keera said.

"What else?" Harrison shifted his eyes to the shelf on which he'd found the stump remover and asked, "How tall do you think that shelf is?"

His thought process became clear. "Anne LaRussa couldn't have reached the container to bring it down from that shelf," Keera said.

"Not from her wheelchair."

"Maybe she used a tool to knock it down?"

"Maybe, but then how did she put it back?" Harrison said.

Keera looked at the sloped lawn. "She couldn't have gotten down here. Not by herself."

"Or back up," Harrison agreed.

"Again, somebody else?"

"Would seem so. If our assumptions are accurate."

"Let's talk with the gardener. Maybe she asked him to get it for her and to store it in here." Harrison grabbed a five-gallon white bucket, turned it upside down, and stood on it. "What are you looking for?" Keera asked.

"I don't know. I didn't expect to find stump remover."

Keera considered her watch. "You better get Patsy if you're going to make your flight."

They walked back up the hill to the LaRussa house and back into the kitchen. Keera considered the stove.

"Something else?" Harrison said.

There was, she knew, but she couldn't put her finger on it. In chess, sometimes her opponents' moves surprised her, as the stump remover had surprised them. At such moments Patsy urged her to let her options gestate until they became clear.

"I think so," she said. "But I don't know what. Not at the moment."

CHAPTER 24

Just after eight o'clock at night, Keera met Patsy and Harrison in the law firm conference room after their flight back from Pullman.

"Spencer Tickman was Vince LaRussa's fraternity brother," Patsy said without preamble. "He said LaRussa was a snake, that he could have talked Adam into eating the apple from the tree of life in the Garden of Eden. A classic bullshitter."

"Did he have anything to back it up?" Keera said. "Or did he just generally dislike him?"

"He disliked him, no doubt about that. He made that clear. But he also backed it up," Patsy said. "He said Vince was the fraternity treasurer his senior year. Said everyone thought Vince would run for president, but Vince turned it down. Said he didn't have time because he had started a car service for students too drunk to drive."

"Ahead of his time," Harrison said. "Uber and Lyft are making a killing."

"Tickman said Vince took advantage of an incident in which a student got killed in a drunk-driving accident on his way back from Moscow, Idaho. He started a company called VLR—Vince LaRussa Rides. According to Tickman, LaRussa drove a beater car and went after the drunks on campus, giving them rides to fraternities, sororities, and their dorms after they'd had too much to drink. He tried to expand by picking up students at the airport, but the taxi drivers got wind that he was undercutting them and ran him off with a pitchfork. He didn't give up though."

Harrison said, "Tickman said Vince then hired students as drivers, bought them pagers, and ran the business four nights a week out of his room in the fraternity."

Keera thought of the tutoring business LaRussa had started in high school and sensed where the story might be going. "How did the money work?" she asked.

"Vince would get a cut of every fare collected from every driver. They charged flat rates. Tickman said Vince showed up at the fraternity one day driving a new car, and when questioned, he said the business had taken off," Patsy said.

"But it hadn't?" Keera asked.

"The fraternity president got a call from the national chapter, which owns the fraternity house on campus. They hadn't received all the rent owed for the semester," Patsy said.

"I can see the plot twist coming," Keera said.

"The president goes down to Vince's room and asks him, 'What the hell?' Vince tells him several guys were late paying their rent, but he'd get after them and get national paid. Well, this went on for several weeks. National would call, say they received a partial payment, the president would confront Vince, Vince would say he'd received a few more rent payments and would make another payment to national."

"Until he ran out of money to pay national," Keera said.

"Tickman said Vince ran out of guys to blame, cleared out his room in the middle of the night, and left school," Harrison said.

"How much money went missing?" Keera asked.

"Just under nine thousand dollars," Patsy said.

"Tickman said it was a real shit show," Harrison added. "National sent an accountant to go through the books, and the accountant determined Vince had used the fraternity's bank account like it was VLR's business account. He used the rent money to keep VLR afloat, writing checks on a bad account, then writing a second check on the fraternity's account to pay the VLR account and make it look like the account had money in it. He'd write these checks on a Friday, and it would take a week before the check bounced. Whenever national bitched, he'd make a partial payment."

"Pretty slick for a college student," Harrison said. "That took some thought."

"What happened to Vince? Was he prosecuted?" Keera asked.

Patsy said, "They ultimately caught up with him somewhere in Idaho. The story was in the local paper out there. Tickman said LaRussa got a lawyer to negotiate a suspended sentence—provided he paid back the money."

"Did he pay back the money?" Keera asked.

"According to the local paper in Pullman," Harrison said. "He likely sold the car."

"Anyone else been asking Tickman about LaRussa?"

"Jack Worthing," Patsy said. "Tickman got a call six months ago, just like Mary Bell and Eric Fields."

"Tickman remembered the name Jack Worthing without being prompted," Harrison said. "Said Worthing told him he was writing a story about LaRussa, all the success he's had. Tickman thought it was bullshit."

"Why?"

"Simple, really," Harrison said. "Tickman figured if somebody wanted to write about Vince's success, why would he get in touch with one of his fraternity brothers who he had ripped off?"

"Makes sense. Did Tickman press Jack Worthing on the question?"

"Said he told Worthing if he was going to write a story about LaRussa's successes, he should write about who LaRussa screwed on his way to the top."

Keera checked her watch. It was too late to confront LaRussa tonight. She'd speak to him in the morning. "Find out if Vince has any kind of criminal record in Oregon or Washington, and get whatever newspaper articles you can find," she said to Harrison.

"Already ahead of you," Harrison said. He pulled copies of the Moscow-Pullman newspaper articles from his briefcase.

"We stopped at the newspaper's offices and at Whitman County Superior Court before we headed back to the airport," Patsy said. "I read the articles on the plane ride home. They corroborate what Tickman told us." He handed Keera the articles and the criminal complaint. "The charges were dropped when LaRussa paid back the money owed."

Keera had another thought. "We should also determine if Vince ever graduated from college, or business school," she said. "Doesn't sound like he did."

"We have no way to track down this guy Jack Worthing?" Patsy asked Harrison.

"The server isn't connected to anyone in particular. It would be a waste of time and likely take weeks," Harrison said.

"We don't have that much time," Keera said.

"Ask for more time," Harrison said.

"The more time we give Ambrose, the more likely he'll find this same crap we're finding," she said, holding up the newspaper articles. "Did Tickman say anyone else had called him?"

"Not yet," Patsy said.

"If Ambrose discovered it, could we get it excluded as a prior bad act?" Keera asked Patsy.

In Washington you couldn't introduce evidence of prior bad behavior to prove a different crime, though there were exceptions.

"Ambrose would argue it proves a motive," Patsy said. "So would I. I'd argue the testimony shows LaRussa has always been obsessed with making money, going so far as to steal to get it. It's thin, but . . . I don't see Judge Hung allowing in evidence of a school play, or Vince selling strawberries as a kid. Stealing from his fraternity brothers though? That's not as clear. She could certainly find the probative value outweighs the prejudice and let it in, but I also don't see Judge Hung risking potentially getting a conviction overturned on appeal. Let's not get ahead of ourselves. We have enough to worry about. If Ambrose finds out, we'll deal with it then. Let's deal with what's in front of us."

"Maybe LaRussa has an explanation," Harrison said.

Keera would find out in the morning.

"On a more positive note," Harrison said, "I spoke to a friend who's a mechanical engineer and an inventor. Has about fifty patents to his name. He agreed to take a look at the evidence and try to come up with a theory of what happened."

"Let's hope he's fast," Keera said.

"Everyone go home and get a good night's sleep," Patsy said.

Keera didn't think a good night's sleep likely, not with her mind focused on all the different nuances in her case.

Jealous mistress.

Keera turned the deadbolt on her front door at just after 9:00 p.m., dog tired. She picked up the day's mail from the floor and carried it to the dining room table. Curiosity won over fatigue, and she hit the space bar of her computer, telling herself she'd make just one move, then go to bed. The Dark Knight had slid his pawn to b4, believing his two rooks were strong enough to defeat Keera's defenses. She thought of Ambrose and his two rooks—Syd Evans and Lisa Bennet. Was their testimony strong enough to convict LaRussa? It looked to be, on first impression.

In a series of fairly quick decisions, Keera took the Dark Knight's pawn at b4. The Dark Knight retaliated and took her pawn at the same square. Now she attacked. Her queen took her opponent's knight at a7. The Dark Knight took her pawn at c5. Keera took his pawn at the same square. The Dark Knight moved his bishop to d6, attacking her knight and pawn. Keera moved her rook to c8, ensuring the Dark Knight's bishop would have to take her pawn at c5. He did. Again, it was a decoy. She was giving up pieces to keep his focus away from the real battle she prepared on the left side of the board. Keera moved her queen to d7, as if to defend her other pieces there.

She thought of the game and her strategy to create a decoy. She couldn't win creating a decoy at trial—arguing Dr. Lisa Bennet killed Anne LaRussa. Ambrose wouldn't fall for it. He'd know Keera couldn't create reasonable doubt. She couldn't explain why Bennet would bring the gun to the LaRussa home that Sunday night. She had no evidence Anne LaRussa had confronted her with the affair before that visit, something Ambrose would point out. It was a losing argument.

"What am I not seeing?" she asked as she waited for the Dark Knight to make his next move. "Am I missing something? Am I distracted? Is Jack Worthing setting up a decoy to keep me from seeing the real battle elsewhere?"

She wondered if Miller Ambrose could be leading her astray.

Her father's voice spoke in Keera's head. *Never defend without a plan to attack.*

She needed to somehow use Ambrose's arrogance, overconfidence, and his intense desire to beat her against him. She'd continue to argue Bennet had killed LaRussa, make it appear she didn't see the holes in that strategy. That might, at the very least, make Ambrose overconfident—until she had another argument or theory.

If she could find another argument or theory. That was not a given, and she was running short on time.

But the battle, ready or not, was definitely on.

CHAPTER 25

June 17, 2023
King County Jail, Seattle

The following morning, Saturday, Keera met LaRussa at the King County jail. He never hesitated when Keera asked him if he'd graduated.

"I didn't obtain a college degree," he said. "And nowhere on the LWM website does it say I did. I had always intended to go back and complete my education, but I didn't need to." He folded his hands on the metal table bolted to the floor. "I have a knack for making other people money. A lot of money. It's what I'm good at. Bill Gates is good with computers. He didn't need a degree from Harvard to tell him what he was good at. Not graduating became a badge of honor for me to run an investment firm that consistently outperformed my bigger competitors with all their degrees. I don't flaunt it, but I'm proud of it. Why is this an issue?"

Keera studied LaRussa as he spoke. Nothing indicated to her that he wasn't telling the truth. She pushed forward another piece, applying pressure to again see how he might respond. "The prosecution will argue your motivation to kill Anne was because she threatened to invoke the prenup agreement and take everything, all your money. They'll argue that money was important to you."

"Money *is* important to me. It's what I do. I make other people money. What does that have to do with my obtaining a college degree or an advanced degree?"

"Why didn't you obtain a degree?" Keera asked, still nibbling around the edges.

Again, LaRussa didn't hesitate. "There was a misunderstanding at the fraternity involving member funds. I was the treasurer, and I was blamed for it. Remaining at school became untenable."

"What kind of misunderstanding?"

"I was accused of stealing fraternity member funds for a car service business I started in college," LaRussa said.

"Did you?"

LaRussa shook his head. "I was young, and I was unsophisticated, but I wasn't a thief."

"What does that mean?"

"It means, my car service had some start-up costs, and I used some fraternity funds to cover those costs. When the car service became profitable, I paid the funds to the national chapter."

"Except for nine thousand dollars," Keera said.

LaRussa stared as if trying to determine what she knew. "I paid that money back, Keera."

"When you were prosecuted."

LaRussa shook his head. "I always intended to pay that money back, and I was doing so at the fraternity. I would have paid back the rest also, but I got run out of Pullman by some guys in my fraternity threatening to kill me. I lost my car service business and the ability I had to pay back the rest of the money. The next thing I knew I was being prosecuted. I didn't want my future jeopardized, so I pled guilty under the condition that the charge and the plea would be expunged when I paid off the debt, which I did, in full."

"How did you pay it back if the car service had ended?"

"I sold my car." He shook his head. "How do you know about this? The charges were dropped when I paid the money owed."

"I received an email," she said, "advising me to speak with a Spencer Tickman."

"He was the guy physically threatening me," LaRussa interrupted. "A football player. Big as a house and frankly, an idiot. He didn't like me from the start because I was running a successful business while going to school, and I didn't need to study a lot to get good grades. He resented me, and he didn't try to hide it. He turned the fraternity against me. He had them all convinced I should be hung. I decided to leave and work it out on my own." LaRussa sighed. "I don't understand. Why would he send you an email? Did he read about my arrest?"

"He read about your arrest," Keera said. "But he didn't send the email."

"Jack Worthing?"

Keera nodded.

"Was it Tickman? Is he the one sending the emails? Is he Jack Worthing?" LaRussa asked. "He definitely has an ax to grind."

"I don't think so. He said someone named Jack Worthing called him," she said. "And I'm not sure how he would have known what happened in elementary and high school."

"I was a kid then," LaRussa said, sounding frustrated. He sat back from the table. "This is ridiculous. Would it even be admissible?"

"If the State finds these witnesses, it will argue it's evidence that you valued money, that you always have, and it's the reason you killed Anne, therefore it could go to motive. I can't be certain what Judge Hung might do."

LaRussa seemed to struggle to maintain control. A vein at his temple bulged, and the muscles in his neck tensed. "Are you telling me that selling strawberries for a couple of bucks is evidence that I would shoot my wife?"

"No," Keera said. "I'm not. But the fraternity issue is another matter. You were an adult. You were prosecuted. My point is, someone thinks these witnesses have information of relevance, and I'm struggling to determine what that is. You have no idea who this Jack Worthing might be?"

"No," he said, now sounding more definitive. "None."

"Well, whoever he is, he's known you a long time or he's researched the hell out of you. The witnesses we've spoken with said he told them he was a reporter doing a story on you and your success at LWM. That was not true. I called the reporter who wrote the *Seattle Magazine* piece. He'd never heard the name Jack Worthing."

"What does he want? Why the character assassination?"

"I don't know. But he does seem to have an ax to grind. I'm trying to prevent that. Before he starts taking off limbs."

"Can you?" LaRussa asked. "Can you prevent him from doing so?"

"I'll work as hard as I can, Vince, but I have no idea what else might be out there, what else this Jack Worthing, whoever he is, might bring to my attention. If there is anything, I need to know about it now, because I can tell you from experience that the next weeks will go by quickly, we still have much to do, and trial will be upon us before any of us knows it."

PART III

CHAPTER 26

August 6, 2023
Seattle, Washington

The trial in the State of Washington v. Vincent Ernest LaRussa was put on standby when a preceding trial Judge Hung presided over went longer than expected. Keera, Patsy, Ella, and their staff worked fourteen-to-sixteen-hour days getting prepared. Keera and Patsy battled through pretrial motions at the omnibus hearing, none of which brought up Jack Worthing or the people to whom he had directed the defense. They were also not listed on the State's preliminary witness list.

On Friday, August 4, Judge Hung conducted voir dire with limited questions from the State and the defense. In the end, Judge Hung empaneled a jury of eight women and four men. It wasn't what Keera had hoped for. The firm's jury consultant had advised against women jurors, explaining that while women were, in general, more compassionate than male jurors, that compassion did not extend to men accused of murdering their disabled spouse while cheating on her.

Despite a jury not entirely to their liking, Keera

had reached a sense of peace, if not calm, that came with being prepared. Before chess tournaments, Patsy would tell her nerves were a sign she cared. He told her it was not possible to anticipate or to predict your opponent's every potential move. You had to trust your ability and your preparation to make the right decisions as the game moved forward. The same was true for trial.

Keera's strategy still centered around creating reasonable doubt by arguing that Lisa Bennet killed Anne LaRussa. At present it was the best she had. Harrison and his friend, the mechanical engineer and inventor, struggled to find a coherent theory to explain all the evidence found inside the LaRussa's home. Until, and if, they came up with a comprehensive theory, Keera would defend by misdirecting Ambrose and the jury while holding out hope she'd have an opportunity to attack, but that looked less likely with each passing day.

Jack Worthing had gone silent.

So had the Dark Knight.

This being the first Sunday of August, and Keera not being out of the country or dead, she drove to her parents' home for the family dinner. She didn't look for street parking on this occasion. She pulled straight into the driveway, though the lack of cars meant she was the first to arrive and risked being blocked in. She removed the German chocolate cake she had baked from scratch and decorated with fresh strawberries, carrying it to the front door.

Tonight, she didn't have that sense of dread she so often felt as she approached what was once her home. She and her father had worked well together these past weeks, and she had enjoyed spending time with him, collaborating with him, even accepting his advice. He'd stayed true to his word, as far as she could tell. She had not detected any telltale signs of his drinking. He arrived at work early and left late. They called in lunch and dinner to the firm.

Keera pushed open the front door and stepped inside. "Mom?"

Her mother came down the hall from the kitchen. "You're early."

"Thought I'd help. Maybe set the table."

"That will hopefully put your sister in a better mood, though I doubt it." Bernadette took the cake box and started for the kitchen. "This is beautiful. Where did you buy this?"

"I made it."

Her mother couldn't hide her disbelief. "You made it? Well, it looks delicious."

"Needed something to keep my mind off the trial."

Her mother set the cake beside a stuffed pork loin tied tightly with cooking string.

"My favorite," Keera said stepping closer. "What did you stuff inside?"

"Prosciutto, Gorgonzola cheese, chopped bacon, minced garlic, fresh parsley, and onions. Put the cake on this," she said, handing Keera a platter.

"How come none of us inherited your skill for gourmet cooking?"

Bernadette waved off the praise like it was the bubonic plague. "Probably because you never had to cook."

"I wish I could now."

"Of course you can," her mother said. "You take a mallet, flatten the pork loin, stuff it with what you like, and tie it back together with string."

"All I'm missing is the mallet, the string, and the talent," Keera said. Her mother smiled. "Is Dad here?"

"He's in his den, working. He's been in there every night this week."

"I hope this hasn't been too much for him."

Her mother scoffed. "Are you kidding? He's rejuvenated. It's like thirty years ago when he tried big cases. This case has meant a lot to him, Keera."

"He told you about the deal we made?"

"He told me. And the cabinet in the dining room has a lock on it and I have the key. He hasn't asked me for it. Not once. I have water and sparkling cider for dinner. I told your brother not to bring beer or I'd flush it, and him, down the john."

Keera laughed. Her mother would do it too.

"I'll go in and talk with him, then come back and set the table."

Patsy sat at his desk. The shelving was mahogany, and the décor dark-brown wood and leather. Seahawks, Mariners, Kraken, and even Supersonics sports memorabilia adorned the shelves and walls, along with a signed set of Muhammad Ali's boxing gloves and autographed baseballs from Joe DiMaggio and Ted Williams, encased in plastic. "You're supposed to take Sunday nights off," she said. "Isn't that the advice you gave me?"

He smiled and sat back. "Hey, kiddo." Patsy looked and sounded tired.

"What are you working on?"

"Just rereading the various pleadings and looking over our direct and cross-examination bullet points."

"Any bolts of lightning?"

"Nah," he said. "This is the hardest part, waiting for Ambrose to make the first move. Then we evaluate and respond. How do you feel? Ready?" He put up his hands as he had when Keera was a kid. She set down her phone and punched his hands like a prizefighter in training.

"I could drive myself crazy thinking about the different scenarios that might play out," she said.

"Better to just get a good night's sleep and take each move as it's played, with a long-term strategy in mind."

She smiled and threw a left hook. "I'm optimistic that, at some point, I'll be the one throwing instead of defending punches, but it doesn't look good at the moment."

Patsy gave her a pensive smile and lowered his hands.

"What?" Keera asked.

"You sound the way I sounded forty years ago. I wasn't afraid of anything or anyone. I'd try any case that came through the door, and I expected to win."

"I'm nervous, Dad. And I'm not half the trial attorney you were forty years ago."

"Stories get embellished with time. It's part of our Irish heritage; the Irish love to tell a good story." He smiled. "And that was a different era back then. We got away with things you could never get away with today. We tried cases from the seat of our pants. Now, with all the rules and the procedures . . ." He shook his head. "It's a different time. But I always had a hunch it would be you who succeeded me."

"Ella's succeeded you, Dad."

Patsy shook his head. "Ella manages the firm, and she does a terrific job. But she's not the trial attorney you've become."

"How do you know what kind of trial attorney I am?" she asked, intrigued.

"The defense bar talks just as much as the attorneys in the PA's office. Word on the street is

Keera Duggan is a brawler, and most dangerous when her back is against the wall. That's when they say you come out swinging."

Keera smiled. "I guess I learned that from you." She sighed. "Our back is against the wall right now. I hate not having a better handle on the evidence, playing defense."

"Opponents make mistakes. Play defense but look for that moment to attack. Games can change with one move, sometimes in an instant. So can trials."

Footsteps shuffled in the hallway. People arriving. "I'd better get out there before the hellions destroy something," Patsy said.

"And I'd better get the table set so Maggie doesn't have the opportunity to play the martyr."

"That role has many iterations," Patsy said. Her father departed. Keera followed but turned back when she realized she'd left her phone on his desk. She looked to the alcove at the back of the room, where she and her father used to huddle beside the fireplace and play games of chess at night. A board was set up. She almost called out to tell Patsy they could play a game after dinner, take their minds off the trial, but the words stuck in her throat when she saw pieces had been moved, a game in progress. She stepped toward the board, wondering whom her father could be playing. Her mother had never picked up the game. A friend, perhaps?

She studied the board and could see each piece being moved, including the captured pieces along each side. She could see the trap being set, and she realized why the Dark Knight had gone silent these past two weeks.

CHAPTER 27

August 7, 2023
King County Courthouse

Monday morning the courthouse buzzed. Patsy and Keera entered through the administrative building tunnel, but they couldn't avoid the media gathered outside Judge Hung's courtroom. King County marshals, having anticipated the crowd, guarded the door to the courtroom and, when it had filled with spectators, directed wannabe viewers and media to the adjacent overflow courtroom. Keera answered few questions from the media, giving rote responses, mindful that Judge Hung had warned both sides not to try the case in the media.

Inside, Miller Ambrose and April Richie sat at counsel table with Frank Rossi between them. As the lead detective, Rossi represented the people of Washington State. Rossi gave Keera a nod. Ambrose, his jacket draped over the back of his chair, ignored her, staring at his laptop computer screen. All business. From experience, she knew he was reviewing his opening statement, which he'd give without notes. The gallery pews were full; Anne LaRussa's family sat in the first row behind counsel table looking forlorn and tired.

The air inside the old courthouse was already warm, and a marshal, behind the curve, set up oscillating fans in the corners.

Correctional officers brought in Vince LaRussa. He wore the blue suit, white shirt, and blue tie Keera had a paralegal drop off at the jail. LaRussa would rotate between three different suits and an assortment of shirts and ties. Keera and Patsy had gone over the clothing with the jury consultant. The officers removed LaRussa's handcuffs, and they all sat.

At precisely 9:00 a.m. Judge Hung's bailiff entered and commanded the room to rise just before the judge ascended to her bench. She wasted little time.

"Good morning, Counsel. Please state your appearances for the record."

Ambrose spoke for Richie and Rossi. Keera spoke for Patsy and LaRussa.

Hung instructed the bailiff to bring in the jury.

Keera had told LaRussa to look at the jury as they entered and took their seats in the jury box, but not to stare down any one particular juror. The jurors had been read a statement about the case during voir dire. A man accused of killing his disabled wife. Human nature would cause them to form an impression from that first look, if not a judgment. They'd ask themselves whether this person, dressed in his suit, could have shot his disabled wife.

Judge Hung greeted the jury, read them the case statement Keera and Ambrose had fought over, referenced a few administrative matters, then looked to Ambrose.

"Mr. Ambrose. Does the State wish to make an opening statement?"

He stood. "The State does, Your Honor."

Ambrose buttoned his suit jacket and stepped to the podium. In some courtrooms, counsel could roam before the jury box. Not in Judge Hung's courtroom. Counsel remained at the podium unless approaching the bench. Ambrose did not carry notes or a computer. He looked to Judge Hung. "May it please the court." He turned to Keera and Patsy, a slight grin on his lips. "Respected counsel." He addressed the jury. "Ladies and gentlemen of the jury. I am Miller Ambrose. My co-counsel April Richie and I represent the people of the state of Washington." He introduced Rossi. Then he said, "A moment ago, Judge Hung read you a stipulated statement of the *allegations* the State has brought against the defendant, Vincent LaRussa." Ambrose pointed and looked at LaRussa.

This was routine, and Keera knew it well. All good prosecutors looked at the defendant, the belief being that if the prosecutor couldn't be certain the man on trial was guilty of the alleged crimes, then neither could the jurors. "The statement read to you did not contain any facts, because there are no facts yet before you. That's my job. My job is to present you with facts through the testimony of witnesses and evidence introduced. I will solicit that testimony from the persons seated in that chair." He pointed to the witness chair. "Police officers; detectives; friends of the victim, Anne LaRussa; the medical examiner; and forensic specialists.

"Through those witnesses you will learn that the *facts* of this case are not complicated. And when the State is finished with our case, I am confident you will have no doubt finding that Vincent LaRussa, with premeditation and forethought, shot and killed his wife, Anne LaRussa."

Miller systematically laid out Anne LaRussa's injury and resulting disability, the witnesses he intended to call, and the evidence to be presented. He did not mention Jack Worthing or the people to whom Worthing directed them. Keera listened intently. She took few notes. She would get a transcript each afternoon from the court reporter. She had opportunities to object, but Patsy taught her to refrain, unless the prosecutor's statement was prejudicial. Too many objections and jurors would think Keera feared the evidence and was trying to hide it.

Ambrose used aerial blowups showing the location of LaRussa's home and, presumably, his wealth. Ambrose was as Keera remembered him—workmanlike. His opening took just over forty-five minutes. It had been efficient, with enough detail to arouse the jurors' curiosity and their suspicions, and to help them empathize with Anne LaRussa, without boring them. He laid out a highly plausible scenario that included a motive, Anne LaRussa's threat to divorce Vince and control the finances; an opportunity, when Vince returned home from his charitable event; and a weapon, the ghost gun. He implied Vincent LaRussa thought he had got away with murder, but the security system proved he had not.

The State would present a simple, common-sense case. Anne LaRussa was alive when Syd Evans and Lisa Bennet left the house. No one else arrived at the house before Vince LaRussa arrived home and claimed he found his wife dead.

Ambrose sat.

Judge Hung looked to the jury. "Ladies and gentlemen of the jury, the defense attorney has the choice to make an opening statement now, or to wait until the State has presented its witnesses and rested its case. You should make no conclusions if the defense chooses to wait to make a statement. Ms. Duggan, does the defense wish to make an opening statement at this time?"

"The defense does wish to make a statement," Keera said.

"Proceed."

Keera similarly made introductions, then got down to it. "The State has just told you about the evidence it plans to introduce and from which the State hopes you will find facts. We don't think you will. The State indicated Anne LaRussa was shot by what is referred to as a 'ghost gun,' a gun purchased online or at a gun show that does not require the seller to run a background check or even, in some cases, an ID on the purchaser. The gun has no serial number linking it to the purchaser. The State did not say Mr. LaRussa owned that gun, or any other gun for that matter. The State did not say he had purchased it. The State indicated the purchase of the gun indicates premeditation. The defense agrees." She paused for effect. "But the State will not provide any evidence the premeditation was by Mr. LaRussa. The evidence will be to the contrary. The evidence will show Mr. LaRussa was speaking at a charitable function until he returned home Sunday evening at 9:17 p.m. and found his wife murdered.

"The State indicated forensic experts will testify, but the State did not say those forensic experts have any forensic evidence that Vince LaRussa fired the murder weapon. Not a witness. Not a video. Not a fingerprint. Not DNA. The State's case will be circumstantial. Yes, this case is tragic. It is tragic that a man who suffered the shocking and crushing blow of finding his wife

308

brutally murdered is now suffering the indignity of being accused of killing her.

"Someone shot and killed Anne LaRussa," Keera said. "But the defense is confident, after you hear all of the evidence, that you will conclude that person was not Vincent LaRussa."

After Keera took time to introduce LaRussa to the jury, she concluded.

They were underway.

Judge Hung instructed Ambrose to call his first witness. Ambrose opened with the 911 dispatcher who fielded Vince LaRussa's call. Ambrose played a recording of that call to the jury, presumably because LaRussa did not sound hysterical. On the other hand, LaRussa did say, *"I just got home, and my wife has been shot."*

The dispatcher kept LaRussa on the phone until the first responders arrived.

Keera approached the dispatcher. "What time did you receive that call?" she asked. LaRussa had returned home at 9:17 p.m., and Keera sought to establish there had not been time for him to wipe the gun clean of fingerprints and DNA, scrub his hands, and change and dispose of his clothes to remove any blood spatter.

"The call was made at 9:24 p.m.," the dispatcher said.

Seven minutes after he had arrived home.

Ambrose briefly redirected, pointing out that while the call was made at 9:24, LaRussa did not walk back outside until 9:34 p.m. Ten minutes after the call was made and seventeen minutes after he arrived home.

Following the 911 dispatcher, Ambrose called the first responder, Officer Carl Olsen.

"What time did you arrive at the residence, Officer Olsen?"

"I arrived at 9:39 p.m."

Ambrose paused a beat. "And where was Mr. LaRussa?"

"He was standing outside, pacing his driveway."

"How did he seem to you upon your arrival?"

"He seemed agitated but in control."

"He wasn't hysterical?"

"No."

"Crying?"

"No."

After establishing what LaRussa had told Olsen, and why Olsen had not called the SWAT team, Ambrose asked, "Did you and your partner go through the house to make sure no one else was present?"

"We did."

"And did you find anyone?"

"Just Mr. LaRussa."

"At some point did you go through the house with Mr. LaRussa looking for signs of a forced entry?"

"We did, at the lead detective's request. We

looked for broken glass, a door or a window pried open."

"Did you find anything to indicate anyone had broken into the house?"

"We did not."

When Ambrose finished, Keera moved to the lectern. "Officer Olsen, did you pay any attention to Mr. LaRussa's clothes?"

"His clothes? No."

"Do you recall what was he wearing?"

"He was wearing a tuxedo shirt with the cuffs rolled up, tuxedo pants. Black shoes."

"Did you notice a tuxedo jacket, tie, and cuff links anywhere inside the house?"

"Yes. The jacket was draped over a chair in the sitting room. The tie and cuff links were on the coffee table."

"Did you check Mr. LaRussa's closet to determine if he owned more than one tuxedo?"

"I did not, no."

"Did Mr. LaRussa smell like soap or, I don't know, Lysol?"

"I didn't notice any smell."

"Did his hands look freshly scrubbed?"

"I don't recall."

"You didn't pay attention to that?"

"Not particularly."

"Did you find any gloves of any kind—latex, gardening gloves, golf gloves—any gloves, anywhere inside or outside the house?"

"No."

"Did his clothes have any blood spatter on them?"

"Not that I saw."

"You said he wasn't hysterical, that he wasn't crying. Do you have any mental health training?"

"No."

"You wouldn't be able to tell if Mr. LaRussa had been in shock when you encountered him, would you?"

"He didn't seem to be in shock."

"But you have no such training; do you?"

Olsen looked confused. "No."

Keera questioned the officer for another five minutes before retaking her seat, abiding by Patsy's cross-examination mantra to get in, make a few points, and get out one question too early rather than one question too late.

After lunch, Ambrose called the attorney, Syd Evans, to the stand. Ambrose used the computer monitors to put up the text message Anne LaRussa had sent to Evans and his response. He also showed phone records noting the calls Evans had made to Anne's family. He took Evans through his legal background and the many years he'd worked for Anne LaRussa's family.

"How did Anne LaRussa appear to you when you arrived?" Ambrose asked.

"She was upset."

"Did you ask her what was upsetting her?"

"I did. She said it wasn't anything in particular."

"Was Vince LaRussa home?"

"No, he wasn't."

"Did you ask Anne where Vince was?"

"She said at a charitable function and that he wouldn't be home for a few more hours."

"Was it unusual for Anne LaRussa to summon you to the home?"

"Very. I'd never been before."

"Did she say why she had in this instance?"

"She wanted to know about a clause in their prenuptial agreement that she and Vince LaRussa signed before getting married."

Ambrose then produced the prenuptial agreement on the various computer screens, and Syd Evans testified he had prepared the document, and he went over the specific provisions, including the forfeiture clause. He explained the reason for the clause, how it was intended to protect Anne LaRussa. He explained that in the event of a divorce, if either spouse were determined to have cheated, he or she would forfeit any right to the marital estate, including business assets. He offered his opinion that those assets would include the assets of LaRussa Wealth Management.

According to the list of witnesses Ambrose intended to call, he would put on a forensic accountant later in the trial who would state that based upon their last filed tax return, Anne and Vince LaRussa were worth in excess of $100 million.

"When you put together the prenuptial agreement, whose idea was it to include a forfeiture clause?"

"Anne's parents."

"Did Anne or her parents say why they wanted the clause?"

"Anne's parents had put aside money for Anne. They were worried about their daughter's well-being, were she and Vince to divorce."

Ambrose asked several foundational questions. Then he said, "Did Anne LaRussa tell you why she was asking about the forfeiture clause in the prenuptial agreement?"

"No."

"Did you ask her?"

"I did, yes."

"But she didn't tell you?"

"Again, she just said she wanted some clarification about invoking it."

"Did you come to any conclusions as to why Anne LaRussa was asking about the clause?"

Patsy rose. He had deposed Evans. "Objection. His speculation is irrelevant."

"Sustained," Judge Hung said.

"What time did you leave the LaRussa house?" Ambrose asked.

"I left at about six thirty."

"And when you left the LaRussa home, was Anne LaRussa still alive?"

"Very much so."

After forty-five minutes, Ambrose turned over the witness to the defense. Patsy rose and moved to the podium.

"You didn't text Vince LaRussa that night and tell him Anne had asked to see you; did you?" Patsy asked.

"No, I did not."

"You didn't call him."

"No."

"You didn't email him."

"No."

"So, to your knowledge, Mr. LaRussa had not been told that his wife spoke to you about invoking the forfeiture clause in the prenuptial agreement."

"Not by me, certainly."

"But you did call Anne's parents after you met with Anne, didn't you?"

"Yes."

"You are the Collinses' tax and estate attorney, aren't you?"

"Yes."

"And have been for many years."

"Yes."

"Fair to say your loyalties are to them, isn't it?"

"I suppose it is, yes."

Ambrose stood when Patsy finished. "Mr. Evans, after Mrs. LaRussa's death, why didn't you try to contact Mr. LaRussa to tell him about the meeting you had with his wife?"

"I don't know. I just . . . didn't."

"Was it because you believed it possible Vince LaRussa killed his wife when she told him she intended to file for divorce and invoke the forfeiture clause?"

Patsy shot to his feet. "Objection, Your Honor. The question is leading and without any foundation that Anne LaRussa said any such thing. Moreover, this witness's belief is irrelevant. Counsel should be admonished."

"Sustained." Hung shot Ambrose a look that told him not to try it again.

Ambrose didn't need to. His intent had been clear to the jury as they broke at day's end.

CHAPTER 28

After trial, back in their law office conference room, Keera and Patsy discussed the day's events and made preparations for the morning, splitting up witnesses to cross-examine. Bernadette had come to the firm and dropped off a pot roast with potatoes and vegetables. Patsy, Ella, and Maggie, all working late, dug in. Keera quickly changed into running gear, put in earbuds, and took off along the Elliott Bay waterfront, dodging tourists with baby strollers and people on skateboards. The heat wave had passed, and the temperature hovered in the seventies with a bit of a chill in the air. She'd run to the grain silos located at the north end of the waterfront and back. The five-mile round trip worked up a good sweat and helped to clear her head and relieve her tension so she could better concentrate on the next day's witnesses.

As she ran, she evaluated the first day. It had gone as well as could be expected. She and Patsy scored points on cross-examination, hadn't been hurt any more than she had anticipated by the State's witnesses, and she set up certain bits of evidence as the basis for arguments she'd make later in trial.

Back in the office she grabbed a plate of pot

roast and a protein drink from the refrigerator in the lunchroom, shaking it as she logged on to her computer. She ate and drank while checking emails. Nothing urgent. The daily trial transcript had come in, and she sent it to her father to review. He would highlight pertinent testimony and decide if they wanted to recall any of the State's witnesses in the defense's case in chief, after the State rested. Patsy would also mine for nuggets Keera could use in her closing.

Having checked her emails, she pulled up her notes of the conversations she'd had with Dr. Lisa Bennet. Bennet would be the most important witness for both the prosecution and the defense. If Ambrose did not convince the jury Anne LaRussa had been alive when Bennet left the house, he would lose. And if Keera didn't convince the jury that a reasonable doubt existed as to whether Anne LaRussa remained alive, she would have a steep climb ahead of her. Given Bennet's importance, Keera had spent days preparing for Bennet's cross-examination, consulting Patsy for his expertise.

Her computer pinged, an incoming email.

Jack Worthing.

Keera stared at the name and the subject line immediately below it.

Re: The Game of Your Life

She debated opening it but reasoned that she could handle anything, if she knew of it in advance. It was the things an attorney didn't know that could do the most damage at trial. She opened the email and read it.

Then she called JP Harrison.

Keera hurried downstairs to where Harrison sat behind the wheel of his BMW, waiting. She pulled open the passenger door and slid inside.

"You sure you don't want me and Patsy to handle this?" Harrison said.

"I've been preparing for Lisa Bennet all week," Keera said. "And this person is close."

"Where is Jack Worthing sending us this time, and who are we going to see?"

"Somerset, across the I-90 bridge," she said, referring to the neighborhood on the east side of Lake Washington, a roughly twenty-minute drive from Occidental Square. "The person's name is Phillip McPherson. He's a wealth manager. That's all I know."

"I take it Jack Worthing did not provide additional details."

"He did not," Keera said. "I had my assistant research McPherson on the internet and call to ensure he was home. I'll read what he found on the way."

The Somerset neighborhood was built on a hill. The residents looked across Lake Washington to the Seattle skyline, and across Elliott Bay to the Olympic Mountains. Homes did not come up for sale often in the affluent neighborhood. Whoever Phil McPherson was, he'd done all right for himself.

Harrison wound his BMW along tree-lined streets to a cul-de-sac atop the hill. McPherson lived in a one-story, suburban ranch-style home with stonework. A long cement walk bisected a manicured garden leading to a wooden porch. Keera rang the doorbell, which immediately set off a chorus of barking.

McPherson, who looked very much like the photograph Keera's assistant had retrieved from the internet, opened the front door. Barefoot, he wore shorts and a plain white T-shirt. He had thick, curly, brown hair, showing gray, that flowed to his shoulders, and narrow features, and what Keera's mom would call a Roman nose. Three dogs stood at his side, keenly watching Keera and Harrison. "Can I—" McPherson started, then stopped himself, his light-blue eyes behind round wire-rim glasses seeming to take in Keera and JP Harrison instantly.

"Mr. McPherson. I'm—"

"I know who you are. Your assistant called, but I also saw you on the television and in the news-paper."

He'd been paying attention to the trial. "Wonder if we could have a moment of your time?"

"Why is that?" McPherson did not sound confrontational, just curious. "Your assistant didn't say."

"Someone told us to speak to you about Mr. LaRussa."

McPherson got an impish grin. "And who would that person be?"

"Jack Worthing," Keera said.

"Never heard of him," McPherson said. "What did he tell you?"

"Not a lot. Can I ask if anyone has reached out to talk with you about Vince LaRussa in the past six months?"

McPherson shook his head and crossed his arms. "No. No one." That was different from the names Worthing had provided. "If you're worried about me breaking my confidentiality agreement, I don't have any intention to do so, unless someone subpoenas me to testify, and the court orders it." Another smile.

"That's not our intent." Keera took in the information and tried to make sense of it but not give away that she had no idea what McPherson was talking about. "We're just hoping to ask you a few questions. You work in the same industry as Vince LaRussa?" The articles from the internet indicated that to be the case.

"That's right."

"Is that how you know him?"

"Vince and I know one another intimately,"

McPherson said. Again, the ironic grin. He showed no sign of inviting them inside his home or slamming the door in their faces, so Keera plowed forward.

"What do you mean, 'intimately'?"

"I worked at LWM for three years when Vince got started."

"What did you do?"

"My title?" His smile broadened. "My title was personal wealth advisor and manager. In actuality? I recruited new investors."

"Why do you say it like that?"

"Because Vince was the only person who dealt with the private investors once I brought them into the firm. Though I didn't know that at the time I took the job and wouldn't have if I had known."

"You didn't actually advise them?"

"No. What I did was write quarterly checks to them."

"What about the other personal wealth advisors who worked for LWM—were they advising investors?"

"There were only a few of us, and Vince was very good at partitioning people and their responsibilities."

"Meaning what?"

"Meaning we only knew what was happening inside our own cubicle. He was also good at sizing up people and their personalities, so he could get what he wanted out of each employee."

"And what do you mean by that?"

"I mean, the squeaky wheel got the oil, or in my case, the money. Whenever I brought up the subject of when I would get to build my own book of business and provide investors with advice, Vince would tell me the process took time, that I needed to learn the business foundations first. Then he'd provide me with a bonus to compensate me for the investors that I had brought in, but I had to sign an agreement that I would not share the amount of that bonus with others in the office. That was the deal."

"Did you ever become a wealth advisor?"

"Not at LWM. Nobody did."

"Were you told that?"

"Guys talk. It's inevitable. I found out from the other advisors that they were doing exactly what I was doing and also getting paid bullshit bonuses. None of us was doing any wealth management or providing investment advice."

"Is that why you left?"

"Ultimately. But it wasn't *the reason*."

"What was?"

McPherson pulled back his hair from his forehead, revealing a scar that reminded Keera of the Z-shaped scar on Harry Potter's forehead, except McPherson's scar was farther to the side. "This."

"What happened?"

"Since you're Vince's attorneys, I suppose it

can't hurt to tell you. But this is where the confidentiality clause comes in. So I need to know this part of the conversation is off the record."

Keera wasn't a journalist and had no intention of broadcasting what she learned; at least she didn't anticipate doing so. If McPherson had something important to say that she wanted to use in court, she'd subpoena him and put him under a court order. "Sure," she said.

"After I spoke to the other advisors and learned they were doing the same bullshit job I was doing, I confronted Vince. I told him he had lied to me and all the others who had joined LWM believing they were going to become advisors. I told him he'd set back our careers by years."

"And he hit you?"

"Hit? No. I would have kicked his ass. Vince was prone to fits of rage. His anger flipped on and off like a light switch. He called me ungrateful. Told me I was making more money than I deserved. He said I was a dumbshit and lucky he had taken me in. He said a lot of crap. I told him to go fuck himself and walked away before I killed him. I heard someone shout and I looked back. Thankfully, I turned my head just in time. Had I not, the stapler Vince had thrown might have taken out my eye."

Keera felt stunned.

McPherson obviously enjoyed it. "That's . . . your Vince LaRussa."

Keera recovered, thinking like an attorney. A paper trail? Could the State get in such evidence? Lost temper? "Did you sue him?"

"I would have, but Vince immediately went into survival mode. He paid all my medical bills and gave me an agreed-upon settlement equal to a year's salary."

He paid you off, Keera thought. Just as he had paid off the national fraternity to get the criminal charge against him dropped.

"I had to sign a confidentiality agreement not to sue him and all that other legal bullshit. I didn't really care. I already had another job. And I wasn't about to sue Vince."

"Why not?"

"Vince is well known in the industry. He does a lot of charitable work. I was afraid filing a complaint could backfire and ruin my reputation, keep me from getting another job with another company. When Vince agreed to the settlement, there was no need to sue. But here's the most interesting part about this whole sordid affair, in my opinion."

"What's that?"

"Vince never apologized. He offered to pay my medical expenses, my settlement. He even gave me a strong letter of reference, but at no time did he admit guilt or fault, and at no time did he apologize. He acted like he hadn't done anything wrong and just went on about his business."

"Do you know if anyone else had a similar experience at LWM?"

"No, but it wouldn't surprise me if someone did and if Vince paid him or her off also. Wouldn't surprise me if Vince had criminal and civil complaints against him either."

He didn't. Keera had checked and didn't find anything except the dropped charge of embezzling the fraternity's funds. She decided to pursue the line of questioning with McPherson. "How would he have an investment firm if that were the case?"

McPherson smiled, coy. "Exactly. How would he?"

"How do you think he would?"

"How much do you know about personal wealth investing?"

Keera smiled. "I'm a defense attorney," she said. "Not a lot."

McPherson looked at Harrison.

"I did some white-collar criminal investigations," he said.

McPherson considered his watch. "Come on in. I got a little time before my wife and kids get home from play practice." He opened the front door wider.

The three dogs sniffed Keera and Harrison in the entry. One looked to be part border collie, half its face black, the other white. The black side had a sorrowful, pet-me, brown eye; the white side, a grayish-blue eye that gave the dog a more malevolent appearance. *Pet me. I dare you.*

"My wife takes in strays," McPherson explained. "She's a bleeding heart when it comes to dogs and cats. I had to put my foot down at three dogs and two cats. They eat and shit more than we humans do. But they're also the best alarm system money can buy. They start barking and, trust me, nobody is coming through that front door."

They crossed a simple entry to a living room. McPherson offered them a seat on a couch. He sat in a white, upright chair across a coffee table, his elbows on his knees. "Might as well use the living room," he said. "It's like one of those rooms behind a rope in a museum." The dogs had stopped their progress at the carpet and sat. The border collie stared at Keera. Sensing her unease, McPherson said, "Can't read that one. You don't know if he's going to lick or bite. Don't worry, though, the dogs aren't allowed in here. He won't bother you."

Keera said, "You were going to explain to me how Vince LaRussa could have an investment firm if he had a criminal record."

"LWM is set up as 'private offerings,' which means it sought sophisticated and experienced investors rather than the general public—and there is virtually no federal or state oversight or protection for that class of investors."

"Why is that?" she asked.

"The theory is that accredited investors have the means and the investment experience to evaluate the private offerings' merits and risks. They don't need the protection that, say, widows and orphans need, and the securities do not need to be registered. LaRussa listed himself as a seller of private offerings under SEC Rule 506, Regulation D. Therefore, he only had to fill out a form that his investors met certain income and net worth thresholds. He does that and he doesn't have to disclose any complaints, if he had any, and he escapes state regulation."

"So it isn't illegal," Keera said. "If that's what he did."

"It's what he did," McPherson said. "I recruited those high-income investors."

"And presumably those high-income investors would be sophisticated enough to perform due diligence, and they liked what they found at LWM," Keera said.

"What those investors liked was the promise of interest rates as high as twelve percent and, on average, eight percent each month. The profits came from mortgage funds, mortgage-backed securities, and private mortgages. LWM's initial clients were relatives and friends, and when the fund did well, they told their relatives and friends and so on and so on. Word of mouth. Then, when LWM better established its reputation, Vince sought out local wealth-advisory firms to invest their clients in LWM funds. The earnings were steady and the payouts consistent. LWM raised five hundred million dollars from investors all across the United States."

"It sounds like you knew his investment strategy well for a guy who never actually handled an investor. How is that?"

"I paid attention. That and the firm that I moved to after I left LWM asked me several times to duplicate what LWM was getting in returns for its investors, and I was never able to do that. I tried a number of different models, and I could never duplicate LWM's returns. When I was at LWM, Vince used to say what he did was a trade secret and centered upon not being invested in the market often or for long. Get in, make money, and get out. If the market wavered at all he invested the money in short-term T-bills and other liquid investments."

"It seems to work."

"For Vince. It didn't for me, or for anyone else in the industry. I don't know of any other companies that are consistently getting their investors the kinds of returns LWM generates."

"So then how do you think LWM is doing it?"

"If I knew, I'd be running my own investment firm," McPherson said with a laugh. "Some people have the Midas touch, and some only appear to have it."

"Meaning what?" She sensed from a pause in the conversation that McPherson was becoming reticent. Did he worry he could be sued? Or did he still fear Vince LaRussa?

"As I said, this is an industry that talks. Any new way to invest and make large profits isn't going to be a secret for long. I don't care how proprietary the company that developed the model keeps it, or what confidentiality agreements employees sign. Advisors switch companies. There's corporate espionage. Guys go out and drink and eat dinner together, attend the same professional gatherings. If someone found a magic pill, everyone would be swallowing it."

"Maybe that's why Vince LaRussa didn't let you or anyone else open your own book of business. He was protecting the business model he'd developed."

"Maybe, but that also insinuates that only Vince LaRussa is smart enough to have found this magic formula. He isn't, not in my experience."

"Then how was he consistently getting his investors eight percent?" Keera asked.

"How indeed," McPherson said. "That is what I think is the real magic pill."

Keera handed McPherson a business card and said if anyone called to ask him questions, she'd appreciate receiving a call.

"I'm not interested in talking to the media

330

about it, if that's what you mean," McPherson said. "If I get subpoenaed to court, then I'll have no choice. If not, I believe it's better to just let a sleeping dog lie." He looked to the dogs. "It's like the strays my wife brings home. We don't really know what they've been through, so we don't know what might trigger them. You let them sleep. That way you don't get bitten."

Keera looked to the border collie and wondered which eye was the true reflection of the dog's personality.

Back in the car, Harrison said, "What he said, in essence, is that Vince LaRussa is a fraud. Everything about him."

"That's what he believes," Keera said, trying not to rush to judgment and instead trying to determine why Jack Worthing had provided her with the lead to this information. "It's what he thinks. Not what he knows. The question is whether his opinions are soured by the stapler incident, by his frustration at not being able to duplicate Vince's investment model and likely having some not-too-happy employers, or whether some truth exists to what he's saying."

"How do we find out if LaRussa is legit?" Harrison said.

"I don't know, but Jack Worthing seems to be leading us down this path." Keera saw a pattern. "He started with people who told us that, as a boy, Vince was beguiling and always interested in and capable of making money. Harmless ambition. Then he directed us to a person with a story to indicate money was more than ambition, that Vince would steal it from his classmates and embezzle funds from his fraternity brothers. Now McPherson suggests it goes beyond embezzlement of funds, to some sort of fraud."

"Don't forget the fits of rage," Harrison said. "If this guy McPherson was honest about what happened, then Vince would hurt someone, or at least lose his temper, to protect what he built, and maybe to hide his criminal acts."

"Which might make it admissible, were Ambrose to ever find him."

"That's not the most disturbing part though," Harrison said.

"No? What is?" Keera asked.

"LaRussa's unwillingness or inability to acknowledge fault."

"When I asked Vince about the fraternity incident, he called it a misunderstanding and said it wasn't his fault," Keera said. "He said he had intended all along to give the money back, so no one got hurt."

"But he only did so when he faced prosecution," Harrison said. "Which indicates he doesn't believe he did anything wrong, or he's incapable of accepting he did anything wrong until he faced very real consequences. The only people I've ever dealt with who felt no remorse for their bad behavior were the sociopaths and the psychopaths. They believe everyone is put on this planet for them to manipulate and take advantage of, that they are smarter than everyone else, and they aren't doing anything wrong. They're just doing what everyone else would do if they could."

"Do you think Vince LaRussa is a psychopath?"

"I don't know, Keera. I haven't spent a lot of time with him. But the guy McPherson described . . . that guy . . . Yeah, I'd classify that guy as a psychopath, or at least a sociopath."

Keera got home late. Beat. She had gone back to the office to talk with Patsy about Phil McPherson. Throughout the evening, her mind kept wandering back to the conversation with McPherson. Was Vince LaRussa a psychopath? A person without a conscience, who felt no empathy or remorse? Had Anne confronted him about his cheating and threatened to take everything LaRussa had earned and sent LaRussa into a fit of rage? Is that what Jack Worthing was trying to communicate? If it was, Keera noted several problems. The first was whether Phil McPherson was credible, or just spouting off the revenge he could not take because the confidentiality provision prevented it. In the end, it had been McPherson who took the money, rather than pursue a criminal or civil complaint against

LaRussa. McPherson chose cash over judicial satisfaction. What did that say about him?

It also still didn't explain the gun. If Vince purchased the gun, he had to have done so before that Sunday night. Before Anne LaRussa threatened him, if she had done so that night. Had Anne also confronted him before that Sunday night, prompting him to buy the gun, or had something else motivated the purchase? Had he felt trapped and tied down by Anne's injury, bought the gun as a way out, and saw his opportunity that night, not knowing about Evans and Bennet coming to the house? Were he and Lisa Bennet having an affair, and getting rid of his wife was a way to be with her and to keep his money? Or had he simply bought the gun for self-protection and used it that night in a rage?

Keera wouldn't sleep, not with her mind scrambling through the various scenarios. She turned to her chessboard to center her. She knew her father would also need a distraction. She brought up their chess game. Patsy had moved his queen to a2. Keera had not yet responded because to do so would tip her hand that she had misled Patsy, that the battle she planned was on the other side of the board. She moved her pawn to f4.

This seemingly inconsequential move freed her queen to slip through the pawn chain protecting

Patsy's king. Patsy would soon realize he had been so absorbed in his attack that he'd missed the real battle. After several minutes her computer pinged. Keera smiled. Patsy knew her better than anyone. He knew she needed this game as much as he needed it. Maybe more.

From: Darkknight
To: SeattlePawnslayer

Queen to f7

Patsy was not giving in. He wouldn't patronize her. He would make her earn this victory. His response was brazen, the same way he had once tried cases. Keera would need to be careful. She was about to attack Patsy's king, but he still had three defenders in position to protect. She needed to stay focused on what was before her so as not to end up in a trap.

From: SeattlePawnslayer
To: Darkknight

Queen to h3

From: Darkknight
To: SeattlePawnslayer

Pawn to f3

From: SeattlePawnslayer
To: Darkknight

Queen takes pawn at g3. Check.

The Dark Knight did not respond. Keera heard Patsy telling her to focus on the problem before her. Her strategy for the morning, for her cross of Lisa Bennet, became clear. Stay the course until, and if, the State made a mistake and gave her a chance to attack. Until then, set them up to believe they were winning the battle.

And pray.

CHAPTER 29

The following morning, April Richie called Keera at the office and advised that the State intended to call Frank Rossi out of turn. Dr. Lisa Bennet was detained at work. Keera suspected that wasn't the reason. Other than just to screw with her, Ambrose wanted to call Rossi to establish that the security tape showed only Syd Evans and Lisa Bennet arriving at the LaRussa house before Vince arrived that Sunday evening. He wanted to establish there had been no break-in, that there had been no third person, no intruder. He wanted to take the wind out of the SODDI defense sail before it actually sailed.

Rossi took the stand looking like an American flag in a solid-blue suit, white shirt, and red paisley tie. Keera didn't know whether to cross-examine him or to salute. He looked nervous and sipped from a cup of water, his tell. Ambrose acknowledged him, established his credentials, and had Rossi describe what it meant to be the lead detective on an investigation.

Ambrose questioned Rossi about his arrival at the LaRussa house with Ford, and his interaction with Vince LaRussa, as well as standard protocols to establish no one else was in the home. He walked him through the forensic team members who arrived and their purpose. Ambrose intended it all to look official, diligent, and systematic. He established that no evidence existed of a forced entry.

"Did the LaRussas have a security system at their home?"

"They did. They had a security camera mounted over the garage that covered the entire front yard leading to the front door, and a second camera that provided footage of the backyard."

Ambrose took time to display photographs, which Rossi authenticated. Then he asked, "Did you review the security footage from those cameras for Sunday night, June fourth?"

"I did."

"What did you determine, based upon your review?"

"I determined no one appeared on the security footage at the back of the house that day or that night. The security camera over the garage captured three cars arriving at the LaRussa home Sunday evening." He explained who arrived and when each left.

"Your Honor, for the record, we would like Detective Rossi to show the video footage to the jury and explain what he saw."

Keera stood. "The defense has no objection."

Rossi played the footage. He testified that his partner, Billy Ford, had run the license plates on the first two vehicles and determined the cars were registered to Syd Evans and Lisa Bennet. Rossi pointed out the clock in the lower right corner that documented when each had arrived and when they had left. He then showed Vince LaRussa arriving home at 9:17 p.m. and reemerging on the driveway at 9:34 p.m., roughly five minutes before the responding officers arrived.

Ambrose methodically took Rossi through his and Ford's investigation, the gruesome scene they encountered in the kitchen, and the evidence he, Ford, and the CSI team had collected. Rossi was on the stand the entire morning. Ambrose passed him to the defense just after lunch.

Patsy approached the podium and Keera could tell it unnerved Rossi, who no doubt had expected Keera to cross-examine him. Rossi sipped again from his cup of water and set the cup down. "Good afternoon, Detective Rossi," Patsy said.

"Good afternoon."

"Detective Rossi, you testified you asked Mr. LaRussa's permission to go through the house to search for a possible intruder and he gave you his permission, didn't he?"

"He did."

"He even subsequently searched the house with Officer Olsen, didn't he?"

"He did."

"He told you about the security cameras and where you could obtain the videotape for the footage for that evening, didn't he?"

"He did."

"He didn't try to hide the fact that security footage existed, did he?"

"No, he did not."

"You asked Mr. LaRussa to provide a DNA sample to the CSI detectives and he willingly did so, didn't he?"

"Yes, he did."

"And he willingly provided you with his fingerprints, correct?"

"Yes."

"He even agreed to have his hands and clothing examined for gunshot residue, didn't he?"

"He did."

"But that was just a ruse by you, a fib, wasn't it?"

Rossi shrugged. "I guess you could call it that."

"You don't actually test for GSR residue anymore because it isn't reliable. Isn't that true?"

"That is true."

"But he willingly agreed to such a test, didn't he?"

"He did."

Keera and Patsy would, later in the trial, cross-examine the CSI detectives to establish that neither Vince LaRussa's fingerprints nor his DNA were found on the gun, and no blood spatter was found on his hands or his clothes. They would use the time that LaRussa arrived home and the time that he reemerged outside the home to argue that he couldn't possibly have shot his wife, wiped the gun clean of prints and DNA, and changed into a new set of identical clothes, though he likely did have sufficient time—had the killing been premeditated.

Patsy frequently changed subjects to keep Rossi off balance and try to catch the detective off guard. Her father was the attorney she had watched as a child, calculating and pointed, but still affable to the jury. Maybe he had slipped, but it was not apparent this morning. This afternoon he had risen to the challenge, proving that the Irish Brawler still had a few more good rounds in him.

"Did Mr. LaRussa advise you that his wife had been depressed and irritable?" Patsy said. The question was off script from what they had discussed, and Keera felt a twinge of anxiety.

"Yes, he said words to that effect."

"And he told you that his wife was on prescription pain medication, opioids?"

"Yes, he did."

"He told you he didn't know what specific medications his wife took or the amount, but that you were free to look for yourself in the medicine cabinet in the master bathroom?"

"Yes, he did."

"And you did that, did you not?"

"I called in a forensic pharmacist to inventory the medications in the medicine cabinet."

"Why didn't you just do it yourself?" Patsy certainly knew the answer, but he wanted the answer to come from Rossi.

"There was a considerable number of prescriptions."

Patsy put up a CSI photograph showing the medicine cabinet with the significant number of prescription bottles. Rossi authenticated the photograph. After several more questions, Patsy established that the forensic pharmacist, Bonnie Kramer, had provided a report of her findings, and he put her report on the computer screens for display to the jurors. Both sides had stipulated that the report and the photographs were authentic, so the pharmacist did not have to be called to testify. Patsy handed a copy of the report to Rossi.

"Would you take a look on the fourth page of that report where the forensic pharmacist noted the medications and the amount of each medication prescribed?" Patsy asked.

Rossi did, and Patsy took him through the medications in painstaking detail. They included oxycodone, or Oxycontin, and hydrocodone, or Vicodin. Patsy had Rossi state the dates on the bottles and the amounts within each bottle. Keera could see from the jurors' expressions that the detailed list was hitting home but also that they expected Patsy to do something with the information.

"Did the forensic pharmacist provide an expert opinion as to the number of or the amount of these drugs she found in Anne LaRussa's medicine cabinet?" Patsy asked.

"Not in this report," Rossi said.

"Did she say something to you like 'Wow, that is a lot of opioids'?"

"No," Rossi said, unable to suppress a smile. The jurors also smiled.

"Did she say anywhere in the report that these opioids are addictive?"

"Yes."

"Did she say these opioids can cause a person to become confused and depressed?"

Ambrose objected. "Your Honor, counsel is testifying."

Judge Hung shook her head. "This is cross-examination. I'll allow counsel some leeway. But Mr. Duggan, you're getting close."

"I'll move on, Your Honor." Patsy had made his point. He addressed Rossi. "Did the forensic pharmacist note the name of the doctor who prescribed these opioids?"

"The name was on the prescription bottles."

"And whose name was that?"

And in that moment, Keera understood what Patsy had done. Having Rossi testify before Bennet had been Ambrose's first trial mistake, and Patsy had just taken advantage of his error. In Ambrose's effort to screw with Keera, he hadn't considered that Patsy would portray Bennet as a doctor who had overprescribed opioids to a woman she would call her best friend. Presenting the medicine cabinet to the jury, with all the many bottles dated one after the other, painted an impression of Bennet in the jurors' minds before the doctor ever took the stand. Patsy had set up the chess pieces for Keera to strike.

"Dr. Lisa Bennet," Rossi said.

"Vince LaRussa told you his wife, Anne LaRussa, was depressed, didn't he?"

"He said that, yes."

"Did he say she was also confused?"

"I don't recall him using that word."

"What about the word 'paranoid'? Did he use that word?"

"I believe he did, yes."

"Did he say what his wife was paranoid about?"

"I don't recall that he did."

Patsy moved on. "At any time during your investigation, Detective Rossi, did you find Mr. LaRussa to be uncooperative?"

"Uncooperative? No."

"Reticent or unforthcoming?"

"No."

"While you questioned him at his house, did he ever refuse to answer your questions?"

"No."

"Did he preclude you from conducting any part of your investigation?"

"No."

"He didn't, at any time, appear to you to be hiding anything, or concerned about what your investigation might find?"

Ambrose objected. "Counsel is asking this witness to speculate as to what the defendant might have been doing."

"No, Your Honor," Patsy said in the tone of a genteel Southern gentleman. "I'm asking this seasoned police detective if my client did anything at any time during his investigation that this seasoned police detective interpreted to be evasive, or an attempt to hide evidence."

"Overruled," Judge Hung said. "You may answer the question, Detective."

"I did not interpret anything the defendant did to be evasive or an attempt to hide any evidence."

"Did he appear to you to be upset or distraught?"

"He appeared to be upset. I can't say whether he was distraught or not."

Patsy cross-examined Rossi for another fifteen minutes, and each question brought an internal smile to Keera's face. As he wrapped up, he asked questions they would need to highlight JP Harrison's testimony when Keera called witnesses to present the defense's case. Patsy asked Rossi open-ended questions, though this was cross-examination, because he knew the answers and he knew Rossi to be a straight shooter, honest. "Detective Rossi, what was the temperature that Sunday, June fourth?"

"Hot," Rossi said, garnering smiles from the jury.

Patsy also smiled. "Not exactly a meteorologist, are you?" he said, garnering more smiles—a trick he had taught Keera. *If the witness gets the jury to smile, go with it.*

"Hardly."

"You did record the temperature in your report. Do you need time to check?"

"No. It was 106 degrees outside."

"Was it hot inside the house?"

"Very."

"Hotter than 106 degrees?"

"I don't know, but it was hot."

"Did the LaRussas have air-conditioning?"

"They did, but Mr. LaRussa said it should have kicked on automatically."

"Did you ask him why the air-conditioning did not kick on?"

"Someone turned off the switch on the control panel."

"Mr. LaRussa told you he didn't turn it off, didn't he?"

"He said he did not."

Patsy pulled up a picture of the burn mark on the oven door found by JP Harrison. "Do you recognize this photograph?"

"It looks like the oven door in the kitchen."

"And what is that dark mark on the handle?"

Rossi looked more closely, then said, "I don't know."

"Did you observe water on the kitchen floor?"

"I did."

"How much?"

"I don't know. A glass was also on the floor, so perhaps eight ounces. I don't really know the quantity."

"Did the CSI detectives at the crime scene provide you, as the lead detective, with an analysis of the water found on the kitchen floor?"

"An analysis?"

"Yes. A chemical analysis."

"Of the water?"

"That's right."

"I'm not sure," Rossi said, smiling.

"There was water on the kitchen counter, wasn't there?"

"There was. Some."

"How do you explain it?"

"I don't know."

"Was there a candle on the counter?"

"Yes."

"Was it lit?"

"Yes."

"Do you know why it was there?"

"I didn't. Not at that time. I subsequently learned that Mrs. LaRussa lit scented candles, that the aroma calmed her."

Patsy left the answer alone. "Did you reach any conclusions, based on the CSI reports, as to where the shooter stood at the time he or she discharged the weapon?"

"The shooter was behind Anne LaRussa. He held the gun barrel between three to five feet from the back of her head."

"Did you stand three to five feet behind Anne LaRussa to determine if that position was feasible for the shooter?"

"I don't understand."

"Let me illustrate." Patsy put up a photograph previously authenticated and taken by the CSI team, which included measurements. "How far is the kitchen counter from the deceased's wheelchair in this photograph?"

Rossi didn't immediately answer. He looked at the sketch. "It appears to be three feet, six inches."

"How wide is that counter?"

"Forty-eight inches."

"So the shooter, you concluded, had to have been standing on the far side of the counter. Here," Patsy said, using a baton. "That's seven feet, three inches, isn't it?"

Rossi smiled. "It is. However, the shooter could have reached his arm across the counter and leaned into the shot before he pulled the trigger."

"Yes, he or she might have done that," Patsy said, as if the answer made sense. Then he pounced, subtly. "Did you find any blood spatter on Vince LaRussa's clothing, his jacket, or the sleeve of his shirt, which led you to believe he had reached his arm across the counter and discharged the weapon?"

Rossi paused. "No, we did not."

"How often in your experience do shooters leave the murder weapon behind at the crime scene, Detective?"

"Not often."

"Can you recall such a case?"

"Just one," Rossi said. He explained the case he and Keera had worked where he found a gun in the woods when the killer dropped it upon fleeing.

"So this is unusual," Patsy said.

"Very."

"You indicated the shooter was likely standing in this location," Patsy said, again using the pointer. "Where was the gun found?"

Rossi pointed to the location alongside the wheelchair. Patsy put up another photograph on the computer monitor. "Wouldn't the shooter have dropped the weapon at his or her side and left out the front door?"

Rossi saw this trap or thought he did. "He could have tossed the gun over the counter."

"Tossed?" Patsy said, his voice rising. "Tossed a loaded 9-millimeter handgun four or five feet onto a tile floor?" Skepticism dripped from each word.

"Yes," Rossi said.

Patsy made a face like he didn't believe it. "That would be very dangerous, wouldn't it?"

"It could be, yes," Rossi said.

"A lot more dangerous than simply letting the gun slip from the hand to the ground, correct?"

"But the person might not have been thinking clearly. He may have panicked."

Patsy smiled. He'd goaded Rossi into a mistake. "This shooter, whom the State has hypothesized shot Anne LaRussa with premeditation and forethought, using an untraceable gun, who either wore gloves or took the time to wipe the gun clean of fingerprints and DNA, then was smart enough to not only change clothes, but to change into clothes identical to the clothes he wore to a charity event that night, and somehow discarded his other clothes, this very deliberate shooter was *so careless* that he simply tossed a loaded gun over the counter onto the tile floor? Is that what you're saying?"

"He could have walked around the counter to ensure Anne LaRussa was dead, and placed the gun on the floor," Rossi said.

"The husband, who knows his wife's hands are crippled, walks around the counter and places the gun on the floor to, what, make it look like a suicide? That doesn't make any sense, does it, Detective Rossi?" Patsy asked.

Rossi shook his head. "Or just to ensure she was dead."

"Anne LaRussa was incapable of holding and firing a handgun, wasn't she?"

"That's what the evidence indicated."

"Her husband would have presumably known that, wouldn't he?"

"Objection," Ambrose said standing. "Calls for speculation."

"Overruled."

"I assume he would have," Rossi said.

"So walking around the counter and dropping the gun would have been idiotic; wouldn't it?"

"People do idiotic things in high-stress situations."

"Did Vince LaRussa strike you as an idiot?"

"No."

"When you interviewed Vince LaRussa, did he at any time indicate to you that he believed his wife committed suicide?"

"No."

"He didn't tell you his wife was talking about killing herself?"

"No."

Patsy paused here, making a face like Rossi's answers were puzzling. Then he shifted gears. "Other than Mr. LaRussa, what other suspects did you consider?"

"We looked at a number of other potential suspects."

"Can you name them for me?"

"Syd Evans and Dr. Lisa Bennet, because of the

close proximity of their visits to the shooting."

Patsy stood for a moment as if considering his notes. He wasn't. He wanted the jury to consider what Rossi had just said, allowing Keera to argue the police, too, had doubt. After a beat he said, "Did Dr. Lisa Bennet purchase the ghost gun found at the site?"

"We found no evidence she did," Rossi said.

"Because that is the purpose of a ghost gun, isn't it? To not leave behind a paper trail?"

"That can be, yes."

"So she could have purchased the gun but there's just no paper trail that she did?"

"There's no paper trail."

"No paper trail Vince LaRussa did either, is there?"

"No."

"Did you verify that Anne LaRussa remained alive when Dr. Bennet left the house that Sunday night at 7:30 p.m.?"

"There wasn't any way to verify it."

"Couldn't verify that either, huh? So it's possible Anne LaRussa was not alive when Dr. Bennet left the house that night."

Ambrose shot to his feet. "Calls for this witness to speculate."

"Sustained," Judge Hung said.

"No videotape inside the house, is there?" Patsy asked.

"No."

"You just assumed Anne LaRussa remained alive, didn't you?"

"We did."

"Hmmm," Patsy said. Then he thanked Rossi, though he did not excuse him, in case the defense decided to call Rossi during the defense's case in chief.

As he walked back to counsel table, Patsy gave Keera a wry smile and whispered, "Let them call another witness out of order to screw with my daughter."

Ambrose made his way to the lectern. "Detective Rossi, did Mr. LaRussa tell you he had looked at the security tape prior to your arrival to try to determine who might have come to the home while he was at the charitable function?"

"No. He didn't say that he did."

"He didn't tell you that the Collinses' attorney, Syd Evans, or that Anne's doctor, Lisa Bennet, had come to the home while he was away."

"He didn't say that. No."

"Did you find it odd that a man with a security system and cameras comes home to, at least according to him, find his wife shot, but didn't look at the security footage to possibly determine who had come to the home?"

Keera almost objected that the question was leading, but she refrained, knowing Rossi would not give Ambrose the answer he wanted. Keera could argue in closing that LaRussa's not immediately looking at the tape proved he hadn't been trying to determine what he could and could not get away with, but rather had been a man in shock.

"I didn't think about that," Rossi said. "I was focused on securing the crime scene and gathering as much evidence as possible."

"Counsel for the defense asked if you'd considered other suspects, and you said Syd Evans and Dr. Bennet because they both arrived at the house Sunday evening. Did you eventually dismiss Dr. Bennet as a suspect?"

"We did."

"Why?"

"Dr. Bennet said Anne LaRussa accused her of cheating with her husband for the first time that Sunday night. That being the case, there would have been no reason for Dr. Bennet to have purchased a ghost gun and brought it to the house that night. Dr. Bennet would not have had any motive to kill Anne LaRussa at that time." Ambrose had, as Keera had predicted, driven a big truck through the argument that no evidence existed that Anne had threatened Lisa Bennet before that Sunday night.

Ambrose sat, and to Keera's surprise Patsy stood and moved to the podium.

"You accepted Dr. Bennet's statement that

354

Anne LaRussa didn't accuse her of cheating until Sunday night and therefore Dr. Bennet had no reason to buy the gun before that moment?" Patsy said.

"Yes."

"What if Dr. Bennet lied?" Patsy said. "You would have been wrong to accept her word, wouldn't you?"

"Possibly, but we had no indication she lied," Rossi said.

"Which is precisely what the liar intends, isn't it?" Patsy said.

Rossi looked to be biting his inner lip. "I suppose you could make that argument."

"More to the point, if Anne didn't accuse Dr. Bennet until that evening, then logic has it she didn't accuse her husband until that evening, and based on your reasoning, then Mr. LaRussa"—Patsy gestured to Vince LaRussa, seated at counsel table—"also had no reason to buy a ghost gun before then, did he?"

Ambrose might have driven a truck through the argument, but Patsy had just driven a train engine through it, along with one hundred railcars and the caboose.

Ambrose stood. "Counsel is asking the witness to speculate," he said.

"Forgive me," Patsy said. "I certainly wouldn't want to be the one to ask the detective to speculate."

. . .

After a short break, during which Keera praised her father and Patsy deflected the applause, Ambrose called Dr. Lisa Bennet, and the courtroom grew silent as the bailiff exited the courtroom doors and returned with the tall, good-looking blonde doctor the jurors had already heard so much about from Patsy.

Bennet took the stand in a conservative brown suit and white blouse.

Ambrose gently took Bennet through preliminary matters such as meeting Anne LaRussa in college, and their continued friendship, before asking her the reason Anne had summoned her to the LaRussa home that Sunday night. Bennet stopped several times to dry her tears.

"And she accused you of having an affair with her husband?" Ambrose asked.

"She did."

"Did she have any evidence to support this accusation?"

"Anne had photographs of me and Vince together at a lunch on a restaurant patio."

Ambrose put the photographs on the screen one at a time, and Bennet authenticated them as the photographs given to her by Anne LaRussa. As Bennet did so, a thought crossed Keera's mind, one spurred by Patsy's cross-examination of Rossi. Why had Anne given Bennet the photographs? It didn't make any sense, did it?

356

Wouldn't Anne have wanted to show those same photographs to her husband, whom she allegedly confronted that same night? Vince LaRussa made no mention of having seen the photographs and seemed genuinely surprised when Bennet produced them at her home. The CSI team that scoured the LaRussa house did not produce other copies.

"Were you and Vince LaRussa having an affair?" Ambrose asked.

"No."

"Did you tell Anne LaRussa she was mistaken?"

"Yes."

"How did you explain the photographs to Anne?"

"I told Anne that Vince and I met for lunch because I was worried Anne had become addicted to her prescription pain medications, and we were trying to come up with a plan to wean her off her drugs."

"What was her response?"

"She thought I was trying to change the subject. She didn't believe me."

"And what did you do?"

"There was nothing more I could do. Anne wouldn't listen to reason. I thought it best that I let her calm down and come back when Anne had a chance to talk to Vince."

"And when you left Anne LaRussa that evening, was she alive?"

"Very much so," Bennet said.

"Did you shoot Anne LaRussa, Dr. Bennet?"

"She was my best friend," Bennet said. "No. I did not shoot her."

Ambrose turned to Keera. "Your witness."

Keera wasted no time, asking her first question before she reached the podium. "You believed Anne had become addicted to her pain medication?"

"Yes."

"Your best friend?"

"Yes."

"The pain medication you prescribed for her?"

"Yes."

"You're an oncologist?"

"Yes."

"You treat cancer?"

"Yes."

"So you know about people in pain and the medications that can help them with that pain, like opioids, don't you?"

"I do."

"You know that opioids are highly addictive, don't you?"

"Yes."

Keera went through the varied and numerous dates on the bottles. "You continued to prescribe opioids time after time, though you believed your best friend was becoming addicted; didn't you?"

Bennet became less subdued and more combative. "Because Anne was in pain. Because I felt incredibly sorry for her, and for what she had been through. Because I didn't realize right away that Anne was becoming addicted. Because you don't cut off an addicted person cold turkey. You have to develop a plan to safely and effectively wean them from the drug." Bennet blotted tears with her Kleenex. "I didn't want to see Anne in any more pain," she said, tears rolling down her cheeks. "I watched my husband die in so much pain; I just couldn't endure seeing my best friend go through something similar."

"You thought it would be better if she was addicted to her opioids?"

"No," Bennet said, her voice more forceful but her tears also more prevalent.

"You're a single mother of three daughters; aren't you?"

"Yes."

"Their sole provider since your husband's death?"

"Yes."

"Your medical license can be suspended for willfully overprescribing opioids; can't it?"

"It's a possibility, but I didn't believe I was overprescribing Anne."

"But if Anne reported you to the Washington Medical Commission for overprescribing opioids, that could be a basis for you to have your license suspended, couldn't it?"

"Anne wouldn't do that. She wasn't vindictive in that way."

"Not the Anne you knew before her accident, perhaps, but perhaps the paranoid, depressed, addicted Anne whom you have described, the Anne who hired a private investigator because she believed you and her husband were having an affair. That Anne could certainly be vindictive; couldn't she?"

Bennet hung her head. "I don't know," she said softly. "I don't know."

CHAPTER 30

Over the next several trial days, Ambrose methodically called witnesses, including Anne LaRussa's father to testify about the reason for the prenuptial agreement, his daughter's accident, and the difficulty family members had speaking to Anne during the last few weeks of her life, outside the presence of her husband. "Seems like Vince was always around," he said. Patsy cross-examined, one father to another, and struck just the right chord. Anne's father admitted that his daughter had never indicated that she and Vince were having marital problems.

Ambrose then called CSI detectives and other expert witnesses to testify as to fingerprint analysis, DNA, and ballistics. Keera and Patsy split the workload cross-examining the expert forensic witnesses, establishing that neither Vincent LaRussa's fingerprints nor his DNA was found on the gun. Ballistics simply confirmed the gun found on the floor was a 9 millimeter, recently fired, and that the striations on the bullet matched the gun barrel and the shell casing located on the floor. They also confirmed that no blood spatter was found on Vince LaRussa's clothing.

Ambrose played the crime scene video, and

several jurors cringed or averted their eyes. Ambrose did not ask about, and none of the State's experts testified to, finding the burn mark on the oven door handle, or that the water on the floor tested positive for potassium nitrate. In short, his experts would not have passed Mr. Cobalt's class. They had not come up with a coherent theory to explain all the variables.

Unfortunately, Harrison and his inventor friend wouldn't have passed either. They were working on yet another theory to explain the evidence but told Keera something remained missing.

Keera, her sisters, and Patsy worked late nights together. Keera often sat in Patsy's office discussing trial strategy, the way they had once discussed chess strategy, the strengths and weaknesses of each of Keera's upcoming opponents. She hardly remembered her father this way—his mind clear, his wit and humor sharp. Ambrose had brought out the Brawler. Her father's cross-examinations of expert witnesses from whom there seemed little to gain, like his cross-examination of Rossi, were works of art. That freed up Keera to focus on the more demanding witnesses and strategize about their case in chief as Ambrose neared the end of the State's case.

Keera knew Ambrose took pleasure in calling witnesses out of order and that Judge Hung would have no sympathy for her. He had messengers deliver bullshit motions at the end of the day intended to make busywork and keep Keera from focusing on the next day's witnesses. It didn't. All it did was piss off Ella, and a pissed-off Ella was a real bitch, and Keera meant that in the most flattering way.

Keera would return to her office and find her sister at her desk, smiling. "What does that asshole have for me today?" she'd ask. Then she'd dig in and go to work. Even Maggie stayed late, typing and formatting the motions and responses, proofreading drafts, and ensuring everything was filed in a timely manner. She called in meals, and they ate together as father and daughters, not Patrick Duggan & Associates. Patsy Duggan and his daughters. On occasion their mother stayed and ate with them. Maggie didn't ask for overtime, and she didn't complain about the long hours, and Keera began to understand that it had to have been extremely hard on Maggie, being the middle daughter. Her complaints all these years were just a cry to be noticed, to feel useful, to be treated as part of the team and not looked upon as the ugly duckling incapable of doing the things her two sisters could do.

Ambrose did what even the Sunday dinners did not. He'd brought them together, gave them a common enemy, made them a family who stood up for one another, and who cared for one another.

They won more motions than they lost and, eventually, Judge Hung, tiring of Ambrose's game, told him in court one morning, before she brought in the jury, that she didn't want to see another motion unless he brought the matter up with her before she dismissed counsel at the end of the day.

At night, Keera returned home and, depending on how late she arrived, Patsy was usually up for one or two chess moves. She didn't tell Patsy she knew his alter ego, the Dark Knight. She sensed the anonymous interaction was important to him, so they could play chess player against chess player, not father against daughter. Keera didn't want to spoil the game either. She feared he would ease up. She needed the challenge to remain sharp.

On his thirtieth move, Patsy slid his king to f1. Keera's bishop, whom she had hidden in the corner, came out of hiding to take his pawn at f3—a sacrificial move. Patsy had no alternative but to use his pawn to take her bishop. When he did, Keera's queen then took the pawn, leaving Patsy's king exposed. The only question now was whether his king could run.

On Tuesday of the second week, Frank Rossi sat at counsel table listening as Ambrose questioned medical examiner Arthur Litchfield about his autopsy and his findings. Ambrose wanted to finish the State's case with a definitive statement from the medical examiner that Anne LaRussa's death had been a homicide.

Litchfield presented himself well in a tailored navy-blue suit, and he looked and sounded professional. His credentials were solid.

"And based upon the body's rectal temperature, what was your estimated time of death?" Ambrose asked. Rossi had heard the question before and knew the answer, which was all about letting Litchfield look brilliant and honest to the jury.

"There is no single factor that will accurately indicate the time of physiological death, absent an eyewitness or a tape that captures the fatal incident. It is always a best guess, an educated estimate. The sooner after death that I can examine the body, the more accurate my estimate will be."

"And what did you estimate to be the time of death when you examined Anne LaRussa?" Ambrose asked.

"The estimated time of death based upon the rectal temperature was between six and nine thirty in the evening," Litchfield said, and he explained the mathematical calculation used to determine this estimate.

"You weren't able to be more precise?" Ambrose asked.

"Not given the temperature inside the house,"

Litchfield said, and Ambrose again allowed him to explain that the deceased lost core body temperature more slowly in such a warm environment, preventing a more precise time of death.

"What about other factors?"

"Rigor mortis and lividity were consistent with my estimated time of death based upon the rectal temperature."

Ambrose asked Litchfield to explain both concepts to the jury, and Litchfield took the next few minutes to do so, and how each also confirmed time of death.

"Let's turn to page twelve of your medical examination," Ambrose said.

This was where Rossi expected things to get more interesting. Keera and her father had done their best, but Rossi thought it a tall order for them to convince even a single juror that Lisa Bennet had shot and killed Anne LaRussa. The motive simply wasn't strong enough or certain enough—the potential impact to her medical license. Ambrose would argue Keera's theory was a desperate ploy, that Keera was grasping at straws, that Bennet was a cancer doctor, a person who helped those grievously ill, some dying. He'd argue that someone so compassionate would not take her best friend's life because of an accusation. Jurors could much more readily understand the potential loss of millions of dollars as a motive for murder, putting LaRussa back squarely in the crosshairs.

Something else didn't sit right with Rossi, though, and he had struggled with it for some time. Bennet was a cancer doctor. According to Litchfield, Anne LaRussa would have died from terminal cancer within weeks. Why hadn't Bennet simply stated she provided Anne LaRussa the opioids because she was in pain from her cancer? Why hadn't Ambrose prepped her to say it? It seemed a simple way for him to defuse Keera's attempt at a character assassination. Keera would likely use the information to argue that Vince LaRussa had no motive to kill a spouse he knew would die in a matter of weeks. But Ambrose could make the same argument about Bennet. Why would Bennet kill her best friend if Anne LaRussa was going to die anyway?

Was it possible Anne didn't know she had cancer, meaning neither Vince LaRussa nor Lisa Bennet had known? If so, that left them right back where Rossi had started: Vince LaRussa killed his wife fearing she'd take the millions he had made.

"You follow the guidelines recommended by the World Health Organization in defining the underlying cause of death, do you not?" Ambrose asked Litchfield.

"I do, yes," Litchfield said.

"And how did you define the underlying cause of death in this instance?"

"The victim was shot in the back of the head from approximately three to five feet with a 9-millimeter bullet, and she died from the concomitant trauma and loss of blood and oxygen that shut down vital organs."

"Did you note any other wound you believe contributed to the decedent's death?"

"No."

"Did you note any disease, abnormality, injury, or poisoning you believe contributed to the cause of death?"

Rossi's ears perked up, but Ambrose had been slick in his question, relating the disease to cause of death. "I did not," Litchfield said.

Ambrose had chosen not to address the cancer. He would argue, through Litchfield's testimony, that the cancer had not contributed to Anne LaRussa's cause of death and was, therefore, irrelevant.

"And did you reach a conclusion as to whether Anne LaRussa's death was accidental, a suicide, from natural causes, or a homicide?" Ambrose asked, again duty bound.

"It was a homicide," Litchfield said.

Ambrose paused as if considering another question. He wasn't. He'd leave the testimony on this high point. As Rossi predicted, Ambrose turned to Keera Duggan. "Your witness," he said.

Keera made her way to the podium and started deliberately. She went through Litchfield's report with him, pointing out some minor inconsistencies.

"You don't know for certain whether Anne LaRussa was capable of holding a handgun, do you?"

"Not with certainty," Litchfield said.

"Was she capable of holding a glass of water, Dr. Litchfield?"

"I don't know," Litchfield said.

Rossi waited, but Keera did not show Litchfield the photographs of the broken glass beside the wheelchair. He concluded Keera did not want to give Litchfield a chance to explain. Rather, she would argue in her closing to the jury that the medical examiner was incorrect about the victim's ability to hold a glass.

"Let's talk about core body temperature. You indicated that it was hot inside the house, is that correct?"

"Over a hundred degrees."

"And if the ambient room temperature is that warm, the deceased loses body temperature slower than if the temperature in the room was more temperate?"

"That is correct."

"So, in this instance, the deceased lost body temperature more slowly."

"That's true."

"Meaning, she could have been dead longer than the estimate you provided."

"That's why I estimated she'd died between six and nine thirty that Sunday night," Litchfield said.

Meaning Bennet could have killed Anne LaRussa, at least based on the estimated time of death. Keera asked questions for several more minutes. Rossi kept waiting for her to bring up Anne LaRussa's cancer.

"Thank you, Doctor Litchfield," Keera said to Rossi's surprise.

"Is Dr. Litchfield excused?" Judge Hung asked.

"Subject to his being available should the defense call him in its case in chief," Keera said.

"Dr. Litchfield, you are excused but are to remain available should the defense seek to recall you during its case in chief."

Rossi couldn't understand Keera's strategy. Did she not want to bring up the subject of cancer because she could not prove Anne LaRussa committed suicide and feared Ambrose would argue the defense was just throwing theories on the wall and hoping one stuck with the jurors? Perhaps she thought her argument that Bennet had pulled the trigger the stronger of the two, especially if Anne had not known she had cancer and therefore neither did LaRussa nor Bennet.

It didn't make sense. How could Anne not have known? And if she did know, why would she have kept that information from her husband?

And how could Bennet, LaRussa's best friend and an oncologist, not have known?

Ambrose stood, drawing Rossi's thoughts back to the courtroom. "Your honor, the State rests."

"Very well. Ladies and gentlemen of the jury, it is now almost four thirty. We are going to adjourn trial for the day. In the morning, the defense will begin presenting its case."

Judge Hung provided her routine admonishment that the jury members not speak to one another nor with anyone else about the case or the evidence, and that they not read any newspapers or watch any news reports. Then she excused them.

As counsel and the spectators stood, the jurors exited to the jury room at the back of the courtroom, and Rossi looked across the aisle at Keera. She had her hand on Vince LaRussa's shoulder, whispering in his ear. Her father, Patsy Duggan, was putting away binders, notepads, and computers.

Ambrose and Richie gathered their belongings and left the courtroom together. The State having rested its case in chief, Rossi did not need to meet with them. He had a free evening. Something didn't sit right with him. He thought back weeks, to when Ambrose made a point of coming to Police Headquarters to discuss the ME's report, something he had never done before.

Rossi started around counsel table for the door, then stopped. He looked again to Keera as she walked out the door. Rossi recalled the phone call he had received from Ambrose asking if he'd turned over the police file, specifically the autopsy report.

Rossi looked to Judge Hung's clerk standing in the well moving papers around and felt the twinge of butterflies in his stomach. A premonition he had learned to trust.

"Excuse me," he said to the clerk. "I wonder if I could take a look at the State's last exhibit? The medical examiner's autopsy report. My copy is back at Police Headquarters and I was hoping to avoid going back to my desk. You know how it is. You go back to your desk with daylight and people will find a million different things for you to do. Ending the day early was an unexpected surprise. I hope to get home and enjoy the evening."

The clerk smiled. "You had me at people finding a million things for you to do," she said and handed Rossi the multipage document. "Here you go."

"Thanks," he said. "I'll only be a minute. I won't keep you."

He opened the ME's report to the section in which he was most interested, cause of death.

CHAPTER 31

August 16, 2023

Wednesday, after Keera and Patsy had put on eight trial witnesses in rapid succession, she worked late preparing to call their final witnesses and adding bullet-point notes to her closing argument. She faced reality. She'd have to argue reasonable doubt and hope to convince at least one juror that Anne LaRussa, angry and paranoid, had threatened Bennet's medical license, and that Bennet had shot her. The problem as to when and why Bennet had purchased the gun still existed, but that problem also existed for the State's case against Vince LaRussa.

Was it enough to create reasonable doubt?

Keera didn't know.

Judge Hung had made it clear she wanted to send the case to the jury at the end of the day Thursday, so the jurors would have Friday to deliberate.

When Keera arrived at home she went through her usual routine, checking her surroundings before exiting her car and putting her keys in her right hand before walking to the front door. She stepped inside. Her shoes found the mail that had been slipped through the mail slot.

After deadbolting the door, she scooped up the letters and magazines and dumped the stack on the dining room table, then went into the kitchen and poured herself a glass of cold water from the pitcher in her fridge. The Chinese food they ate for dinner at the office had left her feeling bloated and dehydrated.

She glanced at her computer, but she didn't want to start playing. Besides, she was certain Patsy, who left the office with her, would also be too tired to play. She decided to get a good night's sleep and get to the office early to make final preparations.

Early Thursday morning, Keera made a strong cup of coffee and took a colder than usual shower to jump-start her body and her mind. She drank her coffee at the dining room table while sifting through the mail, which included a 9-by-12-inch manila envelope amid the junk. It had no mailing address or return address. No stamps. Someone had slipped the envelope through her mail slot.

She thought immediately of Jack Worthing, and a chill ran up her spine. Her address was not a public record. Had someone followed her?

She flipped the envelope over, pulled open the tab, then removed the multipage document. She was initially confused, but as she read, her confusion gave way to astonishment.

Ambrose had just made a mistake, possibly a fatal mistake.

Time to attack.

Minutes before 9:00 a.m. Keera and Patsy huddled in a vacant room at the King County Courthouse, talking on Keera's cell phone to JP Harrison, whom she had tried but failed to reach before leaving home. The document slipped through the mail slot had been Arthur Litchfield's autopsy report, though not the one admitted into evidence. This earlier report indicated Anne LaRussa had been dying from pancreatic cancer. The information was exciting enough on its own, but in Keera's mind, it was also the missing piece of evidence Harrison and his expert needed. When that domino fell, others would also fall, until, Keera believed, she would have a theory of which Mr. Cobalt would approve.

"The potassium nitrate in the water on the floor and in the shavings taken from the oven door handle has to be related somehow; doesn't it?" She was rushing, but she was also running out of time.

"It's a valid theory," Harrison said.

Keera read aloud from the source on her laptop. " 'Potassium nitrate has been used as a constituent for several different purposes, including food preservatives, fertilizers, tree stump removal, rocket propellants, and fireworks.' What does every firework need to explode?"

"Gunpowder?"

"Without you holding it," she said.

"A fuse."

"The firework has to have a fuse. We found the possible source for the potassium nitrate. And you can make a fuse out of cotton string. It's why we found cotton fibers in the water."

"You've lost me, love. Anne LaRussa died of a gunshot. Not an explosion."

"I'm just sticking to Mr. Cobalt's principle. A theory has to encompass every piece of evidence. We found the possible source of the potassium nitrate. We needed to find the cotton. You can make a fuse out of cotton string. I pulled up a YouTube video and sent you the link. Take a look."

"I'm looking at it now," Harrison said.

"We don't have time at the moment to watch the entire thing. The video shows you how to make a fuse out of cotton string and potassium nitrate," she said.

"I'm still not following, Keera."

The autopsy report had changed Keera's thinking about the case. Was it too late for her to change theories? Maybe. But she had deemed the risk less than the risk of the jury not accepting that Lisa Bennet had shot Anne LaRussa, and she decided to take the chance. Her father certainly would.

"Vince told me Anne LaRussa was a good cook after the accident."

"Okay."

Keera had thought of the first-Sunday-of-the-month dinner her family had shared, of the stuffed pork loin sitting on the kitchen counter looking like it might explode, were it not for the string holding it together. "My mother is also a good cook, and she will tell you every good cook has string in the kitchen. Cotton string."

"String?" Harrison asked, still not seeing the connection.

"You use it to tie meat together, to make sausage, to tie the legs of chickens and turkeys after you stuff them. We found the source of the potassium nitrate. Maybe we've found the source of the cotton."

In the YouTube video Keera had watched, the cotton string was soaked in the potassium nitrate, then laid out in a grid pattern on a baking sheet and dried in an oven set on a low temperature. Once the string dried, it could be lit with a match, and it burned like a fuse. It was why that morning when they found the stump remover in the shed at the LaRussa house, it had both scared and intrigued her. Intrigued because she felt as if they were on to something. Scared because she feared they might never figure out exactly what that was.

Maybe she had figured it out.

"Again—" Harrison started.

Keera cut him off. "I know. Anne died of a gun-shot wound, not from a bomb exploding." She considered her watch. She was out of time. "I'm just sticking to Mr. Cobalt's principle. Watch the YouTube video, then read the ME's report I just sent to you. Anne LaRussa was dying of cancer. Ambrose withheld that report. She had four to six weeks to live. Who would have known this?" She didn't wait for Harrison to answer. "Dr. Lisa Bennet, an oncologist and Anne's best friend. When I crossed Bennet, she said . . ." Patsy handed Keera the trial transcript opened to the tagged page, Bennet's testimony highlighted. "She said, quote, 'I just couldn't endure seeing my best friend go through something similar.' End quote. Bennet also had the photographs of her and Vince together. It bugged me but I wasn't certain why. Now I know. Why wouldn't Anne have kept them to show Vince? CSI makes no mention of finding copies of the photo-graphs, meaning Anne gave the only copies to Bennet. Why?" Again, Keera didn't wait for a response. "Because she wanted the prosecutor and us to have them, that's why. And you and I both agreed that Anne LaRussa could not have obtained the tree stump remover from that top shelf in the shed, nor could she have maneuvered the lawn on her own. We both agreed some-one helped her. It wasn't the gardener. It was

Bennet. Bennet helped Anne take her own life."

"How though? Why?"

"I don't know how, exactly, JP. She somehow created a fuse using string and stump remover. Maybe it wasn't to ignite something. Maybe she used the string to pull the trigger of the gun, but wanted to get rid of the string after the fact to make it look like Vince shot her. That's what I need you and your engineering friend to figure out, and fast." She looked at her watch. "I need you to get to the LaRussa house and look through the kitchen drawers for cotton string. If you find it, figure out how Anne LaRussa rigged a ghost gun using string to make it look like she was shot."

"We need time, Keera."

"Unfortunately, we don't have it. I'm supposed to close end of the day. And I need to follow up my direct examination of you with a demonstration you come up with to fully impact the jury."

"I don't know what to tell you," Harrison said. "The earliest we could bring something to court, if we can even figure it out, would be tomorrow, Friday. Can you filibuster with one of your witnesses?"

Patsy checked his watch. "Go," he said to Keera. "You get to court so you don't piss off Judge Hung any more than you're already going to. I'll deal with this."

"I need time, Patsy."

"At the moment, you need to get into that courtroom before Judge Hung sanctions you. Let me handle buying you some time."

Keera exited the conference room and entered the courtroom. Judge Hung had already taken the bench. Ambrose, Richie, and Rossi turned to look at Keera as she entered, as did Vince LaRussa, seated alone at the defense table, two marshals stationed nearby.

"You realize what time it is, Counsel?" Judge Hung said as Keera took her place.

"I apologize," Keera said.

"I will not keep my jury waiting," Judge Hung said. "Do you understand?"

"I do. And, again, I apologize."

"Is Mr. Duggan joining us this morning?"

"Not this morning. No."

Judge Hung's eyes narrowed, and she gave Keera an inquisitive look. "Then let's get started."

Keera remained standing. "I have a matter to discuss with the court."

Judge Hung looked like someone just about to eat her favorite meal when the fork was pulled from her hand. "What kind of matter?"

"I wish to call another witness this afternoon. A matter came up this morning, and I wish to call Dr. Arthur Litchfield to return to the stand. I called Dr. Litchfield this morning and advised him of the defense's intent. He is available and waiting in the hallway."

Ambrose rose. "We were given no notice of this. Counsel didn't bother to tell us last night or this morning."

"The change wasn't necessitated until this morning, Your Honor," Keera said. "I apologize to the State and to the court, but given that the State has already presented Dr. Litchfield in its case in chief, I fail to see any prejudice. And, as Your Honor said in chambers, things in trial can't always be predicted, including calling witnesses out of order. Both sides had to be prepared to move forward, without complaint."

Judge Hung looked to be choking on her own words. She rocked back in her chair several times before she turned her attention to the State. "Mr. Ambrose, you can make an objection if you like, but we will proceed as Ms. Duggan has requested. Doctor Litchfield is a State witness, so I fail to see any prejudice. And the State has called witnesses out of order multiple times. You will simply have to adapt, as I did warn *both* counsel."

With that, Judge Hung asked the bailiff to bring in the jury. When they were seated, she said, "Ms. Duggan, you may continue with the defense's case."

Keera recalled the CSI detectives, nitpicking small items and stalling as much as she dared.

She put on friends of the LaRussas whom JP Harrison had found, and they testified that neither Vince nor Anne had ever indicated the couple had marital problems, or that one or the other was having an affair. They spoke glowingly of Vince and said he showed great empathy and compassion for Anne following her accident. They had gone so far as to invest their money with LWM.

Ambrose objected frequently that the witnesses' testimony was irrelevant, or hearsay, and Judge Hung sustained several of those objections. Again, Keera did her best to string out the testimony and kill time.

Early in the afternoon, during a recess, Keera stepped outside to find JP Harrison in the hallway. He wore his best blue suit. "We're working on it, Keera. We're testing some ideas based on the YouTube video you sent, but we don't have anything definitive yet. I'm sorry. You're going to have to ask for more time."

She wasn't going to get it. "I'll ask, but be prepared to go on after Litchfield."

"Can you filibuster?"

"I'll do the best I can. Where is Patsy?"

"I don't know," Harrison said. "I thought he was inside the courtroom."

Keera looked down the hall, but she didn't have time to hunt Patsy down. She went back inside the courtroom and the trial resumed. "The defense calls Dr. Arthur Litchfield, the State's medical examiner," Keera said.

Litchfield entered the courtroom looking like he hadn't changed clothes since he last testified. He sat and adjusted his glasses with the ball of his thumb.

Keera moved to the lectern.

"Dr. Litchfield, as part of your duties you drew the decedent's blood and did a toxicology screening, did you not?"

"Yes, I did."

"Can you tell the jury what that toxicology screening revealed?"

Ambrose rose. "Objection. This has been gone over in the State's case in chief."

"It has, Ms. Duggan," Judge Hung said.

"It's only to lay a foundation, Your Honor. I'll be quick."

"Do so."

"Can you answer the question, Dr. Litchfield?"

"The screening revealed high levels of opioids, specifically oxycodone and hydrocodone."

"Which are also known as Oxycontin and Vicodin."

"Yes."

"Highly addictive?"

"They can be, yes."

"Was the toxicity sufficient to kill the deceased?"

"No. Not in my opinion."

"What is the primary reason opioids are prescribed?"

"They're used to relieve pain."

"Would that include the type of pain persons afflicted with terminal cancer might experience?"

Ambrose shot to his feet. "Objection, Your Honor. Counsel is asking this witness to speculate. There are any number of reasons for the use of—"

Hung raised a hand. "Dr. Litchfield is an expert witness and a pathologist. The objection is overruled."

Ambrose's objection confirmed what Keera had already suspected. She addressed Litchfield, believing he would tell the truth, maybe even be eager to do so. "Do you need me to repeat the question, Doctor?" Keera asked.

"No. I recall it. The answer is yes, opioids are prescribed to relieve pain such as experienced by individuals suffering from cancer."

"Were you curious why Anne LaRussa had high levels of opioids in her system?"

"No," Litchfield said.

"Why not?" Keera asked.

"My job was to determine the cause of death. I concluded Anne LaRussa died from a gunshot to the back of her skull and the associated loss of blood that resulted in the shutdown of vital organs, not an overdose."

"Was Anne LaRussa suffering from cancer?"

"Yes."

Keera felt her heartbeat quicken. "Do you know what type?"

Ambrose was on his feet again. "Objection, Your Honor. This witness is not an oncologist."

"Your honor," Keera said. "The State established that Dr. Litchfield is a board-certified pathologist and specializes in the diagnosis of disease and the causes of death."

"Overruled," Judge Hung said. Keera could tell the judge was interested. "You may answer, Dr. Litchfield."

"She had metastasized pancreatic cancer."

"When you say 'metastasized,' would you explain that to the jurors?"

"The cancer appeared to have started in her pancreas. Regardless of where it started, it had spread to other organs as well as to her bones and her lymph nodes."

"Was Anne LaRussa's cancer terminal, Doctor?"

Ambrose again stood and objected that the question was beyond Litchfield's expertise. As Judge Hung overruled his objection, Keera thought of the line from *Hamlet*. *The man doth protest too much, methinks.* She hoped the jury thought the same thing.

"In my opinion, yes. Her cancer was terminal."

"In your opinion, based on your autopsy examination, and your experience as a board-certified pathologist, roughly how long did Anne LaRussa have to live?"

"Objection," Ambrose said.

"Overruled."

"In my opinion," Litchfield said. "Four to six weeks."

Keera walked back to counsel table and picked up Litchfield's report marked as an exhibit in the State's case. Vince LaRussa studied Keera. She had not had time to talk to him before trial that morning and tell him of this development. He looked both stunned and curious, and Keera concluded from his expression that he had not known his wife had terminal cancer. She asked the court clerk to provide the admitted exhibit to Litchfield. "Now, Dr. Litchfield, would you direct me to the place in your report where you set forth that Anne LaRussa had metastasized pancreatic cancer and would die in four to six weeks?"

"I can't."

"It is not in this report; is it?"

"No. It isn't."

"It was one of your findings upon performing your autopsy, was it not?"

"Yes, it was."

"But it wasn't set forth in your report?"

"Not in this report, no."

There was the opening Keera needed. "Is it identified in another report?"

Ambrose rose. "Objection, Your Honor. She's

386

asking this witness to speculate about what another report might contain."

"I'll be more specific," Keera said.

"Please do so," Judge Hung said.

"Did *you* identify metastasized pancreatic cancer in another report you prepared, Dr. Litchfield?"

"Yes," he said. "I did."

Keera paused to give the answer time to have maximum impact. "What report did you prepare that listed Anne LaRussa's pancreatic cancer?"

"I identified it in my original autopsy report."

"You listed that the deceased had terminal, metastasized, pancreatic cancer in your original autopsy report?"

"Yes."

"You prepared two autopsy reports?"

"Yes."

"More than two?"

"No."

"Do you normally prepare more than one autopsy report?"

"No."

"Then why is your finding, that the deceased had metastasized pancreatic cancer, not set forth in this document, State's Exhibit 126?"

"I was told to remove any reference to the cancer."

You could have heard a pin drop. The chairs of several jurors creaked as they leaned forward. "Who told you to remove that finding?"

"The prosecutor, Mr. Ambrose."

Keera paused, then turned and pointed to where Ambrose sat, trying to look nonplussed. But Keera knew him well enough to know from his clenched jawline and the dark pinpoints of his pupils that he was anything but. Ambrose was pissed. Pissed that someone had leaked the original report. Pissed that she had obtained it. Pissed that she had called him out in open court, at trial. And pissed that Litchfield's matter-of-fact manner of testifying only magnified that something nefarious had occurred. Ambrose's ego and his burning desire to beat Keera Duggan had pushed him to a colossal error in judgment. Keera didn't have to look at the jurors to know they were staring at Ambrose and wondering why he had gone to such an elaborate extent to cover up Anne LaRussa's cancer.

"Did the prosecutor say why he wanted you to take out the reference to cancer?"

Ambrose objected. "Your Honor, this goes to the State's preparation of this case for trial and is protected as work product."

"Not when the State made the statement to an expert witness, it is not," Keera said.

"Overruled," Hung said in a terse, unforgiving tone.

"Mr. Ambrose said that if the victim's cancer was not a cause or contributing factor in her death, he wanted me to remove the reference from my report."

Keera took a calculated risk with her next question, one she knew Patsy would take. "Have you ever, in your twenty-plus years as a medical examiner, been asked by the prosecuting attorney to remove a fact you noted in your autopsy report related to the decedent?"

"No."

"Then, I take it that this was unusual."

"Yes."

"Highly unusual?"

"Objection," Ambrose said, but it lacked vitality.

"Sustained."

"This was the first and only time?"

"Yes."

Keera considered her notes, but this was again to buy time for the jury to consider Litchfield's testimony, and also to filibuster, to the extent Judge Hung would allow it. After a long minute, Keera thanked Litchfield and passed the witness. As she moved back to counsel table, she looked to the courtroom doors, but Patsy did not walk through them.

Ambrose rose quickly and moved to the lectern. Hopefully he would ask a lot of questions and solve her timing problem. "Dr. Litchfield, in your opinion, did Anne LaRussa's metastasized, pancreatic cancer contribute in any way to the cause of her death?"

"No. Not in my opinion."

"And is it not true that in providing an opinion on the cause of death, if a disease or illness present is unrelated to and arises independently of the victim's cause of death, then it need not be reported?" Keera almost stood and objected that the question was leading, but in a split second she decided not to draw any more attention to the question. She also had an intuition about Litchfield. It was like playing roulette, watching the ball spin and bounce and hopefully land in the tray of a number she had bet on.

"It need not be reported," Litchfield said, "as a cause of death."

Ambrose looked relieved.

"But it should have been reported as a finding, nonetheless."

Keera lowered her head to hide her smile.

Recovering after a stunned pause, Ambrose said, "Does it in any way change your opinion that Anne LaRussa's death was a homicide?"

"No. It does not."

"Thank you," Ambrose said. He moved back to his seat looking both pissed and embarrassed.

Litchfield stepped down from the witness chair and crossed the floor to the courtroom doors. A bailiff manning the door opened it for him and he stepped out. Judge Hung looked to Keera. "Call your next witness, Counsel."

Keera stood, about to call JP Harrison, when the

courtroom door swung open and Patsy stumbled in, swaying from side to side.

Her heart seized.

"Keera," Patsy said, his volume too loud, his words slurred. "I'm here. Not to worry. I'm here, Your Honor. I'm here. I apologize for my tardiness."

Judge Hung looked initially stricken, quickly recovered, and banged her gavel. "The court will be in recess. Bailiff, escort the jurors to the jury room." She covered her microphone with the palm of her hand and spoke sotto voce to one of the bailiffs beside her desk, who moved quickly to remove Patsy from the courtroom.

When the jury had cleared the room, Judge Hung stood, rapped her gavel, and said, "I'll see counsel in my chambers."

Judge Hung devoted equal time ripping into Ambrose, then Keera. Patsy, Keera assumed, was in the hallway, likely waiting for Ella or Maggie to take him back to the office.

"Mr. Ambrose, in my forty years of both practice and as a sitting judge I have never heard of a prosecuting attorney doing what you did, getting an expert witness to manipulate his report."

"Your Honor, manipulation—" Ambrose began.

"Save your breath for the disciplinary board," Judge Hung said. "I expect you are going to need it." She turned to Keera. "Does the defense intend to move for a mistrial, Ms. Duggan? You are within your right to do so."

Not on your life, Keera thought. "No, Your Honor, the defense has no such intention."

Judge Hung then ripped into Keera for Patsy's disruption of her courtroom and her trial. She showed no compassion or empathy for Patsy. Keera didn't expect any. As Patsy had said, he'd made too many enemies in the prosecutor's office, many of whom had ascended to the bench, and they were eager for payback. After Judge Hung's rants, given the late hour, she dismissed the jury and recessed court until the morning, at which time she said she expected both sides to close.

Keera walked down the hill to Occidental Square. The sun was out and the street traffic light. People went about their day, going to restaurants, bars, making their way to public transportation and the journey home. She thought of the recent nights she and Ella and Maggie had shared with Patsy eating dinner; how nice it had been to be a family, to get along. For the first time since she could remember, the nights together didn't feel like the sword of Damocles hung over their heads, threatening to fall and decapitate them at any moment. But again, Patsy had tainted her memories. Her mother was wrong. The law was not Patsy's jealous mistress. That role belonged to alcohol.

Keera shook the thought to focus on the trial—where they were and where she needed to go. She had struck a significant blow against Miller Ambrose, possibly ruined his career, or at least his ambitions. She took no pride in it. He'd done it to himself. But she remained far from winning the case. She'd established that Anne LaRussa had terminal cancer, but Arthur Litchfield had still concluded her death a homicide, not suicide. And there was no guarantee Harrison and his engineer friend would come up with a viable theory to account for all the evidence to explain what Keera now believed had happened, or that the jurors would even accept an argument that Anne LaRussa committed suicide.

After the pasting by Judge Hung in chambers, Keera had spoken with LaRussa in the King County jail. He told her he had no idea Anne had terminal cancer. Neither Anne nor Lisa Bennet had said a word to him. She didn't have time to discuss Harrison's efforts to support her theory, but Litchfield's testimony that Anne was dying had been the piece of evidence missing. Had they known that, the defense would have proceeded with that understanding and tried to determine how she had committed suicide. The question of why she had done it, and likely with the intent to frame her husband, remained a mystery, one only Anne LaRussa and Dr. Lisa Bennet might ever know. She also decided not to tell LaRussa about her interview with Phillip McPherson, not believing it was of any significance to the trial.

She crossed Occidental Square, envious of the people seated at the tables enjoying an evening meal or drink or just the sunshine. The Paddy Wagon's patio was full, and the interior of the bar and restaurant humming. Liam caught sight of her and called out as she passed the wrought-iron railing, inviting her for a drink.

"I'm in trial," she said. "But I'll be done tomorrow. Maybe I'll stop by."

"I'm going to hold you to that," Liam said.

She would no doubt need a drink. And Liam would no doubt hold her to it.

She stepped into the elevator. A part of her hoped it fell three stories, but the elevator rose without incident and stopped on the third floor. Keera stepped out, sick to her stomach as she approached Patrick Duggan & Associates, attorneys at law. Maggie sat at her reception desk.

"You didn't go home?" Keera asked.

"No, I didn't go home. I had to go get Patsy from court. Just like old times."

"Maggie, I'm sorry."

"Can it, Keera. It is what it is."

Keera decided to let it be. "Where's Ella?"

"She's in Patsy's office trying to make sense of his trial materials while he's sleeping it off."

The door to Patsy's office was closed. Keera

debated whether to open the door or to walk down the hall to her office, change into running clothes, and get her emotions in check with a run. She sighed. She wasn't angry, just sad. Her father had an illness. Maybe it wasn't his fault. Maybe she needed to find forgiveness. Bitterness had certainly not made her feel any better. She took a breath and pushed open the door. Ella sat behind Patsy's desk. Patsy lay on his couch, his eyes closed.

"How is he?" Keera asked.

Ella shrugged. "Ask him."

Her father bolted upright and flashed a bright grin, his eyes clear. "For once I thought I'd use my shitty reputation for something positive," he said, his speech crisp, showing no signs of being drunk. "Like you said, they expected me to fall flat on my face, and who am I to not give the people what they want?"

Maggie came down the hall and entered the office smiling, then broke out laughing.

"That was an act?" Keera asked.

"I've had a lot of practice over the years, haven't I? I assume you got your extension?"

Keera smiled, uncertain what had just transpired. "I got it. But, Patsy, what about your reputation? Your career?"

"I'm at the end of my career, kiddo. We all know that."

"Your cross of Rossi was a masterpiece."

"Then let it be my final one. My best role is the one you've put me in—counselor. Someone who can provide advice. This is your show now. You and Ella and Maggie. I'm just glad I got to go out on my own terms."

"The Irish Brawler," Ella said, near tears.

"The Irish Brawler," Patsy said.

CHAPTER 32

August 18, 2023

Friday morning, after a long night of preparation, Keera called JP Harrison to the stand. She, Patsy, Harrison, and his engineering partner had come up with a theory of how Anne LaRussa could have committed suicide that accounted for each variable, and they'd put together a video. That was well and good, but there remained the issue of Ambrose. He would object vehemently to the introduction of the video evidence, and even Patsy wouldn't bet that Judge Hung would admit their videotaped demonstration. It might very well have been a long night for very little reward.

As Harrison entered the courtroom, Keera had to admit, he cut a dashing figure. His suit was a dark shade of gold, and a white shirt complemented his dark skin and made him look both fashionable and competent. He commanded the room's attention.

"Good morning, Mr. Harrison," Keera said.

"Good morning," he said, his English accent full. Perfect.

"Would you tell the jury your background?"

Harrison spoke casually. He sounded relaxed, confident. He told the jury of his education in

England and the United States. He had studied criminal justice at the University of Washington—a local—and he had intentions of attending law school and becoming a lawyer.

"Why didn't you?" Keera asked.

"The police department called to me," he said. "I had a desire to serve and to protect, to maybe make a difference in someone's life."

Keera asked, and Harrison told the jury of his experience during his twenty-five years serving at the Seattle Police Department. He explained how he was a uniformed officer for five years, then sat for and passed the detective's exam. She went through his various stints as a detective in the CSI Unit, where he learned the departments' intricacies: fingerprinting and DNA gathering and analysis, ballistics, and the forensic sciences. From there he worked in a number of SPD detective departments at Police Headquarters before reaching Seattle's Violent Crimes unit, where he had served for fifteen years.

"And then you retired?" Keera said.

"That's the one thing I found I wasn't very good at," Harrison said, smiling. "I'm one of those people who likes to stay busy. I tried golf but found it tedious. I tried fishing but found it too slow. In the end I decided I loved what I did during my career. I loved the forensic sciences, solving puzzles, solving crimes."

"What exactly is your second career?"

"I obtained my private investigator's license, but really I'm more of a private forensic investigator."

"You work for the defense?"

"I work for both the defense and the prosecution, though the prosecution usually has their own experts, like the men and women I assume have testified here during this trial. But police departments have also retained my services when they want a fresh pair of eyes."

It was a rehearsed answer to let the jury know Harrison had no bias. He'd been a cop. He'd served as a detective who worked to put criminals behind bars and still occasionally did.

Keera took Harrison through what she had asked him to do, and he explained, in great detail, what he had done when he went out to the LaRussa home.

"I noted a number of puzzling pieces of evidence. Ultimately my job is to explain that puzzle," he said.

"Would you tell the jury those puzzle pieces of evidence?" Keera asked.

"Gladly."

Keera used slides as Harrison spoke. Each variable came up on the screen as he mentioned it, complemented with a photograph.

"First, there was Lisa Bennet's fingerprint on the locked oven door handle. Second, I noted a burn mark on the oven door." Keera displayed a photograph, and Harrison authenticated it for the jury.

"Detective Rossi couldn't explain the marking. He thought it could have been a wear mark," Keera said. "Do you agree?"

"No. I had scrapings of that mark tested, which refute such an assumption."

"Why? What did the scrapings reveal?"

"Potassium nitrate."

Keera asked Harrison to explain where potassium nitrate came from and what products might contain it.

"What other piece of evidence did you find puzzling?"

"Third, there was the water on the floor."

"There's a broken glass on the floor in the picture," Keera said. "Could Anne LaRussa have dropped a glass?"

"Certainly. In fact I believe she held a glass of water or broke a glass to account for the water on the floor. However, I had the water on the floor analyzed, and the analysis is what I found interesting."

"What did you find?"

"The water also contained trace amounts of potassium nitrate, as well as microscopic cotton fibers."

"Any other puzzle pieces?"

"Number four was the gun, of course. If someone had shot Anne LaRussa, he or she had to have stood behind the kitchen counter, given the blood spatter evidence and the estimated distance of the gun barrel to where the victim sat." Harrison then provided a more detailed analysis of the blood spatter. Ambrose did not object, because his blood spatter witness had testified to much the same thing.

"If the person wanted to leave the gun at the crime scene, the most logical choice would have been to simply drop it and walk out the front door. The location of the gun on the opposite side of the counter, near the wheelchair, was, therefore, troubling. Even rudimentary gun owners know better than to toss a loaded gun onto a hard surface."

"What other evidence puzzled you?"

Number five. "Sunday was one of the hottest days on record in Seattle. Temperatures were well over one hundred degrees in most areas of Puget Sound. One hundred and six in Seattle on that day. The LaRussa home had an air-conditioning system tied into the heating system. That is, the air-conditioning kicked on automatically if the temperature inside the house exceeded seventy-two degrees, which it did that day, but the air-conditioning system was not on. Seemed if there was ever a day to use it, that was the day."

"Anything else?"

Number six. "The candle burning on the kitchen counter."

"What did you find odd about the candle?"

"Nothing, but it was certainly another piece of evidence to consider, especially since I read in the CSI reports that the candle was lit, but CSI did not find a match or a lighter anywhere in the kitchen."

"And did you come up with an explanation for all these puzzle pieces?"

"Not right away. There was a lot of trial and error. But eventually, yes, I believe I did."

"Each piece of evidence?" Keera asked, sounding skeptical.

"I had a high school chemistry professor, Mr. Cobalt, who told us that a theory wasn't a theory unless it explained *all* the variables. If it did not, then it wasn't a theory, it was a hypothesis. We got As for theories. Cs and Ds for hypotheses."

"Let's go through the evidence one piece at a time. First, Lisa Bennet's fingerprint on the oven door handle. What did you conclude from that?"

"Obviously that she touched the door handle."

Several jurors smiled.

"She testified here in court she didn't open the oven door."

"I don't believe she did. In fact, the upper oven door was locked, as if for cleaning, but the knob was not moved to the cleaning setting." Keera displayed another photograph, and Harrison said, "I think it much more likely she slid the latch and locked that door shut."

"I'll come back to that," Keera said, trying not to sound rehearsed. "What about the burn mark on the door handle? Can you explain that?"

"As I testified, we found potassium nitrate in both the scrapings from the mark on the door and in the water on the floor."

"And did you come up with an explanation for the potassium nitrate?"

"I believe so, yes."

Harrison explained, with the use of photographs, how he had gone back to the house, to the gardening shed in the backyard, and located the container of stump remover. He showed where the stump remover was located. Ambrose took notes. He was certain to argue that Anne LaRussa could not have reached the can.

"And what is the chemical composition of stump remover?" Keera asked.

Another photograph displayed the back of the stump remover container. "One hundred percent potassium nitrate."

"You mentioned you also identified cotton fibers. Can you explain those?"

"I didn't find anything to explain the cotton fibers in the gardening shed, but upon reexamination of the kitchen, I located a spool of cotton string in a kitchen drawer."

"Do you have photographs documenting where you found the spool of string?"

Harrison showed the jury photographs depicting

the spool of string in a kitchen drawer. Ambrose sat with legs crossed, pen resting on his note-pad, still confident. He did not know how this fit together and clearly intended to attack Harrison with Anne's physical limitations. Keera was about to ask a question that would change Ambrose's calm-and-collected demeanor.

"And the gun on the floor near Anne LaRussa's wheelchair? What is your explanation as to how it ended up there?"

"I think it would be best if I showed you," Harrison said.

"How can you do that?"

"I have a video that explains each piece of evidence and visually demonstrates my theory as to what happened."

"And do you believe it will help the jury to better understand the evidence?"

"I do."

Ambrose had uncrossed his legs and moved to the edge of his chair as Keera asked Judge Hung for permission to play the video.

Ambrose rose. "Objection, Your Honor. We were given no notice of a video or a chance to review it ahead of Mr. Harrison's testimony. This is highly prejudicial."

"The video was not complete until late last evening, Your Honor," Keera countered. "We're happy to let the State consider it before showing it in court."

"We'll take a recess," Judge Hung said. "I'll see counsel in chambers."

After the jury departed, the court reporter, Keera, and Ambrose walked behind the bench and down the hall to Judge Hung's chambers. "This is bullshit," Ambrose said under his breath.

"No," Keera said. "This is trial."

Judge Hung stood behind her desk. "Explain yourself, Ms. Duggan."

"As the court told both counsel, witnesses might be called out of order, and things come up. We have to be willing and able to roll with them."

"And this video presentation is one of those things?"

"You can ask Mr. Harrison, Your Honor—"

"I'm asking you."

Keera had considered this question and prepared her response. "The puzzle pieces Mr. Harrison identified could not be easily explained. His explanation came only after we realized that the medical examiner's report had been improperly redacted to remove the fact that Anne LaRussa had terminal cancer, and the logical assumption that Anne LaRussa could have committed suicide became apparent."

"Your Honor, this is speculative and ludicrous," Ambrose said.

Keera pressed forward through the interruption. "Upon receipt of this information, Mr. Harrison's working theory made sense, and the video became relevant. Counsel for the State didn't even try to explain all the evidence. We will, with the aid of the video. Mr. Harrison has been working night and day on a theory that explains all the evidence. The demonstration could not be done in court, for a number of reasons, primarily because firing a weapon is dangerous."

"Why wasn't the video presented to the State for an earlier viewing? Why wait until we are in court?"

"Again, Your Honor, you can ask Mr. Harrison, but the answer is everything didn't fall into place until we received news of Anne LaRussa's terminal cancer, which had been intentionally withheld from the defense. It was a very late evening."

Judge Hung leaned back and took in a deep breath. Her nostrils flared, her eyes pinpoints of black. "Ms. Duggan, if I determine that Mr. Duggan's exploits in my courtroom yesterday were somehow a ploy to buy you and your expert time, I will sanction you and report you to the ethics section of the Washington bar."

"I believe that my father's drinking problem is well documented and understood in this building, and by many of the judges who preside over these courtrooms, yourself included," she said, not answering the implied question or lying to the court.

"So are his antics," Judge Hung said.

"My father's alcoholism is not an antic," Keera said. "It's an illness. If you wish, I can call my mother, my sisters, and my brothers to document it for the court."

Judge Hung pursed her lips, duly chastised. Then she said, "We will view the video in chambers. I will then decide whether to admit it in court. Get your witness and bring him in here."

Keera left chambers and exhaled. The butterflies in her stomach fluttered but she suppressed them. The video was, in essence, her queen in this chess game. Her most powerful piece. Now was her opportunity to attack. Ambrose had provided the opening. Lose this argument and she would lose the trial. Win, and she had a chance.

She retrieved JP Harrison and his laptop from the courtroom and together they returned to chambers. After a moment to get set up, Harrison played the video for Judge Hung and Ambrose. When finished, Ambrose strenuously objected.

"This is pure speculation."

"Hardly," Keera said. "It is based on the evidence collected and scientific fact, but if the State wishes to raise that argument on cross-examination or in closing, the State is certainly free to do so. Mr. Harrison has been qualified as an expert witness and therefore may testify in the form of an opinion. This represents his opinion as to what happened. It is relevant, and this video will aid the jury in understanding what the defense believes happened that Sunday evening."

"Anne LaRussa, never could have put these things in place given her physical limitations," Ambrose said, telegraphing his cross-examination. "It would have been impossible."

Keera shrugged. "Again, the State is free to make that argument on cross-examination and in closing to the jury."

"This should not have been withheld," Ambrose countered. "If the State had it, we could have had our experts go over it in detail and conduct their own experiments to determine if this is even accurate."

"And if the defense had Dr. Litchfield's original autopsy report before the State asked him to modify it, we would have known that Anne LaRussa was dying of cancer at the trial's outset, instead of having to change course at the eleventh hour, as it were," Keera said. "The State's actions caused our delay. The State cannot have it both ways."

Ambrose opened his mouth to speak, but Judge Hung raised her hand and silenced him. She closed her eyes and exhaled, opened them, and stared at her desk for a very long minute. Then she raised her gaze to Ambrose and Keera. "I will allow the video to be played for the jury," she said. Keera felt a great sense of relief. "Provided Ms. Duggan can lay a proper foundation. You may cross-examine the witness to challenge his findings and opinions, Mr. Ambrose. If you disagree with my ruling, you may bring an appeal. What you can no longer do is argue a breach of fair play. You reap what you sow. We're done here. I'm not keeping my jury waiting another minute."

Back in court, JP Harrison retook the stand. Keera laid a foundation for the video, Ambrose objected, and Judge Hung ruled the video admissible. She then spoke to the jurors. "I want to caution the members of the jury that the video is a demonstration of what the defense expert *believes* explains the underlying evidence. It is the defense's theory as to what happened."

With that admonishment, Keera played the video and Harrison explained it.

"You will see a mannequin that is the same height as the decedent, Anne LaRussa, seated in Anne LaRussa's wheelchair." Harrison explained that he had taken measurements based on Anne's height and the height of her wheelchair. Then he said, "If one takes cotton string, and soaks it in a potassium nitrate solution, in this case the stump remover found in Anne LaRussa's shed, then dries that string on a low temperature in an ordinary oven, one creates a fuse that will ignite." Again, Harrison showed the process on the video as well as the string burning like a fuse.

"Now the gun. The question that needed to be

resolved was how to get the gun to be upright if not held in a person's hand."

Several jurors looked perplexed by this comment.

"After failed attempts, I realized I was ignoring two pieces of evidence—the water on the floor also contained potassium nitrate. Not to mention the fact that someone had turned off the air-conditioning."

"Meaning what?" Keera asked.

"A simple way to ensure the gun is upright is to freeze the gun grip in a block of ice."

"Did you find any containers that could have been used to hold water while it froze into the block of ice?"

"The gardening shed had many such containers. The container had to be big enough so the block of ice would hold the gun upright with the barrel parallel to the ground."

The video depicted a handgun with the grip in a block of ice in a container.

"Upon setup, the ice is removed from the container and placed on the towel to keep it from sliding from the counter." Again, the video depicted this. "Now. How does one pull the trigger?" Harrison asked. "The first thing to understand is the trigger does not require much pressure. On a 9-millimeter handgun, as was the case in this instance, the required pressure is just three point five pounds."

"So how would Anne LaRussa pull the trigger while sitting in her wheelchair with her back to the gun?" Keera asked.

"She didn't need to pull the trigger. She just needed to pull the string."

Several jurors leaned forward.

Harrison showed a 9 mm handgun of the same make and model as the ghost gun, its grip in a block of ice on a wooden countertop that he explained was the same height as the LaRussas' kitchen counter. Measurements taken proved him accurate. The block of ice was placed on a kitchen towel. The mannequin sat with her back to the counter. Across the wheelchair arm were two ends of a length of cotton string that had been dipped in potassium nitrate, then dried. One end of the string went from the wheelchair arm, across the counter and around the oven door handle, which was locked shut, then returned, wrapping around the trigger of the pistol, and continuing back to the wheelchair.

"What the person needs to do is get rid of the string and the block of ice. On such a warm day, with the air-conditioning in the house turned off, the ice simply melted. The string is a tad bit trickier. But then I recalled the potassium nitrate and the candle. The person in the wheelchair would need only to ignite the return end of the string, which would burn like a fuse. The person puts an end of the fuse in the candle flame, drops that end, places the candle on the nearby counter, then pulls the other end of the string. The oven door provides leverage, like a pulley system; the trigger depresses, and the gun fires. Eventually, the string completely burns, undetectable to the naked eye but for the burn mark on the oven door handle."

"And you performed an experiment to determine if your theory works?"

"Yes. If I may?"

Ambrose rose. "The State will make a standing objection to the jurors viewing the videotape."

"So noted," Judge Hung said.

With that, Harrison played the videotape and explained that the string in the demonstration was pulled from behind bulletproof plexiglass. His friend, the inventor, lit the fuse using a candle. He then tugged on the other end of the string that went around the oven door handle. The string depressed the trigger, and the gun fired. The mannequin's head exploded and fell forward, then listed to the side. The force of the gunshot lifted the grip of the gun from the ice, and it flipped grip over barrel, landing on the floor not far from where they had found the ghost gun.

The jurors looked punch-drunk, so much so that Keera ended her examination on that stunning moment.

Ambrose stood and approached the lectern. "That's a rather elaborate experiment," he said.

"It took how long for you and your friend—I believe you said he was an inventor and a mechanical engineer?"

"That's right."

"How long did it take you and this friend to come up with this?"

"We've been working on a theory to explain the evidence for weeks."

"Weeks. And how many times . . ." Ambrose paused. "How many times did you have to perform this experiment before it worked?"

"We developed this theory and this experiment just last night when we learned that the decedent had terminal cancer. We only had this one chance."

Ambrose quickly pivoted. "You don't think that Anne LaRussa, confined to a wheelchair, thought of this elaborate experiment on her own; do you?"

"I think that is entirely possible."

"What was Anne LaRussa's educational background?"

"I don't know."

"Do you think someone with a degree in English literature could have come up with something so elaborate as you and your friend the mechanical engineer did?"

There it was. Ambrose's arrogance had led him to ask a question he should not have, a question to which he did not know the answer.

"I do, if she knew how to use the internet," Harrison said. "Sadly, you'll find this very contraption on YouTube, available to anyone who can stroke computer keys."

Ambrose's Adam's apple bobbed, but he moved on as if nonplussed. "The shelving in the toolshed where you located the stump remover was just about seven feet tall, was it not?"

"Yes," Harrison said.

"And the stump remover was on the top shelf; yes?"

"Correct."

Ambrose did not ask the next question. He would argue in closing to the jury that a woman confined to a wheelchair could not have reached the stump remover.

"And the backyard is sloped. I believe one of your photographs depicts the shed location and the backyard." Harrison found the photograph and placed it on the computer screen. "That slope would have made maneuvering a wheelchair treacherous; would it not?" Ambrose asked.

"It certainly could have," Harrison agreed.

"And that block of ice. How much did it weigh?"

Harrison answered, and Ambrose refrained from asking Harrison whether a partially paralyzed woman could have lifted and placed the block of ice on the kitchen counter by herself. Again, he'd make that argument to the jury.

Ambrose concluded and sat.

Keera rose. It was time to move her queen and again put Ambrose in check. "Mr. Harrison, counsel intimated that Anne LaRussa could not have reached the potassium nitrate atop the seven-foot shelf."

"I can only say it would have likely been a challenge," Harrison said.

"Or maneuvered her wheelchair down the sloped lawn in the backyard."

"Again, I can't say for certain, but it definitely would have been a challenge."

"And a challenge to lift the block of ice?"

"Certainly."

"Then your experiment did not account for one variable, Anne LaRussa's physical limitations; did it?"

In her peripheral vision, Keera noted the jury turn their gazes to her, with expressions indicating they had misheard her question.

"It does, actually," Harrison said. "We concluded that Anne LaRussa must have had help, perhaps a friend who couldn't endure seeing her suffer from the cancer that would eventually kill her."

Something snapped, drawing Keera's attention briefly to counsel table. Vince LaRussa sat with an expression of controlled rage. She looked down at his hands in his lap.

LaRussa had snapped in half the pen he had been holding.

CHAPTER 33

Ambrose spent the remainder of the afternoon recalling witnesses, especially his forensic
experts, to refute JP Harrison's testimony and his
experiment. Judge Hung had no alternative but to
allow him to do so, though the two sides would
not give their closings now until Monday. The
problem with Ambrose's attack on Harrison was
the experiment had worked, and it had explained
all the variables. In this case a picture, or video,
was truly worth a thousand words.

Keera decided against cross-examining the
recalled witnesses, except for one or two questions. To most she asked, "You will admit, will
you not, that the experiment worked?" They had
little choice with the video staring them, and the
jurors, in the face. Any attempt to disparage it
only made them less credible. Keera was glad
for the additional time to prepare her closing.
She would now argue that Anne LaRussa, dying
of terminal cancer, had taken her own life. She
would argue that because of her physical limitations, Anne LaRussa had to have had help, as
Harrison had testified, that she could not have
set up the device on her own. She would argue
that Harrison's theory also explained why Lisa
Bennet, her best friend, carried the large bag

into the house and why it looked heavy. The bag, Keera would say, likely contained the block of ice with the gun.

She would tell the jury it explained why Bennet left the LaRussa home that night in tears, clearly upset, with a bag not as heavy as when she entered. She would argue that the redacted medical examiner's report explained why Anne LaRussa's best friend would help Anne take her own life, why Bennet's testimony made even more sense. Having witnessed her husband suffer so much pain, Bennet couldn't bear to see her friend suffer during those final weeks. It explained the amount of opioids, pain medication, prescribed and in Anne LaRussa's system. Keera would argue that Lisa Bennet's actions had not been malicious, but merciful.

Ambrose couldn't very well argue that Keera had changed arguments in midtrial, not after withholding the information about Anne LaRussa's cancer.

The only thing Keera did not yet know was why Bennet and Anne LaRussa had gone to such an elaborate length to frame Vince LaRussa and possibly send him to prison for the rest of his life. Anne LaRussa had not acted because Vince had an affair, at least not with Lisa Bennet. Had there been someone else? And if there had been, would Anne LaRussa be so vindictive? Would her best friend, Lisa Bennet? Keera didn't see it.

After trial, Keera told JP Harrison to wait for her in her office. She wanted to speak to LaRussa. She met LaRussa in the counsel room in the King County jail after he had changed back into his red scrubs. He entered the room with a somber smile and slumped into the chair across from her. "That was brilliant," he said.

"Clearly Anne had help, Vince. Lisa Bennet?"

"No doubt," LaRussa said.

"Why, Vince? Why would your wife and her best friend try to put you behind bars for the rest of your life?"

"I don't know," he said, shaking his head vigorously. "I've been asking myself that same question."

It wasn't a good enough answer.

She persisted. "You weren't having an affair, not with Lisa Bennet. Was there someone else?"

"No. No one. You'll have to talk to Lisa."

"No, I don't. Not to create reasonable doubt," Keera said.

"She'd likely lie anyway."

Something in his tone. "Why do you say that?"

He seemed to catch himself. "Because she's been lying this entire time, hasn't she?"

"What ax does she have to grind with you, Vince?"

He stood suddenly, his voice rising. "I don't know, Keera. I wish I did, but . . . I don't know.

You think this comes as a shock to you? Imagine the shock to me. My own wife doing something like this." LaRussa took a breath and took a moment to gather himself. Keera thought of Phil McPherson saying LaRussa's temper could trigger like the flip of a switch. He calmed. "I'm sorry for the outburst. This is all a bit much. It saddens me to think that I could have done something to bring Anne to such a drastic measure. But I have no idea what that was. I really don't."

Keera read his facial expression and his posture. Nothing overt to indicate he was lying or hiding something. Still, her intuition told her otherwise.

Something wasn't right. Something remained missing.

"Okay." She stood and started for the door. "I'll see you Monday morning in court."

"Keera?"

She turned back at the door.

"Brilliant," he said. Then he smiled. "Truly brilliant."

Goose bumps ran up Keera's spine and along her arms, the kind she used to get when Miller Ambrose stalked her.

Keera returned to the office.

"Heard you and JP knocked it out of the park," Maggie said as Keera stepped from the elevator and entered.

419

Keera deflected the enthusiasm. "We got the video into evidence. We're not done yet."

"What's eating you?" Maggie asked.

"I just don't want us to get ahead of ourselves." She started for her office but stopped and walked back to the reception desk. "But whatever the outcome, Maggie, we couldn't have done it without your help. I'm grateful. I know you haven't asked for anything, but I'm going to suggest to Ella that you be compensated for all your extra time. A bonus."

"Thanks," Maggie said, sounding uncertain. "That means a lot, Keera."

"You were invaluable getting all of our pleadings finalized and filed, ordering in food, coordinating the witnesses. Thanks for everything you've done."

"Okay," Maggie said.

Keera stepped forward and, after an awkward moment, she reached out and hugged her sister. She couldn't remember the last time she and Maggie shared a hug. Maggie looked uncomfortable and felt stiff. Keera released her and asked, "JP here?"

"Tall, dark, and handsome is in Patsy's office being debriefed. Any chance he'll be single soon?"

"With JP you never know. Frankly, you could do better."

"Really?" Maggie said. " 'Cause he's like an eleven on a scale of one to ten."

"He can't give you what you want, Maggie. What you deserve," Keera said. Again, her sister looked confused.

Keera found Harrison, Ella, and Patsy in Patsy's office.

"Hey, there she is." Patsy stood from his chair and walked around his desk with his fist up, like a boxer in a ring. "Man, I wish I could have been in court today."

Keera smiled. "I do too, Dad."

"Do you have any idea what a not-guilty verdict will mean for the firm?" Ella said. "We're going to have to hire associates again to handle cases coming in the door."

"Let's not get ahead of ourselves," Keera said. "We still have to close."

Harrison smiled. "You're not serious, are you?"

"I am," she said.

Patsy threw a couple of jabs, then a cross. "I'm going to have to give up my nickname to a new Irish Brawler in town."

"You'll always be the Irish Brawler, Dad. Has today's transcript come in yet?"

"Haven't looked," Patsy said, lowering his fists. "Everything okay?"

"Fine. It's just . . ."

"Why did Bennet and Anne LaRussa do it?" Patsy said.

"We were just having that conversation. What did Vince have to say?" Harrison asked.

"He said he didn't know, but I think he does know."

"Is that what's eating you?" Patsy said.

"Among other things, yes."

"Anne was dying of cancer," Harrison said.

"She was, but that doesn't explain why she and her best friend would try to pin her murder on her husband and put him away for life. That goes well beyond vindictiveness. There's more," Keera said.

"You think he could have been having an affair with someone else?" Ella asked.

"That was my first thought. LaRussa denied it, but I think it's a distinct possibility." She turned to Harrison. "Did you see what happened in the courtroom today when it became clear that Bennet had to have helped Anne?"

"No. I saw you turn but . . ."

"Vince snapped the pen in his hand."

"Heard the snap," Harrison said. "Didn't know what it was."

"It reminded me of what Phil McPherson said, that LaRussa could lose his temper in an instant. That he could snap. He lost his temper in the jail also when I pushed him for an answer."

"But he didn't snap. He didn't kill his wife. You've proven that. He didn't do it. What else is bothering you?" Patsy said.

"I want to know what happened. This is like a

422

draw in chess. You fight this hard and then there's no resolution."

"You only needed to prove reasonable doubt to win," Patsy said.

"It's not about winning. It's about knowing the truth. I'm going to go find Lisa Bennet. Find out why she did it."

"She'll deny it," Patsy said.

Keera knew her father was right. Without more evidence, Bennet had no reason to tell the truth and every reason not to.

"Okay. I just suggested we all go down to the Paddy Wagon and have dinner. The firm's treat," Patsy said.

"Tempting," she said. "You all go. I just want to go home, go for a run, sit in a warm bath, and relax."

"You sure?" Patsy said.

"Yeah." She turned to Harrison. "Do me a favor. Don't sit next to Maggie at dinner."

"No?"

Keera shook her head. "No."

Harrison grinned. "Your sister likes me."

"You go out with her, and . . ."

He raised his hands. "No worries. I want no part of the Irish Brawler."

Keera returned home to an empty house and suddenly felt very isolated.

She was alone.

Unmarried. No boyfriend. No children.

She thought of Ella and Maggie, both also alone, and her two brothers and their divorces. Ella was alone by choice. She chose not to put herself out there and potentially get hurt. At the other end of the spectrum was Maggie. She tried to fill the deep hole she had dug with meaningless encounters, but they would never mend her so she could be whole. Keera didn't want her life to be like either of theirs. She didn't want to run from intimacy or blame her problems on her father's drinking. She realized she had been doing just what her father had always done. She had been making excuses for her drinking and making poor choices. She'd made a poor choice dating Miller Ambrose. The consequences were her fault, not his. She never should have placed herself in that situation.

A person in a gasoline-soaked suit should never play with matches, she thought.

Her father was an alcoholic. So were both her brothers. She suspected Ella was also, but had sought help and conquered it, the way Ella conquered everything—head-on. Alcoholism was in Keera's family genes. She was soaked in gasoline. She walked to the cabinet, to where she kept the match, retrieved the Dalmore Scotch bottle, and took it into the kitchen. She opened the top, tipped the bottle upside down, and let the liquid flow down the sink drain.

She wouldn't light the flame any longer.

She put the bottle in the recycle bin and walked back into the living room. She wished she had someone to talk with. She wished for children who needed dinner, baths, help with homework, anything to take her mind off what had happened in court this afternoon. She had an eerie premonition that Vince LaRussa had gotten away with something. Maybe not the murder of his wife, but something.

An affair?

Something nefarious, as Phil McPherson had certainly hinted? But why would that cause Anne and Lisa to frame him?

Needing a distraction, Keera went for a long run. When she came back, she felt better. She went into the kitchen to get a tall glass of water. Passing through the dining room, she hit the space bar on her laptop. Patsy would know she needed a distraction. He'd made his thirty-second move.

From: Darkknight
To: SeattlePawnslayer

King slides to g1

He was running. Trying to escape the inevitable. But she had her queen.

425

From: SeattlePawnslayer
To: Darkknight

Queen to e3. Check.

From: Darkknight
To: SeattlePawnslayer

King to g2

Rather than an all-out attack with her remaining pieces, even those that once looked trapped, Keera moved her knight.

From: SeattlePawnslayer
To: Darkknight

Knight to f5

From: Darkknight
To: SeattlePawnslayer

Bishop takes pawn at d4

A desperate move now to get away.

Each move she made would keep the king in check to prevent him from moving his queen and taking her bishop, ending the game. Absent a fatal mistake, she couldn't lose.

From: SeattlePawnslayer
To: Darkknight

Knight takes pawn at h4. Check.

No escape. No respite. Patsy could run, buy some time, but he could not get away. What would he do now? Concede? Do something desperate?

From: Darkknight
To: SeattlePawnslayer

King to f1

From: SeattlePawnslayer
To: Darkknight

Queen takes pawn at d3. Check.

Patsy had been so close to winning, he had never considered he might lose. Was it poor planning? A flawed strategy? Or was it ego that led him to this situation? She thought again of Vince LaRussa and couldn't help but think of the parallels, that he, too, was on the run and believed he was about to win.

Her computer pinged. An incoming email. She knew before she even looked.

From: Worthing, Jack
Sent: August 18, 2023
To: Keera Duggan
Subject: Final Move

Keera stared at the subject line.

She'd come this far. The game of her life. Final move.

She'd damn well play it out. Damn right she would. To the very end.

CHAPTER 34

August 19, 2023

Harrison picked up Keera Saturday morning. "Where to?" he asked.

"Beaverton," she said. With no direct or cross-examinations to prepare, with jury instructions finalized and before Judge Hung, and with her closing in good shape, Keera decided to make this drive with Harrison.

"Again?" Harrison asked.

"Jack Worthing says this will be the final move."

"You believe him?"

"We've played the game this far. Let's see what we learn. Where it takes us."

"I was afraid you might say that. Open the glove box."

Keera did. "You brought a gun?"

"If this is going to be the final move, I'd prefer it not to be *our* final move."

"We don't need a gun."

"You sure about that?"

She wasn't. Keera shut the glove box and looked out the window. "What did you find on this woman?"

"Nothing," Harrison said. "She's not on

social media. No property in her name. No car registered to her. No criminal record. No civil lawsuits. I checked all the usual sources. Never found her. Maybe Stephanie Bowers is like our Jack Worthing; maybe she only exists in literature."

"I tried that route," Keera said. "Skimmed the play again. She's not in there. Not that I found."

"You think this could be the woman LaRussa was having an affair with?"

"The thought crossed my mind, but . . . the address makes that unlikely."

"Why?"

"It's a mobile home park."

The Red Rock Mobile Estates, a mobile home and RV park, was located thirty minutes to the west of Beaverton. Keera had seen some nice mobile home parks, with homes relatively new and the community clean and tidy. This was not one of them. The homes at Red Rock were aging and decrepit, some without skirts, rusting. Broken-down cars littered the narrow asphalt roads along with battered bikes and garbage bags. Trees were few and didn't offer much in the way of shade. When Harrison drove his car into the park, the residents, some sitting out in folding chairs, drinking beer and smoking cigarettes, looked at the car like they were looking at an ATM.

Harrison pulled up to the trailer parked on

430

space fourteen—an RV that looked like it hadn't been moved in years. Out front was a folding table and two chairs. A broken awning extended from the RV and had been tied with rope to a tree limb, offering a triangle of shade.

Harrison reached across his car and grabbed the gun from the glove box, putting it in the holster he wore under a thin linen jacket, the sleeves rolled to his elbows.

"This is everywhere, USA," Keera said, smiling at Harrison's discomfort.

"This is a robbery waiting to happen," he replied. "That's what everywhere, USA, has become."

Keera and Harrison pushed from the car. Harrison stopped at the hood, his arms folded, his eyes hidden behind sunglasses. He watched the residents across the way as Keera walked up wooden steps and knocked on the door.

"She'll never hear you," Harrison said over his shoulder. "Knock like you mean it."

Keera balled her hand and banged on the door with the meaty part of her fist. A moment later a woman opened the door, squinting as if the light hurt her eyes. Keera guessed late seventies, and those looked to have been hard-lived years. She wore a white tank top, cutoff jean shorts, and no shoes. Definitely not someone Vince LaRussa was having an affair with.

"Who the hell are you?" the woman asked, squinting into the bright sunlight.

431

"Stephanie Bowers?" Keera asked, still trying to make sense of it.

"I paid my rent yesterday afternoon. You can call the park manager. Better yet, go and see him. Asshole told me I had to pay a twenty-dollar surcharge."

"I'm not here about the rent," Keera said.

"What are you here about then?"

"Vince LaRussa."

The woman looked suddenly fearful. Her eyes widened and her already pale skin looked translucent. "Don't know anyone by that name."

"I think you do."

"Well, you think wrong, honey. So, get off my paid-for parcel of concrete before I call the police."

"No need." Keera pointed to Harrison. "That's a police officer right there."

Harrison held up his private investigator's billfold like a cop held up his badge and identification. His jacket fell open, his gun visible. Several residents watching from across the road found other things to do. Stephanie Bowers looked to be debating what to do.

"I'm not here to cause you any trouble, Ms. Bowers. Just want to ask you a few questions. I actually represent Vince LaRussa."

"For what?" she said, her voice raspy.

"You haven't watched the news or read the newspaper lately?"

"Who do I look like, Barbara Walters?"

"But you do know Vince LaRussa?"

"Look, you're going to cause me a lot of grief and heartache, okay? Not to mention a place to live and food on my table."

The fog lifted. "Vince pays your rent and for your food?"

"I didn't say that."

"Yes, you did. Why does he pay?"

The woman looked like every swallow hurt her throat. "Why are you people suddenly so interested in who I am, after all these years?"

"Did someone else come to talk with you?" Keera asked.

"His wife."

"Vince's wife?"

"Came about seven, eight months ago. I'd never met her."

In her peripheral vision, Keera saw Harrison turn his head. In her mind she calculated that the person who came to speak to Stephanie Bowers did so before that person spoke to Mary Bell, Eric Fields, or Spencer Tickman. "What did she look like?" Keera asked Bowers.

"Tall. Blonde. Dressed well."

Keera and Harrison shared another look. Lisa Bennet. Things were getting more than interesting. "What did she want?" Keera asked Bowers.

"Same as you. She wanted to know about Vince." Bowers shook her head, then stepped back inside the RV, but she did not shut the door. She grabbed a crumpled pack of cigarettes and a butane lighter from a cluttered counter and moved to the tattered and torn lawn chairs beneath the makeshift awning. "Let's get this over with."

Uncertain the tattered chair would hold her weight, Keera sat carefully. The nylon strips sagged underneath her. Stephanie Bowers sat across from her. She held out the pack of cigarettes. Keera shook her head.

"No. Of course you don't," Bowers said. "Hey," she called out to Harrison. He looked back over his shoulder. She held up the pack.

Harrison raised his hand. "I'm trying to quit."

"Why? Something has to kill you, might as well be cigarettes." She lit one, took a drag, and tilted back her head as she blew out the smoke. She set the lighter on the cigarette pack, balancing it on the fragile chair arm. "What do you want to know?"

"Why did his wife come to talk to you?"

Bowers laughed, which caused a coughing fit. When it subsided, she said, "She thought Vince and I were having an affair."

"Did she say why?"

"Found monthly payments Vince has been making to me for years. Thought maybe I was his girlfriend."

"She must have been relieved to learn you weren't."

"Not really."

"No? Why not?"

"I think you better first tell me why you're here. So I'm not doing all the talking."

"I was told to come talk to you."

"Told by who? His wife?"

"Jack Worthing."

Bowers vigorously shook her head. "Not possible."

"Why not?"

She took another hit on the cigarette. Stalling. The fingernails of her left hand had yellowed. She was missing teeth. "I think you better tell me a little more what this is all about."

Keera did. Bowers listened, her eyes occasionally flickering to the ground or off to the left or the right. Uncomfortable. By the time Keera had finished, Bowers had extinguished two cigarette stubs on the ground. "Let's start with why Vince pays for your rent and for your food," Keera said.

"Because I'm his mother," she said, her stare now defiant. "And before you go talking about how wonderful and kind that is . . . It ain't either. He doesn't pay because he loves me or has any sympathy for me."

"Why does he?"

"Because he's embarrassed of me. Embarrassed and ashamed. He pays to keep me quiet and in the shadows. Out of his life."

"I'm sorry," Keera said, not certain what else to say.

"Why are you sorry? Shit, I'm over it. It is what it is."

"Is Bowers your married name?"

"Second marriage . . . No. Third. I can't keep track." She laughed, then coughed again. A smoker's hack.

"And the name LaRussa?"

"That would be Vince's daddy. He was *not* a good man. He preferred the belt and the bottle. Together it got bad. Sometimes *real* bad. I had many trips to the hospital. Vince and me."

"He beat Vince?"

"Welcome to the real world, sweetie."

"What happened to Vince's father?" Keera asked, wondering if he could somehow be Jack Worthing.

"Not sure. Me and Vince took off one day. If I hadn't, he'd a killed one or the both of us. Never seen or heard from him again."

"How long were you together?"

"Hell, I don't know. What the hell does that matter? You want to tell me I was an idiot? Go ahead. I've heard it all before."

"No. I don't. I actually understand."

"How the hell would you understand? Look at you in your nice clothes. Nice car. You don't understand."

"My father's an alcoholic."

"That's a polite way to put it. I'll try using that next time instead of 'drunk motherfucker.' "

"How old was Vince when you left his father?" Keera tried again.

"I don't know. We weren't much on celebrating birthdays. Eleven or twelve, I'd guess." So his father could not be Jack Worthing. Not likely anyway.

"How did he cope with it?"

"Vince? Hell, he didn't care. He always had his nose in a book reading something. Seemed like he didn't pay much attention to anything in the real world. Probably easier that way."

"He was a reader?"

She laughed and coughed and talked through it. "Used to go to the library. Would walk or ride his bike if it didn't have a flat and come home with a stack of books in his backpack."

Keera had a sense where this was headed. "Did he read plays?"

"Plays, comic books, magazines, books. He read everything. Like I said, always had his nose in something."

"When I said Jack Worthing sent me, you said it wasn't possible. Why not?"

"Because Jack Worthing was a name Vince made up and used in his imaginary world."

"Imaginary world?"

"Boy had his head in the clouds half the time. He was always imagining things. He imagined

437

we was rich and everybody at school liked him. Guess it made him feel important. Used to say his name was Jack Worthing. Don't know where he got it. Figured he got it from one of those books, but . . . Hell, I don't know. Never been much for reading myself. My daddy used to read with him though."

"His grandfather?"

"He lived close by. Drove a taxi around town, mostly at night. Slept most of the day, but when he was up, he'd get Vince from school, and they'd read together while I was at work."

"Your father drove a taxi," Keera said, thinking about the car service Vince LaRussa started in college.

"Vince idolized him." Bowers smiled. "Used to sell baskets of strawberries for him. My daddy bought 'em at the store. Thought it would teach Vince the value of a dollar. Sent him off every Saturday to keep Vince out of trouble. When Vince got home, his father would make him hand over the money. He'd beat him if he didn't. I think Vince held back some of the money, though, but I don't know."

Which explained why Vince sold the baskets for more than what was expected. He didn't want to turn over all the money.

"When he got older, he told his grandfather that someday he'd start his own taxi company and make him the boss over everyone." She laughed again and coughed some more. "He was a determined little boy. I'll give him that . . . but I wasn't much help getting him where he wanted to be. He took off after his grandpa passed."

"Did you tell his wife about Jack Worthing?"

"I don't recall. It might have come up. She asked a lot of questions. I figured her being his wife . . . and she'd already found me." She shrugged. "So there was no sense hiding."

"Did you let Vince know that his wife came here?"

She laughed and shook her head. "Yeah, I just fired up my laptop and sent him off an email." She shrugged. "I don't even own a phone, honey. Can't afford one. Besides, I didn't know if he'd be pissed and maybe cut me off. Didn't want to take that chance. I would truly be screwed."

"Did you tell his wife that?"

"I asked her not to let Vince know she'd found me, yeah. You bet."

" 'The truth is rarely pure and never simple,' " Keera said.

Bowers stopped in midpuff. "Vince used to say stuff like that."

"Vince or Jack Worthing?" Keera said.

Bowers looked at her, but this time she didn't correct Keera and tell her Jack Worthing wasn't real.

"I don't know," she said.

・ ・ ・

Back in the car, driving north to Seattle, Harrison said, "Lisa Bennet posed as Anne LaRussa. I think we've proved Bennet was Anne's accomplice."

"But why? Why set Vince up? We still don't have an answer to that."

"You think Lisa sent the emails?"

"I don't know for certain, but it seems logical, doesn't it?"

"Nothing in this case seems logical."

"We know Anne didn't send them. And what reason would Vince have to send them?"

"None I can think of."

"Assuming it's Bennet, what is she trying to tell us?"

"That appears to be the sixty-four-thousand-dollar question, doesn't it?" Harrison looked at his watch. "We could stop by Bennet's house and ask her, tell her what we know. Put it to her bluntly."

"We could," Keera said. But thinking it through, she wasn't so sure that was the best thing. "She clearly wanted us to have this information. I'm not as certain she wanted us to figure out what she and Anne did, framing Vince. It's like Vince LaRussa said in jail—she could just deny it, and what would we have gained?"

"Ambrose might call her again. Get her to say she didn't help Anne set up the gun. If he does, you could—"

"He won't. Ambrose doesn't want to give me another chance to cross-examine her. He's better off arguing his points in his closing. He'll tell the jury the suicide is a desperate theory because we couldn't prove Lisa Bennet shot Anne."

"What then do we do?"

"We go forward and finish the trial," Keera said. "You did your job. Now I do mine. I give my closing. I tell the jury the evidence does not support the finding that Vince LaRussa killed his wife."

Harrison didn't respond. He didn't have to.

Keera knew what he was thinking. The evidence in court exonerated Vince LaRussa for the murder of his wife, of that she was certain. But the evidence Jack Worthing's emails had provided indicated something far less certain.

CHAPTER 35

August 21, 2023

Monday morning, Keera sat at counsel table, Vince LaRussa between her and Patsy. Patsy came despite the issue of Judge Hung reporting him to the bar for appearing in her court drunk. He wouldn't lose his license. More likely he'd be ordered to counseling. Not a bad thing. Patsy told Keera wild horses couldn't keep him out of the courtroom this morning.

LaRussa leaned over until their shoulders touched. "Everything all right?" he whispered. The warmth of his breath was punctuated with the aroma of eggs. What Keera did not smell was the acidic odor of nerves. "You seem quiet."

"Just focused on my closing," she said. She had not told him about Stephanie Bowers. Not yet. Not until she had a better understanding of what was going on.

"You won't let me down," LaRussa said. "I know you can't promise me anything except that you'll give it your very best and fight every step of the way."

She turned her head and considered him, but more his words. He'd just repeated what she'd told him the first time they met in his condominium, nearly word for word.

LaRussa grinned. Then he sat back and faced forward. It sent goose bumps up and down her arms. She had to fight against the urge to shudder.

The bailiff called the courtroom to order. They rose in unison as Judge Hung entered. She glanced at counsel table, no doubt surprised to see Patsy, but refrained from commenting. She instructed the bailiff to bring in the jury. Judge Hung provided the jury a brief statement about closing arguments, what they were, and how the jury should interpret them. She told them the State would give its closing, followed by the defense. The State would then have the final word on rebuttal. The jurors wore their poker faces and their posture was stiff. Their movements robotic. Nervous.

Ambrose approached the lectern. He greeted and thanked the jurors for performing their civic duty. He told them the justice system could not work without them. It was all rote. Keera had heard it many times before.

"I told you in my opening statement this case was a tragedy. I told you the evidence would prove that a disabled woman, Anne LaRussa, was shot in the back of the head by her husband because she threatened to take from him all that he had worked to accomplish. It wasn't inconsequential. You heard our forensic accountant testify that the defendant's assets are in the tens of millions of dollars. What do we now know? What has the State proven? These are the undisputed facts."

As Ambrose spoke, April Richie put bullet points on the courtroom computers.

"Two people came to the LaRussa home the evening of Sunday, June fourth, between 6:07 and 7:30 p.m. Both had been summoned by Anne LaRussa. The first was the family lawyer, Syd Evans. Mr. Evans testified that Anne wanted to invoke the forfeiture clause in the prenuptial agreement she and the defendant had signed at the time of their marriage. Syd Evans testified that when he left the LaRussa home that evening, Anne LaRussa remained very much alive.

"The second person summoned to the LaRussa home was Anne LaRussa's best friend, Dr. Lisa Bennet. She arrived at 7:03 p.m. Dr. Bennet testified on that witness stand, under penalty of perjury, that Anne LaRussa summoned her to the home because Anne believed Lisa Bennet was having an affair with her husband—an affair that would have triggered the forfeiture clause in that prenuptial agreement. Lisa Bennet denied the affair, but Anne LaRussa produced photographs of Lisa Bennet and the defendant, Vince LaRussa, at a restaurant in Madison Park. Lisa Bennet testified the purpose for the meeting was concern about her friend's well-being. Concern that her friend had become addicted to prescription painkillers, opioids.

"I submit to you, ladies and gentlemen, that it doesn't matter whether Dr. Bennet and Vince LaRussa were having an affair." Ambrose paused here for effect. "What matters is what Anne LaRussa *believed*. Was she paranoid? Irritable? Depressed? Was she terminally ill?

"It doesn't matter. All that matters is what she believed."

As Ambrose spoke, Keera fought to remain attentive, to take notes on his statements she would have to counter in her closing. But her mind wandered—which it almost never did. Her ability to intensely focus while contemplating the ramifications of each potential chess move was what made her such a formidable player. Her thoughts drifted back to that first meeting in LaRussa's condominium and her words that Vince LaRussa had just repeated. She had wanted this case desperately, to prove herself both to Ella and Patsy, but also to Ambrose. Now she felt trapped. She thought of Vince LaRussa wanting to put in a gate at the top of his driveway. He said it was to protect Anne, but his wife didn't want it. She said it would make her feel *even more like a prisoner.* That thought made her think of Anne's family, who testified that they rarely saw their daughter the last few months without Vince present. He'd moved his office to the house.

He said he didn't like to leave Anne alone, but maybe he didn't want her meeting with others without him present. What did he fear? Anne LaRussa had clearly been snooping. She'd found the monthly payments Vince made to Stephanie Bowers and she thought he was having an affair. Instead, she learned he had a mother she'd never met, a life she knew nothing about. She had to wonder who the man was who had shared her bed for so many years. What else had she found? Another thought came, and this one sickened her. Had Vince LaRussa killed Anne and made it look like a suicide? Had he drugged his wife with the many drugs in her medicine cabinet, set up the device, and planned to get off for a crime he had committed? One thing Jack Worthing had taught Keera through his witnesses: Vince LaRussa was a survivor. He'd survived his father's beatings, he'd learned how to lie to keep money he'd earned, and he had survived prosecution for stealing.

Ambrose continued. "Dr. Bennet testified she could not convince Anne to the contrary. She said Anne was upset, distraught. She testified that when she left the LaRussa home at seven twenty-nine Sunday evening, Anne LaRussa remained very much alive.

"Now, defense counsel tried, at first, to argue that Lisa Bennet killed Anne, her best friend. The defense argued Lisa Bennet did so because

Anne *might* have threatened Lisa Bennet's medical license for overprescribing the opioids, in retaliation for the affair she believed Bennet was having with her husband." Ambrose paused for emphasis. Then he said, "There are so many problems with that argument. So many."

Ambrose listed the problems while April Richie put them up as bullet points on the computer screens. "If Lisa Bennet didn't know Anne's suspicions until Sunday night, why would she have purchased and brought a gun before then? She wouldn't have.

"With this huge hole in their argument, the defense reversed course and came up with an alternative theory—this time that Anne LaRussa, confined to a wheelchair, thought up, set up, and built an elaborate mechanism to kill herself—a mechanism that took the defense's highly skilled expert witness *weeks* to concoct. The defense told you their theory accounts for all the evidence gathered in the LaRussa home by the CSI team."

Another pause. "But . . . it didn't account for the most fundamental facts. Anne LaRussa was not physically capable of putting that elaborate mechanism in place. The defense also didn't give you a reason why Anne LaRussa would kill herself and seek to blame her husband.

"The defense came up with yet *another* theory. And it is, again, centered on Dr. Lisa Bennet. The defense wants you to now believe that Anne's *best friend* helped her take her own life. The same best friend who testified that Anne accused her of having an affair with her husband?" Ambrose's voice dripped incredulity. "These are fairy tales, ladies and gentlemen. These are fables. Fantasies. This is desperation. The defense is throwing mud on the wall and hoping something, anything, will stick to create reasonable doubt in your minds so that you will free a murderer."

That notion struck Keera in the chest. Was she about to free a murderer?

"Forget the fantasies and the fables. Remember the *facts*. Vince LaRussa arrived at home that night and his wife remained alive. How do we know this? Because Dr. Bennet said Anne LaRussa was alive when she departed the house at seven twenty-nine. There is no dispute about that. We can also assume, because we know Anne LaRussa spoke in detail to Syd Evans about the forfeiture clause, that she confronted her husband, Vince LaRussa, about having an affair and threatened to take all his assets. This isn't speculation. It's common sense. Anne LaRussa's intent came to a head that evening. Are we to believe she didn't also confront her husband? Why then go to all the trouble? Why hire a private investigator to get photographs, proof in her mind of the affair? Of course she confronted Vince LaRussa.

"The defense also intimates the State tried

to hide Anne LaRussa's cancer. You heard the medical examiner. Her cancer had nothing to do with her death. Maybe everything came to a head that evening *because Anne LaRussa knew she was dying and didn't have a lot of time remaining.* So she confronted her husband and swore to bankrupt him. And in response, Vince LaRussa"—Ambrose pointed to LaRussa—"shot and killed his wife. Shot her in the back of the head. A coward. That, ladies and gentlemen, is the only logical conclusion, based on the evidence." Ambrose paused as if to gather himself. Then he said, "Let's go through it together piece by piece."

Half an hour later, Ambrose neared the end of his closing. It had been a strong presentation under the circumstances. Workmanlike. Detailed. As usual. It illustrated how much he wanted to win this case. How much he wanted to beat Keera. But the evidence did not prove Vince to be a killer. Keera was sure JP Harrison had explained and depicted what had happened—a theory that satisfied all the evidence. She was sure Vince LaRussa had not pulled the trigger of that gun. The evidence did not, as Miller Ambrose kept telling the jury, fit.

But could LaRussa have set up the gun?

If not, why then did Keera have so many reservations?

"We'll take a brief recess," Judge Hung said.

Keera looked up from her thoughts. Miller Ambrose was retreating to counsel table. The jurors remained poker faced.

"And when we return, the defense will give its closing."

Keera broke out in a cold sweat, suddenly nauseated. She slid back her chair. "I have to use the restroom," she said and departed the courtroom.

She hurried down the gray-and-white marble floor to the bathroom and pushed open the door. The bathroom, like the building, was more than one hundred years old, with black-and-white terrazzo tiles, wooden bathroom stalls, and porcelain sinks. Keera turned on the tap water at the first sink and splashed cold water on her face, letting it cool her skin. She sensed someone approach the sink beside her. When she looked up, Lisa Bennet's mirrored reflection stared at the water flowing from the tap of the adjacent sink. Keera had not seen Bennet in the courtroom. She likely had been watching the closed-circuit television in the adjacent room.

Either way, Keera sensed this chance meeting had been orchestrated.

"You're Jack Worthing; aren't you?" Keera said.

"No." Bennet rinsed the soap from her hands. "I'm just the messenger. You know who Jack Worthing is."

The door to the bathroom pushed open, and others, some of whom had been seated in the gallery, walked in. Bennet turned for the towel dispenser and dried her hands on coarse brown paper before discarding it in a bin. She glanced once in the mirror, catching Keera's eye.

Then she left.

I'm just the messenger. Bennet had sent the emails.

You know who Jack Worthing is.

Jack Worthing was, according to Stephanie Bowers, Vince LaRussa. So what did it all mean?

Keera returned to the courtroom and retook her seat, aware that both Patsy and LaRussa watched her. Judge Hung had not yet retaken her seat on the bench. The question welled inside her, building until she could no longer suppress it. She turned and faced LaRussa. He didn't look surprised or inquisitive. He looked at her as if he had anticipated this moment.

"You've known who Jack Worthing is all along. Not the person who sent the emails, but the name. You know that name."

She expected him to deny it. She expected him to furrow his brow and look perplexed, as he had done when she first raised that name in the attorney conference room at the King County jail. She expected him to ask what she was talking about. A skilled liar.

He didn't. Vince LaRussa's lips inched into a

thin grin. "What I've known is irrelevant to the job you have sworn to do, Counselor," he whispered. "You promised to provide me with a vigorous defense, every step of the way. To the very end." He leaned closer. His eyes darkened. His stare hardened. His jaw set. "Do your job."

"Ms. Duggan." Judge Hung had retaken the bench. "Does the defense wish to give a closing statement?"

LaRussa broke eye contact and sat back, staring straight ahead.

"Ms. Duggan?"

Keera looked past LaRussa to Patsy, who appeared concerned. Keera took a breath and addressed Judge Hung. "It does, Your Honor."

She moved her laptop to the podium, her mind spinning. She looked to the jurors and somehow pulled everything together. Movement inside the courtroom slowed. She could see every move in the trial unfolding, as she once could see the moves on a chessboard being played.

"May it please the court." She thanked the jury for their service. Then she said, "Like many of you, I have struggled with the evidence in this case, though never with Vince LaRussa's innocence. It's why we are here, in court, because the evidence is perplexing." Her competitive streak kicked in. "My client, Vince LaRussa, is innocent. He came into this courtroom innocent until proven guilty. The State had the burden to prove his guilt . . . but not just to prove it. The State's burden is to prove his guilt to each and every one of you, *beyond a reasonable doubt.*"

She gave her stock comments on reasonable doubt, something she used often in her trials. Judge Hung would provide the jury with a specific instruction after closing arguments.

"I struggled because the evidence seemed contradictory. I struggled to understand how all the variables fit together in a coherent theory. You heard our defense expert, JP Harrison, testify to much the same thing. He said a theory is not a theory unless it accounts for *all* the variables. He learned that in his high school chemistry class from his teacher, Mr. Cobalt. If the theory accounts for all the variables, he received an A. If it does not, then the theory fails. It is just a hypothesis."

Several jurors smiled, no doubt recalling Harrison and his testimony.

"The prosecution failed," Keera said. "The State's theory of this case simply doesn't account for all the evidence and is, therefore, not a theory but a hypothesis. Mere speculation."

She paused a moment for emphasis. Then she said, "Let's go through the evidence Mr. Ambrose did not explain." She hit the computer screen and put up the bullet points Ambrose had used. She used them like chess pieces to attack and deplete the State's position one move at a time.

She paused to give the jury the opportunity to think on its own. Patsy said too many attorneys told the jurors what to think. The good lawyers left the jurors white space and allowed them to seemingly reach conclusions on their own.

It was an art. It was a gift.

"The State tells you to use common sense, but the State never gives you a commonsense answer to these questions," Keera said. "I'm sure the evidence was puzzling for some of you—until JP Harrison presented you with a theory supported by an experiment that accounted for *every piece of evidence*. JP Harrison presented evidence that Anne LaRussa killed herself. He presented a method by which she accomplished this. Mr. Harrison passed Mr. Cobalt's test. He got an A.

"The State, in its closing, asked you to reject Mr. Harrison's theory because the State says it doesn't make sense. The State argues Anne LaRussa could not have physically set up the mechanism on her own. The State argues Anne LaRussa had no motivation to blame her husband. The State anticipated the defense's argument that Anne LaRussa did not set up the device on her own, that she received help from her best friend, Lisa Bennet."

Keera took a deep breath. She parted her hands, holding them palm up. "Anne LaRussa was dying. She had terminal cancer. She had weeks to live, at most. The State did not want you to know this. The State went to great lengths to not let the medical examiner, Arthur Litchfield, tell you this critical piece of evidence. What was the State trying to hide? Was the State trying to hide the fact that Dr. Lisa Bennet, an oncologist who lost her husband to cancer, knew both professionally and personally the pain and suffering her best friend would endure those final, horrible weeks; that it would be a blessing for Anne and for her family if she died quickly? Was it trying to hide the fact that Lisa Bennet would do what her best friend asked, and help her to leave this world on her own terms?

"Instead, in its closing, the State raises another question. Why would Anne LaRussa and Lisa Bennet set up the device that killed her, and why would they seek to blame her husband?" Keera turned and looked to Vince LaRussa. His eyes shifted, momentarily engaging her.

"I don't know," she said. She looked to the jurors. "*We* may never know why. But that isn't my job. And that isn't what you have been asked to determine. I told you in my opening statement that my job was to convince you that reasonable doubt exists as to whether Vince LaRussa killed his wife.

"The State has failed to prove *beyond a reasonable doubt* that Vince LaRussa, with malice aforethought, shot and killed his wife. But I don't have to tell you that. You've figured it out on your own, as was your duty. You know Vince LaRussa didn't do it. Vince LaRussa did not murder his wife, and that is the only question before you. I ask you to do your duty. I ask you to find Vince LaRussa not guilty."

After a brief pause, Keera thanked the jury. She felt physically and emotionally drained as she made her way back to counsel table. The rush of adrenaline she had so often felt at the end of chess tournaments and at the conclusion of trials did not come, nor did the satisfaction.

Ambrose stood to give the final word. Keera thought he would try to provide an answer to the questions she had posed. He didn't. He couldn't.

"The defense would like you to believe this case is complicated," Ambrose said. "They would like you to believe the evidence is complicated. 'It's too complicated to figure out, so let's throw our hands up and find the defendant not guilty.'" He shook his head and stared at the jury. "The defense is the one trying to confuse you. Not the State. This case is simple.

"Anne LaRussa called Syd Evans to her house that Sunday night to discuss the forfeiture clause in the prenuptial agreement. Anne LaRussa called Lisa Bennet to the house that Sunday night to accuse her of having an affair with Vince LaRussa, an affair that would trigger that forfeiture clause. You heard Dr. Bennet testify on the witness stand, under oath." Another pause.

Ambrose was clearly struggling to keep his anger under control. "No one else came to the house that night. No one broke a window or jimmied a door before Vincent LaRussa came home that night. Anne LaRussa confronted him with evidence that would cost him tens of millions of dollars. And he shot Anne LaRussa in the back of the head."

He stared at them. His voice calmed. "Tragic, but straightforward. Simple.

"Don't let the defense confuse you. Find the defendant, Vince LaRussa, guilty of first-degree murder."

Ambrose sat.

Vince LaRussa's fate was now in the jury's hands.

So why did Keera feel like it remained in hers?

CHAPTER 36

Judge Hung sent the case to the jury just after lunch. Vince LaRussa was escorted back to jail to await the jurors' verdict. Keera did not talk to him. She gave Patsy that task. Then they returned to their office. Both expected a long deliberation. Two hours after returning, Keera received word from Judge Hung's court clerk that the jurors had several questions. Judge Hung wanted counsel to brief those questions, meaning provide legal support for their positions, further indicating a long deliberation.

"I'll do it," Ella said in Keera's office with Patsy and Maggie. "I have that research, and I know the trial transcript better than anyone."

"Thanks, Ella," Keera said as Ella headed to the door.

"Not a problem."

"I mean it," Keera said.

Ella stopped and looked back. Her eyes panned from Keera to Patsy, then to Maggie, and finally back to Keera. "This is what family does," she said.

Keera smiled. "And law firms."

"I'll make some fresh coffee and order in sandwiches," Maggie said. "Anything in particular?"

"I'm not hungry," Keera said.

"I'm ordering you a sandwich and you're going to eat it," Maggie said. "That goes for you too, Dad."

Keera smiled. "Okay. But first I'm going to go for a walk to clear my head."

"Take your cell phone," Maggie said and left Keera's office.

"You want some company?" Patsy asked.

"I think this time I'll go alone."

"You have that look," he said.

"What look is that?" Keera said, feigning ignorance.

"That look young defense attorneys get when they realize the person they're fighting so hard to get off is guilty. They wonder what the hell they're doing, what kind of person they're putting back on the street."

"You've experienced it," Keera said.

Patsy smiled, rueful. "I have. And I can tell you it isn't nearly as bad as that feeling you get when you know an innocent client is going to be convicted."

"I'm sure it isn't."

"So, what's eating you, kiddo? LaRussa didn't kill his wife. I think that's pretty clear."

"Is it?" Keera asked. "I'm no longer so certain. Maybe he didn't pull the trigger, but I don't think he's innocent, Dad. I just don't know what he's guilty of."

"Is this doubt coming from Jack Worthing, and all the people he's sent us to talk to?"

"I ran into Lisa Bennet in the bathroom just before giving my closing argument. I said, 'You're Jack Worthing.' "

"What was her response?"

"She said, 'No. I'm just the messenger. You know who Jack Worthing is.' "

"Vince?"

"I think it means she wrote the emails and she helped Anne set up the device. I think she sent me to talk to those people, to his mother, to learn that Vince is Jack Worthing. Just before I gave my closing I turned to Vince and asked him."

"What did he say?"

"He told me to do the job I promised to do." She sighed. "Remember I said there's a line of dialogue in *The Importance of Being Earnest*?"

"I remember you said something. I don't remember the line."

" 'The truth is rarely pure and never simple.' I think that applies here. I just don't know what the truth is, in this case."

Patsy didn't answer right away. After a few moments, he said, "Here's the thing to always remember, kiddo. You were retained to do a job. You can't beat yourself up because you did that job well. It's the State's job to put criminals behind bars. I think you still have some PA blood in you, and it's making you question your job as a defense attorney. It takes time to understand a defense attorney's job isn't to get anybody off. It's to make sure your client's rights are protected. If you do your job, then the outcome—guilty, not guilty, hung jury, is irrelevant." Patsy walked to the door. "Go for your walk. You'll feel better. I'm going to my office and your sister is going to force-feed me a sandwich."

Keera took the elevator to the first floor, but she walked only as far as the Paddy Wagon. She opted for a booth in the back where she would often sit and work on her laptop when she wanted to get away from the office phones.

Liam appeared at her table. "Eating alone?" he said. "That's not healthy."

"Just drinking," she said.

"Even less healthy."

"Club soda with a lime."

He checked his watch. "Too early for Dalmore?"

"Waiting on a jury," she said.

"Been reading about the trial in the paper," Liam said.

"It's in the jury's hands now," she said.

"I'll leave you to your thoughts, then."

He returned minutes later with her club soda and lime, as well as a salad and slices of bread and cubes of butter. "Never good to drink on an empty stomach." He smiled before he departed, giving her privacy.

Keera responded to emails on her phone that required attention. She didn't know what was worse, being in trial or trying to get out from under the mound of work that piled up in her other cases while she was in trial.

She was glad to have the distraction.

At some point she sensed someone standing at her table and looked up expecting to see Liam.

"Thought I would find you here," Frank Rossi said. "Looks like you're getting a head start on everything you haven't done the last several weeks. I know that feeling too well."

Keera leaned back against the seat cushion, curious. As with Lisa Bennet in the courthouse bathroom, she knew this was not a chance meeting. "I would have thought you'd be doing the same thing."

"I'm not as conscientious as you," Rossi said. He gestured to the booth seat across the table from her. She motioned for him to sit.

Liam returned. "Whatever she's drinking," Rossi said. "What is that? Vodka? Gin?"

"Club soda with a lime," Keera said.

Rossi looked at his watch, which caused Keera to look at hers. It was after five. Judge Hung had sent the jurors home. Almost simultaneously, Keera's phone pinged. A text from Ella. The court clerk had called to advise exactly that.

"Club soda with a lime," Rossi said.

"You just in the neighborhood and decide to stop by?" Keera asked.

Rossi smiled. "I called your office. They said you went for a walk. I remembered you telling me you often came here when you wanted to get away from the phone." He looked about. "I always liked this place."

Keera and Rossi had come to the Paddy Wagon when working cases, or to celebrate a conviction. "Yeah, me too." She paused. "Thanks for the ME's report."

Rossi grabbed a slice of sourdough from the basket and took a bite. "I'll deny it."

"I know."

"Puts the nail in Ambrose's coffin to become King County prosecuting attorney though. Judge Hung will hang him for misconduct. No pun intended. Can't say I care, given that he was prepared to throw me under that bus."

"Patsy says Judge Hung doesn't accept anything that puts a stain on the legal profession," Keera said.

"Like a lawyer faking he's drunk to buy his experts more time?" Rossi asked.

"I'll deny it," Keera said.

Liam returned with Rossi's drink. He didn't bring him his own salad or bread.

Rossi took a sip. "Not bad. I could get used to this." He set the glass down. "Crazy case, huh?

Nothing like the cases we tried together. Your closing was excellent, by the way."

"Thank you," she said, still waiting for Rossi to reveal the purpose for his visit.

"Billy Ford said this case was like that riddle. Damned if he wasn't right."

"What riddle?"

"The one about the guy walking into a room and finding the window open, a puddle of water on the floor, broken glass, and Mary has suffocated. What happened?"

"I'm too exhausted for riddles, Frank."

"Mary was a goldfish. The wind came through the window, knocked the fishbowl to the ground." He ate more bread. "You solved the riddle."

"You think so?"

"Harrison provided as good an explanation for what happened as any."

"I'm not sure I solved it."

"He's going to get off," Rossi said. "You know that; don't you?"

Keera gave Rossi's question some thought. "We'll see."

"You don't look happy about it. What's wrong?"

That caught her attention. The reason why he was here? "Do you think he's innocent?"

"Of killing his wife? I thought he did it. I wanted more time to gather evidence, but Ambrose had his panties in a bunch, and your client refused to waive time. Another good move, by the way. So yeah, I thought he did it. But after hearing Harrison's theory, watching that video . . . I think LaRussa's innocent—of killing his wife anyway."

Keera ran her finger down the condensation on the outside of her glass. She raised her gaze and made eye contact with Rossi. He seemed to want to say more.

"The question I keep asking myself is a question I know you keep asking yourself: Why would Anne LaRussa do what she did?" Rossi said. "If she did what Harrison said, she set her death up to look like her husband killed her. Why? And why would Lisa Bennet participate in something like that? There would have to be a good reason; wouldn't there?"

"You talk to Bennet about it?"

"Not yet."

"I wish I knew the reason."

"You don't?"

She shook her head. "No."

"But the same thought occurred to you, didn't it?"

"I'll deny it," Keera said, unable to suppress a grin.

"Someone knows," Rossi said.

"Jack Worthing," Keera said, throwing out the name. Rossi's features seemed to freeze, like a mask. "What?" she asked.

"How do you know that name?"

Keera studied Rossi's facial expression and his body language. He knew the name. "How do *you* know that name?"

"We never released that name to the public, Keera. Where did you hear it?"

"Released it to the public? What are you talking about, Frank? You know that name? You're familiar with it?"

"I think you need to tell me how you know that name, Keera."

"I'm not sure I can."

"Look, Keera, we've known each other a long time, long enough for you to know I'm being sincere. This isn't some detective's ploy to get information out of defense counsel."

She recalled Jack Worthing's first email, telling her she was playing the game of her life. "I can't tell you, Frank."

A flash of understanding crossed his face. "You learned the name during the course of representing Vince LaRussa. Work product?"

"It's complicated. I just know I can't tell you."

"Keera—"

"But I know somebody who can."

CHAPTER 37

They took separate cars and parked at the curb in front of Lisa Bennet's home. Rossi met Keera at the stairs leading to the front door. "I should do this on my own," he said.

"No chance, Frank," Keera said. "She meant for me to have the information. I'm trying to figure out why. If she is going to tell anyone, she'll tell me. But you need to hear it for yourself. I can't tell you."

The summer light had faded, though darkness remained hours away. At the front door, Rossi knocked. Footsteps approached, then silence. Lisa Bennet was debating whether to open her front door, perhaps contemplating that she'd been caught and fearful of having been found out. Rossi was about to knock a second time when the door pulled open.

Bennet looked tired, physically worn down, and mentally drained.

"Doctor Bennet?" Rossi held up his badge and ID. "I'd like a moment of your time."

Bennet looked to Keera, then back to Rossi. She didn't ask *what about* or feign ignorance. She looked resigned. Without a word, she stepped back to allow them to enter.

They went into the front room. Rossi sat and

leaned forward, elbows resting on his knees. Keera took a chair off to the side.

"I'm going to cut to the chase, Dr. Bennet, since I think we're *all* exhausted," Rossi said. "Do you know the name Jack Worthing?"

Bennet nodded.

"Tell me how?" Rossi said.

"Anne first told me."

"What did she tell you?"

Bennet sighed. "Where do you want me to start?" She sounded tired.

"I've found the beginning is always a good place," Rossi said.

Bennet looked to Keera. "If you did as the emails instructed, then you know."

"Tell me," Rossi said. "I need to know."

"Vince LaRussa isn't who he purports to be."

"Explain what you mean," Rossi said. "Who is he?"

Again, Bennet glanced at Keera. "Vince grew up in an abusive home with an abusive father, and a mother who was an addict. Anne found monthly payments Vince was making to a woman named Stephanie Bowers. This was after her accident. It started innocently. Anne was in his office for some purpose and found a record of the payments, every month, on his desk. The same amount. She thought at first it was an investor, but then she noticed the address, a trailer park outside Beaverton, Oregon. Not exactly the high-

468

end clientele Vince sought. It made Anne curious. Given Anne's physical limitations, she couldn't very well go and talk to Bowers, and Bowers didn't have a phone. Not listed anyway."

"So you went," Keera said. "And told Bowers you were Anne LaRussa."

"Yes."

"And found that Stephanie Bowers was Vince LaRussa's mother," Keera said.

Bennet nodded.

"What do you mean she *found* his mother?" Rossi looked up from scribbling notes in a notepad. "Vince didn't know about his own mother?"

"Vince knew about her. Anne didn't," Bennet said. "Vince had told Anne when they married that both his parents were dead, that he had no living relatives. It was a lie. One of many. He was paying his mother's rent and providing her food money to keep her quiet. I went to the trailer park, pretended to be Anne, and spoke to his mother. Bowers said she and Vince took off in the middle of the night after his father nearly killed her. They never saw him again. She described an ugly household and said Vince escaped the abuse by reading about other people's lives and imagining them to be his life. One of those lives was Jack Worthing, a character in a play with an alter ego. It's not unusual for a child subjected to early, repetitive trauma to fail to develop a core sense of identity, and to instead create an alternate identity, possibly more than one, that is radically different from his reality."

"Like multiple personality disorder?" Rossi asked.

" 'Dissociative identity' is the clinical term, though it's not universally accepted by medical and health professionals. In essence, the belief is that the child creates an identity or identities unlike his own to avoid having to cope with trauma. The child creates different memories, different families, even different friends. In Vince's mind, his alternate identity was someone well liked who had lots of money, or would soon, but that person also had a dark side that did the dark things the other identity would not. Vince associated wealth with success, at a very young age. Accumulating money became paramount to him because he believed it represented happiness. Bowers told me all about Vince, all the things Anne didn't know. She told me about his schooling, his friends. All the things a wife should have known but Anne didn't.

"I told Anne what Bowers told me and she dug deeper. She worked backwards and eventually found Vince's schools in Beaverton and his college, Washington State. The more people she talked with from Vince's past, the more she realized Vince was a fraud and a likely sociopath. She learned that Vince stole money from his classmates in elementary school. He hid money he earned selling strawberries so his grandfather wouldn't take it. He embezzled money from his fraternity. He injured an employee, then paid him hush money so he wouldn't sue."

"Anne LaRussa didn't know any of this when she married him?" Rossi asked.

"People with this psychiatric disorder are very adept liars because they believe what they are telling others is the truth."

Keera recalled her inability to read whether LaRussa was telling her the truth when she confronted him about the witnesses, and she had learned to read people's tells. LaRussa never showed one.

"When Anne asked him questions about what his family was like before they died, Vince could speak about them convincingly, as if the people he spoke of had really existed. When I first met Vince, I didn't know what to think. He seemed too good to be true. Good-looking, motivated, charismatic. But when I would ask him personal questions, he would either change the subject or give me short answers that didn't reveal much. I worried for Anne. She came from money. She was going to inherit money."

"You thought LaRussa could be a gold digger," Rossi said.

"I thought it a distinct possibility," Bennet said. "So did Anne's father."

"The reason for the prenuptial agreement,"

Rossi said. "Did you talk with Anne about it?"

"Anne was in love. She truly loved Vince. And she believed Vince was a guy who had pulled himself up from nothing. She also said money wasn't an issue because her parents would insist on a prenuptial agreement and Vince had agreed to it." She turned to Keera. "You know how it is. If you object too strenuously, you run the risk of losing your friend. I didn't want to lose Anne's friendship, so I kept my mouth shut and hoped for the best."

"What does all this have to do with Anne LaRussa's murder?" Rossi asked.

"You're familiar with Bernie Madoff?" Bennet asked.

"Absolutely," Rossi said.

"Madoff became Vince's template for LaRussa Wealth Management."

"It's a Ponzi scheme?" Rossi asked, sounding unconvinced. "LWM is a Ponzi scheme?"

"It's why no one else has been able to duplicate LWM's investment returns," Keera said, recalling Phil McPherson telling her he had tried to put together various models and failed. "Why Vince didn't want his employees handling any of the clients. He wasn't actually investing in the market or anywhere else. He just needed the new investors so he could pay the old investors each month."

"Vince only needed Anne to convince her

family to invest with LWM, then get them to convince their wealthy friends. The family did so, for Anne," Bennet said. "They wanted Vince to be successful. And he was. LWM returned consistent profits each month for its investors. Word spread. No one did a background check on Vince because he was Anne's husband. He had a beautiful office in Pioneer Square, sat on charity boards, and eventually was on the cover of *Seattle Magazine*."

"It was all bullshit?" Rossi said.

"Not initially. Vince initially had some legitimate properties and was making legitimate investments. He is very, very smart. He picks things up incredibly fast. But he always wanted more, and he needed more income to keep paying investors eight percent."

Rossi sat forward. "There would be paperwork, audits, loans, title reports on the mortgaged properties, and other paperwork from the deals made. How would LWM get all the paperwork needed to legitimize all the investments? To legitimize the annual audits?" he asked.

"He falsified the records for the vast majority of those properties. He faked the mortgage papers," Bennet said.

"How did he get past the audits?" Rossi asked.

"He hired accounting firms to send out validation requests for his properties, but the mailing addresses he provided were PO boxes Vince had set up for himself."

"He'd get the validation requests and fill the documents out himself," Rossi said.

"He saw how easy it was, and it emboldened him. He falsified more and more records."

"What about his employees?" Rossi asked. "Did they know?"

"Vince is very good at compartmentalizing his employees," Keera said, repeating what McPherson told her. "And people need jobs. His big break came when the large and reputable feeder firms invested their clients' money with LWM."

"They provided LWM credibility," Rossi said, and Keera recalled that he had been an accounting major and he came from an accounting family. "And feeder firms invest in things like retirement accounts. People can't cash out of retirement accounts to try to redeem their profits without paying a penalty, which would have given Vince his steady cash flow."

"And nobody in those reputable feeder firms looked into this?" Keera asked.

"Why would they?" Rossi said. "The feeder firms get paid a percentage of assets under management. On paper, if the assets are increasing eight percent a year, their fees increase by the same percentage."

"What about the investors?" Keera said, recalling more of her conversation with McPherson. "They were sophisticated. Some of them surely would have figured out things weren't on the up-and-up and reported it."

"If you were consistently getting eight percent return on your investments and knew you could pull your money out at any time, would you complain?" Rossi said. "Many of these high-wealth investors became high wealth because what they care about isn't social justice, equality for all, and a system in which all investors are treated equally. They are high wealth because they care about money. Making money. And Vince LaRussa is making them a lot of it, every month. He's the golden goose." He turned to Bennet. "How do you know all of this?" Rossi asked her.

"Anne figured it out. She told me."

"Anne? She was a literature major," Keera said.

"And always very, very smart," Bennet said. "When Anne had her horses, she ran the entire equestrian business, paid all the bills, every-thing. She was busy and content. She didn't have the time or the interest to look into LWM's business. After her injury, she was home and started looking into things that didn't seem right. It started innocently, as I said. Anne found the payments to Stephanie Bowers. Then she found certain validation requests with PO boxes on them. When she looked further into it, she saw all the validation requests were being sent to different PO boxes but somehow landing on

Vince's desk. She didn't understand why that was. Then she found title reports and loan applications for properties, looked those properties up, and learned LWM had no interest in them."

"Vince manufactured loans using false title reports, loan applications, and other paperwork from proposed deals that were never made," Rossi said. "He created bogus assets, bogus properties to offset the missing cash, then sought out new investors and used their investments to pay the monthly interest to the initial investors. It's a classic Ponzi scheme."

"Anne tested the waters once and asked Vince about the properties," Bennet said. "Vince told her she didn't understand his business and should stay out of it. When she persisted he got angry. Anne told him she was looking out for her parents and their friends who had invested with LWM, but Vince just got more defiant and said he was the best thing that ever happened to all of them, that he had made them a lot of money."

"Why did he keep documents at home if he didn't trust Anne?" Keera asked.

"Probably so his secretary and LWM employees wouldn't find them at work," Rossi said. "In a Ponzi scheme it's important to limit the number of people who have any information on the investment scheme. He likely had two sets of books, one he kept at work that he used when courting new investors, and a second set with more accurate information he kept at home."

"After Anne confronted Vince, he had a deadbolt installed on his office door," Bennet said. "Which only made Anne more concerned." Bennet looked to Keera. "Vince underestimated her. Anne's body was broken but her mind was sharp. Anne called a locksmith, told him she'd locked herself out of her office, and had a spare key made. People are empathetic to a woman in a wheelchair. They don't ask a lot of questions. She found the post office boxes for twenty fake properties and figured out Vince was replying to auditor inquiries himself. She also found an invoice from an accounting firm in Pioneer Square returning LWM's deposit and declining to perform an audit."

"Cliff Larson Accounting," Rossi said. "Bernie Madoff used to choose small accounting firms with names similar to the large accounting firms to make it look like the big firms were auditing him and giving him the stamp of approval. That's why the name was familiar to me. LaRussa did the same thing."

"Why didn't the accountant report LWM?" Keera asked.

Rossi shook his head. "Many auditing firms don't want to take the chance of becoming blackballed. It is not unusual for the firm to simply back out of the job when they find an impropriety, send a letter and say they won't perform the audit. That happened with Madoff."

"When the news broke about the murdered accountant in Pioneer Square and Anne read the name in the paper, she knew Vince had to be involved somehow, that the accountant had figured out the Ponzi scheme and maybe threatened to expose Vince," Bennet said. "Anne didn't know for sure. All she knew was the man had been murdered."

"You're saying Vince LaRussa killed the accountant in the old Pioneer Building?" Keera asked.

Rossi looked at her. "Jack Worthing was Cliff Larson's last meeting that afternoon. At least that's what we believe. We found that name in the receptionist's calendar. That's how I know it. We've been trying to link it to a disgruntled client or former client for more than a year."

"Oh my God," Keera said. "And I just got him off." She felt nauseated, the same feeling she experienced as a teenager when her father came to her tournaments drunk. She stood and paced.

"Are you all right?" Bennet asked.

She breathed deeply, held her breath for four seconds, then released it slowly.

"Keera?" Rossi said.

"I just need a minute," she said. She felt like she needed a long, hot shower to scrub the grime off. She sat back down and nodded to Rossi and Bennet to continue.

Bennet said, "Anne had another problem. Who could she tell? And how could she prove it? She didn't have a lot of time. She was dying." Bennet wiped tears. "Anne told me she believed Vince killed the accountant, but she didn't have proof." Bennet shrugged. "She was my best friend."

"But why the elaborate suicide?" Rossi asked.

Bennet let out a breath of air. "Anne had been in considerable pain, but she had related that pain to her paralysis. When the pain persisted and got worse, I had her brought in and we did a PET scan. That's when I found the tumors. I told her she had weeks to live. Anne was stoic. She told me she didn't want to live the next forty years as she was, in a wheelchair, and especially not with Vince. Without enough time to get evidence that Vince killed the accountant, she decided instead to frame Vince for her murder. She hoped to put him away for the rest of his life, so he couldn't harm anyone else. After we came up with a mechanism that would work, Anne crafted emails for me, if I needed them." She turned to Keera. "Those are the emails I sent to you."

"Why me?" Keera asked. The question had bothered her from the start. "Why not send those emails to the prosecutor or to the police, the detectives investigating the accountant's murder?"

"Once Anne decided to take her own life and to blame Vince, she didn't want me to be prosecuted for helping her do so. And once I committed to helping her, to lie about her accusing me of having an affair with Vince to give him the motive to kill Anne, I couldn't just go to the police or the prosecutor, not without implicating myself."

"So the affair, that was all made up?" Rossi said.

"Anne told me to have lunch with Vince, hold his hand, make it look intimate."

"Okay, so she set Vince up to take the fall for her death. Why send the emails, then, to anyone?" Rossi asked.

"Anne was doubling down. She knew how smart Vince was, how hard it would be to convict him. She also didn't want to take a chance that something would go wrong with the mechanism and Vince would get off. So she put together emails about what she had learned about Vince's past. My job was to get those emails to the right person after Anne's death, if needed. As I said, I couldn't go to the prosecutor or the police without giving away Anne's suicide and my helping her. I sent the emails in Jack Worthing's name using a VPN, knowing Anne had used that name to talk to the witnesses. I hoped to intrigue you, make you think these people had evidence that Vince killed Anne."

"You took a risk that I might ignore those emails," Keera said.

"I know," she said. "But I researched you once I learned you were representing Vince. I learned that you once played competitive chess, which means you're calculating and competitive. It's why I made mention of it in the first email. I hoped it would intrigue you and cause you to follow through with the other witnesses."

"You still have those emails, the ones you sent as Jack Worthing?" Rossi asked Bennet.

"I still have them," Bennet said.

"I want to speak to his mother," Rossi said. "She can independently corroborate that Vince used that name, that it is a name from his past." Rossi took out his cell phone and made a phone call. "Billy," he said. "I need you to pull the Cliff Larson file, specifically the list of his clients. I know it's late. Do it tomorrow. Find out if LaRussa Wealth Management is anywhere on that list. And find the receptionist's appointment calendar. I'll explain more when I have time."

After speaking to Bennet with Rossi, Keera went home and called Patsy. She told him what she had learned, the significance of the name Jack Worthing.

Patsy listened intently. Then he said, "It's like I said, kiddo. If he walks from this charge, it isn't because you freed a guilty man. The PA failed to convict him. You just did your job. What Rossi does in the future with the information he's been given is his job. That's our system of justice."

"Doesn't make it any easier to hear, Dad."

"I know. Are you going to be okay?"

She assured him she would be and asked him not to tell Ella. She didn't see the point.

She set her phone down and instinctively moved to the cabinet beneath the sideboard before remembering she'd poured her Scotch down the sink. She inhaled a deep breath, exhaled, and turned to her other crutch. Chess. Winning was now just a matter of time, but Keera was stalling. She didn't want the connection with her father to again end.

Still, it was inevitable. Patsy was running out of squares to which he could retreat. If she made a move, one out of character for the Seattle Pawnslayer, Patsy would suspect she'd let him win, maybe even that she'd learned his identity and was taking pity on him. Neither he nor she would feel good about it.

She studied Patsy's most recent move, king to e1. Keera moved her rook to e8. Check. She had multiple ways to finish the game but decided to use her rook to bait Patsy's queen and keep the game alive, so he wouldn't resign.

A short time later, Patsy made his thirty-seventh move. His queen took her rook at e8.

Keera moved her knight to g2 and again checked his king.

On his thirty-eighth move, Patsy moved his king to f2. Keera's bishop took Patsy's bishop at d4. Check.

Almost over now. Almost.

CHAPTER 38

August 22, 2023

Tuesday morning, Keera went into the office early but couldn't concentrate on her other files. She kept thinking about Frank Rossi, wondering if he had spoken to Stephanie Bowers or any of the other witnesses and what he had learned.

Just after lunch, she received a call from Judge Maxine Hung's court clerk. She expected the clerk to tell Keera the jury had additional questions.

"The jury has reached a verdict," the woman said. "Judge Hung has requested all counsel in court by 1:00 p.m."

Keera stood from her chair. Butterflies swarmed her stomach. She hung up the phone and hurried down the hall to tell Patsy.

He looked stunned. "So quickly?" he asked.

"Apparently."

A quick verdict was often associated with a finding of guilt. If one or more jurors held out, it took the other jurors time to convince them, or to give up trying. Had no one held out? Had they bought Miller Ambrose's simple argument— Anne LaRussa was alive when Lisa Bennet left the house and dead when Vince LaRussa called

911? Had they not bought Harrison's theory and his video evidence? Not one of them?

"Whatever the outcome," Patsy said. "Know that you just did your job. Nothing more or less."

Ordinarily Keera couldn't temper her intense competitive streak, but this time she couldn't help but think about the accountant who Frank Rossi said had been brutally beaten to death. Maybe this was Vince's just punishment, as his wife had hoped. Maybe she had succeeded in reaching out from the grave, to ensure justice was served.

Keera, Patsy, Ella, and Maggie hurried up the hill to the courthouse. None of them said much. The talking was over. It was time to listen.

The news vans and reporters who had appeared off and on throughout the trial returned in full, lining Third Avenue. Keera and her team used the tunnel through the administrative building, but there would be no avoiding the reporters inside the courthouse. The pack awaited them on the ninth floor, seeking a comment about the quick jury verdict. Keera declined to respond. So, too, did Patsy. She didn't see the need to speculate or posture now that the jury had rendered its decision. It would be what it would be, and they would all know soon enough.

King County marshals cleared a path through the media and escorted the four of them into the courtroom. Ella and Maggie found seats in the gallery, which soon filled, men and women sitting shoulder to shoulder. More people stood in the back. Anne LaRussa's relatives retook their designated place behind Miller Ambrose and April Richie. They looked nervous. Frank Rossi did not sit at counsel table, which was clear of computers, notepads, exhibits, and files. This was no longer the attorneys' show. Ambrose sat with legs crossed, his hands folded in his lap. When Keera and Patsy pulled out their chairs, Ambrose gave a passing glance across the aisle, but he did not say anything.

As Keera and Patsy took their seats, the court clerk disappeared behind the bench. Moments later, corrections officers led Vince LaRussa into the courtroom and removed his handcuffs. LaRussa sat. Keera sensed him looking at her, but she kept her gaze forward. The thought of what he'd likely done sickened her. LaRussa leaned to his left so their shoulders touched. Again, her skin crawled.

"You said a quick decision is often a bad sign," LaRussa said. She smelled the acidic tint of nerves. Good.

"One never knows for certain," she said, not looking at him and grateful when the clerk reentered the courtroom.

"All rise."

The bailiff announced Judge Hung. The courtroom rose in unison, then sat when Judge Hung settled in behind her desk. The jurist also looked unprepared for the jury's quick decision. She sat forward. "It is the court's understanding that the jury has reached a verdict. In a moment I will ask the bailiff to bring in the jury. I want to caution everyone, on both sides of the courtroom, to respect the jury's decision. If I perceive anyone not respecting the decision, if there are any outbursts, I will have that person removed and held in contempt."

With that, Judge Hung instructed the bailiff to bring in the jury.

The air in the room thickened. Movements slowed. The bailiff's shoes snapped against the linoleum floor. A door at the back of the courtroom creaked open. The bailiff's voice shattered the silence. "All rise for the jury."

The jurors walked past the pews and took their seats in the jury box. Some kept their gaze on the floor. Others focused intently on Judge Hung. Not one of them looked at Ambrose or at Keera's side of the courtroom. Keera did not detect a tell.

"Members of the jury, I understand you have reached a verdict," Judge Hung said. She opened a sealed envelope and read the pages to herself. It felt like an eternity. Finally, she looked to the jurors. "Members of the jury, the court clerk will now read the verdict in the case of the State of Washington, plaintiff, versus Vincent Ernest LaRussa, defendant."

The court clerk stood. "Count one. Murder in

the first degree, RCW 9A.32.030." She paused. "We the jury in the above-entitled matter find the defendant not guilty."

Keera felt stunned.

LaRussa made a fist and softly pounded the table. Patsy turned and put his hand on LaRussa's back. Keera heard Anne LaRussa's family gasp, then weep. Murmurs reverberated throughout the gallery, but no outbursts. To Keera's left, Miller Ambrose bowed his head, but otherwise he did not react. Richie had a wide-eyed stare of shocked disbelief.

Judge Hung spoke to the jury. "Ladies and gentlemen of the jury, I am now going to ask you individually if this is your true and correct verdict. Please respond yes or no."

Judge Hung polled the jurors and, one by one, they affirmed the verdict. Vince LaRussa balled both hands into fists beneath counsel table and bowed his head, as if overcome with emotion. He did not cry. When the final juror had been polled, LaRussa turned and shook Patsy's hand.

Judge Hung advised the jury that the bailiff would escort them to the jury room to retrieve their belongings. She would meet with them to discuss their verdict and answer any questions. She also advised them that counsel might ask to speak to them, but the jurors were under no obligation to do so. With that, she released them and adjourned the proceedings.

As Judge Hung departed the bench, the courtroom erupted. Behind counsel table, Keera heard the media on their cell phones, calling in the verdict. Anne LaRussa's family huddled with Ambrose and Richie, speaking quietly.

Keera turned and found Vince LaRussa staring at her. He did not have a tear in his eye. His gaze was intent. He grinned and reached out his hand. Keera took it. LaRussa pulled her in and hugged her fiercely. Keera felt herself stiffen.

He whispered softly in her ear. "You kept your promise."

She pulled back. Stuck to routine. "The corrections officers will take you back to jail for processing. You should be released within the hour. Patsy and I will handle the media."

"It's important my clients know about the verdict as soon as possible and that I am back in charge. Can you set up a meeting with the media for later this afternoon? Send me a text and let me know where to be and when."

Keera nodded. Vince LaRussa was not focused on Anne's family members but on keeping his business running. He'd survived, again. He smiled as the marshals escorted him toward the door.

The media shouted questions, and LaRussa stopped. "I'm just glad this ordeal is over," he said. Anne LaRussa's family looked at him. He spoke as if they didn't exist. "Because of Anne's injuries and her addiction, she was not the same person I married. She had become paranoid and vindictive. I don't know why she did this."

LaRussa said it with sincerity, as if he believed it, and without any thought to his wife's grieving family. Without any empathy. Keera thought again of her interview with Phil McPherson. *At no time did he apologize. He acted like he hadn't done anything wrong and just went on about his business.*

Psychopath.

And he was going to walk out of the King County jail a free man.

Because Keera had won.

As Keera and her team returned to their office, the phones rang nonstop. Maggie was quickly under siege and enlisted a legal assistant to help field calls. Ella handled potential-client calls. Patsy spoke to the media and advised that they would hold a news conference at three o'clock in Occidental Square, outside the entrance to the office. When Maggie came up for air, she ordered some food and some sparkling cider to celebrate after the news conference.

"We should discuss what you're going to say at the conference," Ella said to Keera. "This is a huge verdict, Keera. This is going to be all over the newspapers and the television. It's going to be a substantial boost to the firm's profile, to your profile."

Keera knew Ella meant well. With this verdict they might both break from Patsy's huge shadow and establish their own reputations. Where that might take the firm, Keera had no idea. She thanked Ella, then said she'd be in her office.

"Are you all right?" Ella asked.

She nodded and went to her office. She closed the door, moved to the arched windows, and looked out at the old Pioneer Building between the branches of the maple trees in that square, the leaves partially obscuring the totem pole and pergola. She thought of the accountant, Cliff Larson, beaten to death in one of those offices—a brutal and vicious death. Emotion welled. Her stomach roiled. She turned from the window and threw up what little food she had eaten into the wastebasket beside her desk.

CHAPTER 39

At three o'clock, Keera recognized the three soft knocks on her office door. Patsy stepped in. "Is he here?" Keera asked, turning from the windows.

"Not yet, no." Patsy closed the door behind him. "He has been released though." He stepped in farther, perhaps noticing her sickened appearance, and hugged her.

"What if he kills someone else, Dad?"

Patsy said, "The detectives will gather the evidence needed to arrest him, Keera, and it will be up to the prosecuting attorney to convict him. Not you."

"What if they can't get the evidence?"

"Then he'll walk. That's our system of justice, Keera. Everyone is innocent until proven guilty. Everyone has the right to a vigorous defense."

"That's easier to accept in theory."

"You're right. The public believes in both presumptions in theory, much less so when those presumptions punch them in the face, like the O. J. Simpson verdict. The system isn't perfect. But I still believe it's the best in the world, and I will continue to defend it by defending our clients. That's been my job. It's now your job."

Keera didn't know what to say. So she remained silent.

Patsy checked his watch. "I asked Maggie to let me know when Vince arrives," he said. "Did you want to discuss what to say?"

She shook her head.

He pulled the door open. "I'll head down to the news conference and advise the media we are awaiting Vince LaRussa's arrival. He likely wants to make a big entrance. See if you can reach him and let me know."

Seconds after he left, Keera's cell phone rang. She thought it would be Vince LaRussa, but caller ID recognized Frank Rossi's number.

"Where are you?" she asked.

"I'm in the square with everyone else awaiting the news conference. Where is your client?"

"Did you talk to Stephanie Bowers?"

"Last night," Rossi said.

"And?"

"And we're going to wait a few days until this all dies down. We're getting the feds involved. The US Trustee's office will seek a court-appointed trustee to take control of LWM, freeze its accounts and assets, and try to find the money before LaRussa has a chance to abscond with it. They will pull together all the documents to prove the Ponzi scheme."

"What about the accountant, Cliff Larson?"

"I'm working on a charging document with Rick Cerrabone." Rossi named another senior prosecutor in the Most Dangerous Offender

493

Project. Cerrabone was well regarded and respected by the detectives. "We don't want to give that away just yet. We'll take LaRussa into custody on fraud and corruption and other charges. Then we'll bring the charging document to ensure he doesn't get out of jail. So where is he?"

"I don't know," Keera said.

"Try calling him. Call me back."

Keera disconnected and pulled up LaRussa's cell phone number. LaRussa did not answer. The call rang through to his voice mail. She redialed Frank Rossi's number. "He's not picking up his calls."

"I don't like this," Rossi said.

"He has access to a Learjet at Boeing Field," Keera said. "He suspects I know something, and he has to know Lisa Bennet helped Anne. He could already be running."

"I've got people watching Boeing Field to make sure he isn't going anywhere. And we're sitting on his condominium at Rainier Square and his home. Any other ideas?"

Keera thought of her chess game against Patsy, about his king, who had nowhere left to run. LaRussa, too, was running out of squares to which he could retreat, but unlike Patsy, when cornered, LaRussa wouldn't resign. He wouldn't admit defeat. He was not a man of honor. He'd do something drastic—to the bitter end.

"He won't surrender, Frank. It isn't in him."

"Meaning what?"

If LaRussa couldn't flee, he'd have no choice but to fight. "He'll attack."

"What?"

"He'll attack the piece he believes is his most dangerous pursuer in one last bid to survive."

"The piece?"

"The person, Frank." The thought struck her like a gut punch, so powerful she nearly dropped the phone. "Stephanie Bowers or Lisa Bennet," she said. "You have your car?" She was already moving to her office door.

"No, but I can get a pool car."

"No time. Meet me behind the building in the pay parking lot."

Keera rushed from her office into the hall, walking quickly, then jogging, and finally sprinting. Animated voices echoed, people talking loudly. She blew past reception. Maggie looked up from the phone and covered the receiver. "Is he here?"

"Let me know if he calls," she shouted as she reached the lobby. "Patch him through to my cell phone."

"Where are you going? Keera?"

Keera descended the interior staircase as quickly as she could. In the lobby she looked through the glass doors to Occidental Square. A crowd had gathered. She turned for the back of the building, hit the handle on the door beneath the red exit sign, and hurried into the parking lot. Rossi waited. Keera unlocked her car with the key fob, slid behind the wheel, and they drove from the lot, heading west, toward Elliott Bay. She turned right onto Alaskan Way and drove parallel to the water to get away from downtown Seattle's traffic.

Rossi was on his phone with dispatch, telling them where he was going and asking that they alert the police in Beaverton and get a unit to Stephanie Bowers's RV home. He provided dispatch with Lisa Bennet's home address and requested any available unit meet him at the house.

Keera cut over Denny Way, weaving in and out of cars and turning whenever she encountered traffic. She turned left on Tenth Avenue, drove down the block, made a right, then another left. No patrol cars.

"Where are they, Frank?"

"Should be on their way," Rossi said.

"We can't wait."

She stopped in the cutout in the curb and pushed from the car. Rossi grabbed her arm as she came around the hood. "There is no 'we.' You wait here."

She pulled her arm free. "The hell I will." She darted up the concrete stairs, Rossi right behind her.

The front door was ajar. A bad sign.

Rossi pulled her behind him, removed his gun, and stepped inside. They moved systematically from room to room on the first floor. Rossi shifted, pivoted, took aim around each corner, but saw no one. Keera didn't hear a sound.

They passed through the kitchen to a hall with a narrow staircase. Keera noted something on the carpet and pointed to it. Blood? Rossi acknowledged it, then shuffled forward to the banister. He aimed up the stairs. No one. He climbed the first step, then the second, eyes and barrel focused above, at the second story.

As they ascended, Keera saw more blood on the carpet. On the second story they proceeded down a hall. Rossi put his back against a wall filled with framed photographs that had been knocked askew. One lay on the carpet, the glass shattered. Lisa Bennet and her daughters stared up at Keera through cracked glass as she stepped over them.

Rossi followed the blood trail to the room at the end of the hall, the door also slightly ajar. In the crack of the door opening, Keera saw a bed with a white comforter. Rossi reached out and gently pushed the door open, bringing more of the room slowly into view. He stepped in and took aim at the person sitting on the bed.

Lisa Bennet.

The doctor turned her head but did not raise

the gun in her hand. On her bed was a suitcase, haphazardly filled with clothes. On the ground lay Vince LaRussa. Near his outstretched hand was a metal rod. Blood soaked the carpeting beneath him.

Bennet, who looked to be in shock, turned her gaze back to her bedroom window. Keera heard cars screeching to a stop and saw red-and-white police lights reflected in the window. Rossi approached Bennet slowly, cautiously. He reached and removed the gun from her hand. She looked up at him as he did so. Rossi stepped back, knelt, and put two fingers to LaRussa's neck.

Then he stood, securing his weapon. "I'm going to go down and let the uniforms know," Rossi said. "Don't touch anything." He left the room.

Keera sat on the bed beside Bennet.

"I knew he would come," Bennet said softly. "You did too."

Keera nodded. "I thought he might."

A pause. "It was Anne's suggestion that I purchase a second gun," Bennet said. "Maybe she never truly believed she would get Vince, and if she didn't . . . She wanted me to be safe." She let the thought fade, looked at her suitcase. "I thought of leaving. But where was I going to go? My daughters are here. My job is here." She shook her head. "Leaving would have made Anne's death meaningless. Anne could have run. She didn't. She fought. To the end." Bennet wiped tears from her cheeks. "I waited for him to come. I knew it was just a matter of time." She looked at Keera, sighed, and shook her head. "When you lose your husband . . . it hardens you. The scars toughen you. You have to protect your home, your children." She sighed again, wiped additional tears. "He came into the house. He didn't think I'd pull the trigger. He didn't think I would do it."

She looked Keera in the eye.

"The first time I pulled the trigger for me and shot him in the shoulder. When he didn't stop, when he followed me up the stairs, into the bedroom, I pulled it again.

"The second time was for Anne."

EPILOGUE

It had been more than a week since the LaRussa verdict and his subsequent shooting death, but things had not slowed for Keera. Lisa Bennet had retained the law firm, specifically Ella, to represent her in the fallout—the assisted suicide of Anne LaRussa and the shooting of Vince LaRussa. Ella's initial conversations with the King County prosecuting attorney indicated they would decline to prosecute her on either charge.

Reporters continued to call Keera incessantly, and to flock to the story of Vince LaRussa like pigeons to crumbs of bread. With good reason. Initial indications revealed LWM's Ponzi scheme to be the largest ever in Washington State history. A federally appointed trustee had seized LWM's bank accounts and all of Vince LaRussa's personal assets, including his home, his condominium, his Learjet, and his cars, but the initial valuation, at least according to Frank Rossi, indicated millions remained missing. Investors in LWM, including those who had been honestly naïve, as well as those who had been willfully silent while they collected checks each month, were out thousands or, in some cases, millions of dollars. That alone warranted media attention. But the most attention centered on LaRussa's childhood. As the facts came out, the interest was piqued, and his upbringing had already been the subject of several news articles, with more certain to come. Those few who knew LaRussa—his clients, and his employees—expressed dismay at the extent of his fraud. Those who had known him growing up expressed no dismay. They said the Ponzi scheme was consistent with the man they had known.

Regulators called for tighter controls in the investment arena to protect investors. Frank Rossi was not optimistic. The *Seattle Times* quoted him. "Greed causes people to do things they wouldn't ordinarily do, and to turn a blind eye," he said. "So long as people are making money, these types of scams will not go away."

Keera fielded or deflected numerous phone calls before finally assigning that task to Maggie. She was a fierce gatekeeper. The media wanted to know how much Keera knew during her representation of LaRussa. Upon Patsy's advice, she made one media statement and said that she knew nothing of LaRussa's alleged violent murder of Cliff Larson, and only learned of his past through her legal representation. She did not know of LWM's fraudulent acts while she defended LaRussa. She declined to answer questions and directed all further inquiries to the investigating detectives, Frank Rossi and Billy Ford.

Patsy told her that, eventually, Vince LaRussa

501

would fade from the public's consciousness and become just another blip in Seattle's history. Likely so, Keera thought, but he'd linger long in her memory.

She had spent much of her time at home, contemplating the chessboard and what to do. His thirty-ninth move, Patsy's king took her knight at g2. She moved her queen to g3. Check. The queen had the honor of finishing the game.

But Keera's heart wasn't in it.

His fortieth move, Patsy retreated his king to h1.

Keera contemplated her final move. She reached for the piece, then pulled back her hand.

Twenty minutes later, she parked in her parents' driveway, pushed out of her car, and made her way to the front door. Her mother answered. She looked and sounded surprised to see her. "Keera? What are you doing here on a Saturday afternoon?"

"Dad home?"

"He's in his den, reading. Is everything okay?"

Something not being okay had always been the assumption at the Duggan home. *What's wrong? Is everything okay? What happened?*

"Everything is fine, Mom. I just want to talk to him."

"Come on in. I'll get him."

"That's okay," she said. "I know my way." Keera smiled to put her mother at ease, but she knew it only went so far in a family that had too often assumed the worst and too often had been right.

She walked down the hall to the den. Patsy sat in his oversized brown leather chair, feet raised on an ottoman, light streaming through the windowpane. He read a legal thriller, one of his passions.

He smiled when Keera entered, but his smile faded to concern. "Hey, kiddo. What brings you here on a beautiful day? Everything okay?"

"Everything is fine, Dad. Just wanted to talk with you."

"Sure," he said, shutting the novel. "Something come up?"

She smiled. "Haven't we had enough?"

Her father laughed. "You can say that again." Patsy removed his feet and Keera lowered to the ottoman.

"I noticed the liquor cabinet is still locked. Will it stay that way?" she asked.

Her father didn't immediately answer. Then he said, "If I want to stay alive."

Keera studied him. It wasn't a bluff. "What do you mean?"

"Your mother's been after me to go in and have a checkup. I haven't had an annual physical since . . . I don't know when. Decades. I went after the trial."

"Is everything all right? You're not sick; are you?"

"The doctor says I'm in surprisingly good shape for my age . . . except my liver, which he says I've managed to pickle."

"Is that a medical term?" she said, seeking a ray of light.

He smiled. "I've destroyed liver cells and have significant scarring. Cirrhosis that could lead to cancer."

"Could?"

"He told me if I wanted to live to see eighty, and hopefully beyond, I had to give up the liquor. Cold turkey."

"Can you?"

"I've done it for a month."

"You've done it for a month before . . ." Her father would not infrequently give up drinking for Lent, forty days, then be so drunk come Easter he couldn't celebrate with the family.

"I know, kiddo. And I've disappointed your mother and you kids. I'm a binge drinker. Since I was seventeen. It's who I am."

"You sound like a defeatist. You don't sound like the Irish Brawler."

"Maybe I should have said, 'It's who I was.' Sometimes it takes the fear of God to change your behavior. Like I said. I've been sober a month. That's a start."

"I poured a bottle of Dalmore Port Wood down the drain," Keera said.

"That's an expensive statement."

"I haven't had a drink in a month either."

"I didn't know you drank."

"I made a lot of bad decisions when I drank, Dad." She wiped at a tear. It surprised her, and it surprised Patsy. Seeing his baby girl cry led to his own tears.

"Miller Ambrose?"

She was not surprised her father knew, not with all the eyes and ears Patsy still had inside the courthouse, the prosecutor's office, and at the police department. She nodded, but words stuck in her throat.

"Not so bad," her father said, allowing for a weak smile. "It brought you to the firm."

"That it did." She pulled herself together. "I made a lot of excuses to justify my drinking, Dad. Too many. None good enough. I'll make you a deal. The court is going to order you to go to counseling because of that charade you pulled. I'll go to AA meetings with you."

"You?"

"I found a group that meets close by Tuesday nights. I can pick you up. We can go to dinner beforehand and talk. The way we used to when we played chess."

Her father fought back tears. His lower lip quivered, and he rubbed a hand over his mouth. "I made a mess of things; didn't I?"

"Like you said, that's in the past, Dad. We can look to the future."

"I'd like that. I just don't know, Keera . . . I don't want to disappoint again."

She reached out and held his hands. "None of us do, Dad. We do the best we can." Keera looked to her right. To the alcove with the fireplace and the chessboard. "Looks like you have a game in progress." She rose and stepped to the chessboard. "Are you light or dark?"

"Light," he said, following her.

"Doesn't look good, Dad."

"The person I'm playing is better than me," he said.

"He'd have to be, to beat you."

"She," he said. "The person I'm playing is a she."

Keera smiled. "What do you say we end this game and start fresh? A whole new game."

"The game isn't finished."

"I think it is." She reached and put her finger on the dark king, laying it on its side. "I resign."

He stared at her, hard, until understanding. "You knew."

"I figured it out the last dinner of the month. I saw the board and recognized the moves."

"You could have won. Queen to h3. Checkmate."

"Playing chess was never about winning or losing, Dad. It still isn't. I just wanted to spend time with you. I just wanted to play."

Bernadette came into the room. She looked

worried, more so when she noticed Patsy's red eyes. "Is everything all right?"

"Everything is fine, Mom. Dad's going to go to AA meetings with me; right, Dad?"

Patsy nodded. "But not right now . . . Right now we're going to play a game."

Her mother lowered her head, clearly holding back tears. The Irish were tough, hardscrabble. She cleared her throat. "You'll stay for dinner, Keera?"

"Depends on how long it takes me to beat the Irish Brawler," she said, moving her pieces into position to start another game. "What do you say, Dad? Let's retire the Dark Knight."

ACKNOWLEDGMENTS

I often sit down with my editor at Thomas & Mercer, Gracie Doyle, and discuss my next writing project, what issue I'm looking to tackle and in what genre. Gracie brought up the subject of returning to my roots, a legal thriller, which I haven't written in some time. I like to joke to friends that I am a recovering lawyer, and I did start my writing career with a Seattle lawyer protagonist in a series of novels now referred to as the David Sloane series. I love courtroom dynamics and can appreciate the really good lawyers—maybe because I didn't get a lot of opportunity to try cases and I never felt seasoned. But I also love family dynamics, perhaps because I'm one of ten children. I wanted to blend both.

Too often lawyers in novels are seen only as combatants in the courtroom, but we rarely see the daily lives they lead. A good example is a deposition I attended. The attorney taking the deposition was a father and had forgotten to help his son make a soapbox-derby car for an upcoming race. So there he was, in the deposition, asking questions while affixing weights and graphite to the wheels to increase the speed of his son's derby car. I never did find out how he did in the race.

The issue of addiction is a serious one in the legal profession. The various state organizations have classes for lawyers who develop problems. I don't know if the illness is any greater than the percentages in the normal population, or for other occupations. Divorce also seemed prevalent when I practiced. Being a lawyer is not a job; it is a profession. It is not a nine-to-five endeavor. When lawyers are not working on their cases, they're often thinking about them, strategizing, and working on ways to resolve the dispute. There are also the hours they spend developing their reputations and bringing in clients, and participating in the legal organizations of which they are members. It is a lot of work, and I admire those that do it well.

When a lawyer is in trial, everything else comes to an end. The real world doesn't exist for those days, sometimes weeks, that the lawyer is in court. It puts tremendous strain on the lawyers, their law firms, and their families.

I can't imagine being a prosecuting attorney or a defense lawyer. The stakes in civil litigation, often millions of dollars, were high enough. Whether or not my client would go to prison, and for how long, would have been truly frightening, but not as frightening as thinking that someone guilty of a crime would walk free from the courtroom because I didn't do my job well enough. I've sat in on several criminal trials to watch the lawyers and the defendant, including a death penalty case. The facts were gruesome. Multiple murders by a man who didn't even know the family he had killed. I left that courtroom each day sickened, and I had nightmares about protecting my own family. I can't imagine what it can do to attorneys who deal with it every day. It has to change you, living in that world. It has to be very difficult to turn off the case and try to focus on a normal life. Again, I have great respect for those who try and defend criminal cases, including several friends I went to school with in California.

This past year I lost my legal mentor, Doug Harvey. Doug was the attorney for whom I worked for thirteen years at Gordon & Rees in San Francisco. He was a tough son of a gun, full of fire and brimstone—what one might call "a man's man." When I left the legal profession to pursue writing novels, Doug left to pursue another of his passions, producing wine. He and a partner bought land, grew grapes, and even built the Dumas Station winery in Walla Walla, Washington, where Doug had been raised with his brothers. As with the law, Doug made that venture a success. The Dumas Station wines are some of the best in the state of Washington. His daughter, Ali, is intimately involved in the business. Doug's other passions were golf and fly-fishing, and he had planned to do a lot of both in Walla Walla with his brothers and his wife, Jane. But things don't always work out as we plan.

I recall Doug telling me he lost a brother unexpectedly to cancer. Shortly thereafter, Doug had trouble with his vision, learned he had an aggressive cancer in his brain, and spent almost a decade fighting for his life. He used to come to Seattle for treatment with Jane, and I would often pick him up at the airport and take him to his doctor's appointments or meet him and Jane for dinner. The cancer took a lot out of Doug. It was sad for me to see. Even more sad when Jane called to tell me that he had finally succumbed to that battle. I remember Doug telling me one night at dinner, "Nothing is guaranteed. If there is anything you want to do in life, do it. Don't wait."

Words to live by.

I will miss him.

As many of my loyal readers know, each novel I give myself a challenge. In the novel *Her Deadly Game*, I wanted to create a protagonist who came from a dysfunctional family, but who had escaped by becoming a chess prodigy. Why chess? Because I knew very good trial attorneys, like my cousin Maurice Fitzgerald, who were also very good chess players. Did the two go together? They thought so. They told me in law and in chess you strategized not just about your next move but for the many moves your opponent might make and how you might combat those moves. Doing this prevented you from being blindsided and helped put together a long-term strategy on how to resolve the game—or a case. I'm sure that the skills learned in chess are also applicable to many other professions and to life in general. Don't focus on the problem. Focus on the solution and how to get to it.

The problem is: I don't play chess. What to do? Rely on the kindness of friends and strangers. A friend of mine, Rourke O'Brien, spent many of his professional years running a nonprofit chess foundation. Rourke put me in touch with Elliott Neff, the founder and CEO of Chess4life, as well as a national master. Yes, a very smart guy. The connection was perfect. I told Elliott what I was trying to do, that I wanted to create a game within the courtroom game that my protagonist, Keera Duggan, would be defending. I wanted the chess game to represent what was going on in the trial, the battle between the prosecuting attorney and Keera, the defense attorney. Elliott was kind and patient with me. He listened to what I wanted, and then he literally created a game for me, move by move, by both players. Check out the Chess4life website. They do amazing things for kids, and I'm sure they could use your support: Chess4life.com.

I truly hope you, loyal readers, enjoy the

game within the game. I did everything possible to include each move, but as writers know, sometimes in the editing process, which is as arduous as the writing process, things can get removed or changed. If there is a mistake in the chess game, that mistake belongs to me and only to me, not to Elliott.

I am grateful that Elliott and Rourke were part of my team. They made the creation and writing of this novel a lot of fun.

I also wanted the challenge of writing a novel with a huge twist. I wanted that twist to be in the victim's manner of death. I won't give away any spoilers, but I think I succeeded, and I could not have done so without the help of former police officer and good friend Alan Hardwick. Alan is a Renaissance man. A talented musician, he is a member of the band One Love Bridge, as well as a writer. He was a Boise, Idaho, police detective and founded that department's criminal intelligence unit. In Edmonds, Washington, he served as a sergeant and acting assistant chief of police with the Edmonds Police Department. He was a member of the FBI Joint Terrorism Task Force and the Washington Homicide Investigators Association. He now runs the Hardwick Consulting Group. Alan listened to what I was attempting to do, and then said he had a friend who was a mechanical engineer with numerous patents. He volunteered to run my idea by him and see what he could come up with. Again, I was fortunate. Alan called me back a few days later and explained to me what his friend had devised. It was brilliant. I also knew I could use my own discovery process for the discovery process of my protagonist, Keera Duggan, in the novel.

Again, this collaboration was a challenge but also a great deal of fun.

As with all the novels in the Tracy Crosswhite series, I simply could not have written this one without the help of Jennifer Southworth, Seattle Police Department, Violent Crimes Section. After a distinguished career that included working CSI and then investigating homicides, Jennifer has retired. She remains invaluable in helping me to formulate interesting ideas, and with the daily police routine, as well as the specific tasks undertaken in the pursuit of a perpetrator of a crime. Though this novel was more courtroom drama than police procedural, I have learned that there is a tremendous amount of interaction between detectives and the prosecutors, and they often work hand in hand within the criminal justice system. I hope that I portrayed this accurately.

To the extent there are any mistakes in the police aspects of this novel, those mistakes are mine and mine alone. In the interests of telling a story, and keeping it entertaining, I have condensed certain timelines, most notably the time it takes to bring a case to trial and other aspects.

Thanks to Meg Ruley, Rebecca Scherer, and the team at the Jane Rotrosen Agency. They do just about everything to make my life easier, and for that I am eternally grateful for their continued representation. They are with me every step of this process, from story ideas, to drafts, to titles and cover concepts.

Thank you to Thomas & Mercer, Amazon Publishing. I'm losing count of the number of books I've written for them. People ask me how I'm putting out more than one novel a year. The simple answer is I work every day, I love to create stories, and I get a lot of support from my writing teams at the literary agency and at Amazon Publishing. They have helped to counsel me on my approach to writing multiple series, and they work tirelessly to make each novel the very best that it can be. They have sold and promoted me and my novels all over the world, and I have had the pleasure of meeting the Amazon Publishing teams from the UK, Ireland, France, Germany, Italy, and Spain. These are hardworking people who somehow make hard work a lot of fun. What they do best is promote and sell my novels, and for that I am so very grateful. Some of you may have seen the social media tweets of the covers of my novels *The Extraordinary Life of Sam Hell* and *The World Played Chess* on billboards in

Times Square in New York City. No one was as excited as me to see those billboards! I was both shocked and thrilled. But it is just a small part of what the team does for me and my novels.

Thanks to Sarah Shaw, author relations. Thanks to Rachel Kuck, head of production; Rachael Herbert and Nicole Burns-Ascue, production managers; and Adrienne Krogh, art director. It's getting redundant, I know, but I love the covers and the titles of each of my novels. Thanks to Dennelle Catlett, and congratulations on her promotion to head of publicity, Amazon Publishing. Dennelle is always there, always available when I call or send an email with a need or a request. She actively promotes me, helps me to give to worthwhile charitable organizations, and makes my travel easy. Thanks to the marketing team, Andrew George, Lindsey Bragg, and Erica Moriarty, for all their dedicated work and incredible new ideas to help me build my author platform. Their energy and creativity is wonderful. They make each new idea a great experience. Thanks to Mikyla Bruder, head of Amazon Publishing, and publisher Hai-Yen Mura for creating a team dedicated to their jobs and allowing me to be a part of it. I am sincerely grateful, and even more amazed with each additional million readers we reach.

I am especially grateful to Thomas & Mercer's editorial director, Gracie Doyle. As mentioned above, Gracie and I work closely together on my ideas from their initial formation to print. Beyond that, we have a lot of fun when we get together and were recently able to renew our annual Christmas dinner with spouses. So much fun.

Thank you to Charlotte Herscher, developmental editor. All of my books with Amazon Publishing have been edited by Charlotte—from police procedurals to legal thrillers, espionage thrillers, and literary novels. The woman can edit anything and make it better. She never ceases to amaze me how quickly she picks up the story line and works to make it as good as it can possibly be, often by persuading me to make some difficult cuts. There is often a lot of gnashing of teeth when I get the editorial letter, but after a day I realize Charlotte is right, and the book will be better for it.

Thanks to Scott Calamar, copyeditor, whom I desperately need. Grammar has never been my strength, so there is usually a lot to do.

Thanks to Tami Taylor, who runs my website, creates my newsletters, and creates some of my foreign-language book covers. Thanks to Pam Binder and the Pacific Northwest Writers Association for their support.

Thanks to all of you tireless readers, for finding my novels and for your incredible support of my work all over the world. Hearing from readers is a blessing, and I enjoy each email. You can find me at www.robertdugonibooks.com and at Amazon.com/robertdugoni. I am also on twitter @robertdugoni, Facebook AuthorRobertDugoni, as well as Instagram amazon.com/RobertDugoni. Thanks to my mother and father for a wonderful childhood and for teaching me to reach for the stars, then to work my butt off to get there. I miss my dad. As with Doug, I lost him to cancer.

Thank you to my wife, Cristina, for all her love and support, and thanks to my two children, Joe and Catherine, who have started to read my novels, which makes me so very proud.

I couldn't do this without all of you, nor would I want to.

ABOUT THE AUTHOR

Robert Dugoni is the critically acclaimed *New York Times*, *Wall Street Journal*, *Washington Post*, and Amazon Charts bestselling author of the Tracy Crosswhite series, which has sold more than eight million books worldwide. He is also the author of the bestselling Charles Jenkins series; the bestselling David Sloane series; the stand-alone novels *The 7th Canon*, *Damage Control*, *The World Played Chess*, and *The Extraordinary Life of Sam Hell*, *Suspense Magazine*'s 2018 Book of the Year, for which Dugoni won an AudioFile Earphones Award for narration; and the nonfiction exposé *The Cyanide Canary*, a *Washington Post* best book of the year. He is the recipient of the Nancy Pearl Book Award for fiction and a three-time winner of the Friends of Mystery Spotted Owl Award for best novel set in the Pacific Northwest. He is a two-time finalist for the Thriller Awards and the Harper Lee Prize for Legal Fiction, as well as a finalist for the Silver Falchion Award for mystery and the Mystery Writers of America Edgar Awards. His books are sold in more than twenty-five countries and have been translated into more than two dozen languages. Visit his website at www.robertdugonibooks.com.

Center Point Large Print
600 Brooks Road / PO Box 1
Thorndike, ME 04986-0001 USA

(207) 568-3717

US & Canada:
1 800 929-9108
www.centerpointlargeprint.com